THE
FAR AWAY
GIRL

BOOKS BY SHARON MAAS

Of Marriageable Age
The Lost Daughter of India
The Orphan of India
The Soldier's Girl
The Violin Maker's Daughter
Her Darkest Hour

THE QUINT CHRONICLES
The Small Fortune of Dorothea Q
The Secret Life of Winnie Cox
The Sugar Planter's Daughter
The Girl from the Sugar Plantation

Sharon Maas

THE FAR AWAY GIRL

Bookouture

Published by Bookouture in 2021

An imprint of Storyfire Ltd.
Carmelite House
50 Victoria Embankment
London EC4Y 0DZ

www.bookouture.com

ISBN: 978-1-80019-238-6
eBook ISBN: 978-1-80019-237-9

To my granddaughters: Aliya, Grace and Margo

Grandmothers (extract)

Only these grandmothers can raise their rifles over the gates
and shoot into the trees where the limbs of young men
flail into the foliage.
Only these grandmothers can halt the slingshots aimed at birds
in the knitted palms of their hands.
Only the grandmothers can look down the long roads travelled
into the histories of yesterday
and back to the future where the children test the waters
with their toes
and languages ricochet like gunshots.

Only these grandmothers can stand between yesterday
and tomorrow

From **Only These Grandmothers**
By Maggie Harris, Writer

Georgetown, Guyana, 1977

Dear Diary,

Hello. Now I am six. My name is Rita Maraj. I live at Number Seven, Kaieteur Close, Georgetown, with Daddy and Mildrid. Mildrid is the made. Daddy gave you to me today. He said You will be my Freind and I can write Things to You. I like the puppy on your cover. I also got a bisicle, its red, I can ride my bisicle almost alredy. I had a party with Polly and Dona and Brian Coolij and some others. And we played coloured girl in the ring and I chose Brian as partner but I didn't kiss him. I had a cake with six candles and I blew them all out. I made a wish. I wont tell you my wish but I'll tell you everything else about me. A lady gave me a dolly but I threw it in the rubbish. Georgetown is in Guyana. It used to be called British Guiana. It was a British colony then but now it is an Independent Nation. It is the only English Speaking country in South America, but it is a Carribean country but it is not in the Carribean. It has 701,718 people. I am one of them. It has 76000 square miles so it is bigger than England. It has only four people per square mile but they all live along the coast. It has three counties, Berbice, Demerara and Essequibo. It has many rivers. Guyana means Land of many Waters. I learned all that in History and Geography. I have 2 dogs and three cats. I fownd them by myself. I like watching ants. My Mummy ~~dide dyd~~ dyed when I was a baby. I love anamals and ants and Daddy says I can have lots of them. I like to read. Daddy didnt come home to read my Story for me tonight that's why im writing to You. I learnd to read and write at the Mary Noble Primary School but I still make some speling mistakes but not meny. I like school but Im always getting into truble I cant help it. Janet Focks said I look like a black ragger Muffin so I throo her books out the window. Miss Lee made me leve the room. I wrote my name on the wall. She gave me a letter for Daddy. I ~~read~~ red it and throo it away. She told him to kome my hair before I go to school but Daddy sleeps in the morning so he cant so Mildrid komes it for me sometimes but she says it has got two many nots and it hurts when she komes it thats why I bit her hand today but I didnt mean to. I was going to kome it myself but I entirley forgot. Miss Lee said I look like a Sensa fowl that's a fowl that has fethers growing backwards. Donna said I killt my Mummy but I don't believe her so I pullt her hair. Sorry for my speling mistakes.

Goodbye, Rita

PS I hope you like me I hope we get to be best Freinds.

Part One

Small Days

Chapter One

(Eight months later) Doomsday

'Either they go,' Chandra said firmly on Doomsday, her very first day at Number Seven, 'or I.' She laid the silver knife and fork primly together beside the chicken bones on her china plate, daintily lifted the white damask napkin from her lap and pressed it to her crimson lips. The silver and the china and the damask were all her own: they were part of her trousseau, prime weapons in her war against the established disorder at Number Seven. She pushed the plate forward, placed her elbows on the table, rested her chin on clasped hands and stared at Rita across the table with the narrowed eyes of a cat. Rita was just about to say, 'Then go,' but Daddy leaned sideways and put his arm round Chandra.

'It's all right, darling. I'll have a little talk with her.' He looked at Rita and smiled and winked, and instead of speaking out, Rita stared at her plate and bit her top lip and pushed out her bottom lip, and Chandra said, 'Look at her, she's pouting again! That girl's spoilt silly!'

That evening, Daddy came to sit on Rita's bed and explained everything to her. 'Chandra doesn't like ants,' he said. 'And we need Chandra. You know why, don't you? Because you need a mummy. I told you. Most people don't like ants, you know, most people don't have ant farms in their homes. So please be a good girl and don't vex her, sweetheart. Let's keep the peace, OK? Just do what she says.' And he bent down and whispered in Rita's ear, 'My favourite little girl!' Rita pulled away, sulking. He didn't have any other little girls, and anyway, it wasn't just the ants, it was the dogs and cats and everything else.

'She kicked Frisky. I saw, I was hiding but I saw. And she called Dolly a dirty old bitch. She's a bitch herself!'

Daddy chuckled. 'Where you learn words like that, eh? Come now, go to sleep. Y'all going to get used to one another. You got a nice new mummy, soon you going to have a little brother, you going to have a real family again!'

'Go 'way!' Rita flung herself down upon her pillow, twisting in mid-air so her back was turned to Daddy.

Serve him right.

The very next day Frisky was dead. The day after Daddy married her and brought her home, the day after Doomsday. Frisky was the first sign of terrible things to come. Frisky had mange, and the vet had given Rita a solution to bathe him in and she had been doing so lovingly each day, but when Rita came back from school the day after Doomsday, Chandra said Frisky was no more.

'Put to sleep,' she said. 'That mangy old thing!' And Rita heard Chandra telling Daddy, 'I'm not going to have any animals in the house and she'll just have to get used to that. You've spoiled that girl completely; she's running wild, like one of those children raised by wolves. What d'you call them?'

'Feral children,' said Jitty mildly. 'You have to understand, it was very difficult for her, the poor thing, and if you're just kind—'

'Don't make excuses. If you're kind to a spoilt child, it just gets worse. I'll have to take her in hand. I'm sure this place is full of fleas. She had that mangy old thing in her *bed!*' That was the worst thing about stepmothers, Rita concluded after several weeks had passed: they hated animals. Especially stray puppies and kittens. Not to mention ants, tadpoles and caterpillars kept in shoeboxes with lots of green leaves. Daddy should have known that before he married Chandra. Now it was too late. Take ants, for instance. Rita loved ants. She could watch ants for hours, marching in straight lines along the windowsills, *march march march*, looking at them through a magnifying glass and wondering just what they were thinking. Did ants think? Or did they just thoughtlessly, wordlessly know, feeling what they had to do, *follow follow follow, sugar sugar sugar*? You could put a piece of pink sugar-cake on a table with no ants and in no time, one would be there sniffing, then two, and then an excited scurrying crowd crying *look look look, come come come, sugar sugar sugar*, then the marching ants carrying pieces of sugar-cake bigger than themselves, *march march march, carry carry carry*, back to their homes. They marched around the house, up and down the walls and doorframes and table legs, and Rita's eyes followed them, knowing where they came in and where they went out; she kept them in jars filled with sand and watched them marching through labyrinths of underground tunnels, carrying the crumbs she fed them, *carry carry carry*, waving their antennae, singing their march songs. Rita gave them names, but mixed them up. She imagined herself small, ant-size, and marching and singing with them. She strained her ears to catch their cries of sugar and their march songs, sure that if she tuned her mind fine enough, she could hear. She had been running her successful ant farm for a good three months. Then Chandra, on her very first day, came pumping a red can of Flit and the ants were gone. Forever.

After that, Rita kept her pets in the yard. Under bushes, behind a heap of planks, on the back seat of the Morris wreck. A litter of kittens she found drowning in a trench. A kiskadee with a wounded wing that died. Polly Wong's dog Rover for two weeks when the Wongs were in the Islands, Barbados, or Antigua, on holiday. She moved her Animal Clinic to Polly Wong's garden. When she grew up she was going to be a vet, live in a big house and fill it with animals.

The second worst thing about stepmothers was they made you tidy up behind you. Wherever Rita went now, she had to be picking up this and that and putting it here and there. Walking and turning round to pick up whatever she had just dropped. In the good old days of just her and Daddy you could walk around the place in your underpants leaving a nice comfortable trail behind you: sweetie papers, comic books, bits of string you no longer needed; and nobody cared – least of all Daddy, because he did the same. Sometimes Mildred would pick up the things and put them in their proper places but in a house the size of Number Seven there were a whole lot of proper places, and you couldn't find the things again when you most wanted them, so what was the use? Chandra put an end to all that. She brought a maid with her when she moved in and the maid was supposed to clean, but Chandra wouldn't let her clean up after Rita. She made Rita wear clothes, and as for hair, she took her to the barbershop and had it cut down to an inch all over, like a boy.

'That girl needs training,' Rita heard her telling Daddy. 'A real little ragamuffin you got growing up here. Nothin' doin', not in my house. What visitors goin' to think? I didn't become Mrs Maraj to let people call me a slattern.'

The third worst thing about stepmothers was that they didn't fret quietly like other people, sucking their teeth and shaking their head. No, they yelled the place down if you did something wrong. Like when Rita made herself a pawpaw milkshake and not only used one of Chandra's best heirloom silver spoons to scoop the pawpaw meat into the shaker, but left the spoon in the shaker and switched on the motor, which broke the shaker and bent the spoon. Chandra yelled so loud the whole neighbourhood came running, and Rita ran and hid up the backyard mango tree till Daddy came home.

'That child better not touch a single one of my things again!' Chandra shrieked at Daddy, and poor Daddy just smiled and said yes, yes, and took her in his arms and guided her upstairs to the bedroom.

*

The one good thing about stepmothers was that Daddy was home earlier each day. The trouble was, when he was home, he only had eyes for Chandra, cancelling out her one good point. In other words, Chandra was a catastrophe, in capital letters. Rita wrote it in her diary, two months after Chandra came.

Dear Diary,

Daddy said I'm getting a new mummy but all I've got is a CATASTROFEE.

Chapter Two

Jitty, 1956–70

There were poison-tongued people in Georgetown who would whisper, behind upheld hands, that Jitty Maraj himself was a catastrophe, that even the best of wives couldn't settle him down.

People waited eagerly for the next catastrophe, which had to come the way the sun had to rise. Jitty had always liked his drink, not a fitting preference for a member of a devout Hindu–Christian family. This predilection was a curse, weaving its way through his life, causing a mishap here and a slip-up there, and little knots along the way, and no one in his family escaped its loops. The slip-ups sometimes had far-reaching consequences: Rita's conception, for instance, had been such a slip-up. But perhaps Jitty's entire eat, drink and be merry act could be traced back to an enormous slip-up, back when he was three and his mother, father and three siblings were killed by a drunk driver.

Jitty couldn't be blamed for the accident, of course, but if he'd been a good little boy he'd have been killed too. After all, it was his very *naughtiness* that kept him home from church the Sunday they were killed, driving home from mass. He liked to pinch the bottoms of the ladies in the pew in front of him or crawl under his own pew to escape into the aisle, and so his parents finally left him at home with Granma while they all drove off in the grass-green Vauxhall that fatal day.

The two cars slammed into each other at the corner of Brickdam and Camp Street and nobody had the remotest chance. Jitty's father never even had time to brake. Neither did the driver of the other car, packed full of fun-loving, rum-drunk young men back from an all-night party. Jitty's mother lived a few hours in the hospital, and one of the young men survived to swear off drink for the rest of his life. Everyone else died on the spot. It was Georgetown's worst accident that year.

Little orphan Jitty was left behind to be raised by Granma and Aunt Mary at Number Seven, Kaieteur Close, the Dutch colonial white wooden mansion round the corner from the Canadian Embassy in Kingston. Kingston, one of Georgetown's greenest, breeziest neighbourhoods, just a stone's throw from the Sea Wall, the 280-mile wall that runs along much of Guyana's coastline, and all of the coastline. Built by the colonial powers that be between 1855 and 1882, it protected the capital city and the coastal settlements – six feet below sea level – from flooding. Kingston wrapped itself protectively around Kaieteur Close, this quiet oasis at its hub, and life there was a pleasant, mellow-paced affair, slow, good-natured, and not a little complacent. The accident was a shock to the community's very nerve.

Kaieteur Close itself was a town planner's miscalculation in a city of orderly grid-worked streets, for it was a cul-de-sac, jutting into one of the blocks with no other purpose, it seemed, than to lead up to Number Seven. Numbers One to Six and Eight to Twelve, on both sides of the leafy close, were pristine fairy-tale white wooden mansions decorously hidden behind well-trimmed hibiscus and bougainvillea hedges.

They stood sedately on stilts, orderly sentries gazing silently at each other across the short street, whispering primly to each other through jalousied windows over fragrant oleanders, reminiscing about the Dutch and French and British colonial lords who'd once lived in their spacious halls.

Number Seven stood aloof, displayed in brazen grandeur at the stub-end of Kaieteur Close, a two-storey misshapen matron with broad hips and several long spindly legs keeping watch over the street, making no attempt to hide behind foliage. An ugly matron at that. A monstrosity of a house, people said, put together higgledy-piggledy, as if the past generations who had lived there had each had different ideas as to how to construct more room for growing families, servants, maiden aunts and ageing crotchety grandmothers. Rooms sticking out here and there; stairs going up and down, some wood, some wrought-iron, some painted, some left in their original state turning silver with age and weather.

Most Georgetown mansions of its era, built in the Dutch colonial heyday, were objects of beauty, sedate and white and many-windowed, resting on tall pillars with long staircases leading to their front doors. You could get glimpses of them, nestled as they were in beautifully tended gardens where hibiscus bushes vied with bougainvillea towering up trellises and up walls to produce the flowers of the most vivid colours: pink and purple and red, yellow and orange and violet. Where butterflies, bees and hum-mingbirds flitted among those flowers, and jasmine and oleander and frangipani provided softer accents as well as fragrance.

These beautiful houses were not the only legacy of the Dutch. Central Georgetown itself was an oasis of quiet old-world charm. Its wide avenues with central walkways between grassy verges shaded by towering flamboyant trees, the atmosphere of timeless serenity, the Promenade Gardens at its heart and the Atlantic breeze that swept in from the coast: all of this earned it the title of Garden City of the Caribbean. Number Seven could have belonged to this collection of vintage architectural wonders, but it didn't.

Many old Georgetown houses had towers – built by sea-captains, it was said, so they could keep an eye out for ships entering the Demerara from the Atlantic – but none quite like Number Seven's, a single ugly tooth jutting from the roof of an upstairs room, with a ladder leading up to a quadrangle just large enough for one thin person to stand upon, doing nothing except perhaps holding a telescope to one eye to search the horizon. Hideous, naked and unashamed, its paint peeling, since Granma, hidden away in her upstairs quarters, never bothered to refresh it, Number Seven glowered in an oversized, unkempt yard. In no way could this be called a garden. No hedge to cower behind, no neat herbaceous border along her driveway, no false modesty, only an enormous mango tree rising from a tangle of weeds and dishevelled bushes on one side of the messy drive of sand and weeds, and a cluster of coconut trees on the other. And behind the house a veritable jungle, left to its own designs, with a star-apple tree, a genip tree, and another, smaller, mango tree next to Number Six.

Granma and Aunt Mary had both given up on gardening, given up on Jitty, and, at least in Aunt Mary's case, given up on life itself, if life meant marriage, as it did for any well-brought-up Indian girl. Aunt Mary, almost in her forties now, worked for a British charity on a voluntary basis. She 'sorted out', as she put it, orphaned children, waifs and strays, and had little time for the waif in her own home, her own family.

The one thing she had done for Jitty was to have him secretly (for Granma would not have approved) baptised soon after the crash. So, Jitty, born a Hindu, was quite officially, albeit secretly, a Christian. Aunt Mary informed him of this when the time came for him to be confirmed; but he decided not to comply. And as he grew into adolescence, he found his own spiritual footing: 'I'm an agnostic,' Jitty said, and that was that.

At Number Seven Jitty had enjoyed a carefree, pleasant childhood. The lack of parents and siblings was no handicap, for Jitty had the gift of making friends, and among the boys and girls in numbers One to Six, Eight to Twelve, he was the undisputed king. They were always a wild lot, those Kaieteur Close children; their loyalty to each other was legendary, their unspoken 'us-against-the-rest-of-the-world' philosophy a fact of nature. But being born to Number Seven was at once a legacy, a responsibility, a challenge and an honour. Jitty shouldered that duty with good-natured insouciance.

Unlike Jitty, the children of Numbers One to Six, Eight to Twelve, were disadvantaged. They had parents. Parents who disapproved of insouciance in general and, in particular, of little Jitty Maraj and his two-woman Hindu–Christian household, of the doubly inept reins of guardianship held too slackly in the Maraj home, the lack of discipline therein: the lack, in other words, of a *man*. Disapproved in general of the country's political confusion and the threatened end of colonialism. Disapproved in particular of their children's association with a cooly. The problem was solved in various ways as the children entered puberty and the country gained, at long last, independence from Britain. A few children were sent to boarding school in England. Many of the remaining families did not remain long; they emigrated to England, America, Canada, places collectively known as Abroad, seeking a better life. The Kaieteur Close Band broke into scattered fragments, leaving Jitty behind.

The Maraj fortune was too much bound up in the country for them to leave: it lay in forestry and hardware. For generations the family had owned forestry rights of a large swathe of rainforest in the country's Interior, founded by Jitty's great-great-grandfather, Doodnauth Maraj, who had come with the first batch of Indian indentured servants; not as a labourer, but as a businessman, curious to make his fortune halfway across the world. And make his fortune he did, and built this house. To this day, the money flowed; Granma, in her enclave on the upper storey, kept an eye on the books, and was satisfied.

Jitty had grown up with the benefit of two religions. Granma was staunchly Hindu; but her daughter Rohini, under the influence of a dedicated English mistress at Bishops' High School, not to mention daily Christian assemblies with hymns, prayers and Bible readings, had converted to Christianity at an early age and changed her name to Mary. Hinduism and Christianity had been practised with equal fervour in an uneasy yet peaceful coexistence in Number Seven. Both religions, and both of Jitty's female guardians, Granma and Aunt Mary, were hostile to Jitty's freewheeling predilections, but their hostility had absolutely no effect on the growing young man. Even as a schoolboy, Jitty liked his girls, his rum, and his loud music, in that order. He revered Ringo Starr, bought himself a drumkit and for six long months set his sights on becoming the drummer of one of Georgetown's several bands. Number Seven and the whole of Kaieteur Close boomed and rattled at all hours of the day or night. But Georgetowners were a very tolerant people, and nobody ever complained, and Granma, who only wore her hearing aid when she had to, was oblivious to it all until, tired of the effort, he gave up drumming.

When Jitty was fifteen Aunt Mary married an older widower (an Englishman, inspector of the charity she worked for) of solid standing, who swept her off to London, leaving Jitty entirely in Granma's morally upright but to all practical purposes incapable hands. Occasionally she emerged as a dragon from its lair, to lay down the law in no uncertain terms, and at such times Jitty quaked. She handed him money as if it grew on trees. It kept the peace. She hired a string of servants to take care of the boy and retired to her room up in the eaves beneath the tower, to her prayers and mantras, her ledgers and business files. Her business manager came to see her every day, keeping her updated. Her doctor came when called; she had heart issues. She had her own live-in Lady's Maid, who lived in a small upstairs side-room and hurried up- and downstairs attending to her immediate needs. It was possible to ignore her very existence, for Jitty had his own room and a bathroom downstairs; he did, however, exert himself to visit her every Sunday afternoon, at her specific request. He kept those visits short.

Granma bought him, at his request, a motorbike, a 100cc Honda, for his sixteenth birthday. With his new wheels, Jitty was the star of the town. Girls giggled and flirted in his presence; he teased them and 'followed' them on his motorbike on their way home after school, which was, of course, strictly forbidden both by the headmistress of Bishops' High and the nuns of St Rose's and St Joseph's. But the girls liked it, and so did Jitty. They hitched up their uniforms to inches above the knee, loosened their school ties (if their uniform required one) and put on lipstick after school and limed at Bookers' Snack Bar and watched out for him. Life was good.

Chapter Three

After walking out the school gates for the last time, aged nineteen and still slightly shell-shocked by the dramatic events of the last few months, Jitty worked at a variety of short-lived jobs. He helped out at a garage for three months, loaded and unloaded ships at the dock for five weeks, and did a stint at stacking shelves at Quang Hing's Supermarket. But stacking supermarket shelves was simply not good enough.

A-level results came in, and he was relieved to find he had passed them all. Not brilliantly, but at least he'd passed. English Literature, Geography, History. He was all set to move up in the world, and fate played into his hand: the *Daily Graphic* advertised for trainee reporters. Jitty cut off his hair, stopped smoking, put on a clean white shirt and tie and new black trousers and shiny black shoes, applied for the position, took the test, and got the job.

And in journalism Jitty found, eventually, his personal professional niche. Journalism proved to be the ship that sailed him into respectability. He was a good writer, but even more so, he was a good interviewer; even the most cranky and reticent of subjects, charmed by his genuine affability, opened up to him and shared with him stories and secrets never before revealed. He became the *Graphic*'s star feature writer; whenever a personage of note came to visit the country, Jitty was sent to prise them open. He met the famous and the notorious. His feature on Mahalia Jackson was moving, on Muhammad Ali funny-serious, on Fidel Castro provoking. He was sent to meet the Beatles in Tobago; he couldn't get much out of them, unfortunately: they were all high as a kite. It wasn't much of a feature, but a good story to tell at the high-profile receptions and dinners he was invited to as representative of the press.

As a good-looking, well-dressed young Indian man, affable in temperament and always smiling, successful at his job and polite to everyone, Jitty had them all fooled. Nobody would suspect it was all a mask. If there was anything at all unpleasant, traumatic, guilt-inducing, shameful, hidden in Jitty's soul, nobody would ever suspect it, for the face he presented to the world was one of unmitigated bonhomie. He was, as ever, the quintessential Sunny-Boy, but this time a mature, responsible one.

By the time Rita, aged five, moved into Number Seven, Jitty had reformed himself, pulled himself up by the legendary bootstraps, turned over the legendary new leaf: now a leading *Graphic* journalist with a fine reputation. Number Seven, meanwhile, had fallen more and more into disrepair. Granma had not renovated or repainted the house since the death of her only son, a result of her burying herself away in her upstairs bedroom; once pristine white, it had turned grey. All over the place, inside and out, the old paint was preparing to fall off, flaking away from the wall in smaller or larger slivers.

Soon after she first moved in, Rita proceeded to help peel the paint away from those parts of the wall she could reach, sitting on the front stairs or cross-legged on the veranda, sliding overgrown fingernails or even a knife under the layer of old paint and prising it away. It was like picking at a scab, but in a way that did not hurt.

She could sit for hours, scratching away at the paint. No one prevented her from doing so; no one cared, not Jitty, and certainly not Mildred.

For the entire first six months, Rita refused to speak to Jitty, or anyone, in fact. She just sat there, day after day, scratching at the peeling paint, or else wandering around the backyard, looking at things, sometimes touching. Never properly playing.

Jitty found he had no idea what to do with a little half-orphaned girl. There'd never been a man in his life, never a father figure, no father, grandfather, or even an uncle. Granma and Aunt Mary simply did not mix with men, apart from Granma's business adviser, her solicitor, and Aunt Mary's future husband.

Before Rita's arrival, he had so looked forward to his role as father. He'd been sure he could be father *and* mother to her. He'd be a good father. He'd always liked children, and living on Kaieteur Close had proven it: the children there – and there were always children there – liked him back. He'd always stop to have a word with them, bought them sweeties and cricket balls and little knick-knacks he came upon. Once or twice, he'd played cricket with the boys. He'd once taught a little girl to ride a bicycle. He brought them gifts at Christmas, and once had dressed in a Santa costume to their delight. But all of these tactics did not work with Rita.

He bought her dolls and dolly prams and dolly houses, but she refused to even look at them. She would not wear the clothes he bought for her, lovely pink frilly dresses with matching shoes and socks, preferring the clothes she'd arrived in and brought with her, until they were literally too tight to fit. After which Mildred was sent to Stabroek Market to find similar things: simple shorts and T-shirts.

There was a private nursery-cum-primary school in Kingston, the Mary Noble school, which took children from four to ten, and, rather insecure by now, Jitty enrolled her. But the teacher said it was wasted on her, since she spoke to nobody, adult or child. She did not play with the children of Kaieteur Close. She played with nobody, preferring to roam about the backyard, inspecting insects and leaves and flowers, and sometimes putting them into jars. She climbed trees, and could spend hours up in the branches of the mango tree.

For this reason, she did not seem particularly unhappy, Jitty thought. One day she'd grow out of it. So, he let her be. She seemed so self-sufficient. She got herself up in the morning, washed and dressed herself, took herself to bed at night. Then, Jitty would come and read her a bedtime story. He wasn't sure if she was listening, but always she was asleep by the time he finished. He'd kiss her, then, on her forehead, and whispered that he loved her. 'I'm sorry,' he'd also whisper.

Once, a few months after her arrival, two ladies came to visit, in their Sunday best, probably after church. They knocked on the door and Rita opened it to them and stared. The younger lady, who wore a powder-blue dress with a lacy bodice and smelled of Johnson's Baby Powder, bent down so that her face was on Rita's level and smiled. 'Hello, darling!' she'd said. 'How you've grown! Remember me, Aunty Penny? And this is Aunt Mathilda.'

Rita only stared, frowning. By this time Jitty had rushed over, and now stood protectively over Rita. Just like her, he glowered.

'What do you want?' he said in his most threatening voice.

'We just wanted to see her! We just want her to know us! After all—'

'After all, nothing!' said Jitty. He pulled Rita away and shut the door in their faces. Jitty was not normally a rude man – after all, they called him Sunny-Boy – but this time his customary charm was miles away. He trembled with rage.

Later, Aunty Penny telephoned him, and Rita picked up snippets from his end of the conversation. Though she was only five, of course she understood. 'I told you, Penny: no contact! No, she's fine. No, I won't change my mind.'

To Rita, he said: 'Don't bother with them, they're just old ladies.'

*

Yet deep inside he knew there was a problem, and after six months had passed and Rita's favourite pastime was still peeling off paint, Jitty decided to do something about it.

Looking out of the window, he saw Mrs Wong from next door getting into her car, parked under the house. He waved and shouted and asked her to wait, then ran downstairs. They spoke over the fence; he told Mrs Wong about the problem. Mrs Wong wasn't as sympathetic as he'd hoped.

'You mean, you just brought her here, just like that? Tore her away from her grandparents? And she didn't know you? Just plonked her in the house?'

'But I am her father! And I have custody! And—'

'Custody blablabla! Do you think a five-year-old child respects custody?'

'But I—'

'However, what's done is done and you can't undo it, short of sending her back. I don't suppose you're willing to do that.'

'No! I just want her to love me!'

'Your granma never told you: *I want never gets?*'

'Yes, but—'

'Jitty, I don't have time now. I have to pick up Polly from nursery and then go shopping and then cook lunch. But I'll come over when I'm back home, all right? And see what I can do.'

'That's wonderful! Thank you so much, Mrs Wong!'

'You might as well call me Jenny, seeing as I called you Jitty. I'm sorry about that. You just always seemed like a boy to me. A teenage boy. But now you're a father and you need to become a man.'

'Yes, yes. You're right. It's what I want too.'

'Good. See you later, then.' Satisfied, Jitty went back indoors. Rita was right there where he'd left her, curled up next to the dining-room wall, scraping off the chipped paint. It looked as if she'd be there for the rest of the day, and she probably would be.

He sighed again and called: 'OK, Mildred, I have to get back to the office. Look after her and try to get her to eat. I gone.'

Then: 'OK, darling, I'm off to work!' he called to Rita. 'If you're hungry, just go and tell Mildred. She'll be here if you need anything.'

Not that Rita ever needed anything, or drew attention to what needs she had. She was amazingly independent. Every morning, she'd get up early, go to the toilet and bathroom, have a shower, get dressed. Rita refused to wear any of the new garments, specially obtained from the market by Mildred. Dressed only in her underwear, she had found her old clothes in the rubbish bin, fished them out and put them on, all silently, and wore them till they no longer fit. Only then did she deign to wear the new ones.

Mildred tried her best to get her to eat at mealtimes but she refused everything cooked. She drank orange Ju-Cee soft drinks, and ate peanut butter straight out of the jar, and Cow & Gate powdered milk, dry, straight out of the tin. She loved fruit, however, and was extraordinarily dexterous with a knife – far more so than was suitable of a child of only five. She could dissect a mango, peel it meticulously, and grate it to make chow-chow by adding salt and a little pepper sauce, which she would eat sitting on the back stairs leading down from the kitchen. She could also peel a pineapple perfectly, leaving only the tiniest eyes and then slicing it. Mildred made pineapple drink from the skins, and that, too, Rita deigned to drink. It took her a little time until she discovered the fridge and the treasures it held – there was no electricity where she came from, so no fridge – but once she *had*, she raided it occasionally and ate whatever might be available there, cold. Patties and chicken legs and plain rice, all without asking, all silently. And then she'd make herself comfortable somewhere where the paint seemed loose, and peel it away with her fingernails.

Later, as promised, Jenny Wong knocked on the door and Mildred let her in and pointed to Rita.

'There she is. She don't speak to nobody. She don't say a word.'

Mrs Wong nodded and walked over to Rita, greeted her. Rita did not reply, so Mrs Wong squatted down next to her and said, 'What are you doing there, Rita? It looks like fun,' and proceeded to 'help' Rita peel away the old paint. Rita said nothing and they worked in silence for a while. Then Mrs Wong said, 'Our cat just had kittens! They are two weeks old now, and so cute! Why don't you come over and see them?'

She spoke casually, nonchalantly. As if it really wasn't anything Rita might be interested in at all, as if she'd said nothing more than 'the sun is shining today' or 'the kiskadee is singing today'.

Rita did not react, not verbally, but she did quickly glance up and away, and Mrs Wong took her cue and her encouragement from that.

'I have a little girl just like you, and she loves those kittens! She is trying to find names for them. Perhaps you could help her?'

Rita frowned, which was a good sign, but said nothing and continued to peel the paint. So did Mrs Wong. She did not speak again for a while, and then she said, 'I think we've done all we can here. All the loose flaky paint has been removed. We need to go somewhere else to work, where the paint is peeling. Or else we can go over to my house, and I can show you the kittens. What would you like to do?'

At that, Rita did look up. She met Mrs Wong's eyes, and gazed into them with long and serious intent. The older woman could almost see the little mind working behind those deep dark eyes. Finally, Rita nodded, and Mrs Wong understood the nod to mean 'kittens'. She stood up and held out her hand for Rita and pulled her to her feet. She loosened her grip on Rita's hand, but the little hand remained where it was, and closed around hers. Together, hand in hand, they walked towards the door. Mrs Wong looked back at Mildred, standing in the open kitchen door, and put a finger on her lips, and Mildred nodded.

There were four kittens, and Polly Wong was in two minds as to whether to call the white one with a spot on its forehead and one black paw Spotty, or Blackpaw. The other kittens were already named Frisky, Kitty and Lucky.

'Dot,' said Rita, and that was the first word she had spoken since arriving at Kaieteur Close. Polly agreed with that name, and even agreed, later that day, to rename Frisky, Kitty and Lucky according to Rita's advice – because in the course of that day Rita had revealed herself to be something of a chatterbox with strong ideas of her own. In fact, Polly agreed that the names Boots, Pepper and Whiskers were MUCH better names than the ones she had chosen.

'Would you like one?' Polly asked and Rita actually smiled, for the first time since moving to Town.

'You can choose!' said Polly generously, and Rita chose the one named Dot.

'He'll have to stay here for a few more weeks – he needs his mummy still,' said Polly, and Rita's eyes filled with tears and Polly thought she was going to cry, but she didn't. She picked up Dot and hugged and kissed him all over, then handed him back to his mother.

Afterwards, Mrs Wong served the girls tamarind balls and sorrel juice, and both were delicious, and she managed to get a few words out of Rita, and the next day a few more, and the following day, Rita was a chatterbox with her as well, and firm friends with Polly.

'She'll come round,' said Mrs Wong, or Jenny, as Jitty now managed to address her. (There was something scary about Mrs Wong; it took him an age to be that familiar with her. And her husband scared him even more: Dr Wong was a highly respected doctor at a private hospital, and he never smiled.) 'Give her time. But be warned: she's quite the bossy-boots!'

As Mildred was to agree, later, 'That girl! She too hard-ears! What she need is some licks on she backside!'

But Jitty only laughed and shook his head. He didn't believe in hitting children, and certainly not a child like Rita, a 'difficult' child. What she needed was infinite love and affection.

'If you want the moon, I'll get it for you, somehow,' he promised, though he knew he could never keep *that* promise. But 'whatever you want' became the watchword at Number Seven Kaieteur Close, and that was how he and Rita eventually made friends – or, at least, reached a level of communication they both could agree on.

Mrs Wong disapproved of Jitty's methods.

'That girl needs a mother!' she told Jitty. 'You better provide one!'

Jitty knew that she was right. He had finally become respectable and settled down, for Rita's sake, but there was still one thing missing: Rita needed a new mother. Which meant that he needed a wife. That would be the next step in the reformation of Jitty Maraj.

And yet, and yet. He took his time. Marriage was not a matter to rush into, even if you had a little girl desperate for a mother. Even if your life was in a shambles and you didn't know how to be a proper father and you didn't know the first thing about how to be an adult.

Marriage! How his friends would tease him! They teased him enough about having a daughter at home. And there were things hidden in Jitty's mind, hidden deep in shadows, that he cared not to disturb, and marriage – the very idea of it – would certainly cause major disturbance. It seemed like a betrayal of every step he had taken through this life, every development that had made him what he was today. A betrayal of his most deep-seated convictions, his resolutions. He had vowed to be a father to Rita; she had turned his life upside down. But could he, should he, go this path alone? Did he really need help?

But the question was not did he need help. The question was did *Rita* need help. And she did.

A child needs a mother, Jenny Wong had told him, and he believed it was true. *He* had needed a mother, and a father for that matter, and had ended up with a cranky Granma and a pious aunt, and a big hole in his life that, in quiet moments, he felt was sucking him in until he quickly climbed out again. He had had to grow himself into responsible manhood, even if it had taken a turbulent and, towards the end, disastrous path.

But disaster had sobered him, and he was pleased with the result. Yes, he had his deep, deep secrets, hidden flaws and major slip-ups and one really, really bad decision. But that was in the past, and there's where it would stay, hidden away from everyone including himself. He was a good man now, not one of those ruffians you read about in the papers, who beat their wives and children! No, Jitty was kind and good and gentle, a New Man, as they said these days. Jitty also had a reputation to preserve, that of Sunny-Boy, which had been the natural development from Hippie. Surely he could be a Sunny-Boy as a father, too? And a husband, once he'd found the right mother for Rita.

Upstairs, among all of Granma's old ledgers, files and notebooks (which he had never got round to clearing out) was that one dreaded file named 'Marriage'; she had shown him it years ago. But he was not ready to go there. He wasn't *that* desperate. He was Jitty Maraj, the biggest catch in Town. He'd taken himself out of the dating market years ago, ever since the first flush of self-reformation ardour. Jitty had been celibate now for almost seven years – a thing he had never thought possible, but really, he'd had no choice. He might be a bit rusty at this dating game, but surely he hadn't lost his appeal? All he had to do was unpack his old bag of seduction tricks, and descend on the pretty young single girls of Georgetown, this time promising a walk down the aisle.

To his astonishment, it didn't work. A single, freewheeling Jitty Maraj with a cheeky boyish grin and bad-boy reputation was one thing; a boring journalist who wrote serious articles, who had catastrophically messed up his life (as every girl in Town knew) and with a ragamuffin of a daughter: that was a different matter altogether, not worth the trouble, even for a ring on the finger.

After several months of failed attempts to secure a wife, Jitty went into Granma's room and retrieved the Marriage file.

Chapter Four

Jitty, 1977–78

Granma had researched Georgetown's marriage market well, and had created a short-list of three girls. Their details, as well as their family connections, and pros and cons for each, were all collected in that blue file marked Marriage. She called it the Marriage List, and reminded him of it from time to time. Jitty had dismissed the whole thing as a joke; now he knew it was a short-cut.

It took him some time to reconcile himself to the very serious idea of marriage to a girl of Granma's choice. But he had to admit, it would save a lot of time; as he'd already seen, running the hopeless gauntlet of trial and error on the open dating scene was not an easy task. This was the only way. Granma had done good work, and these were all very viable choices, judging from the photos (they were all extremely pretty) and the notes. Granma had already weighed up the pros and cons of every eligible Hindu girl in the country, and singled out these three prime candidates.

Hopefully, these three were still all unmarried; he knew that Granma had chosen girls five years younger than he himself, so they would all be around twenty now. Indian girls tended to marry early, even in these modern days. The notes attached to each photo listed each girl's pros and cons, all precisely documented without sentimentality or coyness. One had to be factual about these things: that was Granma's stance, and Jitty, now, agreed. No love-marriage for him. Love could always be fostered and grown, albeit a different kind to the one he'd always conflated with lust. Those days were decidedly over. He opened the file, read Granma's notes, and went on the marriage prowl.

The first girl had to be removed from the list immediately. She had been a top student at Bishops' and had immediately enrolled at the University of Guyana, where she now studied law. She informed him with little tact or consideration of his feelings that she was not in the marriage market, and if she were, wouldn't be marrying *him*. Jitty had to bite his tongue to stop him from speaking his mind: she wasn't the prettiest one anyway. He could do better.

The second girl was already married.

The third girl was perfect. She was beautiful, still unmarried, and her greatest *pro*, as noted by Granma, was that her family owned a thriving construction business, Jha Constructions, which went extremely well with the Marajs' own logging and sawmill business; not that that was thriving, these days, with all this nationalisation going on, and people turning to concrete to build new houses, but sawmills and construction (in a city where most houses were of wood) went together like milk and honey. What's more, she was from the county of Berbice, a further *pro*, since the people from up there were completely unaware of Jitty's dubious reputation. Her name was Chandra Fogarty-Jha.

This girl's only *con* was that she was not pure Indian; her mother was white, a Fogarty, from the famous English Fogarty family that owned the second-largest department store in town, opposite Bookers' Universal, a store with a furniture department, thus opening avenues for further business connections.

Not that Jitty knew anything about business – that was all Granma's thinking. It was why she could forgive the girl's mixed-race heritage. At least the mixture was socially enhancing, rather than a downgrade. It was always good to have a white person in the family, in terms of social mobility and reputation.

Not that Jitty thought in terms of racial hierarchies, but reality was reality. Chandra Fogarty-Jha was an excellent match.

With his easy charm and good looks, Jitty's bid was successful. Chandra was charmed by his legendary charisma, as he expected, and even the fact that he already had a daughter didn't put her off.

'Oh, a little girl! I *love* little girls! They're so cute! I can't wait to be best friends with her and go shopping for pretty dresses!' She almost clapped her hands in glee. Jitty grimaced internally and determined not to let the two meet until it was too late.

Marriage was agreed between them on the second date, and with her parents' approval, wedding plans went ahead according to Hindu rituals. A small wedding, it was decided, as the groom had not a single relative apart from his daughter, and his friends were not the type to enjoy the hoo-ha of an extravagant Hindu wedding (apart from the food).

To his joy, Chandra wasn't too fastidious about 'waiting till we're married', as most Indian girls would be. He was lucky enough to have his cake and eat it too; his long celibacy, he realised, was not written in stone, and its breakage was long overdue. He had paid the penance for his misdeeds.

A bit unfortunate that Chandra proved to be exceedingly fertile; he hadn't been particularly careful, but he *had* thought they'd wait for a child. But there it was. They had to bring forward the wedding date for the sake of propriety. Actually, all the better, Jitty thought. She might demand to meet Rita if they left it too late, and what good would that do? She might even back out altogether. Her main role in life, after all, was to be a stepmother, and better not to leave too many options open.

Rita did not attend the wedding. Jitty took care of that. He thought that both sides would profit from this: the bride's party would not have a scowling, rudely silent little girl spoil their festival of joy, and Rita herself would not have to be forced into a party dress: she hated all parties and the clothes to go with them.

A little white lie was necessary; Jitty was good at little white lies. And so he told them that she, sadly, had chicken pox, and could not attend. A white lie to protect them all. Straight after the wedding, he and Chandra flew off to Barbados for their week-long honeymoon.

And so stepmother and stepdaughter only met each other after the fact, when it was indeed too late for anyone to back out. 'Anyone' being, of course, Chandra.

Unfortunately, Chandra and Rita were at loggerheads from the start.

Chapter Five

1978: Anihilashun

The first time Jitty brought Chandra home, just after their honeymoon, Rita hid behind the curtains in the cupboard beneath the stairs and watched and listened. Daddy had called her several times already, shouting down the place, and walked through all the rooms looking for her, but she had not answered.

'I can't think where she is,' Daddy said to Chandra. 'I told her to be home this afternoon because I was bringing you to meet her. I'll just run over to that Polly next door and see if she's there. Wait here. *Mildred!* Mildred, I'm just going over to the Wongs' to see if Rita's there, please bring some tea and cake for Mistress Maraj.'

'Why don't you send the servant to get her?' Chandra grumbled.

'She might need some persuading,' Daddy replied, and walked out of the door.

Rita, holding her breath and peering out from behind a crack just one finger wide, watched Chandra alone in the drawing room. Luckily, the staircase was placed in a back corner of the living room so that, clutching the two curtains above and below her peephole and turning to follow Chandra as she moved about the room, Rita had a full view of what went on.

Chandra started to investigate the set-up, but was interrupted by Frisky, who came bounding through the front door, which Daddy had left ajar, and enthusiastically began investigating her, Chandra, sniffing up her legs and writhing around in ecstasy, flinging himself in rapture against Chandra's silky brown calves while giving short little yaps of delight. Chandra yelped herself, but in annoyance, then began shouting, 'You bloody bitch! Get out, you rascal! Go on, get out, get out! Go away!', beating at Frisky with her handbag and kicking at him. Rita was just about to jump out and rescue Frisky, who after all was only living up to his name, when Mildred rushed out of the kitchen shouting, 'Out! Out! Out!', grabbed Frisky by the scruff of his neck and flung him out of the door so that Rita could hear the poor thing tumbling down the steps outside. She suppressed the overwhelming desire to rush out and push Mildred and Chandra out of the door in turn, vowed to have it out with Mildred later, and commanded her heart to stop pounding so loud, which it did. She watched. Chandra was brushing at the hem of her dress with little flicks of her hand, her mouth, or what Rita could see of it, turned down at the corners in an expression of utter disgust.

'That animal has mange! Did you see his back! Why you allow that child to… Jitty told me she has a dog but that mangy beast… Why didn't he tell me? And I'm sure it's full of fleas, and…' On her way back to the kitchen Mildred said, 'A dog? That girl got at least four dogs, las' time I count, an' dis one is de latest. She bring it home the other day because de people want to put it to sleep, an' if you arsk me—'

'Four dogs? And you allow them in the house? But what kind of a place is this? My goodness, he didn't tell me, and look at the condition of everything! I thought you were housekeeper here?'

But Mildred just sniffed loudly and disappeared behind the curtain of threaded shells that inadequately shielded the drawing room from the kitchen. Chandra gave herself over to the more rewarding task of continuing her investigation of the drawing room.

She stood on the threadbare carpet in the middle of the room, facing Rita's hiding place, and looked around, frowning, her gaze glancing on and off the sundry pieces of faded furniture and other miscellaneous items arranged haphazardly around the room, her brow gaining a new wrinkle at each station. It lingered on the large oval dining table. Except for the little space at one end where Jitty took his meals (Rita always ate sitting on the Berbice chair in the gallery, looking out of the window, a bowl of food in her hand). The table was completely covered with papers, school books, old newspapers, comics, paper clips, a dog collar, an empty bottle of Old Spice, a broken porcelain cat, all the clutter of daily life at Number Seven. In one corner stood a rusty metal dome of fine wire mesh designed to keep the flies off food, but which was especially good for *catching* flies so you could watch them buzzing around excitedly for a while, and then magnanimously set them free.

At the moment Priscilla, a bluebottle Rita had caught after lunch and was feeding up for later release, was throwing herself in suicidal despair against the mesh. Chandra seemed to cringe when she took that in, and her eyes wandered off to the bits of furniture arranged about the room. Rita's pyjama trousers still hung over the back of the Berbice chair, where she had hastily flung them that morning in her hurry to dress for school (Mrs Wong had been blowing the horn outside the gate). Inexplicably, one of Daddy's shoes lay sole-up on a windowsill – Rita vaguely remembered using the shoe to try to coax a lizard down from the rafters several weeks ago; she'd placed a juicy living spider in the heel of the shoe, hoping the lizard would come for it and she could keep him a few days as a pet, but he hadn't.

Chandra's gaze lingered longest on Rita's ant farm. That was in place of honour in a corner of the gallery; Rita had been working on it for several months. Her friend Kalaam Farouk had given her a small, unused aquarium, which she had filled with sand and placed in an old plastic blow-up paddling pool. The water wasn't deep, but made an adequate moat around the glass fortress that housed the ants, and within that fortress Rita had constructed for them a complete little world, a paradise, where they could have all the food they wanted without having to go out to look for it; for

Rita fed them all the sweetest delicacies she could get her hands
on – a piece of this and a crumb of that – and, kneeling before the
farm, watched them, *march march march, carry carry carry, follow
follow follow*, and listened to them singing their march songs and
their follow songs. She did that for hours. Nobody minded. Except
Chandra. Rita could tell by the pull of the corners of her mouth.
She didn't like Rita's ant farm, just as she didn't like Frisky. So,
Rita didn't like Chandra.

Chandra wore a tight-fitting red dress that stopped at her knees,
made of some smooth shiny material flawed by a series of creases
in the lap area, caused by sitting. Three spaghetti straps on each
shoulder seemed a mite too tight, but matched perfectly the array
of straps and spikes on her high-heeled, red patent-leather sandals.

Gold-brown shoulders, gold-brown ankles, silky gold-brown
skin everywhere. Soft gold-brown orbs trying to burst out of the
bodice of the dress, and as Chandra turned round, Rita could see
the orbs of her buttocks (invisibly gold-brown) contoured against
the seat of the dress. She wore gold bangles and a gold chain round
her neck and carried a purse of sequinned gold.

The face that topped this vision of red and gold might have
been pretty if it hadn't been marred by the downturned mouth and
wrinkled brow and narrowed eyes, and the expression of vexation
so clearly written across it. Peering through the curtain, Rita saw
Chandra looking intensely at the floor and then digging at it with
the point of her sandal, and wondered what was going on. When
Chandra bent down and scratched at the floor with a long curved
red fingernail, she knew: Chandra had discovered one of the blobs
of chewing gum trodden into the floorboards. There were so many
of them in the house Mildred had stopped grumbling and trying
to scratch them off and simply left them to merge into the wood,
as was proper.

Chandra crouched just two yards before Rita; her red dress
slid tightly up her thighs, so that Rita could see the triangle of

her crotch, and it was bright lacy red, which somehow gave Rita a comforting feeling of utter disdain. She shrank back for a moment as the slit of Chandra's eyes raised suddenly and looked straight at her cubbyhole, not daring to let go of the curtain lest it move and give her away. Had Chandra seen her eye gleaming? No. Chandra stood up, having confirmed her suspicion of chewing gum, wiped the palms of her hands on the hips of her dress, smoothing it down as well as drying them of sweat (Rita could see the damp flecks they left on the material) and stalked, tottering on her heels, over to the cabinet where they kept their crockery and glassware. She glanced over her shoulder, as if aware of being watched, opened the cabinet, removed a glass, and held it up to the light. Rita couldn't see her face, but saw the round black helmet of stiffly sprayed hair nod, as if confirming another suspicion. The glass was replaced, the cabinet closed, and Chandra stalked back across the room, directly towards Rita, just as if she had suddenly received information as to Rita's hiding place and was coming to sweep back the curtains with a dramatic flourish. Rita pressed herself flat against the back of the cupboard and held her breath, and just then Mildred walked through the shell curtain, balancing on one hand a tray on which two tall glasses of lime juice wobbled precariously. She placed the tray on the little round purple-heart table next to the Berbice chair, smiled at Chandra and said, 'Why you don't sit down, madame? It might take some time to find the chile! An' here's some nice cold lime juice!'

Chandra nodded and sat down on the sofa next to the Berbice chair. She raised one of the glasses to her lips just as Daddy walked in.

'I can't find her anywhere,' said Daddy, and he sounded really disappointed. He plonked himself down on the Berbice chair and took the second glass. 'I went to all the houses and none of the children have seen her. And I *told* her to be at home, I *told* her I was bringing you!'

'Well, if you ask me, that's probably the reason why she can't be found,' Chandra said, sipping at her juice. 'You know what people are saying about that child? People are talking, you know, and they warned me several times. My own father said—'

'Yes, I know, dear, you told me, but when you move in she going to tame down; I know it, a lovely mother like you! She needs a family life again. Once she got that, she'll settle down. I promise.'

'Hmmmph! We'll see about that. It's one thing to have your own children but when you take on other people's hard-ears children, you got your hands full. What with my own little one coming along soon…'

At those words Rita felt a hefty thud inside her chest. *What* little one coming along?

'An angel like you! She might be a little worried and that's why she's not here now but I'm sure when she meets you…'

'What exactly does she know about me?'

'Well, not much. I told her I was bringing a friend along. A lady-friend.'

'A lady-friend? That's all?'

'Well, I didn't want to get her too excited. We should take things slowly.'

'That's what you've been saying the last three months, Jitty Maraj. Whenever I asked to meet her. "Let's just postpone it a few months," not even bringing her to the wedding! What's wrong with you? And now we're married and all and she still don't know? You told her I was a *lady-friend*?'

'Well, I thought it best to wait as long as possible. If she knew in advance, she might be a little worried and make a fuss. I still think it's best to confront her with a done deed. It's a little bit much, you know, you and the baby and all.'

'So, you going to tell her a "lady-friend" come to live in the house? And when you going to tell her about the baby? When this belly swell up so big, she think I'm a rain barrel, or what?'

'Don't worry, darling. It will all be all right. Come now, calm down and don't fret so.' He leaned over and Rita knew that he was kissing her. She felt such disgust, she squeezed her eyes shut, but opened them on hearing Chandra's petulant voice.

'Jitty Maraj, don't think I don't know you. I can see right through you. If it wasn't for the baby…'

'Darling, you know I do love you. It's just that Rita—'

'Rita, Rita, Rita is all I hear! That girl got you wrap round she little finger.'

'No, no, dear, it's you who got me round your little finger.'

'If I didn't know you were rich yourself, I would believe you only marrying me for my inheritance.'

'What bosh, darling. You know Granma left me everything. This house, the business, the Maraj fortune…' He leaned over towards her again, and she pulled away once more.

'Yes, and you pulled the Maraj name through the mud. Look at how you let the place go to pieces. And yourself too, I might add. It's going to take all my energy to get the house and the yard looking like something to be proud of. I mean, with all your money you could have done something to keep it up. Just look at the place! I never saw such a dump in my life, it's like a homeless shelter! And you didn't even make the effort to clean it up for me! And look at the yard! Nothing but weeds, and rubbish everywhere; you even have a rusty car under the mango tree! What's it doing there?'

'Oh, you saw that? Yes, that used to be mine. I had an accident with it.'

'Why you don't take it to the scrapyard?'

'Well, you see, Rita likes to play in it. It's a nice place for a child to play. Our son will like it too, you'll see!'

'Oh no, he won't! The first thing I do when I move in here is get that rust-heap out. I telling you, Jitty Maraj, now you got me as your wife I not taking no nonsense! That old wreck got to go! First thing, you hear?'

'Yeh, right; whatever you say, darling. Whatever you say. First thing.' He leaned over again and third time lucky: this time she let him. But the first thing that went was Frisky. The day after Doomsday. Along with the ants, eradicated with a mist of Flit, along with the cats, the caterpillars and the tadpoles, unceremoniously carted down to the yard and dumped.

'Out, out, out,' said Chandra, walking around with a scowl and a tight round swelling belly, pointing here and there and creating havoc in Rita's kingdom. She ordered the mango tree cut down.

'Mango trees are for backyards,' said Chandra. 'In my front garden I want canna lilies, roses, a hibiscus hedge. Oleander, of course. Croton and fern. That group of palm trees can stay, they'll look lovely growing in an English lawn. Daddy's gardener Ramsingh is sending round his cousin with his wife and children. They'll do a good job, we'll soon have this place looking all spick and span.'

Rita bred frogs and fish in an old tyre sunk into the ground in the backyard. When Chandra saw that, stepping over the knee-high weeds that protected it from view, she turned up her nose and said, 'That's a breeding place for mosquitoes. Out!'

The palings along the back boundary hadn't been painted for years. The wood was silver with age, crumbly with mould and wood-ants. Chandra had braved the jungle protecting them from view and found the place where Rita had broken through so as to gain access into the gutter behind, where you could catch as many fish and tadpoles as you wanted. The water there was a little stinky but it was worth it. You could put the baby frogs on pieces of wood and float them downstream, right down to the Lamaha Canal.

'This place is an utter disgrace,' said Chandra to Jitty, who had trailed shamefacedly behind her. 'I'm going to pull down those palings and build a nice high concrete wall with barbed wire along the top. You never know what kind of choke-and-rob ruffians might break in. Really, Jitty, if you had any respect for me, you would never have allowed me even to see a disaster area like this.

The house was an absolute mess – thank goodness it's coming together now. We just need some fresh paint everywhere, inside and out, and it will be as good as new. But the yard is a complete shambles. That daughter of yours is trouble with a capital T, she's the next thing I have to take in hand. I'll teach her manners if it's the death of me.'

Rita, hiding up in the far reaches of the jamun tree, her face stained purple from the plump juicy jamuns she was stuffing in her mouth, heard every word. She spit out a jamun stone, carefully aimed, and it hit Chandra on a tender spot. 'EEEE!' shrieked Chandra, twisting around to rub her bottom and frowning accusingly at Jitty. 'Do you have marabuntas in this yard? One just stung me!'

That night, Rita, lying on her tummy on her bed in the room where the walls had been painted pink and where brand-new pink-and-white flowered curtains danced in the salty moonlit breeze drifting in from the Atlantic, chewed her pencil and tried to think of a word terrible enough to fit the Chandra effect. 'Ruin' was not strong enough; 'Destruction' was worse but still not quite right, and even if you wrote 'Complete' in front of 'Ruin' and 'Destruction' you only proved how weak those words were. She crept down the stairs to the bookcase and pulled out a falling-to-pieces dictionary smelling of wood-ants and residue of Flit, and carted it back to bed with her. She looked up 'ruin', but that wasn't bad enough, though it was certainly true that Chandra had ruined her life.

She looked up at the photo of Mummy on her wall. It was the only photo she had, a black and white one of her Upper Sixth school class at Bishops' High School. Mummy's face was circled in black. She had pigtails hanging over her shoulder. Rita had asked Daddy for another photo, but he said he didn't have any – this was the only one.

'I hate her,' she said to Mummy. 'I wish you were here. Why did you have to leave me? Please punish her for me!'

She chewed her pencil some more, scratched at the scab on her knee, and turned back to the dictionary. Under 'ruin' she had found 'destruction', so she looked that up next. And there, under 'destruction', she found just the word she needed. The definition, she saw to her satisfaction, was 'complete destruction of body and soul. The word stuck forever in her mind. She closed the dictionary and finished her diary entry. Rita used the dictionary for meanings, not spellings. The important things about words were what they sounded like and what meanings they held so she never bothered to copy them from the dictionary; she said a word to herself, and wrote it the way it sounded.

> Dear Diary, this woman is a wicked witch. She has brought ANIHILASHUN.
>
> My life has turned so terrible. Everything is destroyed. Nobody cares about me. All Daddy cares about now is Chandra.
>
> Chandra Chandra Chandra. Whenever I hear that name I want to scream!!!
>
> It is just so tragic that I don't have a mummy. I wish with all my heart she was here. I miss her so much.
>
> Love Rita

Chapter Six

Going to See the Queen

On the third day after Doomsday, Rita vanished. Nobody knew when and nobody knew how; most of all, nobody knew where to. And because nobody could remember having seen her since breakfast, nobody knew how long. Mildred was the first to notice, when the chicken drumstick she had placed on the table for Rita's lunch grew cold and white with coagulated fat. She went over to Polly Wong's, but Polly hadn't seen Rita all morning. Mildred shrugged and went on with her work, and it was only when Rita wasn't back by four that any kind of alarm shivered through Number Seven.

Jitty was telephoned at the *Graphic*, and came home early, frowning, and asked Chandra wherever could she be, and Chandra shrugged and said she must be gallivanting with her friends, and messages were sent out to Numbers One to Six, Eight to Twelve, to ask who last had seen her.

Nobody. A search party was organised, but brought no results.

Rita returned just before dusk. Mildred saw her first, from the kitchen window, slipping through the bushes in the background as quiet as a shadow, and raised the alarm. Jitty was there to meet her as she slunk through the back door. She was just about to sneak upstairs when Jitty gathered her up into his arms, chuckled out his relief, carried her over to the Berbice chair and pulled her onto his lap, where he teased and tickled her the way he used to do before Chandra came. But instead of wiggling and giggling, she shook her head sullenly, slithered out of his grasp and ran upstairs, where she wrote secret things in her diary, which she hid in a very secret place. So, Jitty just grinned and shrugged his shoulders and said to Chandra, 'She was always a bit wild, but she's a good girl, she'll settle down and get used to the changes.'

Chandra was annoyed because she didn't like being outma-noeuvred by a little chit of a girl. She went up to Rita's room and pulled her out by her upper arm and said, 'Where have you been, where have you been?'

'To see the queen, to see the queen!' yelled Rita, and she squiggled and squirmed, she kicked and pulled, she pinched and bit so that Chandra had to let go; and Rita in a trice was out of the house and up in the mango tree and looking down, making faces at Chandra. Chandra rubbed the place on her arm where Rita had bitten her and she too shrugged her shoulders and said, 'Jitty, you better lock that minx on a chain. Me, I had enough.'

Rita stayed up in the mango tree till it was dark. Then she sneaked into the house again – they had left the back door unlocked – and up to her room, unseen. Then Chandra came up and told her about the boy she was going to have.

'Go and have a talk with her,' Jitty had pleaded, after Rita ran outside screaming, having bitten Chandra. 'Just go and try to be nice to her, like a mother. Please, Chandra.'

Chandra frowned, rubbing the spot where Rita had bitten her. There was still a circle of tooth marks; Rita had almost drawn blood. And now *she* was supposed to make the first move! Swallow her justified anger and reassure Rita. And Rita had not even apologised. The child should at least apologise first, before any sort of talk could take place.

Very well. She would talk to the child – when Rita had calmed down. The child must know the facts. No use filling her head with a pack of lies and mushy sentimentalities about happy families. The child was a barbarian, spoiled silly. It was time she faced the truth.

So, Chandra told Rita the facts.

'Your father is longing for a son,' Chandra told her when she came down from the mango tree. She sat on the edge of Rita's bed, still rubbing the bite-spot.

'Every man wants a son, and especially Indian men, to pass on the name and the blood. Your blood is anyway mixed; your father is desperate for a boy of Indian blood, a Hindu like him. Did you know that a Hindu man without a son is a disgrace to the whole family? He's not really a man. Of course, you couldn't know that, you grew up with coloured people and you never learned Indian ways the way Jitty and I did. Jitty doesn't expect anything from you, you're only a girl. Don't be hurt, he is very fond of you, of course, but you know what it's like with men, they're very particular about having a son. And the baby is kicking a lot so it's bound to be a boy. My Grandmother Jha knows about these things and she says the way it's kicking, it's a boy. So don't be hurt when he's born and you get the feeling your father has lost interest in you, it's just that his dearest desire has been fulfilled. I'm telling you this so that you can get accustomed to the idea. You've played first fiddle for a long time, Rita, but you must know it's not natural and it's only because he hasn't got a son so prepare yourself.'

After that Rita came and went as she pleased, establishing a pattern that nobody bothered to break. Nobody knew where she went to, but as it was still the August holidays it didn't really matter, since sooner or later, she always came back. The Kaieteur Close children felt abandoned; life hadn't half the spirit without her. Not even Polly knew where Rita spent her hours, or if she did, she wasn't telling. The girls played boring things like hopscotch and jacks, and the boys set traps for lizards, and the holidays lazed by without Rita.

Meanwhile, Chandra was putting the house in order. Initially, she had had something of a shock to find there was hardly a fraction of the Maraj fortune left. She had ranted and raved against Jitty, threatened to leave, threatened to get her father to sue for breach of contract ('What contract?' asked Jitty innocently) and finally faced the reality and used her own capital for the renovations that needed to be made. It was a matter of saving face: Chandra had coveted the Maraj home and the Maraj name for years, and she wasn't about to make a fool of herself. She wouldn't have Georgetown society sniggering behind their backs and pointing at her: 'She married a drunk and a pauper and lives in a hovel.'

Jitty liked his drink but he wasn't a drunk; and as for him being a pauper, she'd see about that. Her great-grandfather William Fogarty hadn't founded Georgetown's second-biggest general store for nothing. She wasn't an only child of an only child for nothing. She hadn't been her grandfather Jha's beloved for nothing. Her grandfather hadn't been quarrelling with her father for years on end for nothing. Grandfather Jha hadn't left acres and acres of prime Guyana rainforest to her for nothing, and Grandfather Fogarty hadn't left her a bursting bank book for nothing.

Chandra Fogarty-Jha, now Maraj, was rich, so the appropriate changes were made, and Number Seven came into its own. Reforming Jitty was easy: he was easy-going to a fault. He only needed guidance. He caved in to every suggestion she made, so that she soon no longer made suggestions, she gave orders, to which he was obedient. He had slatternly habits, but with the help of her own personal maid, Chandra managed to remake his image so that she could appear at his side at this reception or the other without feeling ashamed.

Dressed up in the clothes she chose for him, he cut a dashing figure; he was good-natured and likeable and had a certain charm people fell for, and they laughed at his corny jokes, the same sort of jokes that laced the frothy entertainment articles he sometimes produced for the *Graphic*. He tended to drink one or two too many at parties, but Chandra had methods of steering him in other directions, if necessary bringing him home and into her bed, before matters got out of hand. So married life would have been quite pleasant if not for the one little fly in the soup: Rita.

Chapter Seven

No Dolls, Please!

Every year on Rita's birthday, a package arrived for her, and every time she opened it, she found a doll inside it, and a gift card from someone called Aunt Mathilda. And every year she threw it to one side, almost angrily, and refused to play with it, and Jitty passed it on to St Anne's orphanage.

'Just tell her I don't play with dollies,' said Rita. 'I despise them.'

'It would be a bit rude,' said Jitty.

'I don't care,' said Rita. 'I don't want no blasted dollies.'

'Language, little madame!'

'Sorry. Damned.'

'That's just as bad. And you used a double negative. So, one negates the other, so you DO want dolls!'

'Oops!'

She also received cards. Birthday cards, from 'Granny and Granpa', and 'Aunty Penny and Uncle Douglas and the children', and 'Aunt Mathilda and Uncle Patrick'; and Christmas cards from the same lot of people.

'I don't even know these people,' she said to Jitty. 'Why they send me cards?'

'Maybe they're thinking of you,' he replied.

'But they don't even know me, either,' she said.

They do, in a way, Jitty thought to himself, but he said nothing.

'Do you want to know them?'

'No.' Then she thought again. 'Are they Mummy's relatives?'

'Yes. Her parents and sister and aunts and uncles.'

'So, they all knew her?'

'Yes.'

'Aunty Penny came once, didn't she? I remember.'

'Yes. She came with Aunt Mathilda.'

'And you were cross and sent them away?'

'I did. The time wasn't right.'

'Right for what?'

'It's complicated, Rita. One day you will know everything. I don't want you to be confused. You're getting older now, though, and perhaps you could meet them, under certain conditions. When you're more settled.'

Rita thought about it. She really did not like adults. Not at all. Except for Daddy and Aunty Jenny and the East Indian gardeners on the Lamaha Canal. Not even Mummy's relatives. They were mostly just old ladies anyway, who thought she played with dolls, which was insulting.

'No,' she said. 'I don't want to see them.'

Jitty breathed a sigh of relief.

'Good,' he said. 'What would you like instead of dolls?'

'Books. Books about animals.'

'I'll tell Aunt Mathilda.'

Another person sent cards and barrels of food at Christmas: Aunt Mary, the former spinster aunt who had finally found love and run off to London. She also wrote the occasional letter, in which she spoke of her happy life in her big house in London, and her kind husband, and how much more advanced England was than the backwater Guyana. Her Christmas barrels were filled with all sorts of good things you couldn't get in Guyana; yet still, Chandra was offended.

'She think we's poor people, or what?' she complained. There was some truth to the complaint. It was a well-known fact that those lucky citizens who had managed to escape to those fantastical places like London, New York, Toronto lived Shangri-La lives in places flowing with milk and honey. They generously sent barrels of goodies home at Christmas; there were companies that expressly dealt with the supply and import of barrels. It was families taking care of their own; and many a poor family depended on the regular arrival of a barrel packed full of wonderful and unavailable items of food.

Because even Chandra had to admit: food was getting scarce. It was a mystery how, in a country whose economy was mostly based on agriculture, many people had not enough to eat. The supermarket shelves were often empty.

'Only matches and bleach available, madame!' Mildred, would say after a shopping trip. You couldn't get this or that. No Kellogg's Corn Flakes or Cadbury's Chocolates. You couldn't live on yams and eddoes and bora beans… and rice, endless rice! And sugar! Plenty of rice and sugar but you couldn't live from rice and sugar! All the government's fault!

'We should have stayed British!' some people began to murmur. 'Colonial times were better!' and: 'These government people are incompetent: stealing all the goods! Thieves!'

It was at this time of scarcity, fuelled by Aunt Mary's letters and her generosity, that Chandra first began to murmur that maybe they, too, should think about emigration. After all, anyone who was anyone was leaving the country for good, to live lives of luxury in those fabled places. Already one of her Jha cousins had made the move, settled in Canada, and wrote smug letters home detailing the new life she had built with her new Canadian husband. Chandra was a woman much given to jealousy and envy; this didn't help. Jitty, however, managed to keep her in check.

'Maybe we'll go and visit Aunt Mary one day,' he consoled her. 'Or your Cousin Sita. I promise. And don't you have an English grandmother across the pond?'

Duly placated, Chandra kept the peace for now. Rita could have told her there and then that Jitty never kept his promises.

*

Rita slipped through the hole in the palings and followed the trench
to the place where it emptied into the Lamaha Canal, the main
irrigation channel in a city that could only stay above water level
due to a complicated irrigation system. A coastal town one metre
below the high tide level, and with two rainy seasons a year, was
a town in constant danger of flooding. But the Sea Wall kept the
ocean out, and an intricate network of canals, built by the former
Dutch colonial powers, kept it dry; a system of *kokers*, sluices,
opening and closing at the appropriate times, drained the city of
excess water.

To Rita, Lamaha Canal was a refuge. She climbed a few more
fences and found herself in a place almost like the countryside:
patches of gardens tidily laid out in handkerchief-size beds, interspersed with banana trees. East Indian gardeners worked these
bountiful allotments, and kept their produce watered with canal
water. Now, Rita sat down on a patch of grass to think. She did
a lot of thinking these days, ever since Chandra's arrival. There
were so many problems to solve. Like what she was going to do
about Chandra.

Chandra had emptied the world of everything worth living for,
and there was no getting rid of her: Chandra was here to stay. Daddy
wouldn't listen to her, Rita, any more. Daddy, who had always
done everything Rita ever wanted, had lost his mind to that witch.

All the animals were gone. Exiled from the house first, then
thrown out of the yard. Some things were just too hard to bear. Rita
didn't so much mind about the ants and the tadpoles because they
were safe; they could go on living in some sort of way – but Frisky
was dead. She had almost cured him but Chandra had killed him.
Murdered him. Mildred had taken the other dogs away to be given
to friends and relatives in La Penitence. They were watchdogs now,
tied on a string and spending their days barking at strangers. The

cat and her kittens had been given away and nobody knew where
they were and nobody cared, except Rita, and nobody cared about
Rita either. Nobody in the whole wide world.

'How yuh doin', beti?' Rookmini, the East Indian allotment
owner, was waving and smiling from the callaloo patch. Rita waved
back but she didn't smile.

Rookmini stooped down, bunching her skirt between her spread
knees and hacking at the black earth. She had forgotten Rita. Rita
stood up and continued on her way. The East Indian gardeners
were all out, working in their tiny plots along the canal, digging
and hoeing to coax vegetables from the soil. Rita knew them all
by name now. They were her friends. They waved as she went by,
calling a greeting as Rookmini had done.

'Come, girl, come, have some genips,' said Bashir's wife, and
Rita went up to her and held out her blouse in a pouch into which
Bashir's wife poured bunches of plump genips. Mrs Bashir helped
Rita squeeze the genips into her side pockets, which now bulged
like great knobs on her skinny hips. Then more genips were poured
into the pouch, straining the material so that it stretched right
down to the tops of her thighs.

'Careful when you eatin' them, they does stain bad! Otherwise
you mummy gon' be too vex!' said Mrs Bashir.

'It don't matter,' said Rita. 'I don't have a mummy.'

'You don't have? What? Who does look after you den, beti?'
asked Mrs Bashir compassionately, but Rita only shook her head.
Her eyes filled with tears and she stuttered her thanks for the genips
and went on her way.

Ranjeet Singh was loading the donkey cart with pumpkins.

'You late today,' he said, 'I thought you weren't comin' at all!'

'Course I comin'!' said Rita. She clasped the bunched-up material of her blouse in her left hand and approached the little grey
donkey harnessed to the cart. She fondled it behind the ears, the
neck, and when it raised its head, she kissed the muzzle.

'If you mummy see that she gon' be vex,' said Singh, but Rita wasn't listening. She was running her hands along the donkey's swelling belly. It was taut and very big.

'I don't have a mummy. I'm sure it's coming today, she's much fatter!' she said, turning to Singh with huge pleading eyes. 'You shouldn't take her out today. What if she gets it on the street? Please, please keep her here today! I will look after her!'

Singh only laughed and shook his head. 'An' how you expect me to get dese pumpkins to de market?'

'But…' But Singh wasn't listening. He had gone down to the canal with two rusty buckets and he was dipping them into the tea-brown water.

'Don't worry, Lucky, I'll come with you and help when you get your baby,' Rita whispered into the donkey's ear.

Rita spent the rest of the day beside Singh, her legs hanging over the front of the donkey cart. She had to train Singh not to whip Lucky, and Singh allowed himself to be trained. He also allowed Rita to take the reins and drive Lucky, clucking her tongue and calling 'giddy-up, giddy-up' whenever she stopped to pull at the grass on the roadside.

They delivered the pumpkins to the market and then they loaded manure on the cart and carried that to somebody's garden, and then they went to the Promenade Gardens and loaded the cart with coconut branches, which hung out so far behind the cart they almost swept the road. (Singh tied a red flag to them.)

Rita ate the genips as they plodded through the streets, cracking open the stiff green shells and plopping the peachy-pale balls of flesh into her mouth. When the stones were sucked dry, she spat them onto the road, aiming at the passing cars. She, Singh and Lucky carried all sorts of loads all over the town, and at lunchtime they had fish-and-rice with Singh's wife at Stabroek Market (but Rita wasn't very hungry for she was full of genips), and drank mauby, and then they carted some more things here and there, and by the time dusk came and it was time to go home Rita was burned a little browner and felt as exhausted as if she herself had pulled the cart around town. And Lucky hadn't had her baby yet.

Perhaps it would be born tomorrow.

Chapter Eight

August 1978: Rita's First Job

Chandra, Jitty, and Mildred first realised that the August holidays were over when Miss Higgins, the class teacher, rang up to ask if Rita was sick, and why wasn't she at school? Rita had missed three days already, and no letter of excuse.

Rita knew school had reopened, because Polly Wong had told her, but she hadn't told any of the grown-ups.

'Aren't you coming to school any more?' Polly had called over the palings.

Rita glanced up at the kitchen window. 'Shut up, silly, or they'll hear you.'

'But aren't you going to come? Please come, I miss you. Look, here's some chow-chow, Mummy sent it for you. She saw you from the window and sent me down and she wants to know why you don't come round any more. But tell me if you're coming to school tomorrow, or if you're sick or something.'

'No, I done with school,' said Rita importantly, scratching a scab off her arm. 'I got a job now. I go to work every day.'

'Work? True, Rita? You're working already?' Polly stared at her friend with wide-eyed envy. Then reason got the better of her, for Polly was a sensible child, well grounded in adult thinking.

'No, no, I don't believe you. Chirren don't go to work. You're only seven. You need to be fifty to go to work, like my daddy. Don't dig that scab – look, it's bleeding now. It never going to heal if you keep digging it off. You should let it dry out and fall off by itself. Otherwise it leaves a nasty scar. Here, you don't want the chow-chow?'

Rita raised her arm and put the bleeding wound in her mouth, sucked, lowered it and looked at the wound. She wiped the spit off with the back of her hand and as an afterthought took the bowl of chow-chow Polly was holding out. With dirt-smeared fingers she shovelled a heap of it into her mouth. It was delicious, the salt tangy, the pepper fiery.

'You don't believe me?' she said between chews. 'Then just go to the market tomorrow morning, you gon' see me sellin' pumpkin and greens! And I get to eat genips all day, for free.'

'And your daddy allows it?'

Rita shovelled two more loads of chow-chow into her mouth before answering. 'Course he does! You don't know my daddy does whatever I tell him? My daddy said if I want the moon he's going to climb up the sky and bring it down for me. He told me.'

'Yes, but…'

'You know he does, he always does. I'm my daddy's favourite person, his very favourite, he's always telling me that and I can have whatever I want. And he doesn't want a son, he likes girls better. An' it's true. He don't like boys at all.'

'Rita, don't talk with your mouth full, it's disgusting. You should come to school, you know. I miss you, and all the chirren asking, and Mrs Clark, and anyway, if you don't go to school you get stupid, and—'

'I finish with school. School is for babies. I hate school. Here, take this.' Rita pushed the empty bowl at Polly and ran away to check on a secret horde of ants, a mini-farm she kept in a guava-jelly jar, hidden from Chandra's prying eyes on a bottom-house rafter. You could only get to it by climbing up the heap of rotting planks Daddy was storing for the bicycle shed he never got round to building.

A few days later, Chandra had the planks removed, for she was starting work on beautifying the yard. And Rita was yanked back off to school, which put an end to the days of genips and donkeys.

You can send a girl to school but you can't make her learn. Rita was at best a mediocre pupil. She hated facts; numbers even more. She forgot history dates and no matter how often she hammered the words 'seventy-two' into her brain, eight times nine remained an inaccessible enigma, and she never stopped counting on her fingers. The droning of her teachers bored her; certain keywords were all it took to set her off floating in a fantasy of her own. Learning by rote was torture; she felt herself pressed into a mould from which the only escape was dreaming.

'She seems preoccupied,' said Mrs Clark, the headmistress, in a confidential telephone call to Jitty. 'Have there been any changes in her life lately? She's an extremely bright child, one of our brightest, but her class mistress tells me that this term she simply refuses to work. She just sits there dreaming. She won't write a word. She doesn't take anything in. It's like trying to teach a stone wall.'

'Well… ah, we've been having a little bit of trouble with her lately,' admitted a stammering Jitty. 'She's slightly unsteady at the moment but I'm sure it will pass. No need to worry.'

'Well, I certainly hope it passes soon. It's always such a shame when a child doesn't live up to its talents.'

'Talents? What talents?'

'You must know that Rita has a way with words, a gift for language – her own and foreign ones. She's top of the class in English, and so good at French, and she's learning Spanish just like that.' She snapped her fingers. 'In fact, Rita has an extraordinary gift for expressing herself in writing,' Mrs Clark continued. 'I mean, as a writer yourself, you must have taken an interest. You must have seen the exercise books she filled last year. Even when she first started school, we didn't have to teach her: she could write already. I thought you had taught her, that you had been encouraging her! And all those little stories she used to bring to show the teachers, they're so good! That story about the Queen Ant and her birthday cake, for instance. Surely you were some kind of a co-author?'

'Well, er, as a matter of fact, no, I wasn't.'

'All the more astonishing, then, and all the more a pity. I can't believe – I mean, I wrote her a glowing school report at the end of last term, so it can't possibly be new to you, Mr Maraj. I think you should come round and we should have a long chat about your daughter. I read in the papers that you married recently, could that be at the root of the matter? Perhaps you'd like to bring your wife, Rita's stepmother, so that we can consider together how to give Rita the support and encouragement she needs?'

Jitty was silent for so long Mrs Clark thought he had hung up. 'Mr Maraj?'

'Yes, I'm still here. Mrs Clark, I'll speak to my wife and I'll ring you back in a day or two, is that all right?'

'Very well, I'll be looking forward to that. I'm sure it's just a passing phase, so I wouldn't worry. If we all pull together then we'll soon have her back on form, I'm quite sure. We should have that talk as soon as possible though, in the next day or two.'

'Yes, yes, of course.' But Mrs Clark never heard from Jitty Maraj. Jitty drew encouragement from Mrs Clark's words, 'I'm sure it's just a passing phase,' because that was what Jitty wanted to believe, and if Mrs Clark confirmed this belief, then it was better just to let things be. The phase would pass by itself; no use upsetting Rita by making a fuss. And why upset Chandra? She had enough on her hands already, what with builders and labourers and gardeners who failed to turn up, Mildred who refused to cook according to instructions, and all the troublesome side effects of a swelling belly.

He decided the best thing to do for Rita was to give her an enormous birthday treat. She would turn seven in mid-September, and Chandra happened to be visiting her parents in Berbice for several weeks of the month.

'I'll tell you what,' said Jitty to Rita. 'Why don't you and I go on a special trip to Kaieteur, for your birthday?'

Kaieteur Falls, the world's largest single-drop waterfall by the volume of water, four times higher than Niagara, hidden away in the depths of Guyana's rainforest, was a sight worth seeing. Foreigners came from far and wide to see it; Guyanese themselves vowed to go, but, inaccessible by land as it was, delayed and delayed, and most never made it. It was the visit of a lifetime. Their own close had been named after it, in a post-Independence flurry of getting rid of British names. It had previously been Forsythe Close, named after a past very much disliked governor, who had built the first house in the cul-de-sac and lived there until recalled, and had since received a lordship.

'Ooh, yes!' said Rita. 'Maybe I'll see the golden frog!'

'You'll certainly see the waterfall. It's magnificent! It's a date! I'll buy tickets for us, for your birthday.'

And he did. However, just two days before their flight to the Interior, Jitty received news that Stokely Carmichael, the black American civil rights leader and activist, and his wife, the South African singer Miriam Makeba, were visiting the country, and, of course, that was an opportunity he could not miss. An interview was scheduled for the very day of the Kaieteur trip, the only time it could be slotted in.

'I'm sorry, darling,' he told Rita. 'We'll do the trip another time, later this year.'

'You promise?'

'I promise.'

But Jitty had never been good at keeping promises. Over the next few weeks Rita kept reminding him, and he kept postponing. Eventually, she managed to commit him to a date in November, and he even went ahead and bought tickets.

It was going to happen. Rita would hold him to it.

Chapter Nine

Gangleader

Over the rest of that year, Rita managed, somehow, to settle into an uneasy relationship with Chandra. Simultaneously, she slid effortlessly into her role at the helm of a new generation of Kaieteur Close children.

They called themselves the Kaieteur Close Kids, which had a nice ring to it, and she was their undisputed leader. It was, after all, her birthright.

The cul-de-sac was a wide, friendly, tree-shaded one, with a gutter running in front of the house fences, crossed by wide bridges leading to the Bottom Houses, the space between the columns on which the houses stood, where everyone parked their cars. There were no cars parked on the street, where they could be hit by a stray cricket ball or scratched by a wobbly bicycle. The street belonged to the kids. They played hopscotch on chalk grids in the middle of it, or jacks on the bridges, or fished for tiny minnows and tadpoles in the gutters, or played cricket and tag and hide-and-seek, in and out the open gates. A sign at the entrance to the close said: DRIVE CAREFULLY, CHILDREN PLAYING, and every car that turned into it slowed down to a walking pace, and the children scattered to the bridges to wait its passing.

Every morning, quite early, first of all the smaller children walked out, hand in hand with their mothers or nannies (some of them pushing prams), to be taken to the nearby nursery school in Parade Street, just round the corner. The next batch to leave was a horde of primary school children, on their bicycles: Rita had received a beautiful red one for her sixth birthday, and taught herself to ride it, and she and Polly sailed off together to the Mary Noble school; while the much-older children, in their green Bishops', or blue St Rose's, or khaki Queen's College, or grey St Stanislaus uniforms, cycled off to their specific secondaries. Later still, it was time for the cars to leave: dapper daddies in white shirts and striped ties, some of them with their young children bound for primary schools further away, St Margaret's on Camp, or Stella Maris on High.

After school each day, the children, fed and watered, their school uniforms discarded, would emerge from their separate gates to play, and the close would bounce with energy and echo with childish screams and laughter. At the end of each day the mummies and nannies, and sometimes daddies, emerged to clear the street of discarded scooters or roller skates or hula hoops or bicycles, and sometimes school ties and shoes and socks and other miscellaneous items of clothing or toys.

As for the adults themselves, it was as if they had come to a silent agreement to put aside all differences of race, politics, religion and background for the sake of their children. At Diwali, the Hindu festival of light, all the mothers placed *diyas*, clay lamps with cotton wicks resting in ghee, in the windows; at Christmas, artificial Christmas trees covered in fake snow and blinking lights and coloured baubles lit up those same windows, and every year, Santa visited all the houses with presents, even the Hindu and Muslim ones. And on Easter Sunday they all flew kites with the rest of Georgetown on the beach, because Christ had risen. And at Phagwah, everybody ran around throwing coloured powder on each other and laughing, because it was the Hindu festival of spring. And at Eid al-Fitr, the end of the Ramadan fast, the two Muslim families, the Khans and the Husseins, put on a sumptuous feast for everyone, and everyone celebrated, a huge street party, and everyone gave each other presents. These were their delicious

Small Days, that would be with them all their lives, however far away they wandered. Small Days were good in Kaieteur Close.

There were no shops in Kingston, but the children didn't need them, because the things they needed came to them. The Shave-Ice-Man, shaving his blocks of ice and squirting them with coloured syrups, or the Sugar-Cane-Man, who sold them sticks of delicious cane or squeezed cane-juice out of his grinding cogwheels. There was an Ice-Cream-Man who dropped by most afternoons, and a woman who sold pine tarts and coconut cake and tamarind balls, who also came round each day.

A man with a donkey cart laden with water coconuts came once a week, and all the mothers would buy heaps of coconuts with their tops hacked off for easy access, and of course for the kids, there was a round of coconut water right away, a hole hacked into the top of the coconut and a straw stuck in.

Every morning, the paper boy made his round, with his rhythmic yell: *Chronicle-Argosy-Graphic*-Papers! And late afternoon, he returned, and the kids would chant: '*Evening Post*, Holy Ghost!' Sometimes the children squabbled, of course, as children do; but mostly they played well together, and they all loved and accepted Rita; even the older ones, the ten- and eleven-year-olds, who generally placed themselves above the 'babies', as those under ten were referred to. Rita was still officially a 'baby', but there was *something* about her that earned the respect of even the older ones – everyone knew it.

Rita, some adults whispered, shaking their heads and tut-tutting, was a strange child. Taciturn in the extreme, she radiated a mercurial intensity and authority that challenged the world to ignore her at its peril, while also displaying a complete indifference towards that world. She focused her attention exclusively on those living beings she deemed worthy of such single-minded attention, and only a few hand-picked adults were in that privileged circle: her father Jitty, when he made himself available, their housekeeper Mildred, and Polly Wong's mother. Towards almost all other adults Rita maintained an icy silence, speaking only when she was spoken to (that is, if an answer was required), and then in monosyllables. She hardly ever smiled, and she never laughed if there was any danger of an adult seeing or hearing her. And it was good so. Adults deserved no better.

But it was different with children; other children naturally admired and looked up to her and accepted her as someone to listen to, whether they were her schoolmates at Mary Noble School or the Kaieteur Close Gang, or random children she met on other occasions – at parties, or at the playground, or flying kites on the beach at Easter. Children were drawn to her, and she was kind to them and looked after them.

But her heart belonged to animals, animals of every variety. Her entire inner being focused on their needs. Her very life revolved around the puppies and kittens she brought home to nurture. She had a secret place, at the back of the garden, behind the provisions section managed by the gardener, Singh, behind the toolshed, where Chandra never went, and that's where she tended her furry patients.

With them, she would lose herself, ignoring the rest of the world; and the world – that is, the boys and girls who had gained admission to her world – would gaze on her in admiration, ask questions, which she answered crisply and cleverly, and offer their services.

Helpfully, they brought wounded or stray animals to her, sometimes going far out of their way to find such presents: a puppy with a thorn in its paw from Aunt Ida's home all the way across town, or a tailless lizard, victim of some sadistic boy's torture.

Rita would douse their wounds in mercurochrome nicked from the medicine cabinet, then wrap them generously in (also nicked) bandages. She had found interesting uses for methylated spirits, witch hazel and calamine lotion. The Dettol bottle on the bathroom shelf seemed to empty itself at breakneck speed and the room itself developed a permanent and pungent smell. She had found out through trial and error that Band-Aid didn't stick on feathers or fur, and that cats were less-patient patients than dogs. And she knew the power of a soothing voice and a caressing hand.

But even animals were not enough to completely tame Rita's adventurous spirit, and even Kaieteur Close was not world enough for her.

Chapter Ten

Lots of Ways to Die

Chandra was out visiting one of her friends or relations, and Jitty and Rita were sitting on the back stairs eating chow-chow – grated green mango with salt and pepper sauce, Rita's favourite. It was a rare moment of togetherness; it seemed to Jitty that he hardly ever had time to talk to his daughter. But if he had hoped for some light chit-chat, he was to be disappointed. Rita had other ideas.

'Daddy, what was my mummy like?'

'Oh, she was wonderful, darling. She was beautiful and charming – you would have loved her!'

'Yes, but what was she *like*? Was she clever?'

'Oh yes, that too! She was so, so clever, just like you.'

'I'm not clever.'

'Yes, you are!'

'Teacher says I'm a scallywag.'

'Well, you are, a bit. But scallywags can be clever too!'

'Was she a scallywag?'

He sighed. 'No, not a bit. She was a quiet girl.'

'Tell me more about her. What she was actually *like*?'

'Well, she loved flowers and birds and good food. She also loved music. You should listen to my record collection sometimes – she loved all that music. I'll show you how to play records, if you like. If you're careful with them and don't let them get scratched.'

'What was her favourite music?'

'Oh, just popular music; everything! The Mamas & The Papas, the Beatles, of course, the Bee Gees, John Denver – everything! She also liked all those corny old-fashioned crooners: Jim Reeves, Pat Boone, and so on. I tried to wean her off those, introduce her to the hits. We had it all on cassette and we'd sit in the car on the Sea Wall and listen. She would sing along and sometimes we went to a fete and danced to live bands. The Young Ones was our favourite band. And she would watch the kiskadees and sing "Yellow Bird" – she thought that was what the song was about, the kiskadee, flying away.'

'I love kiskadees too! There's one that sings every morning in the tree outside my window: *kisk-kisk-kiskadee!*'

'We have so many of them! Do you know what kiskadee means?'

'No, what?'

'It's French! Kiskadees speak French! They're saying *"Qu'est-ce qu'il dit?"*, which is French and means "what's he saying?"'

She laughed. 'So, if I ask *what's he's saying*, in French, the answer is *what's he's saying?* That's so funny!'

'Isn't it! The French must have named the bird. You know that Guyana was once French, don't you? You must be learning that in history class? French, and Dutch, before we were British, British Guiana. That's why we have so many Dutch and French names of places. And in the end, they each got a country of their own, French Guiana, Dutch Guiana, and British Guiana. Dutch Guiana is now Suriname, and we are Guyana.'

Jitty always loved to insert a history or geography lesson into his conversations with Rita. She was so thirsty for knowledge; he liked to encourage that. But this time:

'Yes, but Daddy, I wanted to talk about Mummy, not about history. Did she love other animals, like me? I love animals best of all! More than I love people!'

'Oh, yes, she loved animals! She used to have a cat and a dog, just like you. And she loved wild animals, too. You know, she was from the country, and there are lots of wild animals there. She told me she used to have a pet monkey! A sakiwinki!'

'Can I have a pet sakiwinki, just like her?'

'I wouldn't mind, but don't think Chandra would allow it, darling.'

'I know. She hates animals. But I love them. I don't know if I prefer cats or dogs, it's possible to like both the same, isn't it, and I do. But cats a bit more, I think, because I'm a bit like them. They like to roam and be wild and run free and so do I. Cats don't like to be controlled, and I'm like that too.

'Daddy, can we go to the zoo again soon? I want to feed the manatee and see that jaguar. I feel so sorry for him, in a cage like that, walking up and down. He looks so sad. He should be free, in the jungle! You can't keep a jaguar as a pet, but some people keep ocelots, did you know that, Daddy? They're like small wild cats and they live in the rainforest, in the Interior. I want to go to the Interior one day and maybe I'll see an ocelot and make friends and keep it. But Chandra wouldn't let me, would she? And I might get bitten by a snake, a labaria. Or a bushmaster. Or get squeezed by a boa constrictor. I know all about snakes. I read about them in a library book called *Wild Animals of the Amazon*. And we have a thousand million animal and bird and insect species in Guyana and most of them haven't even been discovered yet.

'I want to be a zoologist when I grow up, and discover them. Or a vet. If I discover a new species, like a new insect or spider, I can get it named after me. It would be the maraj spider, for instance. I wonder if somebody named Tarantula discovered the tarantula? Maybe the maraj spider would be even more poisonous. Or bigger. Bigger than the Goliath bird-eating spider, which is the biggest spider in the world. It's a tarantula. If you discover a star, you can get it named after you. Did you know that?' She stopped for breath.

'Sort of.'

'But tell me more about Mummy.'

He sighed. 'What else do you want to know about her?'

'Was she looking forward to having a baby, having me?'

'You can't imagine how much! She was looking forward to you so much! She would have loved you so, so much!'

'And if she had lived, you wouldn't have married Chandra, would you?'

'Oh, sweetheart! If she had lived, everything would have been different. I'm so sorry you didn't get to know her.'

A long pause as they both reflected on those last words. Then: 'Daddy – how did she die?'

Jitty hesitated.

'Well, darling, she was ill and the doctors couldn't save her.'

'What was she ill with? Was it cancer? Brian's granny had cancer and she died.'

'No – no. It wasn't cancer.'

'Well then, what was it? Donna deSouza said her mummy had a friend who committed suicide. That means she killed herself! Isn't that awful?'

'Yes, it's very awful.'

'She must have been so sad. Donna said she hung herself. I'm sad too, a lot, but I don't want to die or hang myself.'

He shuddered, reached out and pulled her close. Then Rita whispered, very quietly, into his ear: 'Donna said I killed Mummy. That when I was being born, her tummy split open and killed her. That's how Mummy died, Donna said.'

He pushed her back, and stared at her. 'What?' Donna told you that? When?'

'Daddy, let go of my arm! You're hurting me. A long time ago. In March, I think. But it's not true is it, Daddy? I didn't kill Mummy?'

There were tears in her voice, and Jitty was quick to put her at ease. He put his arm round her, pulled her close.

'Of course not!'

'I knew it wasn't true. There are lots of ways to die, like cancer and suicide, like I said. And some people have accidents. They drown, or a car smashed into them, or they fall out of a window and break their necks, or something. Or it's a plane crash. Or somebody murders them. With a knife or a gun. People even get their throats cut, you know! It must be horrible! And if you're a queen, you might get your head cut off. It's called execution. In some countries like America they execute people who did bad things, like murder people, did you know that? They shoot them and hang them. I read it in the papers. And you could get bitten by a poisonous snake, like a bushmaster, if you go walking in the jungle, or else if you go swimming in a creek you might get attacked by piranhas and they eat all the flesh off of you. Or you could be a soldier and get shot in a war. And if you climb up a tall ladder to paint a window, or to break into a house like happened to the Khans, you might fall off the ladder and break your neck. Or your house could be on fire, and you live on the top storey, and you have the choice either to die in the fire or jump – what would you do, Daddy? I would jump, because maybe there'd be people standing in the yard telling you to jump and they'd be holding out a big white sheet to catch you. And animals die. They get put down by vets. Chandra had all my animals put down. And sometimes I find dead birds in the garden, or my little fish die. There are lots of ways to die. A thousand million ways.'

'Yes, but – you said you're sad. Why are you sad?'

Jitty knew he shouldn't have asked that question the moment he asked it. Rita was a past master at taking a conversation on long winding routes and then bringing it right back to the beginning, but this time it was his fault. She could switch from flippant diversions to earnest in a heartbeat. Usually he managed to divert her, at least temporarily, but this time he had given her just the opening she needed.

'Because I miss Mummy so much. I think about her all the time. Is she in heaven? Polly's mummy says she's in heaven, and she's watching over me as an angel. Is that true?'

'It probably is, Rita.'

'And she says I can talk to Mummy and she'll answer, and I do, I always do, but I don't think she's in heaven. I think she's in my heart. Inside me. That's closer than heaven, isn't it?'

'Much closer.'

'So, I talk to her, and she answers, and she's watching over me. And she doesn't want me to die.'

'Of course not!'

'And maybe she isn't dead, either. Maybe she just wandered into the jungle and got lost, and is living with an Amerindian tribe somewhere in the deep jungle, a tribe that nobody knows about, but Mummy discovered them but doesn't know the way back. Or maybe when she wandered into the forest, a bad man found her and captured her and kept her captive all these years. That happened to a woman in America, I read it in the papers. And if that's what happened, we should go looking for her. But maybe she really *is* dead. And you know how she died, but you won't tell me. So why can't you tell me now: how did she die, if she did die?'

Jitty stiffened. There it was again. The question that should not be asked and never be answered.

'I told you already. She – she was ill, darling.'

'If it wasn't cancer, then what was it? Granma died from a heart attack. Was it that?'

'No, sweetheart, she didn't have a heart attack.'

'What, then?'

'It was – well, it was her blood. A blood disease. Her blood turned bad.'

'How can blood turn bad? You mean like spoilt milk?'

'Oh, darling! Please let's not talk about this now! It's a bit difficult to understand but one day you will, when you're all grown up. I promise. It's all in the past. Let's talk about the future.'

'But the future is with Chandra! And I don't like Chandra!'

'You have to try a little harder with Chandra. She is your new mummy and it might be a bit difficult for a while but I'm sure you'll grow to love each other.'

'When she has her baby, she'll hate me!'

'Don't say that! Of course she won't!'

'She will, Daddy. I know she will.'

Actually, Jitty was quite enjoying married life. Occasionally Chandra had a little tantrum but she was easily mollified by a few hugs and a candlelit dinner at Palm Courts. She was happy if he went window-shopping with her, her arm hooked into his – though she complained steadily that these days, there wasn't anything to look at in the windows – and she had quickly accepted the fact that it was her money paying for everything.

Jitty had little more than his own salary, which didn't go very far, but Chandra not only had shares in Jha Construction through her father, she had come into a quite respectable trust fund upon her marriage, the Fogarty trust fund left her by her Fogarty grandfather, whom she had met only once, as a child, on one of his rare visits to the country. On his first visit, many years previously, he had brought his young daughter, Chandra's mother, who had fallen in love with an Indian man and, to the horror of the family back home, married him. Grandfather Fogarty, on meeting his only grandchild, had fallen in love with her and, returning to England never to see her again, decided to leave his everything to her. This was the very trust fund, in fact, that had lit up Jitty's grandmother's eyes back in the day when she'd been looking for prospective wives for her wayward grandson. It was this trust fund that had coaxed her to overlook the fact that Chandra was only 50 per cent Indian. The other 50 per cent was English, but *well-heeled* English, which meant it could be excused.

Chandra was all for leading the kind of agreeable life Jitty liked. They spent their Saturdays at the Pegasus poolside, sitting with friends old and new at one of the shady tables, where Chandra would sip a piña colada and Jitty enjoyed a rum and Coke or two, cracking jokes. Once he had suggested they bring Rita along – she would have fun swimming in the pool with the children of their friends – but Chandra had wrinkled her nose and told him why that would never work.

'Rita would not enjoy their company,' she said. 'You don't know your own daughter. Rita has a way of talking that would immediately make her unpopular. The other children might tease her and she would feel left out. And anyway, she much prefers running wild in the yard covering herself with dirt or running off wherever she runs off to. It would be wrong to try and tame her. Let her be.'

'We could maybe all go up to Buxton beach next weekend,' Jitty suggested amiably. 'She always used to like that. The Allicocks have a beach house they let us borrow, we could sleep there Saturday night. She enjoyed watching the crabs, and playing cricket on the beach, and…'

But Chandra wrinkled her nose even more, and shook her head vigorously. 'Jitty, you know how I hate Guyana seawater. That awful dirty brown water!'

'It's not dirt, it's only mud, from the Amazon! People say it's good for the skin,' Jitty joked. 'It will make you even more beautiful than you are. Maybe we should try putting it in jars and exporting it as the latest beauty potion.'

He stopped abruptly when he saw Chandra's expression, and continued in a conciliatory tone, 'But if you don't like the beach, we could go up to Red Water Creek…?'

'That's even worse! Do I look like the sort of wild woman who goes swimming in those bush creeks? You never know what snakes and alligators are going to bite off your toes. Not me, you won't catch me dead up there!' Chandra rubbed her cheek, frowned, and then smiled, showing two rows of sparkling white teeth.

'Now if you really want to go to the sea, we could go and visit my Uncle Vincent in St Lucia. What you say to that?'

'Great idea!' Jitty enthused. 'We could go in the Christmas holidays, Rita would be so excited! She always wanted to travel!'

'Christmas holidays? Are you mad? I would be… let me see… eight months pregnant by then, I would be enormous. You don't think I would be seen gallivanting on the beach in that condition? No, if we go at all, we have to go soon, maybe next month. And that so-called honeymoon we had – do you remember the rats in that cheap hotel? I was scared out of my life! October would be perfect. Or November. Let me book it.'

'But then Rita – school…'

'Rita this, Rita that! Mildred is perfectly capable of looking after that girl; she does whatever she wants anyway. All she needs is a bowl of Corn Flakes in the morning, a chicken leg for lunch, and half a jar of peanut butter in between. And a bed at night. That's settled then. I'll write to Uncle Vincent tomorrow.'

All in all, Jitty thought, he had a very harmonious marriage.

They hardly ever quarrelled. Any differences they had were quickly reconciled, for Chandra always had some very good sugges-tion that would more than adequately solve any problem. She was a genius at that. If only Rita would come to her senses. If only she and Chandra would make friends. But once Chandra had a baby of her own, he said to himself, all her motherly instincts would surface and everything would turn out for the best. After all, he had given Rita a proper family at last.

He had developed regular ways, the ways of a proper husband and father, and he had stopped hanging out with bachelor friends and coming home drunk – Chandra would never stand for that sort of behaviour – and when his son was born, they would finally be like all the other Kaieteur Close families: father and mother, boy and girl, grand house, lovely garden. Granma, had she lived, would have been proud of him (except for in the matter of Rita, of course).

He kept his promise to Rita, to introduce her to the music Cassie had loved. One afternoon, after work – Chandra was out visiting a neighbour – he sat her down next to the Grundig stereogram, opened the compartment where he kept his old records, and showed her how to stack them above the turntable and let them play one after the other. He showed her how to hold them carefully, touching the edges only with delicate fingers or the palm of her hand, and placing the needle ever so gently on the surface. He sorted out the records – singles and LPs – that Cassie had most loved and played them for her. She leaned against the stereogram, a dreamy expression on her face, and watched the turntable spin, and listened to the lyrics. Jitty sat cross-legged on the floor next to her.

'I have to go,' said Jitty suddenly. She looked up. Jitty was scrambling to his feet and his face was wet.

'Daddy! You're crying! What's wrong?'

'Nothing, nothing.' He wiped his face with his shirt-tails. 'You listen. This was her favourite song. Keep listening, choose the ones you like best. I'll record them on cassette for you, so you can listen whenever you want, in your room—' His voice broke, and he got up and walked away. Rita frowned, shrugged, and leaned against the Grundig once again. She'd never understand adults.

Aunty Penny came to visit again, against Jitty's explicit instructions. She came when Daddy was at work. Rita opened the door to her again, scowled and stared for a moment again, and, remembering Daddy's response last time, shut the door in Aunty Penny's face, even before Aunty Penny had finished greeting her. She didn't like adults anyway, and this was an adult Daddy didn't like either. All the more reason to reject her.

'Quite right,' Jitty said when she told him that evening.

'What did she do wrong?' she asked casually, and Jitty replied, 'Everything. I'll tell you one day.'

It was a white lie, but white lies were fine, Jitty reminded himself. In this case, it was a white lie for Rita's protection. He'd do anything to protect Rita. Lie the hind legs off a donkey, if need be.

Chapter Eleven

November: The Hello-goodbye Plant

Hunkered on the grass verge beside the gutter outside the Wongs' home, totally immersed in the soul of the hello-goodbye plant, Rita didn't hear the footsteps approaching from behind, and she didn't look up when Mrs Wong – Aunty Jenny, she was meant to call her – crouched down beside her, laying her tennis racquet on the grass. Mrs Wong – Aunty Jenny – didn't speak; she only watched.

Rita squatted firmly in her favoured position, bare bony brown knees tucked snugly into her armpits. One arm hugged her legs for balance, her left hand cupped one knee, the right held a long stalk of grass, which she held forward, slowly moving it from one tiny branch of the hello-goodbye plant to the other. Her lips whispered the words hello, goodbye as she worked through the clump of grass. The hello-goodbye plant was really nothing but a tangle of weeds, consisting of hundreds of tiny branches like miniature palms. Most of the time they were open, but when you touched them, they slipped into motion: the palms moved their branches upwards, reaching up to clasp each other in long tight nodes, refusing to unclasp till the plant was perfectly certain that danger had passed. Rita ran her grass-stalk gently from palm to palm, barely touching them, yet even such slight encounters sent each one into withdrawal.

Absorbed in the spectacle, Rita made not the slightest gesture to acknowledge Aunty Jenny's presence by her side, other than to stop whispering her hellos and goodbyes and only mouth the words, her lips moving in rhythm: hello as her stalk approached a new palm, goodbye as it closed up, and on to the next. Aunty Jenny watched, saying nothing. Though she had not glanced up, Rita had felt at once when Aunty Jenny entered her space, and closed up herself, drawing an inner cloak around her being. However, when Aunty Jenny did nothing, said nothing, but only watched, Rita felt an inner release of tension; and now it seemed certain there was to be no assault she first glanced sideways up at Polly's mother, and then she slightly turned her head. Aunty Jenny did not look back at her; she was as absorbed in the hello-goodbye plant as Rita had been, for now the tiny palms had not been touched for several minutes and they were slowly, hesitantly, opening up again. Aunty Jenny pursed her lips and blew gently, touching one branch with her breath, and right away, the plant took fright and drew its leaves together. Only then did Aunty Jenny chuckle softly, and turn her face towards Rita, who smiled slightly and turned her face away so she wouldn't see.

Aunty Jenny spoke then, in almost a whisper. 'Rita,' she said, 'you've been here for hours. I saw you when I went to tennis and you've not moved an inch. If you sit here much longer, you'll turn into a plant yourself!'

'I could have gone in the house just after you left and come out again just before you came back, couldn't I?' said Rita.

'That's very true,' Aunty Jenny agreed. 'But wouldn't you like to come in for some ice cream? Polly would love to play with you again – she's not home right now, she's at her ballet class and so's Maxine, but you could come in and have some ice cream with me, and then we'll go and pick them up. They'd love to see you. You haven't been over for ages! We all miss you so much!'

'Ice cream makes you fat. That's what *she* says.'

'Who's she? Oh, you mean… Well, I wouldn't worry much what she says, Rita, she's a grown-up lady and maybe she worries a lot about her figure. Some ladies do that, you know, but someone like you, you're so thin, you can eat as much ice cream as you like! Soursop ice cream, really delicious!'

Rita turned then and looked up into Aunty Jenny's eyes, because if there was one thing she loved in the world, it was soursop ice cream. Aunty Jenny caught Rita's gaze in her eyes like night and they looked at each other for a whole minute without saying a word, without smiling, though the edges of Aunty Jenny's lips twitched once.

Aunty Jenny had a lovely face. She had the same skin like creamed cashew that Polly had and her wide-apart eyes were big enough and steady enough to hold you and keep you safe. When she smiled, it was like when you watched the sun rising over the Atlantic from your bedroom window, a warm clean feeling. Rita wished she would smile now, so she could get that warm clean feeling, for inside she was crumbling. Last night she had written a poem in her diary, and looking at Aunty Jenny, the words rose in her mind:

> *When I think,*
> *it's like sand.*
> *When I feel,*
> *it's much too bland.*
> *When I cry,*
> *it's like stones.*
> *When I laugh*
> *it's made of bones.*

Aunty Jenny smiled, so Rita smiled back, and said, 'OK.' She climbed to her feet, stretching her limbs slowly like a cat because they hurt from crouching so long. Aunty Jenny got up too, and bent to pick up her racquet. She wore a white blouse and a white pleated skirt that stopped halfway down her thighs, showing bare legs that were creamy like her face and just as smooth.

'Come,' she said cheerfully, and held out a hand, and Rita took it and followed her over the gutter-bridge and through the gate and up into the house.

The Wongs' house wasn't a bit like theirs. At least, not a bit like theirs had been before Doomsday. Since Doomsday, their own house was changing every day and soon it would look just like the Wongs', at least inside. The floor was polished to a high dark gloss, and a couch and two armchairs were placed around a square carpet with a low purple-heart table in the middle, and on the table was a purple-heart ashtray and a vase with sweet-smelling flowers.

Rita immediately walked over to the aquarium on a table against the far wall; she knew the goldfish well, but she hadn't been over for such a long time she was surprised by the changes.

'Where's Slippy?' she asked.

'Slippy? Who… Oh, yes, Slippy died. Didn't Polly tell you?'

'Why did Slippy die? Was she sick? If she was sick, why didn't you call me over? I could have taken care of her and made her well. And you've got two new fish. Do they have names yet?'

Aunty Jenny came over to watch the fish. 'No, I don't believe they have names – at least, Polly never told me if they do. Would you like to choose some names? And then if she hasn't given them names already, she might like to use yours.'

She didn't have to ask Rita twice. 'Aaaah…' Rita said, her brow creased in concentration. 'That one there with the black stripe, I think he should be called Flush. And the other one, the one that looks like Slippy, she's… aaah…' She held a finger against the glass and peered closely at the fish in question. 'She's Pinky.' She swung her head round to look up at Aunty Jenny with radiant eyes.

'Flush and Pinky. Those are good names, very good names. I'm sure Polly would like those names,' said Aunty Jenny, adding cautiously, 'if she hasn't given them names yet.'

Aunty Jenny left Rita looking at the fish and went into the kitchen to get the ice cream. She brought two bowls of it back and together they sat in the gallery on the rattan chairs, in front of the open window where the sea breeze swung through smelling of salt, and in companionable silence they ate. Rita took time to eat hers, savouring the tangy, sweet-sour flavour of the soursop.

There were small bits of slithery soursop flesh mixed up in the ice cream and those were the bits she loved most. Absorbed in the flavour, she spooned tiny pieces of ice cream and fruit into her mouth and felt it melting and becoming part of her, and then she licked the bowl clean with her tongue (Chandra said you weren't supposed to do that, but Chandra wasn't here now) and then she looked up and saw Aunty Jenny was watching her, but not in the mean old sourpuss way that Chandra did, but in a nice quiet warm sunrisy way. So, she smiled.

'Thank you,' she said simply.

'It's a pleasure,' said Aunty Jenny, and then she looked sort of worried, and said, 'Your daddy and… and your… your…'

'Stepmother?' Rita offered.

'Yes, stepmother. They've gone away, haven't they?'

'Oh yes, they went to a place called St Lucia. It's an island. They're staying in a horrible big hotel with a swimming pool. It's called the Blue Waters Beach Hotel, because the water there is blue, not brown like here. They sent me a postcard. It looks really horrible. I'm glad I refused to go.'

'You refused to go?'

'Yes. Daddy really wanted me to come, he begged and begged but I said no. I told him I'm busy, I have things to do. 'Portant things. And I like it here and I hate those places. Broad places.'

'Broad places?'

'Yes, broad. Those broad far-away places. I don't want to go broad.'

'Oh, yes, you mean abroad.'

'Yes, that's what I said. Broad, places. So, I told Daddy to go with her and he went. He wanted to stay with me when I didn't want to go but I told him no, I want to be here alone. With Mildred, alone.'

'But aren't you… just a little bit, sometimes, you know, lonely? I mean, you haven't got any animals any more, and you're not playing with the other children…?'

'No. I like being alone by myself.'

'But what do you do alone by yourself all day?'

'Well, you know, I do some thinking. Sometimes I think about things.'

'What things?'

'Just things. Sometimes I think about my thoughts, and sometimes I think about being something else, like a plant or an ant. She killed all the ants in the house, you know, with Flit, but there are still plenty in the yard.' Rita grinned in a sly way, and whispered, 'I even know where the wood-ants are eating up the house, but I won't tell her, so the house will fall down. And I can climb up in the mango tree and think up there. I can pretend I'm a tree and wave my arms like branches and be the sky.'

Now that she had started to speak the words came pouring out, as if Aunty Jenny had pressed a button and a dam of communication had burst open. Aunty Jenny sat silently listening, nodding, now and then smiling. Then she looked at her watch and interrupted Rita's flood of words. 'Rita, it's getting late,' she said. 'I have to go and pick up Polly and Maxine from their ballet class. Would you like to come? It's only round the corner in Lamaha Street, just a short walk.'

Rita hesitated, not knowing what to say. It was a funny thing with friends. Sometimes you stopped speaking to them and you didn't say a word even when they came out of the gate with their housekeeper and walked right past you, talking to the hello-goodbye plant. You heard them walking by, but you didn't turn round and say hi, just pretended they weren't there, and they didn't say hi either. So, you weren't friends any more. But you wanted to be friends again and you didn't know how to go about it, and you didn't want to be the first one to start being friends again, but you were the first one to stop being friends, and you had forgotten why exactly, so perhaps it was only just if you were the one to start talking again, and going to pick them up from ballet class?

'Polly doesn't like me any more,' she said.

'Of course she likes you! I told you she's dying to play with you again, and Maxine too. She thinks you don't like her. She said you stopped talking to her a week ago and you just ignore her at school, and I told her perhaps you're preoccupied.'

'What kind of pie is that?'

'Pre-occ-u-pied. It means lost in thought so much that you don't notice things going on around you.'

'Say it again?'

Aunty Jenny did so.

'Pre-occ-u-pied,' Rita repeated. 'Is it one word or more?'

'It's one word,' said Aunty Jenny.

'And it means all those things at once?'

'Yes. The prefix is pre, which means "before", or "prior to", which is the same thing, and you know what occupied means. So, preoccupied means you were occupied with something before the thing you're supposed to be occupied with.'

'Pre-occ-u-pied,' Rita said, memorising it. It was a nice word, a useful word, that made sense and was relevant to much of her present life.

A big word with a big meaning, not like all the silly little in-between words the language was full of, words that by themselves meant nothing. Preoccupied held all kinds of little words together and meant them all at once. Rita knew exactly what preoccupied meant, and she resolved to write it in her diary that night and use it as often as she could.

Aunty Jenny looked at her watch again and said, 'But, Rita, I really have to go now, so if you're preoccupied, I'll leave you here to do some more thinking, otherwise let's go!'

When Rita, moving her lips to memorise the wonderful new word preoccupied, didn't make a move, Aunty Jenny added craftily,

'We'll take Rover with us. You can hold the leash.' And she held out her hand and Rita took it, and jumped to her feet, and held Aunty Jenny's hand all the way to the ballet school in Lamaha Street, and the end of Rover's leash in the other, and after that she and Polly were friends again.

'Why weren't you friends with me for a whole week?' Polly asked later, for Polly was a frank, outgoing girl who never kept her thoughts to herself like Rita.

'I was preoccupied,' said Rita grandly, 'but now I'm not any more. Those two new fishes you have – what are their names?'

'They don't have any names – yet,' said Polly. 'I was thinking we could name them together. You're so good at names, what d'you think?'

'Pinky and Flush,' said Rita immediately.

Chapter Twelve

The Scoop

Rita no longer slept in her bedroom. Since Jitty and Chandra's departure for St Lucia a week ago, the house had more or less returned to its pre-Chandra state of comfortable disorder, and Mildred didn't mind in the least when Rita dragged her mattress to the top of the stairs, sat on it, and whooshed down to the bottom like on a flying carpet. Nor did she mind when Rita dragged the mattress to a corner of the drawing room and declared she was going to sleep there from now on, at least till Chandra came back and raised objections.

'You got de big house all to youself,' said Mildred dismissively. 'For all I concern, you could do what you want. You is de mistress.'

In a way it was nice having the big house all to herself, all alone in all the space. On the other hand, it was a bit spooky if you didn't have someone to talk to. It wouldn't have been so bad with animals around. She knew there was no point starting an ant farm all over again, but she did bring up a jar full of tadpoles, who all died after two days, floating soft-belly-up on the water. Which made it even more spooky, for the tadpole ghosts swam through the rooms at night, trying to talk to Rita, blaming her for their baby deaths.

So, the evening after she and Polly started talking again, Rita was still awake when she heard the gate creak open. At first, she thought it was Cyril, Mildred's boyfriend, who, since Jitty and Chandra had left, had begun to visit Mildred at night sometimes, like he used to do before Doomsday. But she hadn't heard Cyril's car so she wondered if it was a ghost, not a tadpole ghost but a people ghost. Maybe it was Granma, or Aunt Mary. Though Aunt Mary wasn't dead, she was in England, but maybe she came back secretly, as a ghost, to check out what they were up to. But no, ghosts didn't need gates – they just walk through walls, like Casper.

Then she heard a gentle knocking on Mildred's door through the open window, and then voices talking, and it definitely wasn't Cyril's voice; it was another woman's voice. Funny, Rita thought, but she was far too sleepy to analyse it. And then she fell asleep.

But next morning there was a big surprise waiting for her. She was going to be late for school as usual and was gobbling down her breakfast sitting in the Berbice chair with a flustered Mildred goading her on when Polly burst through the door.

'Rita, Rita!' she shouted. 'Rita, you can come and stay with us!' Rita's mouth was full of peanut butter and bread, so she made some strange gulping noises in the process of trying to get it down.

'Mummy spoke to your daddy last night. She rang him up in his hotel on St Lucia and he said it's fine with him if you want to. Oh, Rita, Rita, please come! Wouldn't it be wonderful? You can come and sleep in my room, we have a mattress for you but you can sleep in my bed even!'

Mildred, picking up Rita's pyjamas from the carpet, said laconically, 'Oh, yeh, I forgot to mention it, Rita. Aunty Jenny came over last night to arsk if it would be all right and I give she you daddy's telephone number. So, she done telephone already?'

'Yes, yes!' cried Polly. 'She spoke to him last night when we were all sleeping, and he said yes, and you can move in right away! After school! And we're going to have such fun! A whole week!'

And they did. Living with the Wongs was like having all the whole world reach out and say hello, and not say goodbye again, and at the end of the week when Daddy rang from St Lucia, Rita prattled on so long, Daddy had to shout to get a word in.

'Rita, just be quiet for one minute please. Listen, dear, I'm glad you're happy there. I thought you would be, and Aunty Jenny told me she likes having you, that's why I know you won't mind if Chandra and I stay a week longer, will you?'

'No, no, it's all right, Daddy, I like living here... Oh!'

'What?'

'It's my birthday trip next Thursday! To Kaieteur! The one you postponed, when it was really my birthday!'

'Your... Oh, hell, yes, I forgot.'

'You promised!'

'Yes, I know, dear, and we will, we will, I still promise! Just another day, not on Thursday.'

'But you already changed the date once, and you forgot, and now you forgot again, and you'll forget again!'

'No, darling, I promise, cross my heart, we'll go up next weekend. I'll book it the moment I get home. No, not next weekend because we're coming back on Saturday, but the weekend after that... Oh hell, no, that's the Miss Guyana contest, I have to cover it, but I promise, dear, we will do it some time. Soon.'

'You always promise but you never keep your promises! Never!' And she banged down the receiver.

Aunty Jenny found her an hour later, up in the mango tree.

'Are you feeling better now, darling?'

Rita nodded.

'Would you like to come down? I've got some soursop ice cream.'

Rita nodded again, and came down.

'Would you like to tell me all about it?'

Rita nodded. 'Daddy promised. He promised we'd go on my birthday in September but then something at work came up and then he booked for next Thursday and I was looking forward to it, and I would take the day off from school and he would take a day off from work, and we would fly up to Kaieteur Falls, just me and him and not Chandra, and we would spend the day there, and then we would come down. It was to be my delayed birthday present. He promised me ages and ages ago, even before she came, and now he says we can't. Because of *her*. And I didn't even have a party!'

In the end, though, Jitty and Chandra did return in time for the trip to Kaieteur, which was booked for 20 November. But there was no trip to Kaieteur. Nobody even remembered that the tickets were booked, except Rita herself.

On the afternoon of the eighteenth, Jitty burst through the door in a state of high excitement, followed by a scowling Chandra. Rita was at home because Polly and Maxine were at ballet class; she was sitting on the floor in front of a bowl of water, trying to coax baby frogs to sit on floating corks, but she jumped up and ran to him, crying, 'Daddy! Daddy! You came for my birthday trip! We're going to Kaieteur!'

She couldn't believe it: he had made a decision to come home for her birthday, chosen *her* before Chandra!

But after a hasty hug Jitty pushed her aside. 'Not now, darling, I'm really busy. I have to dash off to the newsroom – haven't you heard the news?'

'What news? Tell me!'

'Oh, darling – not now. Chandra will explain. It's a big, big thing. The whole world is watching Guyana. I have to dash.' And dash he did, leaving Rita dazed and Chandra visibly upset, too upset, even, to be cross with Rita, yet more than excited and eager to talk and answer questions.

'What happened? I don't understand!'

'A lot of people committed suicide! In the jungle! They say over a thousand! You know what suicide is, right?'

'Of course! But how? Why? I don't understand!'

'Nobody does, that's why Jitty had to go, to investigate.'

'How can a thousand people kill themselves, all at once?'

'It seems they all drank some drink, Kool-Aid, they say, and it was poisoned! So, they all died at once!' Chandra sobbed. 'Even women and children! The mothers gave the children the poison to drink, and now they all up there in the jungle, lying in the hot sun, the bodies rotting!'

'But why, why? Why would they do that?'

'I don't know, I just heard it on the radio myself. They say it's some American man, a preacher, who told them to do it. It's like a religion – they're saying it's a cult.'

'What's a cult?'

'It's like a made-up religion, a new religion, with a new leader that everybody has to follow and do what he says. And this man, this leader, told them to kill themselves!'

'I still don't understand. What were they doing in the jungle, a thousand people?'

'Nobody knew about them. They came from America – mostly black people. They came to settle in Guyana because they thought it was paradise. I don't know, Rita, I don't know. Look, it's nearly four o'clock. Let's turn on the radio. You can listen too. It will be in tomorrow's papers, and when Jitty comes back, he'll tell us more.'

Chandra switched on the radio and they both listened, stunned, as a breathless announcer, falling over his words, repeated over and over again the salient points of the story: almost a thousand people, almost all black Americans, had drunk poison together and their bodies lay roasting in the sun in a remote camp far away from civilisation. Television crews and newspaper reporters from all over the world were pouring into the country, and for once in its humble life, Guyana was centre stage internationally, and for all the wrong reasons.

Rita didn't quite follow the story – it was just too complicated, too unbelievable, too utterly outlandish. One man, it seemed, was responsible, an American called Jim Jones. He had brought these people here, told them it was paradise, and then told them to drink poison, and they did. Children first.

Rita and Chandra, for the very first time, found themselves having something like a normal conversation, as Chandra, grappling with the truth herself, tried again and again to interpret the story for Rita.

'I don't know,' she kept repeating as Rita fired questions at her. 'I don't know any more than anybody. Jitty wants to get up there if he can – try and get a scoop – but till he come back, we just don't know.'

Jitty was gone all night and all of the next day, but at least there were photos in the *Graphic* and the *Chronicle* the next morning – of bloated bodies, hundreds of them, all on top of each other, lying in a field. There was also an article with Jitty's byline. Though no journalists were allowed into the actual disaster area as yet, he had managed to get an exclusive interview with one of the locals, who declared that the people living in the place called Jonestown were 'weird' and had kept to themselves and they, the locals, had been hearing gunshots and screams for weeks and they had always known that 'something bad' would happen.

Jitty came back that night for a shower and a change of clothes but was off again in a matter of minutes, leaving them both frustrated and hungry for more news, the radio blaring incessantly. Chandra took Rita over to the Wongs, where the excitement was just as raw and frustrated and the radio blaring just as loudly. People were coming and going, all the neighbours, all overwhelmed and thirsty for information that simply was not forthcoming. What a pity, they all said, that there was no television in Guyana as yet! Everyone wanted to *see:* see the bloated bodies, see the doctors and investigators and politicians milling about in that field of death, holding cloths over their noses, bending over to inspect the swollen corpses.

'The stench must be abominable!' said Aunty Jenny.

'How are they going to get them out?' Rita asked. 'They going to need excavators to carry them out!'

'They don't even have roads out there!' said Chandra. 'It's all jungle!'

The stories tumbled over each other. Now there was talk of an American senator and several journalists, who had come to investigate, gunned down at an airstrip near the death camp. All dead. Another story, of a townhouse affiliated to the camp where everyone had shot themselves and cut the throats of three children. Jitty was in the thick of things, here, there and everywhere, getting stories and scoops and interviews, clacking away on his typewriter in the *Graphic* newsroom. He looked dishevelled, distraught – who wouldn't be at such a terrible thing? – his hair a wild mess, but his eyes ablaze, filled with a fervour and excitement nobody had ever seen before.

They hardly saw Jitty over the following week. He popped in and out only to shower and change clothes; once he just packed a small bag and disappeared for three nights; he had a source, he said, and he had a big story. He was almost shaking with excitement, incoherent, dismissive of both of them, in and out of the house before you could even blink.

'Well,' said Chandra at the end of the week, 'this thing has certainly put Guyana on the world map. They won't be saying "Ghana? In Africa?" any more. They'll be saying, "Guyana? Where everybody committed suicide?"'

'Not everybody,' Rita corrected. 'Just a bunch of Americans.'

'A bloody big bunch of them,' said Chandra. 'Why they had to come here to do it?' Strangely enough, the catastrophe of Jonestown drew Chandra and Rita together as nothing had before. They called a truce, a fragile one, to be sure, but a truce nevertheless. Rita tried to follow Chandra's rules, and Chandra stopped her nagging.

As for Jitty: he got the scoop of a lifetime. He had known one of the cult members who lived in a house in Georgetown – or rather, *had* lived, for an aftermath of the tragedy was that all the household members in this external branch also committed suicide, including three children whose throats were slit by their mother. The night of that discovery, Jitty came home for dinner and cried all through the meal. 'The children! The children!' he wept. 'I knew them! I knew their mother!'

Halfway through the meal, he stood up, rushed to the downstairs bathroom and threw up.

Up to this point, Jitty had considered himself apolitical. Guyana had been a political mess since long before independence in 1966: divided by race, led by corrupt politicians. Elections were a fiasco – people voted according to their race, African against Indian. In Jitty's words, a pox on both their houses.

After Jonestown, Jitty went through a further transformation. He deeply suspected CIA involvement in the whole catastrophe, with the express support and encouragement of government, and he set about investigating. Perhaps this was the scoop that would make his name in international journalism; he aspired to working freelance for the big American and British newspapers and magazines. If fatherhood had made him turn over a new leaf, become serious and settled and all those boring things he'd once despised, his career as a political journalist was the icing on the cake.

After Jonestown he flailed around in search of a political home, but finding nothing worthy of his alliance, instead put all his effort into his work. This earned him a promotion to Senior Newsdesk Reporter, and a big rise in pay. Jitty was finally becoming a Man.

He aspired to the position of Political Editor-in-Chief, and kept his eyes fixed on Walter Rodney, a new political star just rising on the horizon. Rodney, he declared to anyone who asked, was Guyana's best hope. Rodney was black, with a PhD in African History from the School of Oriental and African Studies in London. A good man; intelligent, influential *and* ethical, an unusual combination in any politician.

Rodney was *the man*, Jitty declared. The man we could all unite behind; all Guyanese, Indian, black, Chinese, Portuguese, Amerindian, all races. 'We have to progress beyond race, beyond skin colour, or we are lost!' he told anyone who would listen, and always, always, he remembered Rita's mother. Racial prejudice had meant the ruin of her, and it was his sacred duty to put that right.

Chapter Thirteen

1978: The Abyss

Dear Diary,

I listened to this band called The Mamas & The Papas and I discovered that one of the singers is called Mama Cass!!! I couldn't believe it. That's my mummy's name. So sometimes I pretend that Mama Cass is my mummy. She has the most beautiful voice in the world and Daddy recorded one of her songs on my cassette player and I play it over and over again, and it helps me feel better. It's called 'Dream a Little Dream of Me' and I know, I just <u>know</u>, Mama Cass is singing it for me and every word of it is just for me. When she sings that each night, before I go to bed, I know that Mummy and me are going to meet in my dreams and we are thinking of each other.

Oh, Mama Cass! When I hear you singing that I just have to cry and cry into my pillow. I love her so much! And her other songs too. All of them. All The Mamas & The Papas, but especially Mama Cass.

So that's what I do. And if I didn't have Mama Cass, I would die. I really would. I miss her so, so much. All the children in Kaieteur Close have mummies, except me. I want her! I want her back!

Oh, Diary, I'm so scared. Chandra's baby is going to be born soon and it's going to be a boy, she says, and

Daddy always wanted a boy. I'm scared he won't love me any more if he has a son. I don't know what to do. But I listen to Mama Cass and I always feel better afterwards. That one about dreaming of me, and about saying a little prayer for me. It really helps.

Love Rita

Rita was seven when Luisa was born. The annihilation she had predicted had not come to pass. The world she had created at Number Seven had been eradicated, it was true; now there was not one fly too many in the house and not one stray cat too many in the yard. But there was order, even if only Chandra's order, and even if she missed her ants and cats and dogs, in her own little way she thrived.

The house had been painted; she had already stopped chipping away at dried paint anyway, but now there was no more dried bubbling paint; everything was in fresh pastel colours, except for her room, which was bright orange, as she had wished, and Chandra had granted her wish: a miracle. Parts of the building had been taken down, other parts built up, brought into harmony with the bulk of the building.

The ugly spindly legs on which it stood had been reconstructed into smart thick brick pillars, and the whole Bottom House enclosed in a latticework with a garage built in. Bougainvillea in a variety of colours climbed up the latticework, almost reaching into the gallery windows, and, to the right, had been coaxed higher to enclose a shady porch. The gardener, his wife, and his brood of five children, ranging in age from five to fourteen, had created a miracle of growth and colour. The flower beds had been dug and re-dug, and cartfuls of manure poured into the hungry earth, seeds strewn, seedlings planted, water poured, weeds pulled. There had been prunings of roses and tyings of vines; what had once been a tangle of overgrown weeds and wild bushes was now a luscious spreading park of emerald green lawns artistically sliced by beds of rich brown earth bearing an abundance of flora; luxuriant brilliance spilled from green foliage in a sumptuous riot of colour, hibiscus petals of shocking pink in joyful contrast with shrill orange cannas. This was the crowning glory of their Garden City; people made pilgrimages to Kaieteur Close to stand before the immaculate palings and peer through the hedge to the lushness beyond. 'Lovely,' the appreciative said. 'That woman has worked miracles. She has style.' 'Nice, but a bit overdone,' said the envious grudgingly.

And as the jungle had been tamed, so had Rita, the jungle princess. She had acknowledged defeat, and, hiding behind a veneer of sullen acquiescence, found new friends in books, the books she devoured in the privacy of her own room or in the branches of the star-apple tree (which Chandra, miraculously, had left standing).

'You've got such a nice home now!' people exclaimed.

'It's OK,' Rita replied. She missed the tadpoles, all the same.

She and Polly Wong were still the best of friends; Aunty Jenny had tided her over the worst times, and Polly's animals had received a double portion of love.

'She's settled down nicely,' said Jitty to Chandra. 'She's like a real daughter now, she don't give no trouble no more.'

'I told you all she needed was a tight rein,' said Chandra.

'Daddy, what's a half-caste?'

'It's somebody who is half one race, half another. But where did you hear that word?'

'From Chandra. She said I'm one.'

Jitty looked up from the newspaper he was poring over: the *Chronicle*, full of lies, as ever.

'Chandra told you that you're half-caste?'

'No! She didn't tell me, she told someone else. I heard her talking on the phone.'

'What did she say?'

'She said I can't go somewhere because I'm a half-caste.'

'Go where?'

Rita shrugged. 'I don't know. She was talking about dresses and what she was going to wear and if she could bring a nanny for the baby or leave her at home or something. And she said I can't go because I'm a half-caste.'

'Oh – she must mean her cousin's wedding. Those Jhas are terribly racist.'

'What's racist?'

'It's if you think one race is better than the other. Like here in Guyana, we have six races, like me and Chandra, we're Indian, and you are mixed-race because of your mother.'

'So, I'm half-caste, and that's a bad thing?'

'It's not bad at all! It's just different but some people think it's bad. It's when somebody of one race marries somebody of another race. Then their children are mixed-race. We don't say half-caste any more.'

'So that's why the Jhas don't like me.'

'They don't even know you – how can they not like you? See, that's racism, Rita, not liking somebody because of their race and not because of their character. Racism is a bad thing. Being mixed-race isn't. It's your character that counts, not your race. If you're a good person or not.'

'Am I a good person?'

He chuckled. 'Well, you're a bit of a scallywag! But you're only a child. It's allowed.'

'Is Chandra a racist?'

'A bit. All the Jhas are. They're very orthodox.'

'What does ortho… whatever you said – mean?'

'Orthodox. It means narrow-minded, believing and doing only one thing according to your religion. It's the opposite of open-minded. I'm open-minded and I want you to be too.'

'But if she's a racist, and racists are bad, then Chandra is bad?' Jitty scratched his head.

'No – no. I didn't say she was bad.'

'But you said racism is bad and you said she's a bit racist. So, she's a bit bad.'

'I suppose everybody's a bit bad. We're all a mixture of bad and good.'

He was happy with that explanation. It was perfect. But Rita wasn't finished.

'Is the baby going to be half-caste? Like me?'

'No. The baby will be Indian, because both parents are Indian.'

'But Chandra isn't, is she? Chandra is half-caste. Because she's half-white. She's always boasting about being half-white. So, she's half-caste too!'

'Mixed-race. Don't say half-caste, it's not nice.'

'But she said half-caste and she said I'm bad, but she's half-caste too, if it's a bad thing!'

'Oh, Rita! There's a lot more to it than that! You see, racists believe that some races are better than others. They think that white people are better than black people. So, it's good to be mixed-race white like Chandra…' He paused, searching for the right words, but Rita got there before him.

'But not mixed-race black, like me?'

Jitty didn't want to admit it. Didn't want to concede in any way.

'And *white* people would think *she's* mixed-race-bad, because she's half-Indian? So, she's half-caste too!'

'Well, people think all kinds of things, darling. The racists think all kinds of things. But racism is bad, and it's wrong, so I don't want you ever to think it's a bad thing to be mixed-race. Or black. Or anything else but perfect, just as you are.'

'But I'm *not* perfect! You just said that everybody's a mixture of good and bad!'

'Oh, sweetheart! Look at this ad! *Robin Hood*! Walt Disney! Showing at the Strand this weekend! Shall we go, just you and me?'

'Wheeeee! Yes, of course!'

Chapter Fourteen

Ol' Year's Nite

1 January 1979

Dear Diary,

It wasn't a brother after all, it was a sister, and I'm so glad because that was what I was wanting. But I haven't seen her yet because of Ol' Year's Nite. I'll tell you how it happened.

Her Royal Majesty was peeved all day and didn't let me go out and I was fretting all day because I'd promised Polly and Donna I'd come round and we'd go liming on the Sea Wall but forget it. I had to ring them up and tell them to go without me. And then I had to run behind Her Royal Majesty... well, not really run behind her, because Her Majesty never left her royal chamber all day. But run all the same.

Rita, my back is hurting, bring me some cushions from the settee downstairs. Rita, run quick and tell Saraswati to serve me lunch in bed. Rita, the noise is terrible, my head is killing me, go and get some aspirin and close the louvres. The sunlight is terrible! And the noise! Turn off that radio! No, turn it on again but not too loud, I forgot my story is coming in a minute. No, Rita, please stay home today, I may need you, I feel so unsettled and my head is killing me.

Anyway, after lunch she fell asleep and I took a deep breath and I went over to Polly but she was still at the Sea Wall. So, I spent the whole afternoon staring out the window till she woke up again and began bossing me around again.

Daddy didn't come home all afternoon. And he didn't come home all evening and he didn't come home all night. And when she began screaming in the middle of the night, he wasn't home either. Only me and Saraswati. Saraswati is the new maid Chandra hired after she sent Mildred packing. I prefer Mildred.

So, when I hear her screaming, I run to get Saraswati from downstairs and then Saraswati got up to see what she's screaming about. But of course we know. So, Saraswati burst out of her room and yell at me to ring Daddy and ring the doctor because 'de baby comin''.

So, how'm I supposed to ring Daddy? Daddy gallivanting around town, working hard at reporting on all the parties. So, I ring the hospital instead and they say Dr Cameron is off duty and they say to send Her Majesty over in a taxi. So, I call for a taxi and they said, no taxis right now, we'll send one over as soon as one is free.

And Chandra screaming screaming screaming.

So anyway, we wait ages and nobody comes so I ring back and taxi service engaged, and engaged all the next half-hour. And then when I ring back again, nobody answers. So, I ring hospital, and they say, big accident on Regent Street, drunk driver or something, no ambulance available.

Meanwhile, Saraswati still up there with her and between calls, I run up to tell her what happening, and to see what going on, if baby come or what.

Saraswati holding on to her and wiping her forehead, and she breathing heavy like, and hissing at me whenever

I poke my head round the door. <u>Where is that man?</u>
(Meaning Daddy.) <u>When is that man coming?</u> (Meaning
Dr Cameron.) <u>Why's he taking so long?</u> (Meaning the
taxi driver.) And all I got is bad news, and she wanting
to kill me for it.

An hour passes or maybe five, and she get real vex.
She throw a tantrum and yell the place down about
bloody doctor and bloody taxi driver and bloody baby
and bloody everything else, except she didn't say bloody.
Lord, I feel sorry for Saraswati! Then Saraswati say, all
calm and sensible, 'Girl, run over to Aunty Jenny and
ask if she would drive her to hospital.'

And I do that, but of course Aunty Jenny not home, at
some fete, no car, only a babysitter. same in all the houses.
Nobody home except servants and babysitters and house-
keepers, nobody with a car. Plenty of bicycles, but no car.

'*Bloody Ol' Year's Nite!*' she scream. Then Saraswati say
I should boil some pots of water and I know things are
getting serious, because in all the books the first thing
you do when a baby born is boil water.

And then she really start screaming; till now it was
just shouting.

After that, the screaming don't stop. You'd think she
was being murdered, and all she was doing was having
a baby! Well, right there and then I swear that if I ever
get a baby, I not going to scream like that.

OK, so now I got four big pots of water on all the
four burners boiling away and I run up the stairs and
knock on the door to tell Saraswati. Nobody answer my
knock and all quiet so I open the door just a crack and
poke my head in, and I see her lying on the bed in a
naked sweat and then she see me and scream, 'Get out
of here, you stupid idiiieeeeeaaaaghl.'

I slam the door and stand there trembling in the corridor for ages, listening to the screams, and then one real long loud scream, and then a wail, and then Saraswati poke her head round the door and say, 'Well, dear, you have a sister, and is the hot water ready?'

So, dear Diary, that's how my sister was born. Aren't you as pleased as me? That she didn't get a boy, like she wanted?

Love Rita

'Rita, what are you doing?'

Daddy never knocked at Rita's door, but she didn't mind so much with him. Chandra never knocked either, but that she *did* mind, though she never said so. This time Daddy came in with a wide grin all over his face. Rita hastily shut her diary and shoved it under her pillow. She sat up on her bed.

'Writing your diary, are you?' Daddy said. 'Well, at last you've got something to say, haven't you? What do you think of her?'

'Oh, well, she's – well, she's so, so – isn't she?'

'Like a little doll. That's what newborn babies are like, girl. That's what you were like too, you know! So, what you think?'

Rita simply stared at him. She wasn't going to let on. She had seen her sister before breakfast, before anything and anyone. Chandra had sent for her. She had waited at Chandra's door, hardly daring to go in because Chandra might snap off her head, and then she had knocked, and Chandra had called out languidly, 'Come in!' So, she had gone in, and stood before the crib next to the bed, and seen her sister for the first time.

Staring at the baby, Rita had known all sorts of things all at once. Something gripped her. From inside.

Rita had no words for what it was; she had never felt like that before, but it was a bit like when you found a kitten half-drowned in a sack in a gutter, and you took it up and it meowed, and you wanted to press it to you and keep it for ever and ever and let it know that everything was all right. That's how she had felt.

She couldn't take her eyes off the little scrap of humanity sleeping in silent serenity on the pillow, soft and creamy rose-petal skin, perfect little hands with upturned palms in a gesture of complete surrender on either side of a little head capped in black silk. Minuscule fingers too fragile to be true, a face of ineffable innocence, perfection so complete that a lump rose in Rita's throat. She gulped to swallow it down.

It was love at first sight.

From the moment she set eyes on her sister, Rita loved her with an embracing love that was all things at once: reverence and protection; a love too sweeping for a ten-year-old to bear.

'A girl,' said Chandra. 'It's only a girl. So much trouble for a girl. Rita, I expect you to pull your weight and help Saraswati look after it. If you want, you can take it away. I think it's hungry.'

Rita stared. Take it away? Touch that fragile wonderful living being that looked as if it might break? How could she ever?

'Go on, pick the baby up. Just pick it up and take it away. It's only sleeping because it screeched itself into a coma. It's been squalling all night, I didn't get a moment of shut-eye… Saraswati is making some milk down in the kitchen, take it down and feed it. Just leave me in peace. When your daddy gets home, if he ever does, tell him not to bother to wake me.'

And she yawned and turned away from Rita, pulling the sheet over her shoulders.

There was no way Rita could share that, and all that happened afterwards, the picking up and the holding and the carrying downstairs and the feeding and the tiny lips moving, sucking, and the spellbound awe of beholding, with her father. He didn't deserve it. She looked up at Jitty now, rolled her pencil in her palms in impatience, and said, to get rid of him, 'Oh well, I suppose she's

OK,' pulled her diary out from under her pillow and ostentatiously began to leaf through its pages.

Jitty took the hint. He shrugged and turned to leave.

It would be the longest, most important entry she had ever made in her life. When Jitty left the room, she got up, walked over and latched the door, and before returning to her bed, fetched the dictionary, for there were a thousand million feelings in her she had no words for.

Chapter Fifteen

Born a Star

Luisa was born under a lucky star; born a star. Born to shine, eclipsing her big sister who didn't mind in the least; for Rita, from the very first moment, belonged to Luisa as she had never belonged to any human being, or even any animal, till then. Loving animals had been an apprenticeship; this was the real thing. And over the next year she watched with great wonderment as the tiny little thing, no bigger than Polly Wong's favourite doll (Rita herself perfectly despised dolls), grew under her very eyes, from day to day gained size and movement and perception, and she who had raised countless puppies and kittens up from scratch promoted herself to sole guardian of what must surely be creation's crowning glory: Luisa.

Who could resist Luisa? Her father, certainly, couldn't; she thoroughly usurped Rita's place in Jitty's generous heart (or so Rita thought), for she was helpless and cute and soft, needing Daddy's protection, whereas Rita was tough and caustic and bristling with self-preservation. And as for Chandra...

Jitty, are you never going to be ready? My goodness, where is that man? I suppose he's under the bonnet of the car again.

Jitty!... Jitty, there you are! I told you to change out of that old greasy shirt ages ago. Look at the time, it's almost ten fifteen! I told Mrs D'Aguiar I'd be there at eleven, you know how she's particular about time. Did you bring roses from Tulsiram, no, I'm sure you forgot, you expect me to go with my two long empty hands or what? Come on, haul your backside upstairs and get changed right now. Oh gawd, husbands! Why did I ever marry? People say women take so long to get dressed, they don't know you, man, and please go and bathe – I know you, putting your best clothes on stinking skin. And where is that girl, Rita? There you are! Have you got the baby dressed yet? Then go and bring her.

'Oh, there's my little cushy-pushy Luisa! Come to Mummy, darling, come on; who's a little birthday girl? Come into my arms like a bundle of charms. Mmmm, you smell so good, darling! You're one year old and a big little girl, but your hair! Rita, what a mess! Why didn't you brush this child's hair? You know I don't like it when the curls fall over her forehead like a puppy! Run and bring me the hairbrush and that new pink ribbon I bought yesterday. Come, darling, sit still on Mummy's lap now. No, don't grab the hairbrush! Mummy needs it to style your little curly-wurlies, and I'm going to tie this lovely ribbon on the very top. We're going for a lovely birthday walky-walky in the Botanical Gardens, just you and Mummy and Daddy, isn't that nice, on a lovely Sunday morning, and your little friend Suzie is going to be there. You can play in the sand with her, and this afternoon, we'll have a lovely party. Look, hold the ribbon but don't put it in your mouth – it will get all soppy. There we go… Now give Mummy the ribbon. Come on, give, let go, darling. No, I said not in your mouth! Open your teeth. If you bite it like that it's going to tear, the lovely pretty ribbon Mummy bought for your hair. Come, open up now, open up, like a dear girl… Oh, gawd, Rita! Come and see if you can get her to let go. Baby, darling, open your hands and give Mummy the ribbon. RITA! Are you deaf? She's going to bite that ribbon to shreds, come and help me. Stop fighting up like that, Luisa, sit still, sit still and stop wriggling, I tell you, and give me the ribbon right now. Rita, if I hold her wrist, you can prise open her fingers… There! Luisa, darling, open your mouth and let go of that ribbon. Mummy's going to smack you in one minute and then you're going to cry, there! You see! And next time it's going to hurt.

'Take this bawling child, Rita, at least she let go of the ribbon now. Just look at the way she crumpled up my dress, I'm going to have to

change. Just take her away and get her quiet, she ruined that ribbon, look at it! Just look at it! And it was so expensive, it's full of spit. Take her away, take her away, I can't stand that bawling. Take her away and get her quiet, put on her sunbonnet and go into the yard with her and wait there till I come down, but careful and don't get burrs on her clothes. Oh that child is a headache, I tell you, why did I ever think of having a baby?

'Jitty, oh there you are! That was quick, did you bathe in that short time – are you sure? Look, I have to go and change my dress, it's all crumpled up and my make-up is a mess, I need a quarter of an hour. What's the time? What? Oh Lordy, we're going to be late! I'll just rush upstairs. Go down to the car and wait for me but don't start messing around in the engine again, you hear? I hate going places with my two long empty hands. Why did you put on that shirt? It's not starched. I put a shirt for you on the bed, are you blind or what? And you know I hate white socks. Oh, Jitty, when are you going to learn? Go and see if the baby is quiet yet, she was bawling her head off and you know how… That damned telephone, it always rings at the wrong time! Get it, will you? I'm going upstairs. If it's Cheryl, tell her not now, later, I haven't got a minute's time now…'

Down at the bottom of the garden Luisa and Rita inspected the tadpole pond. Luisa had stopped crying; she had done so the minute they were out of Chandra's sight, and it was with a cool smug feeling of satisfaction that Rita had carried her down the stairs into the garden, taken her by her two little hands and held her up as she stumbled forward along the sandy path between the cannas. As they moved along, Luisa hobbling from left foot to right in the vee of Rita's legs, Rita spoke soothingly to her sister.

'She hit you, didn't she? She's an ol' meanie. Don't bother with her. I would never hit you, would I? She's a silly old lady, isn't she? Cretinous. Trying to tie that stupid old ribbon in your hair! You would have looked horrible. She thinks you're a little dolly to dress up and tie up in ribbons but you're not, you were right not to let her! Anyway, you know just what to do when she's silly, don't you? Just start bawling! She can't stand it when you bawl. She likes you all smiley and silly like some cretinous baby girl in *Woman's Own*, but you hate that, don't you? Here we are. Careful you don't slip, it's a bit muddy round the edges 'cause it rained early this morning – better take off your shoes so they don't get dirty or she's going to start screaming again. There…'

Rita threw Luisa's little white shoes and white frilly socks back towards the house; they landed on the path. She settled Luisa on the edge of the pond. It was a home-made pond, Rita's invention, an old car tyre sunk into the earth, the circle at its bottom laid out with a plastic sheet to hold the water, carefully hidden from Chandra in a bushy corner of the backyard she never deigned to inspect, way beyond the compost heap and the gardener's precious manure pile; a secret shared with the gardener, who fully approved of the rearing of frogs. Behind the bushes. You couldn't see it from the house. That was the main thing.

Rita was well aware of the danger of Luisa's frock getting dirty. Such a ridiculous pink frock, with white frills all the way down the front and around the hem, and a wide white satin sash round the waist; Rita rumpled her nose in disdain as she pulled the hem up and tucked it into the sash so that it wouldn't dangle in the water by mistake. Luisa wore matching pink bloomers, the backside white-frilled, and Rita, responsible as ever, pulled these off so that Luisa could sit in safety on the tyre-rim in her plastic pants all puffed out from the cloth nappy they enclosed. Rita gave her a twig and happily, Luisa, gurgling and exclaiming in glee, stirred the water with it and tried to touch the tadpoles flitting about beneath the surface. Rita watched her, and as she watched, she talked.

'Don't let her get you,' she told Luisa. 'You're mine. She's a silly old frog and she thinks she can make you into some silly dolly-girl she's dreamed up. But you're not a dolly, are you? You're Luisa. Say it. Luisa. Loo-ees-a.'

'Oo-ee,' Luisa agreed.

'That's right, Loo-ees-a. Say it again, Loo-ees-a.'

'Oo-ee.'

'Right. Your name is Luisa. Want to know a secret? I gave you that name. I chose it. Because she didn't want you when you were born. She didn't like you at all, she didn't even want to see you and she hadn't got a name for a girl. Only a name for a boy. Sebastian! Imagine that! A boy called Sebastian. Sebastian Maraj. She said it was an elegant name, and a boy with that name would go far, just imagine! So, she hadn't got a girl's name and Daddy had to have a name for the birth certificate and he knew I was good at names so he asked me, but I told him I'd do it only if he promised not to tell her it was from me, and he promised so I said Luisa, and he told her he had thought it up, so it was OK. It's a lovely name. Come on, try again. Loo-ees-a.'

'Oo-ee. Oo-ee. Oo-ee.'

'That's right. And my name? What's my name?' She pointed to her chest. Luisa smiled up at her and pointed too.

'Ita.'

'Almost, Rrr-ita. And… Oh Lord, she's calling! Come quick, we've got to go.'

Rita stood Luisa on the rim of the tyre, stripped off her T-shirt and wiped off the muddy streaks from the plastic pants. She carried her over to the path, bending to pick up the frilled bloomers as she went, pulling them on over the plastic ones, drying Luisa's kicking feet. At the path, she hurriedly pulled on the child's shoes and socks.

Chandra wrenched Luisa out of Rita's arms. 'Where on earth have you been? What have you been doing? Look at this child, she looks like you dragged her through a bush backwards!' She pulled the hem of the dress out of the sash. 'My word, Rita, can't I even leave you one minute alone with this child? And how often do I have to tell you not to run around half-naked at your age? You look like a servant's child, no wonder… Oh hell, she's starting up again! Jitty, take her quick.'

She thrust the whimpering baby at Jitty's chest, and he, taken by surprise, grabbed her a little too heftily and a little too late, digging his fingers in under her arms by mistake. Luisa began to scream.

Chandra stamped her feet. 'Oh no, you idiot, why can't you… Give her to Rita, quick, quick! Rita, take her. Oh Lord, what are we to do? We're so late already and you know those D'Aguiars. Rita, you'll have to come with us for goodness' sake but keep your mouth shut, do you hear? Run upstairs, give me the baby, no, take her with you. Grab some clothes – the yellow dress you wore at the May Day parade. Don't put it on, there's no time, you can do that in the car, and bring a hairbrush, your hair's a mess. Loosen the plaits and brush it out, quick time now, run!'

Rita flew up the stairs, Luisa, no longer screaming, dangling under one arm.

It was only later, after a hasty backseat change and a slapdash brush of hair, two corners before the D'Aguiars' home, that Rita realised she was still barefoot. Barefoot, in a cretinous yellow satin dress chosen by Chandra. Toes stained with mud. She smiled in deep satisfaction, leaned into the back seat and jiggled Luisa on her knees. It wasn't her problem. Not at all.

By the time Luisa was three, she and Rita were a team – closer than twins. It was hard to tell who adored whom more: on the one hand, Luisa had Rita on a string, dancing to the tunes she played from the moment she woke up in her sun-splashed room, all through the day to evening, when she laid her silky mop of black curls on a white frilly pillow and rubbed her charming little fists into eyes heavy with sleep, yawning, stretching up those darling arms to pull doting big sister down for a final kiss.

On the other hand, Rita was the centre of Luisa's universe. Rita held sway over Luisa's moods – with a few words, Rita could calm a tantrum before it even broke out. It was Rita who toilet-trained Luisa. Rita who got her into bed at night with the promise of a goodnight story. Rita she respected and – to a certain degree – obeyed. If Rita said be still, then Luisa, somehow, was still. When Rita said, 'Sing, Luisa!' then Luisa sang. She sang 'Twinkle Twinkle Little Star' and 'Frosty the Snowman' in the purest baby voice, and everybody clapped and said how sweet she was. Luisa wouldn't sing for any other person in the world.

Rita was as proud as any mother. And if Chandra was responsible for the initial forming of Luisa's body, then surely Rita was responsible for the thriving of the same, for its care and nourishment and general well-being. And if she wasn't jealous of the attention Luisa earned by the mere fact of being, she certainly was jealous of anyone who dared to intrude by taking on any of the little essential tasks she considered hers, and hers alone. Only she should feed Luisa. Only she should bathe her, cuddle her, kiss her, take her by the hand as she learned her first steps, help her repeat her first words. She made faces at Saraswati, who came at eight to replace her during school hours, but the moment she pranced into the house after school, Luisa was all hers.

More than all of Chandra's badgering and rules and attempts at child-taming, more than any punishment she could administer, it was responsibility for Luisa that brought Rita into line, tamed her, and bestowed a veneer of domestic harmony on the household. Yes, there was the occasional squabble, but attention going on Luisa distracted from Rita and also, she found, calmed her own tempests.

As for Jitty: from the beginning, he hardly noticed what was going on, whether stormy or peaceful. He weathered domestic squabbles by treating them as the type of drama females commonly engaged in, beneath the need for intervention, and kept himself out of the same for the sake of impartiality. He was a householder, a father, a husband, and as far as he was concerned, he played his role well.

But beneath the veneer of harmony something smouldered. It was well concealed, for ugliness does not show its face willingly. An undercurrent of smouldering hostility. There was something sly, underhand, scheming about Chandra, and Rita felt it, quite distinctly. Rita's internal antennas were finely tuned.

Rita knew.

Chapter Sixteen

The Brat

Rita took to spying on Chandra. Well, it wasn't exactly *spying*, she reasoned with herself, it was just keeping her eyes and ears open. Chandra had a loud voice and loved to chat on the phone with her many Jha cousins and aunts. The phone stood in a room set aside as an office, just next to the stairs, and it gave a little ping whenever someone picked up the receiver; or, of course, sometimes it rang and it was for Chandra. The office window was just above the back stairs leading to the garden from the kitchen.

If you sat on the back stairs you could hear everything.

It didn't take long for Rita to understand that Chandra had a thorn in her side, and that thorn was she herself. Even though she no longer made trouble for Chandra. Even though she kept Chandra's rules and tidied up after herself and even though she took such good care of Chandra's baby, with whom Chandra seemed not to have much of a connection.

When Chandra chatted with her cousins and aunts, inevitably she brought the conversation round to 'that brat', and the brat, Rita understood, was she herself. Chandra complained and grumbled and whined. She didn't like sharing the house with the brat, she didn't like sharing Luisa with the brat, but she had to admit, the brat was good with Luisa, better even than Saraswati, so she had to put up with her; it really helped having someone who actually enjoyed the baby.

On and on went the complaints; she managed to edge them into every single telephone conversation. Even the one about moving to

Canada. One of her aunts was doing just that, joining her daughter who had already made the move, and was encouraging everyone in the family to join them. Rita had already picked up that much at dinner conversations: Chandra nagging Jitty to think about moving to Canada, 'get away from this dead-end country with its dead-end black government'. Every time she said the word *black*, she'd glance at Rita. Rita noticed things like that; Jitty didn't.

And now, when she discussed Canada with this aunt of hers, it was always, 'You know I'd love to come but it's not just me. Jitty would insist on bringing the brat as well.' The person on the other end said something Rita couldn't hear, and then Chandra said, 'You know, Parvati, I would love nothing better than that, sending her back where she came from. But my hands are tied. Jitty would never allow it. He adores that brat. But maybe I can come for a holiday, just me alone.'

In another conversation with the same Parvati person, Rita realised with some astonishment that this was not because of brattish *behaviour* – of which there was none, as far as she could see (she was trying really hard to be good, because of Luisa) – but almost entirely because of her *hair*.

She didn't understand it. How did hair make you a brat? But there it was. Chandra had said it, out loud.

'If it wasn't for that *hair*, she could even pass as an Indian,' Chandra said one day. 'I wouldn't mind so much. But it's so embarrassing. I can't go anywhere because that crinkle-hair is like a red flag, it screams scandal. People point their fingers and talk. I try to explain that she's not my child, she's Jitty's bastard, but you know how it is. People talk. If it wasn't for the hair I could pretend, but—'

The other person must have interrupted because Chandra stopped speaking. A few interjections followed: 'You think so?' and then 'Uhuh, uhuh,' and then 'Really?'

And then, 'Let me write down the address, hold on a minute' and then, 'Oh, I think I know the place. Opposite Bettencourts.

Yes, I've seen it. I don't go there, of course. It's a black-people place, I wouldn't be seen dead.'

Silence again. Rita ran her fingers into her mass of hair. Chandra had had it cut very short when she first moved in, but it was rapidly growing back and was now at a stage where it wasn't long enough to plait and not short enough to keep tidy. It was thick and black, a mass of crispy, wiry spirals, each strand determined to do its thing. It knotted and tangled easily, and keeping it tidy enough for school was a major chore. Saraswati helped, but Saraswati wasn't always around, and anyway, Sarawati, being Indian, had no idea how to tame hair like hers. Chandra refused to touch it. Chandra was already hinting it needed to be cut down to the roots. Again.

Chandra said now: 'Well, yes, of course. It will feel a bit uncomfortable going in there, but if you think…' and then: 'I suppose she'd have to shave herself bald?' Then, 'Oh, oh good. I just have to convince Jitty. Maybe if I buy the thing first and try it out at home and Jitty can see how lovely she looks. Good, well, I have to go now, Parvati, but thanks for the idea. It's a bit extreme and I have to see what the two of them think of it, but it would help a lot. Bye!'

Kissing sounds, and then the chink as she replaced the receiver.

Rita ran into the backyard and up the mango tree and wondered what *that* was all about.

'Daddy, what's wrong with my hair?'

'Why, nothing, darling. Why you ask?'

'Oh, nothing. But somebody said I could pass as an Indian if it wasn't for my hair.'

'Who told you that?'

'Nobody. I mean, nobody *told* me, I just heard it.'

'You heard it? How did that happen?'

'I was just walking past this person and they said it. What does it mean? What's wrong with my hair?'

'Nothing. I love your hair.'

'I don't. It's so hard to comb and gets so knotty and tangled.'

'But I love it! It's growing back nicely now and it really suits you, all loose and all wild around your head like a mane! Like a lion!'

Jitty made a snarling sound and made a very bad lion-attack gesture, his fingers curved and stiff.

'Maybe I should shave myself bald?'

'Don't be silly! What gave you that idea?'

She shrugged. 'Somebody said it would be better.'

'I think Chandra mentioned it's time for it to be cut short again. I'm against that; I'd like you to grow it out. Girls should have long hair. But if it's bothering you…'

'It's not me who's bothered.'

Jitty did not follow up on that, but the next day, Chandra came home smiling from an outing to Town and all day looked like the cat who'd got the cream. Then, just after dinner, while Saraswati was clearing the table, she held up a bag she'd hidden at her feet under the table: held it aloft and said: 'Tada! Surprise!'

'Oh! What you got there, darling?' said Jitty, but instead of answering, Chandra produced a head of hair. Just hair. Silky, black, luscious hair; hair without a head.

'A wig!' announced Chandra. She looked at Rita and said, with a syrupy, crooning voice, 'A child-sized wig! It's for you, darling! I bought it for you! Come, let me try it on – you'll look lovely in it!'

She grabbed Rita – who had stood up to pick up the baby, who lay in a bassinet beside the table – by the arm, pulled her over, and before Rita could say a word was pulling the wig over her head, tucking in the abundant curls so that not even a strand of Rita's own hair was visible. Then she held Rita back with both hands on her arms and in a voice filled with wonder said:

'Oh! Oh, look Jitty, isn't that wonderful? It suits her so much! Why, she could really pass for your daughter now! Absolutely! She looks just like an Indian! That hair is so beautiful, just feel it, Jitty, so silky, and the way it falls over her shoulders and waves up! I bought it just for you, darling!'

This last was addressed to Rita. Rita stood in stunned silence. Jitty, too, seemed stunned for a moment.

'Well, darling, aren't you going to say anything? Doesn't she look sweet? Turn round, sweetheart, let's see the back of it – oh look, look how it falls down her back! You can wear it in a ponytail! Come, let's go over to the mirror, you have to see for yourself!'

But before she could manoeuvre Rita over to the mirror in the hallway, Jitty had risen to his feet, grabbed the wig from Rita's head, dashed it to the floor. He glared at Chandra as he said:

'You take that – that *thing* back to wherever you got it first thing tomorrow! How dare you *insult* my daughter like that!'

Later that night, Rita woke up to hear them shouting at each other. She'd never heard them argue before and it was a bit shocking. She crept out of bed to listen at their door, but she could not make out what they were saying.

She *did* hear the word Canada.

And beneath it all she *felt*, rather than heard, or saw, the ugliness. And knew it was coming to the surface, showing its face, edging up beneath the veneer of calm respectability.

Chapter Seventeen

Naughty Words

'Daddy, what's a bastard?'

'It's a child whose parents are not married. But it's a naughty word. You mustn't say it, ever. Where did you hear it?'

'Somebody said I'm a bastard. But I don't understand. I thought you had to be married to have a baby. I don't understand how…'

'What? Who? Who called you that?'

'Daddy, don't shout! It's all right, she's just silly. It's only that girl at the corner house. The Indians who just moved in? The Persauds? Chandra went over yesterday to welcome her to the close. She took a cake. Anyway, they have four children and me and Polly went to the house this afternoon to ask if the youngest one would like to play. She's about our age. We saw her playing in the yard. But then this big girl, her big sister, came to the door and told us to go away. She said Sita – that's the girl's name – wouldn't be allowed to play with me because I'm a bastard. She said Polly could come by herself if she wants to, but not me. But I don't care. Polly said she would never do that. She said I'm the best friend she ever had and she doesn't care if I'm a bastard or not, she'll… Daddy, where are you going?'

Jitty, his face beetroot-red with rage, had set down the bowl of chow-chow on the steps and was making his way down.

'I'm going to have a word with that girl's mother, Mrs Persaud! How dare she!'

Rita ran behind him, grabbed his hand.

'Daddy, don't! She's Chandra's friend and she'll tell Chandra and I'll get into trouble for telling tales! It's not true anyway, is it? You have to be married to have a baby. Everybody has a mummy and a daddy, and even if one of them dies, they're still your mummy and daddy, aren't they? So, she's just being silly! She maybe doesn't know that my mummy died. So, I'm *not* a bastard!'

'I said, don't use that word!'

'But I'm not it, am I? *Am* I? Mummy died, so I'm not a b— that word I'm not supposed to say? Why is it naughty anyway? Because everybody has a mummy and daddy. That's how babies are made. I know because Polly told me.'

'Sweetheart, it's a bit complicated. When you're older, you'll understand. What did Polly tell you about how babies are made?'

'She told me that the man puts his lolo in the lady's peepee and that's how they make babies. Her mummy told her. And her daddy's a doctor and so they know. And that's the only way. And animals do it too, make babies. And you have to be married to make babies, a man and a woman, a mummy and a daddy, and I have you and I had a mummy, but she died. So, I'm not that naughty thing.'

Jitty stopped striding towards the front gate and bent down and hugged her, his anger melted. He could talk to the awful Persaud woman another time. Maybe he could let Chandra deal with her, if she and Chandra were friends. This was more pressing. It was the day that had to come, as he always knew it would.

He took Rita's hand and walked her back to the kitchen stairs. He sat down, and pulled her onto his lap.

'Yes, dear, you're right – partly right. A man and a lady can make a baby together. But being married is a different thing. It means that they go to a building and promise to stay together and look after each other and be there for one another. That's what marriage is: it's a vow. And most people when they get married, they have a wedding – that's a big celebration, and they go to a church if they are Christian to get their union blessed, or if they are Hindu, a priest comes to bless them and they walk round a fire together, or if they are Muslims – well, I'm not sure what Muslims do, but that's a wedding too. And it means they have promised to stay together and love each other and live together and – and make babies together. And the union is protected by law. But some people make babies without a wedding, without being married. And those children… Well, horrible people call them naughty names like the one that horrible Persaud girl said. But it means nothing, darling. It's just a word. You should never worry about words. You know what I told you about sticks and stones?'

'Yes! *Sticks and stones can break my bones…*' she started to chant, and Jitty joined in:

'*…but words can never hurt me!*'

'But words *do* hurt, Daddy! They hurt inside.' She put her hand on her chest. 'In here.'

'Indeed, that's why you must be kind to other children and not call them names. But there are always some people who will say things that might hurt your feelings. And if that happens you must be strong and brave and not feel bad. Because they are just words, and words are just like bubbles. Empty. They are just blowing empty bubbles at you. That's what that girl did: blow bubbles at you.'

'But, Daddy, is she right? Were you and Mummy not married?'

'Well, in a way… we didn't get married, no.'

'You didn't vow to love each other and stay together? You didn't get God's blessing?'

'Um – no. We didn't.'

Rita was silent for a while, and then she said: 'So I *am* that naughty thing she said? And that girl was right. I *am* a… that naughty word. Is that why I'm so… so bad?'

'Oh, darling! You're not bad at all! Just a little bit naughty, sometimes!'

'Chandra says I'm bad! She says I'm a bad girl. A brat. A brat is somebody who's bad. She's always saying it. And Miss Lee says I'm a little scallywag. Maybe that's why. Maybe it's because I'm that naughty word. And it hurts when she says I'm a brat. It hurts inside. Like sticks and stones.'

'I'm going to talk to Chandra and tell her not to say that any more. She shouldn't be calling you a brat, because you're not. You're just a little...'

'A little what?'

'A little wayward, that's all. A little hard-ears.'

'It's because I'm a bas— that naughty word.'

'Oh, darling! You're not...'

'But I am. It's the truth. If it's the truth, you have to say it.'

'But it's not a nice word.'

'It doesn't matter if it's nice or not. Is there a nice word for that thing? That thing it means?'

'For a child whose parents aren't married? Let me think...' He thought for a while, then he said, 'You know, actually there isn't. It's the only word that means that, I think.'

'But then, if it's the only word, we have to say it, don't we? Because words have to have meanings, to save us saying lots of words instead? That's what words are for. And if it's the *only* word, then we have to say it?'

'Well, put like that, maybe you're right. But I still don't want you to...'

'And maybe if we didn't think it was a bad word, it would stop being a bad word? And I could say it: *bastard*.'

'Rita! I said—'

'No, Daddy, let me finish! I said it because it's true, it's what I am. A child whose parents aren't married. Or else we have to invent a new word for that, so we didn't have to use so many words.'

'Oh, darling! Please, please don't tell anyone you're a... that naughty word. It wouldn't be good.'

'Is Luisa a ba… I mean, that naughty word?'

'No, she isn't.'

'So, you married Luisa's mummy but not mine? So, you love Luisa's mummy more?'

'Darling, it's not like that. When you're older, I'll explain everything to you. It's a long story, very complicated.'

'You didn't love my mummy?'

'I did, I did, but—'

'But you didn't marry her, and she had me and I'm a bastard, but Luisa isn't, so you love Luisa more because she's not a… that naughty thing, and I am?'

'Darling, I don't love Luisa more!'

'Chandra says you do.'

'I'm going to talk to Chandra and tell her not to tell you such nonsense.'

'You'll tell her that you love me just as much as you love Luisa?'

'Of course, darling.'

She nodded in satisfaction, and continued: 'So Dr Wong's parents were also unmarried, and he's that naughty word too,' said Rita with some finality.

'What on earth are you talking about now? What's Dr Wong got to do with it?'

'Well, I heard them. Arguing. Polly's mummy said it, she called him that. She shouted at him and called him… that naughty word.'

'Really? Well, dear, you shouldn't be listening to grown-up conversations.'

'I wasn't listening. Everybody could hear. It was when I spent the night with Polly. They were in the next room, shouting. And Aunty Jenny called him that.'

'Did you – um – hear anything else? No, no I don't want you to gossip. Forget I asked you that. Let's not talk about this any more. Come, let's finish this chow-chow. I'll talk to Mrs Persaud later.'

'Oh, don't bother, Daddy. If she won't let her daughter play with us then she'll just be all alone, won't she? Because I bet Polly doesn't care if I'm a – that naughty word – or not, and none of the other parents, so that girl is not going to have anybody to play with. Poor thing.'

And Rita dug her spoon deep into the bowl of chow-chow and lifted it, heaped over with the stringy, salty, yellowy grated green mango with bits of red pepper in it, opened her mouth wide, and plopped it straight in.

She looked up at her father. 'But you still haven't told me how I came to be a b… that naughty thing!'

Jitty sighed. There was no escape. 'I'll tell you one day, when you're bigger.'

'How big?'

'An adult.'

'Like you? Really old?'

'No – maybe when you finish school.'

'But that's a thousand million years away!'

'No, it's not. The time will just fly past.'

'You promise? You won't forget?'

'I promise, I won't forget.'

How could Jitty ever forget? It preyed on his mind day and night, and the more he tried to forget, the more the past seemed to twist itself into the presence. Rita's very existence reminded him, day and night. She looked so much like her. Every time he looked at Rita, he saw *her*.

Chapter Eighteen

Jitty, 1970

Jitty was in his final year of schooling when he met Cassie Gomes at one of the popular house fetes hosted by his various friends every weekend. Cassie was a mixed-race girl from a poor up-country family, and it was her first fete. She was shy, and it showed, and he noticed. She looked as innocent as a rosebud that had never been sniffed; Jitty could tell at a glance, so he slotted her into the back of his mind – a 'possible'. Meanwhile, there was music, and dancing, and flowing Coca-Cola and other soft drinks, and private bottles of rum passed among the boys. As always at these private fetes, the girls sat on straight-backed chairs arranged against the four walls of the living room while the boys gathered in a huddle near the kitchen, glasses in hands, surreptitiously glancing over to assess which girls were available, which weren't, and which were new, and to discuss them among themselves.

Jitty was in his element: laughing and joking with the boys, eyeing the girls. He wore his favourite pair of blue bell-bottoms: tight on the thighs, flaring out at the knee to extra-wide flaps around the ankles. He wore an open-necked multicoloured short-sleeved shirt with a loud pattern of hibiscus flowers. These were all the rage that year. He wore his best pair of yachting shoes, washed clean and then spruced up with white roll-on cleaner.

His hair was now below his shoulders, much to the disapproval of Granma. His call-name among the boys (for everyone had a call-name) was Hippie – but he wasn't really a hippie. Not a real one. Not the kind that roamed about and dropped out and lived in communes, growing their own food and rejecting society – that was going too far; he loved his home too much, and had no intention of ever leaving it. He didn't want to reform society. Hippie style was a fashion, not an ideology; he loved the colours and the long-hair part of it, and the free love, and the peace, and the doves and the flowers, and the occasional joint. *Make love not war*: now THAT was a philosophy he could agree with. He was, of course, like every sane person, against the Vietnam War, but it didn't really affect him. Life was good, but he wanted a girl.

Cassie was new, but she wasn't particularly pretty, a few of the boys declared as they eyed up the newcomer, and too dark. A few others made jokes about her 'boobies', which seemed to be larger than average; although it was hard to tell because she was also wearing the latest fashion, a 'granny' dress, a cotton loose-fitting frock in pastel colours patterned with tiny flowers, with a high neckline, tiny decorative buttons and lots of frills. Hers was a hand-me-down from the friend who had brought her, who had a new dress custom-made by a seamstress. She looked awkward, her hands twisting in nervousness or jabbing at her hair, which was held in place by two tight plaits wrapped round her head.

The girl sitting next to her was her friend, and they seemed to be making some attempt at conversation. Jitty made an internal note to attend to her later, perhaps, depending on his success with Denise Vaughan, his current flame. But Denise was beautiful, and the crush of many of the young men, so his chances there were fifty-fifty. He had to keep his options open. A new girl was always a good option; a good *last* option.

In a corner sat the hired disc jockey at his table piled high with 45s. At present he was wiping off the records and placing them in piles: slow-dancing, instrumentals, reggae, Beatles, ska, bawdy calypsos, and so on, but the boys were becoming impatient, so one of them walked over and gave him a nudge. He nodded, placed a record on the turntable, and the music began. He had chosen 'Apache', an instrumental by the Shadows; always a good starter, for it was catchy without being romantic, and you could dance slowly to it without getting too close. At the very first note the boys streamed forward, spreading out across the room as each headed for his dance partner of choice. A moment later the floor was filled with couples dancing. Jitty was too late: Denise was taken, swept off her chair by a tall Portuguese boy known to be popular with the girls.

Jitty looked around for his second choices, but they too were all gone, picked early. About five girls remained seated, the new girl among them. Jitty decided not to go for her just yet. It would make him seem desperate, and desperate he wasn't. He picked another girl, and for the next dance yet another. The new girl remained on her chair, looking more nervous and more awkward by the second. The longer you stayed seated, the more undesirable you became; that was the unspoken rule among both the girls and the boys, and by the fourth dance it looked that this new girl was set to be the big loser of the night. Nobody would want her. Jitty had danced each of the three dances with a different girl and was having the time of his life; the music alternated between fast and slow and the dance floor was full of exuberant youth moving lithe limbs to music so infectious it made you sway or jump or wave your arms, according to the beat. But none of the girls he'd danced with really caught his fancy – if he couldn't have Denise, he really didn't want one of the others, girls he'd already kissed and, in some cases, even fondled. He was out for something fresh, undiscovered. He hadn't yet seen the new girl on her feet, but it looked as if she might have a good body. Those boobies...

And so, as the fourth record blared out over the loudspeakers, he made a beeline for the lonely little wallflower with twisting hands. The music this time was The Mamas & The Papas: 'Dream a Little Dream of Me'. Perfect. Slow, dreamy, romantic, a little sentimental. He stood before her and extended a hand and gave her his best smile: 'Care to dance?'

Cassie looked up, startled. She'd reconciled herself to the probability that nobody would ask her to dance. That coming here – invited by one of her schoolfriends, a relative of the hostess who didn't like walking into parties alone – had been a mistake from the start. She'd felt awkward from the first moment, sitting here against the wall like one of those prizes at a fair stand that nobody aimed for. It was humiliating, and she was just considering whether to leave, which posed new problems, because how would she get home?

The fete was in Bel Air Park and she lived with Aunt Mathilda, Daddy's married sister, in Peter Rose Street, not too far away, yet too far to walk home in the dead of night. It was so embarrassing, sitting there in the middle of a row of empty chairs – a reject.

But now here was this handsome East Indian boy, smiling down at her, a hand held out; and now pulling gently to help her stand up, and leading her to the middle of the dance floor. One hand rested lightly on her waist, the other held her hand. She placed her left hand on his right shoulder and fell into the rhythm. There wasn't much to it, you just kind of slid your feet back and forth in time to the music. She kept her gaze straight, over his shoulder. She didn't want to meet his eyes; it was too embarrassing. But then he spoke.

'I haven't seen you before! What's your name?'

She told him: Cassandra Gomes. He laughed. 'Cassandra? That's quite a mouthful! A bit unusual.'

She smiled. 'People call me Cassie.'

'Well, I'm Jitendra Maraj and people call me Jitty,' he told her. 'You're a friend of Janice?' Janice was the hostess, a popular girl who never sat out a dance and whose circle of friends was always expanding.

'No,' said Cassie. 'I'm friends with her cousin and she invited me.'

She should have said more, made conversation, but it was if her tongue was stapled down to the floor of her mouth. The best she could do was answer questions. But that was all right, because Jitty wasn't short of questions.

'So, where do you live? Are you working? What school do you go to?'

She told him: Peter Rose Street, Bishops' High, respectively.

More probing questions revealed that she was seventeen and from out of town; that her parents lived far off in the Essequibo District, on the Pomeroon River, to be exact; that she was basically a country girl, sent to town to complete her schooling.

'You must be very clever if you got into Bishops'! So, you'll be sitting A-levels soon?'

'Next year. Maths and Biology and Chemistry.'

'Oh, a Science girl! I bet you're clever! I'm sitting for English Literature, French and Geography. Hoping to scrape through. So, your parents let you come to town on your own?'

She told him about Aunt Mathilda and her husband, Uncle Patrick, who were unfortunately childless and who were happy to have her.

'Gomes – you're related to Victor Gomes? He was my classmate, Putagee boy.'

She shrugged. 'I don't know him. Gomes is a common name. Lots of Portuguese people up in the Pomeroon.'

She spoke so *properly*, very little Creole dialect. You could tell by that that she took her education seriously. Proper English was a sure sign of class and education, more so, even, than race.

'In Georgetown too. But you don' look Putagee.'

'My dad is half Portuguese, half black. And my mum is pure Amerindian.'

'Ah.' He nodded, though he was surprised. He'd have thought she was half black. But then, racial mixtures often produced surprises and African blood was said to be dominant. That was why she was so dark and had that stiff, frizzy hair.

'Lots of Amerindians up that side?'

'Yes. The Warau tribe is up there, that's where Mum's from. There's a reservation near to Charity.'

'What do your parents do?'

'They're farmers. But Dad also does some pork-knocking, in the Interior.'

'A pork-knocker! He ever found any gold?'

She laughed.

'Not yet, but he's very hopeful.'

The song came to an end, but he didn't escort her back to her chair. They stood on the dance floor, talking – that is, he asking questions and she answering. Then the next record started: the Bee Gees with 'Massachusetts'. She knew all these songs from the radio – she didn't have any records herself, but her aunt and uncle had given her a small cassette recorder for her last birthday, the biggest gift she had ever received, and she had been busy recording all the songs she liked. This was one of them.

You couldn't call it dancing, not really – just shifting from foot to foot. It was the talking that held them there, a discreet distance between their bodies, hands clasped or lightly resting on waist and shoulder. The more they talked, the more she relaxed. Mummy had warned her about boys, and so had Aunt Mathilda, and told her to be careful because they only want one thing, but this one was so kind, so charming, and he was really interested in her. There was an ease to him, a genuine charm. A sort of magnetism that melted her self-consciousness and soon had her smiling back at him. Her initial shyness dissolved under his gaze that seemed so kind, so interested. His eyes were warm, and so was his voice. There was nothing to be wary of.

A third dance: the Beatles with 'Michelle', and then there were some faster songs, calypsos, The Mighty Sparrow of Trinidad and the Merrymen of Barbados – quite bawdy. She felt embarrassed by the lyrics, and all the wiggling and jiggling and winding of bodies. She had no idea what to do but looking around, she saw there wasn't much to it, so she just fell into the rhythm and let her body do as it pleased, but modestly.

She laughed, and she was beautiful when she laughed, so Jitty laughed with her. And she had a good figure, and she moved well; she had stepped on his toes once while slow-dancing, but that was all right. She was a little smarter that the usual girls he went with – that much was obvious. But it was head-smartness rather than street-smartness. She was just as innocent as he had surmised. It was her first fete, she'd revealed. Where she lived was the back of beyond, on a remote creek on the Pomeroon River – a real country bumpkin. A girl from Behind God's Back, as they said.

There was a pause in the music and he led her onto the balcony and brought her a plate of chow mein and a Coke. She sipped at the Coke, and looked up.

'There's rum in this?'

'Just a drop,' he said. 'It's all right.'

'I thought drinks here were alcohol-free?'

He chuckled. 'Officially, yes. But one of the guys brought along a bottle of XM. It's just a drop, try it!'

She did. He could almost feel her inhibitions melting. That was the nice thing about these country girls come to town; they were like butter. So malleable, so pleasant. He could feel her opening up to him.

He liked her. She had so much *potential* – these up-country girls were like open books you could write your own story into. Mould her into the shape he wanted. Girls like her, they didn't have any fancy ideas. They weren't angry and demanding and uptight; they were soft and yielding. Sweet and kind and simply delightful. Such *potential!* This could go far. But he had to take it slowly, not overwhelm her. It would be great fun taking her here and there to places she'd never been before. Why, she'd never even been to the cinema! (Not lately, at least. She said she'd been to see *Fantasia* as a child, in an Essequibo cinema.) Never been on a date. Never walked along the Sea Wall, hand in hand with a boy… never even kissed a boy, that's for sure.

They went back inside, back to the dance floor, and the music was even slower and more romantic: Elvis Presley, and the Drifters. Otis Redding with 'My Girl', and Percy Sledge with 'When a Man Loves a Woman'. He pulled her even closer, so close he could feel her heartbeat as they danced. Their feet hardly moved. They simply swayed. He nuzzled her neck, but he wouldn't kiss her. Not tonight.

The fete came to an end at midnight. She was getting a drop home with the friend who had invited her. Jitty wrote down her phone number, and promised to call her, and he did. They had long telephone conversations. It was true that she didn't have all that much to say, because life in the country doesn't exactly fill you up with exciting experiences you want to discuss, but he liked hearing her voice and he knew well how to talk himself, and about what.

The following weekend he took her to the cinema: *Love Story*, at the Strand. He met her after school, at Bookers' Snack Bar, and bought ice cream sodas and milkshakes and hot dogs. Sometimes he just visited her at home. They would sit in the gallery at the Peter Rose Street house and Aunt Mathilda served them lime juice and chow-chow. He chatted easily with both Aunt Mathilda and Uncle Patrick and they approved of him – 'Such a nice polite boy!' They'd been a bit sceptical at first, because of that long hair he now wore tied back at the nape of his neck, tidily. But they put it down to a passing fashion. He wasn't one of those awful American hippies one read about in the newspapers – the Maraj family name was well known, a respectable family.

Uncle Patrick drove to Kingston one day to inspect the house, not realising it was in a cul-de-sac, which led to some reversing problems. But it was a solid, big house. The boy was decent. He brought Aunt Mathilda hand-picked roses from one of the wild bushes in his backyard, which charmed her all the more, and he obeyed all the rules, such as never keeping Cassie out past ten o'clock, or midnight if there was a fete.

Everyone approved of him. Cassie discovered that she had, quite unintentionally, landed one of the coolest boys in town, cool in himself and not because he'd just come back from London or New York or Toronto. To make things even better, Aunt Mary had left behind a perfectly fine, if a little old, Morris Oxford when she went off to get married. It had stood there unused, undriven but locked for many years, but Jitty managed to break open a door (by breaking a window) and could entertain his friends, male and female, in its interior. Out of the blue, Aunt Mary sent him a fat envelope containing the key and documents, and told him it was now de facto his, if he paid for the insurance, and got his licence; he was old enough to drive, and hopefully would be sensible about it.

'It's safer than a motorbike,' she wrote. 'I never liked the idea of you tearing around on two wheels. Drive carefully.'

Jitty got his licence, and in the weeks to come took Cassie everywhere under the sun – even as far as Buxton Beach, up the east coast, where they lay on the sand and held hands, or drifted in the black inner tube of a lorry. Cassie was a good swimmer, strong and fast; she said she'd been swimming since she was a little girl, in the creek outside her home. So, he took her to Red Water Creek, near the Atkinson Field airport, and they swam there, too, in the cool red water overhung with forest trees.

She would sit in the gallery of her house and wait for him. One of the car headlights was out of order, and she could see his 'one-eye car' coming down the road from Kingston even when it was streets away. She'd see it coming and her heart would beat faster and she finally understood what they were all singing about.

But sometimes he didn't come, and she'd sit at the gallery window watching for him till late, her heart breaking into pieces, and she wondered what had held him back, and if he had another girl. She never asked him, though, and simply accepted it. Jitty never apologised for missed appointments. It was almost as if he hadn't noticed. So, she never mentioned them herself, never accused him, never confronted him.

She was such an easy-going girl. That's what he liked best about her. So accepting, so tolerant – because Jitty was well aware of the dates he missed. A Georgetown girl would have had a yelling fit after he stood them up – that was what he didn't like about *them*. Jitty believed in tolerance. Tolerance was the bedrock of his own personal philosophy. Live and let live. That's what he liked about the hippies. Live and let *love*, he thought with a laugh; that was more like it. His own personal motto.

He took to 'following' her home from school. He'd wait on his motorbike, liming with a few of his pals, outside the Empire cinema where Cassie would ride her bicycle home after school. There they'd come, flocks of Bishops' girls in their green uniforms, green-red-white striped ties, their panama hats with the green hatband. Girls would eye him up, smile, even wave; and he'd wave back, but he was waiting for only one: Cassie. If she was riding with a friend she'd drop behind and he'd ride his Honda slowly beside her, and he'd 'follow' her all the way to Queenstown, to Peter Rose Street, all the way home. It was an honour – but strictly forbidden.

The headmistress, Miss Dewer, summoned Cassie.

'It's been brought to my attention,' she said sternly, 'that a person of the male sex has been accompanying you home in the afternoons. You have been seen by a member of staff, several times. You should know that this is strictly against school rules. As long as you are in school uniform you are to behave in a decorous manner. This has to stop, it brings the school into disrepute.'

Cassie told Jitty, and he laughed and agreed to stop it. She was a well-brought-up Christian girl: quiet, and of sound morals, and he respected that. Wild girls were hard to handle. She needed time, and kindness. But she was worth it. She became his project. For the first time in his life, Jitty had a steady girlfriend. He found it relaxing; Cassie gave him balance, and a sense of peace. A pity, though, she was so old-fashioned. He'd take it slowly, and educate her.

Chapter Nineteen

Jitty, 1970–71

Cassie Gomes turned out to be just as sweet-natured and kind and pliable as Jitty had suspected that night he met her; his instincts had told him the truth. She was indeed the well-brought-up Christian girl he had immediately observed, and he had been right to take things slowly. But she was also that trusting, innocent country girl who had never encountered male wiles or known male desires, a girl with a heart yet unwounded and unscarred and ready to give itself, wholly and completely, to the first kind person to invade it. Jitty was astute enough to know just how this was done, and how to slowly overcome any deep-seated moral reservations that might have been planted in her by her old-fashioned parents.

In the past, before he had the car, Jitty's seductions of well-brought-up girls had suffered through the lack of suitable locations, coupled with strict parental monitoring: curfews and company (it wasn't always easy to get a girl alone) had done the rest. He had had to make do with a lower-class type of girl who might have a room of her own and no parental oversight, or even a professional from Tiger Bay.

Now that Aunt Mary's car was at his full disposal, all of that changed in a wink. The car was his own private seduction chamber, and he made good use of it. Cassie was his long-term project, but there were any number of very pretty girls he'd softened up in the past, modern, fun-loving girls who'd shown promise, and this was a good time to home in on them, to make good on the preparatory steps he had taken: they were, in his own words, 'ripe for the plucking'. As it turned out, in fact some were, some weren't, but he enjoyed the game as any young man in his prime would.

But Cassie Gomes was different. Any other young man in his prime might not bother to waste time on a naive and prudish schoolgirl who still wore her Bishops' uniform at the approved length (just below the knee) instead of rolling up the skirt at the waist to raise the hem to mid-thigh; on a girl who rode her bicycle straight home after school instead of parking it in front of Bookers' Universal Store and hanging out at the snack bar, with a gaggle of classmates, panama hats dangling down their backs, elastic tight against their necks, laughing and joking and flirting. Such girls were a dime a dozen. Cassie was different: she was a project. There was more to her than met the eye, but he had to take it slowly, carefully.

So he began by showing her Georgetown and its environs. He took her to all the cinemas: the Globe, the Metropole, the Empire, the Plaza and the Strand; and sat with her in the back rows of their balconies, doing no more than holding her hand and fondling her fingers. He took her to house fetes and public ones at the Palm Court and Bamboo Gardens. He took her to the Pegasus swimming pool and bought her Cokes lightly laced with rum. He took her to the Promenade Gardens and strolled with her between the flower beds, hand in hand. He took her to the Kissing Bridge at the Botanical Gardens, held her close, and kissed her on the lips. She giggled shyly, and allowed him to do so.

'You've never been kissed properly, have you?' he murmured into her neck.

She giggled in response and said, 'No, of course not.'

'I'll teach you,' he said, nuzzling her neck, and he did, afterwards, driving her up to the Sea Wall – that established rendezvous for amorous couples in cars who had nowhere private to go – and parking there and walking with her along the wall, then sitting with her, facing the Atlantic, his arm round her, pulling her close, complimenting her, tracing his fingers over her lips, telling her again and again how beautiful she was.

So, he taught her how to kiss, sitting in the back seat of the car, parked along the Sea Wall. And they walked along the Wall, the cool ocean breeze whipping at his hair and her dress, holding hands, and they kissed standing up. Once, he took a joint out of his shirt pocket and showed it to her.

'I don't smoke!' she said. 'You know I don't!'

'Ah, but this isn't *tobacco!* he said. 'It's better! You've heard of marijuana?'

'Is it – is it *drugs?*' She was obviously horrified, so he put the joint back in his shirt pocket, changed the subject, and kissed her again, and again. She seemed to like it.

Granma gave Jitty, at his request, a very nice Nikon camera for his nineteenth birthday, and Jitty proceeded to photograph Cassie. He photographed her on the Sea Wall, after persuading her to un-plait her pigtails so her hair, usually so prim and tidy, blew all around her like an enormous mane, whipped by the wind, and she tried to hold it down, and laughed. 'You're so beautiful when you laugh,' he said, and he was right. He photographed her in the Promenade Gardens, standing before a bougainvillea trellis bursting with purple flowers and laughing. He photographed her on the Kissing Bridge, leaning on the rails and laughing. He photographed her when she wasn't looking, when she was eating, when she was pensive, when she was reading a book. He finished one roll of film and replaced it with another, but one day, walking down Main Street, not in the central walkway but on the street itself, a passing motorcyclist grabbed the camera strap so that it snapped, revved his motorbike and sped away. It was the last Jitty saw of the camera – he'd only had it for three weeks.

Over the following weeks further romantic interludes took place within the car, on the back seat, after the romantic walks on the Sea Wall. In the car it was all private, and there was music, carefully chosen by him. Who could resist the sweet croonings of Otis Redding and Percy Sledge? Not him, and, eventually, not even Cassie Gomes.

Finally, he was there. 'Don't worry,' he murmured, 'I have protection.'

When it was over, the first time, she cried, and he comforted her. Nobody could comfort and reassure as well as Jitty Maraj. He reassured her of his love and his care, took her in his arms and stroked her back and dried her tears. He flung the used French Letter over the Sea Wall. It would be carried away by the tide of the vast waters of the Atlantic, and he was supremely happy. He really liked this girl; her shyness was charming. She was truly special, this girl: so refreshingly unsophisticated, so lacking in artifice and stratagem.

Chapter Twenty

Cassie, 1971

First love is a delightful thing, and Cassie Gomes blossomed under its spell. What girl wouldn't? Jitty knew how to make a girl feel special, cherished, beloved, even without whispering those three precious words in her ear. But he came very near to doing so. Surely 'you're the sweetest girl in the world' meant the same as 'I love you'? Cassie couldn't be sure, but she could hope, and she knew that she loved him, and she clung to that hope. She knew he wasn't perfect; she knew he wasn't even always truthful, because her friend Sandra said she'd seen him at a fete the very night he had said he couldn't take her to the Metropole to see *Butch Cassidy and the Sundance Kid* because he had to drive his Granma to the hospital because of heart palpitations and stay with her half the night.

But Cassie's was a forgiving nature. She knew that Jitty was not the kind of young man a girl like her could tie down. She was grateful for his attention, for every moment he spent with her. And if he said she was the sweetest girl in the world, then she should be rejoicing because nobody had ever told her that before – except Mummy – and she shouldn't expect too much from a Town boy. Not place restrictions on him. Jitty's entire character reflected his love of freedom, a personality set free from the old-fashioned mores and moralities of previous generations. That was what she loved about him.

'You're like a flower, opening in the sunshine of love!' he told her, nuzzling her neck. She giggled. There, he'd said it! That pre-

cious four-letter word. Cassie felt wanted, desired, adored. Jitty
made sure she knew she was beautiful, inside and out, and that
he appreciated her beauty. She felt unworthy of him, and so, so
grateful. It was as if she'd been living in a shadow, up to now, and
here she was, dancing in the light.

She would love him forever. Her studies drifted into the background. Her teachers 'had a word' with her guardians, who had a
word with her parents – a warning one, this time. They no longer
approved of Jitty. They were worried. Cassie was flouting the rules,
staying out late, coming home looking dishevelled. Cassie's father
came down from the Pomeroon to have a word with her, and he
found a changed daughter, a daughter who was no longer obedient,
a daughter who no longer listened. He met Jitty, who displayed his
usual charms and laughed and was nothing other than respectful.

'But what are your *intentions* with my daughter?' said worried
Mr Gomes. They were sitting on the terrace of Palm Court – Jitty
had invited him there, knowing he was a poor country man of little
means. Mr Gomes fidgeted in his chair, glancing from side to side. He
was far out of his league, in this setting, with this young man dressed
in a white shirt and tie, clean-shaven, handsome, well-spoken. A fine
figure of a man, this Jitendra, and were it not for that hair anyone
would have taken him for perhaps a well-situated businessman. Jitty's
hair had by now grown to several inches below his shoulders, but
for the occasion he had tied it into a knot on the nape of his neck
so that it wasn't too conspicuous. Usually, he just let it flow; just as
usually, he wore brightly coloured bell-bottoms and tie-dye T-shirts.

'I have only honourable intentions,' replied Jitty. He reached
out and took Cassie's hand.

'Am I not good to you, Cassie?' he said, and they exchanged a
look that would have convinced the most sceptical father that here
was a match made in heaven, Cassie gazing at him in adoration,
and he receiving her devotion with manly chivalry. He lifted her
hand to his lips and kissed it.

Mr Gomes felt humbled, and presumptuous to even think of questioning the motives of such a man.

'Well, she is the apple of our eye so I am trusting you to treat her with respect and honour,' was all he could say, and he hoped that did not sound rude.

By the time Cassie realised she was pregnant she was six weeks gone. She was shocked, at first, but as the idea sank in – she was thrilled. A baby! They were having a baby, she and Jitty!

Delight took hold of her. Jitty was due to take her out that evening, to a little place on Camp Street he had discovered, where they could sip a drink or two under soft lights, accompanied by romantic music, before driving off to park at the Sea Wall. The only thing that marred their relationship was this little detail: their trysts were limited to the car's back seat.

Cassie's eyes shone as she reached out and closed her hands around his.

'Jitty!' she said, 'You'll never guess!'

'Guess what? You won the lottery?' He laughed at his own joke.

'No, no, much better than that! Nothing to do with money!'

'Well, I'm no good at guessing. Just tell me.'

'We're going to have a baby!'

He pulled his hand out of her clasp. 'What? A – a baby? You-you're pregnant?'

'Yes!'

'You're sure?'

'Yes. Absolutely.'

'But – but I've been using – you know. Protection!'

'I read in a magazine that no protection is perfect. And you use that cheap brand. Durex is the best. I read it in a magazine: sometimes they burst.'

'But still… how far along are you?'

'I don't know exactly – it has to be about six weeks, two months.'

'Did you go to your doctor? For confirmation?'

'How can I go to the doctor, as a single girl? He would think I'm a slut!'

'I can get you an appointment with a good doctor who won't think bad of you, and you can take care of it in no time. You don't have to worry.'

'Take care of it? What do you mean?'

'Er, well, you know. Make it not happen. There are people who do that sort of thing.'

'You mean get rid of it? My baby?'

'Sweetheart, please don't call it a baby. It's just a little tadpole right now, not a baby.'

She frowned. 'How can you say that, Jitty? It's a baby! *Our* baby!'

'You haven't – haven't been with any other boy, have you?'

Tears gathered in her eyes. 'Jitty, how could you even think that? What do you think I am? You know I love you, only you!'

'Yes, but…'

'Jitty, you are going to do the right thing, aren't you? I don't understand…'

'Yes, yes, of course I'll do the right thing but we must consider all options, look at the problem from all sides…'

'Don't you want a baby?'

'Of course! Just – just not right now. We're so young, darling, we should wait a few years. I don't even have a job. I'm still basically a schoolboy! How will I…?'

'But you could easily get a job! You'll be doing your A-levels in a few months and then with your connections, I'm sure you could walk in anywhere and get a good job!'

'Yes, but…'

'And you have that nice big house. We could be together all the time, Jitty! A proper family!'

Jitty couldn't bear for her to think the worst of him, to think of him as a cad. He wasn't, not really. It's just that he had never ever, even in his dreams, thought of himself as a father. He was a lover, a charmer, a man in the prime of his life. A baby simply didn't fit. And yet, he wasn't a cad. He had promised her father, he had his honour.

'I need to think about this,' he told Cassie that night. 'It's all so new. I promise you, I'll help.'

'You – you'll do the right thing, won't you, Jitty?'

Her worried eyes searched his for doubt, for vacillation, for all those things that would prove he wasn't man enough. He couldn't meet that gaze; he looked away.

'I promise you, I'll help!' he repeated, and that was really all that he was in a position to promise.

Everyone knew what doing the right thing was. Already, two girls in Cassie's wider circle of friends had had shotgun weddings, and one was due to give birth next month. The boys in question had done the right thing; fortunately, they had both quickly found jobs and the young families had by now settled in with their parents – in one case the boys' parents, in the other case with the girls'. It was the right thing to do, the honourable thing. The *obvious* thing.

But Jitty had mentioned 'taking care it' – *it*, as if her baby was just some kind of foreign body, an unwanted thing that had found its way into her belly by some mysterious and magical process! – and that worried Cassie. Because there were other girls, too, and rumours swirled around them. One girl who had suddenly been whisked away for a week or two (they said to the USA) and returned, sad and withdrawn, broken of spirit, and, rumour had it, she'd had a procedure, the very dreaded thing Jitty was hinting at; and another girl who had gone away and never returned, and, rumour had it, was now a young unmarried mother in a foreign country.

No, she would not 'take care' of it! And it wasn't just a tadpole! The very idea of it, once planted in her mind, had sprung forth and created a reality, a future living being, beloved and precious. She would not, not ever, *take care of it!*

It was true that a baby would drastically interfere with her plan to study medicine, become a doctor, return to the Pomeroon to work there – a neglected area as far as medical care was concerned. But it would only be an interruption, not a cancellation. A delay. She'd be taking her A-levels in a few months, and once she had those, she could still go to university in a few years. She had aunts and cousins in Town who would help, and anyway, surely Jitty could afford help with childcare? As long as they were together, they could do this.

But Jitty didn't sound as if he were willing to take responsibility, and that was worrying. And disappointing. In fact, the more she thought about it, the more terrifying it was. If she alone were responsible, what on earth would she do? She had to confront Jitty, no matter how embarrassing, how humiliating, that would be.

'Jitty, you're going to be a father! You have to take responsibility! We have to get married!'

'But I – I'm not…' He hung his head, still not meeting her eyes.

Cassie, that meek and mild and so timid girl, sprang to her feet and for the first time in his life, Jitty learned that even if a girl is mild in manners and presentation, that mildness might just be a costume, a decoy; that in every kitten lurks a tiger and there is no force so mighty in the world as a mother, or a mother-to-be; and that you'd better not tamper with a tiger.

'Jitendra Maraj, you're going to be a father and you'd better raise your head. Look at me!'

He slowly lifted his head. His eyes, finally locking with hers, showed now not cowardice, but terror. Placing hands on hips, she said, loudly, so that people at other tables turned and stared:

'If you can't get up on your hind legs and be a man then I gonna have to do it for you!'

He paled visibly, his dark skin taking on a ghostly grey pallor as the blood rushed from it.

'What – what you mean?'

'I mean, I'm going to go to your Granma and tell her everything. Tell her about your behaviour and what you did and that you made a baby and don't want to take care of it.'

'No! No, don't do that! Please! Please, Cassie, I gon' do it. I'll talk to her, I'll sort it out, I promise! Somehow…'

And Cassie had to be satisfied with that. She didn't know exactly what 'sort it out' meant, but time would tell.

Chapter Twenty-One

Jitty

Jitty raised his fist, hesitated a moment, then knocked on Granma's door.

'Come in!' she called, and he stepped into her bedroom, the upstairs corner room where she now spent the entirety of her life. Next to it was her own private bathroom, and across the hall in Aunt Mary's old room was the live-in nursemaid, the woman who took care of her and her needs day and night, and adjoining the bedroom was her private office, its walls lined with cupboards and shelves and filing cabinets. There was a desk, too, with an ancient Olympia, several of the keys worn away so that the letters were no more than vague outlines. This is where she received her lawyers and the various businesspeople who dropped in and out of the house. There were two further, empty rooms upstairs, plus the Tower, all unused.

Granma spent most of her days sitting in the Morris chair next to the window in her bedroom. She had had the carpenters in to lower the window frame so that she could see out from a sitting position – not that there was much to see from up here; she couldn't see the street and the goings-on on Kaieteur Close, but between the rooftops there were glimpses of the Atlantic Ocean, ships coming in and leaving the Demerara estuary and disappearing over the horizon, and there were treetops and kiskadees hopping in the branches, and flocks of crows coming in to roost every evening.

All entertainment for Granma, along with the radio planted on the little side table next to her chair.

Jitty had the entire downstairs to himself: a bedroom, a bathroom, kitchen, drawing room, gallery – all his, for Granny never came down, the stairs proving too much for her arthritis. Theoretically he could do as he pleased there – invite girlfriends, throw parties, lounge all day in his pyjamas – but he never did. It was as if Granny's ghost still held sway in these downstairs rooms, watching sternly to see if he broke her stringent rules, and he never did.

He hardly saw her, these days, but Granny had always liked a rum-swizzle, and they had their established routine whereby Jitty would bring her up a rum-swizzle, and himself a bottle of cold Banks beer, every Sunday afternoon, and they would chat over non-essentials – things that had been in the papers that week (Granma read every single edition of the *Chronicle*, the *Graphic*, the *Argosy*, the *Evening Post* and the *Catholic Standard*, cover to cover), local gossip (who had married whom), whatever Mr Burnham or Mr Jagan (the Prime Minister and the Opposition Leader) had said or done in the week gone by.

Granma also had a particular penchant for the British Royal Family, and followed their antics and scandals religiously. Not that there was much of the latter: she heartily approved of the queen and her impeccable behaviour, but loved to speculate as to the future marriages of her children. And as for Princess Margaret – well, she certainly provided a bit of colour. Granma was convinced that colonial times were the best, and the way an independent nation would go could only be downhill. Especially now that 'that Burnham' was in charge.

'Those black people have it in for us Indians!' she would say, again and again; and though she couldn't approve of Opposition Leader Cheddi Jagan entirely (after all, he was a self-defined Marxist) at least he was 'one-a-we', of Indian heritage.

But that was all by the by; Jitty and Granma now lived separate lives, and their Sunday conversations were little more than idle chit-chat, Granma complaining about this and that and Jitty sipping his Banks and nodding approval to everything she said. More was not needed. They skimmed lightly over the surface of current events, and certainly, Granma's business dealings were of no interest whatsoever to Jitty. As long as he received his generous weekly allowance – sent down to him in a manila envelope religiously every Friday afternoon – he was happy with the status quo.

But today was different. Not only was it not a Sunday afternoon, he had potentially explosive news. A girl was pregnant, by him, and was demanding marriage. If Granma, too, demanded marriage – as any responsible parent or guardian of a young man would – his life as he knew it today would be over. But he had the feeling she wouldn't…

Granma had the makings of a matriarch – a frustrated matriarch. She had lost her only son, Jitty's father, in that tragic accident years ago, which had wiped out an entire branch of the family and the legitimate succession. Her daughter, Aunt Mary, had married late and had no children, so Jitty was the last of the Maraj line, a line of succession that went all the way back to India in the early days of indenture. And the first Maraj had not been a sugar labourer, imported to the colony to replace emancipated African slaves. No, their noble ancestor who had come over on one of the early ships had been a businessman of the Vaishya caste, a merchant with the ambition to establish trading routes with the emerging economy, and had found success and built up a fortune in the timber industry. All Granma's hopes and ambitions now rested on Jitty, and he was aware of her plans for his eventual revitalisation of the family. She had made initial plans for his marriage years ago, given him a list of the three girls who came into view, daughters of prominent Indian businessmen with whom a lucrative alliance could be established, and the Maraj line built up again.

True, she had lost control of Jitty during his wild teenage years and eventually given up, retired to her upstairs quarters, and allowed him to run free, sow his wild oats, whatever it was young men did these days. But everyone, including Jitty, knew that eventually he would be brought back into the fold. And in spite of his present freewheeling lifestyle, Jitty, too, knew what was required of him. And behind it all he was terrified of Granma. She might be old and arthritic and withered, sitting there in her Morris chair with the cushions worn hard and almost flat, and her legs up on a footstool, but he was not in the least fooled. Perched beside her on the windowsill was a large bottle of Limacol, the mentholated lime-based astringent lotion no Guyanese over the age of forty could live without, and in her hand was the folded Limacol-soaked handkerchief with which she now and again swabbed her forehead – it helped clear her head, she always said, though Jitty was in no doubt that Granma's head was permanently clear, and possibly even clairvoyant. She could read him like a book. That was the scary thing.

Now, she turned to watch him in silence as he crossed the room.

'Jitty? What you done now?'

It was a familiar greeting; it had started way back when Jitty was a rambunctious boy always in trouble with this neighbour or that, though it was not so often needed now. Jitty sighed and planted himself in the second Morris chair, facing Granma. He was quaking inside, but tried not to show it; he exhibited his usual breezy charm, to which Granma had always been susceptible.

'I'm in a spot of trouble, Granma,' he said. 'Got a girl knocked up and she raisin' a bit of hell.'

'Jitty! I don't believe it! What I told you, when Mr Evans came round that time?'

Jitty had flirted outrageously with a St Rose's girl called Jennifer Evans, a good Catholic girl, and her father had had no other option than to come complaining to Granma. Granma had given him a good talking-to and that had been the end of it, with Jennifer as well as his more ostentatious behaviour. He had learned discretion, over time, and to pick his girls wisely – those with strict parents were to be avoided at all costs – and to make sure Granma was kept out of it; those two conditions were actually co-dependent. Fathers were especially troublesome. It was a wonder they didn't keep their daughters under lock and key (Jitty supposed they would love to, being men themselves and thus knowing what went on in the minds of fellows such as he himself).

'Is a bit different this time, Granma.'

'Look over there on my desk, bring me my address book. There's a lady in there could help. She knows all the ins and outs of these matters.'

Jitty wondered how and why Granma had the telephone number of such a 'lady', but didn't ask.

'It's not like that, Granma. She refuse to have an abortion, she want me to marry her.'

Granma sighed. 'These girls nowadays! They think they got to trap a boy into marriage with a baby. In my day you didn't even meet the boy before marriage.'

'Times have changed, Granma.'

'The old ways were much better. People had morals. Boy, why you can't keep your pants on?' She shook her head, then continued. 'But maybe marriage will settle you down. An Indian girl, I assume. Hopefully, a Hindu. Or at least, not a Muslim.'

'Actually, no. Her name is Cassie Gomes.'

'Gomes? A Portuguese girl, then. Any relation to Frederick Gomes of Carmichael Street? That's a respectable family. Why you had to go playin' around with the daughter?'

'She's not Portuguese, Granma. She's a country girl from the Pomeroon. Her father is mostly African, with some Portuguese mix. Her mummy is Amerindian.'

'What?! What kind of cheap girl you messing around with? Those girls are only after one thing, a ring on they finger. It's probably not even your child.'

Jitty sighed. You just couldn't please Granma. If you got a 'respectable' girl pregnant, it meant she'd tricked you into marriage. But get a 'cheap' girl pregnant, they only wanted a ring and had tricked you with another man's child. Which all boiled down to the same thing: girls were tricksters. What kind of girl were you supposed to get pregnant, then, if any? But Granma had her answer to hand.

'If I told you once, I told you a thousand times: keep your hands off these girls! Keep your hands to yourself and your pants zip up! What is wrong with young men nowadays? In my day…' and off she went on another of her diatribes, about the moral collapse of society, and how it was all down to girls' lack of self-respect and boys' lack of self-control, and parents' lack of control. It was one of Granma's favourite topics, though, thankfully, the diatribes had become rather less frequent over the years due to Jitty's well-planned discretion. But then, in the middle of it, she stopped suddenly and said, abruptly: 'The girl's father is black, you say? You met him?'

Jitty nodded. 'Yes, Granma, I met him. A black man, with some Portuguese mix in.'

'So, you gon' have a black bastard, then? Because I swear to God, Jitendra Maraj, you ain't marrying no black girl.'

'She's insisting, Granma! But I—'

'She can insist till her face turn blue, you ain't marrying that girl. Not so long I'm alive.'

He nodded. 'It's what I told her. I don't have a job, and I haven't even finished school yet!'

'No matter that – if you got to marry, you got to marry, and damn education, you just got to find a job. You got the girls in the Marriage List. But I not havin' the Maraj blood desecrated.

No surree, not this time! This time, you gone a step too far, Jitty. Why you have to go with a girl like that?'

Jitty felt the need to defend Cassie. 'She's a nice girl, Granma. A good girl.'

'Well, obviously not. Look what she did! Why she didn't keep her legs together?'

'But, Granma, is not her fault alone!'

His conscience was not only pricking him right now, it was a sword in his hand, held upright to defend Cassie. Because whatever the predicament they were in, he had been the one to lead her astray – if that was what had happened. Cassie loved him with all her heart and all of a sudden, he felt that love and a need to defend it.

'Hrrumh! Is always the woman's fault unless she was forced. Did you force her? I mean, rape?'

'No, of course not! I…'

'Then she should have said no. No morals, these young girls nowadays.'

'She didn't really want to, Granma, it was me who—'

'Don't make excuses for her! And how you know is *your* child?'

'It is! I just know!'

'These girls full of tricks. She probably see your big house and car and money. For all you know, she got ten other boyfriends.'

'No, Granma! Is not like that! She's a good girl, a special girl, a really fine person and I think—'

'She's a cheap slut!'

'No, no! Don't say that! She's a wonderful girl, really special, and she loves me, and – and better than any other girl I know, and I want to marry her!'

The last words sprang from his lips even before he knew what he was saying, and all of a sudden, it was true. Just like that. A surge of light. Yes, he wanted to marry Cassie and make her happy and make everything right and mend his ways. And have a baby, a child! And be a father, a man! Something was swelling in his heart, an emotion he'd never known before, evoked, perhaps, by his very need to stand up for Cassie; there it was, filling him with a sweetness and light he'd never known before. Yes, surely this was love, that thing they spoke of in every romantic movie he'd ever seen with every single girl he'd kissed on every single back seat in every single cinema in Georgetown. This was it.

'I'm going to marry her!' he repeated, loudly and firmly.

'No, you are *not!*' Granma rose, shakily, to her feet and her response was louder still, a command, a shout. She began again: 'If you marry this black girl, I-I-I…' But then she stumbled and fell back in her chair, gasping, gripping the armrests with white fingers.

'I-I can't breathe! Pain! The pain!' Jitty rushed to her side, put an arm round her.

'Granma! What's wrong?'

Granma gasped out some more words:

'Water! Bring water! And-and call Dr Balakrishnan! Nurse! Nurse!' There was a bell-pull next to her chair; she reached for it, but her hand shook too much and so Jitty pulled it instead, and a distant bell jangled, and the nurse came rushing in from next door.

'Madame! Madame, what's wrong?'

'Water! Water! And the doctor!' The nurse was calmness personified. She turned to Jitty:

'Master Maraj, please pour her a glass from the jug. Madame, I'm calling the doctor right now.'

Jitty, having been petrified into immobility, suddenly sprang into action and followed the nurse's directions. He dashed over to the wash-hand stand in the corner of the room; there stood an ancient ceramic basin with matching water jug, and several glasses downturned on a white towel. He picked up one of them, filled it with water, and walked back to his grandmother. The nurse had already picked up the receiver of the phone next to the chair and dialled; as she waited for a reply, she watched as Jitty held the glass to Granma's lips and the old lady sipped. Then she spoke:

'Ah, good evening, may I speak to Dr Balakrishnan, please.' Her voice was calm, as if she had all the time in the world. Granma pushed the glass away and continued to breathe heavily, her eyes closed, her lips moving as if she were praying. Her right hand now gripped her left upper arm, squeezing it rhythmically.

'Hello, Dr Balakrishnan, Maraj residence here. Mrs Maraj appears to have had an incident of some kind.'

She was silent for a moment, and then said, 'Yes, yes, she seems out of breath and in pain. Very well. Thank you.'

She replaced the receiver and said to Jitty:

'Doctor is coming. Please go downstairs and wait for him. What you said to disturb her like that? You know she got a weak heart.'

'I didn't— I mean…'

'Well, obviously it was too much for her. Poor lady.'

'Shouldn't we – shouldn't we lie her in the bed, or something? I'll help.'

'Just go downstairs. Wait for doctor. If we need your help, we will call you. He will be here in five minutes.'

Jitty nodded, and obeyed, calmed by the nurse's brisk efficiency. He did as he was told: went downstairs to wait for the doctor. Dr Balakrishnan lived in Duke Street, just round the corner. He'd be here soon. All would be well.

Hopefully, too, this little health crisis would wipe Granma's mind of their last conversation. All would be well.

Later, much later, Dr Balakrishnan came downstairs and spoke to Jitty.

'Your grandmother has had a heart attack,' he said. 'I am arranging for her to go to the hospital for observation. They are likely to keep her for a few days.'

'Is she going to be all right?'

'Let's hope for the best. She has been having palpitations and minor incidents for some time now. This is not the first. Let's hope, let's hope.'

And Jitty *did* hope; but his conscience pricked terribly, because he found himself hoping, not for a full recovery, but for the very opposite, and that was a terrible thing to hope for. In spite of his shortcomings, Jitty *did* know right from wrong, and it was wrong, so very wrong, to hope for the death of your own grandmother. Even if she was a horrible person you'd never, ever been close to, who had never shown you affection. Even if her death meant you were free of her command, and never had to listen to her creaky voice again, and didn't have to ask her permission to marry the girl you loved.

But even if she recovered, hopefully this incident would have driven the unfortunate conversation from her mind; hopefully she would have forgotten the entire matter. Jitty had approached the whole matter wrongly. He should have been more subtle, used more charm, wrapped Granma round his little finger the way he had as a boy, used the tricks of manipulation he had mastered so well.

Chapter Twenty-Two

But Granma recovered, had not forgotten, and came home from her three days' sojourn at the hospital more determined than ever to prevent this dastardly union.

Two days had not passed by before she summoned him again. Jitty took a deep breath, told himself to stay calm, and went up determined to talk it through with Granma and somehow persuade her at least to *discuss* the matter reasonably with him. Perhaps if she met Cassie, and saw what a lovely, sweet, decent girl she was, she'd change her mind. Jitty was going to suggest such a meeting, but Granma's first words put paid to that, admittedly far-fetched, possibility.

'So, I hope you made it clear to this girl that marriage is out of the question. I'm willing to free up a bit of money to help her out and get her off your back. Then you can wash your hands of her and her little bastard.'

All of Jitty's diligently practised reasonableness flew out the window. This was *his child* she was speaking of. Red-hot rage consumed him. He yelled at her:

'I will marry her, and there's nothing you can do to prevent it! I am nineteen and not a child any more!' And he turned on his heel and marched out. Just before he slammed the door, Granma shouted: 'We'll see about that!'

This time, there was no heart attack. Granma meant business. He could hear it in her voice. Her time in hospital had given her the respite she'd needed to think things through and gather her strength and now, not taken by surprise as she was the last time, she had all her guns lined up.

'We'll see about that,' she'd said, and she did see.

A few days later, Granma's lawyer knocked on the front door. Mildred let him in and he marched across the drawing room to the stairs leading to Granma's domain. An hour later, he left. That evening, Granma summoned Jitty.

'I wanted to let you know, Jitendra, that I have changed my will. As you know, you have been up to now my sole heir, to everything: the business, this house, my savings. But I have now made certain conditions. If you marry this girl, the will becomes null and void. You will get nothing. Not a cent. It will all go to the Maha Sabha for their charity work. Furthermore, if you marry this girl now, you will be requested to leave this house immediately and set up your own household. I will not have her living here.

'In addition, I have stipulated in my will that, should I die before you reach the age of twenty-five, you will be required to marry one of the three young ladies I have selected for you in order to inherit. However, I have allowed you some leeway – I am aware of the modern phenomenon of love-marriage, and I will make allowances for such a decision on your part, provided you marry an Indian girl, or at least half-Indian. In fact, one of the girls I have chosen for you is indeed only half-Indian, but her pedigree is otherwise impeccable and so I have decided to be somewhat flexible in the matter. But those are my conditions.'

And that was that. Really, Jitty had known it from the start. Somewhere, among all Granma's papers in her office next door, was a file with the names and details of the three girls she had selected years ago, when he first showed signs of immoral behaviour and weakness of character. Granma had told him, back then, that he was free to pick one of them as a wife; they had all been inspected and found suitable, and their parents had agreed to a possible match when the time came. And that was that. He'd always known it, just

as he knew that twenty-five was the age at which he was expected
to be settled enough to settle down.

That was how Granma put it: *settle yourself, then settle down.* But
the magical age of twenty-five had always seemed aeons away, and
Jitty, while knowing that 'settle down' meant marriage, and taking
over the Maraj business, had never come even close to coming to
terms with those expectations. It was like another world. He was
young and virile and full of charm and fun, and he was determined
to make the most of these carefree halcyon years. And he had,
and he'd enjoyed his freedom, but now hard reality had somehow
stepped into the midst of his freewheeling life and put an abrupt
stop to it. It had been the last thing he'd expected, but now that
that reality faced him, stark and unavoidable, he had, inexplicably,
found himself yielding to it. Willingly yielding. The conflict with
Granma had brought it all to a head.

Perhaps it was her unabashed racism, the supercilious way she
had dismissed Cassie – dear, sweet, innocent Cassie! – not only
for her race, but for the names she had called her, the insults,
the insinuations. Righteous indignation rose up in Jitty, but not
only that... Something else swelled within him. It was as if a new
idea, rising as a bubble within him, at first alien and terrible, had
suddenly burst open, revealing a shower of glorious fragrance that
swept through his being.

A child! A baby! His baby! He would be a father! And Cassie's
face, the way it had crumpled in disappointment when he had so
cruelly spoken of *taking care of it*, the hurt in her eyes – all of a
sudden there grew in him a tenderness, a protectiveness, a need to
respond in kind, a sense of great loving-kindness. *Cassie, I will take
care of you! You and your baby!* he cried out in silence.

But this, now, was an entirely new reality. He had always
assumed that, once Granma passed away, this all would be his
and he would be a free man. Her heart attack had brought such
an eventuality even closer. Even without being mercenary, the fact

remained: Granma was nearing eighty years of age, she had a weak heart, one day she would die. One didn't have to be cold of heart to face that reality. What had the doctor said when she was in hospital?

'It could happen again, any time. Tomorrow, or in a year. Maybe in five years, though that would be pushing it. The best thing is to keep her calm and happy.'

Granma's death was inevitable; no use being sentimental about that. And it would solve the problem, or so he had believed. But, now, she'd seemingly anticipated that outcome and outwitted him.

Now, she stopped for breath and, perhaps, to gauge his reaction. Jitty tried to get a word in: 'Granma, I—' But she cut him short: 'Those are my conditions. The choice is yours, Jitendra. You can marry this black girl and raise her child as your own – though it probably isn't – but you are out of a home and future if you do this. That is my last word.'

'But, Granma, I—'

'Not one word more!' she bellowed, and pointed to the door with a trembling finger. Jitty was sure he even saw sparks flying from her blazing eyes, and the loose flesh beneath her chin wobbled and her lips tightened. His legs turned to jelly and he all but fled the room.

There was nothing he could do or say. If Granma threw him out of the house they were both lost. He would be homeless, without an income; even if he left school now, months before sitting his A-levels, he would be unlikely to find a job because of one thing he was certain: if Granma threw him out – and he had no doubt that she would do exactly as she had threatened, should *he* do as *he* had threatened – no employer of any standing would hire him. He would be reduced to selling newspapers on the street corner – or water coconuts, or *dhal puri* rolled up in newspaper, or even working on the docks or as a sugar labourer – his imagination ran wild as he conjured up all the various manual jobs he was aware of, jobs beyond his little bubble of upper-class privilege. It all came down to one thing: he would not be able to provide, and all his newly discovered sense of responsible fatherhood shrivelled to a dry husk of nothing. Evaporated into mist.

Basically, his decision was between his house and his family. He had grown up in this house, knew every nook and cranny of it and the surrounding garden. Friends had come and gone, neighbours around them had moved in and out. People had died – his parents and siblings – or moved away – Aunt Mary – but the house remained. It was his home. His every sense of security was bound up in this house. He could not lose it!

Whereas he had known Cassie not even a year, and he didn't know his child at all, not yet. It was just an idea, a dream, this family of his. Something nebulous he played with in his mind, a future not yet realised or understood.

If he could not have both, if he had to choose – well, how could he possibly let go of the very foundation to his life? And yet – Cassie's faith in him, her eagerness for that future together, her love for this child not yet born...

Eventually, Jitty, too came to a decision, one that satisfied his conscience. He wouldn't tell her. He'd cross that bridge when they came to it. He'd keep the house, and if he couldn't marry Cassie due to the terms of the will, well, there was such a thing as common-law marriage, and as far as he knew, that kind of marriage was not mentioned in the will. True, it was really only practised in the lower strata of society – no self-respecting girl would agree to it, for it gave a woman, a mother, no legal rights – but in their case it would have to do. He would promise marriage to Cassie, and she would certainly agree, not knowing it was a third-class union he was promising. It would keep her happy, at least for the time being, and when she *did* find out, it would be too late, and she wouldn't have much choice. Cassie was a flexible girl. She would not be too upset. She would realise that there hadn't been any other option – not if they wanted a home of their own.

His home.

In the meantime, Cassie would have to go back to the Pomeroon and have the baby there. They would wait for Granma to die. She could stay up there with the baby until then. And then, well, that was soon enough for Cassie to be told the truth.

It had always been a tricky thing, discussing Granma's inevitable death with her, and the freedom it would give them, and it was no easier now. Cassie was just too *ethical*. For the time being, it was enough that she still believed that, once Granma died, they could marry and all would be well, as he had told her from the beginning. No need to rectify that notion.

'She has a weak heart,' he'd told her, back then. 'It could happen any time, the doctor said.'

'You shouldn't be wishing her dead!' she had said. 'That's so unkind!'

'I'm just being realistic. We all have to die one day.'

'But I don't want to wish somebody dead, or build my future on that wish. Let's just marry and live somewhere else until… well, until the situation changes.'

'You mean, until she dies.'

Cassie ignored that remark, and continued.

'We can rent a place. It doesn't have to be huge. I would be quite happy to live in a small cottage with you as my husband.'

'OK. But it will take time to get married. You know, paperwork and stuff. Why don't you go and stay with your parents until then?'

'But I need to sit my exams in June!'

'All right then, sit your exams first, and then go to your parents.'

'Jitty, I can't believe it will take that long to get the paperwork sorted out?'

'It takes ages! You have things like banns and so on, and there's a backlog at the registry office, a long waiting list. It will take a few months at least.' He was making it up as he went along; she wouldn't know the difference.

'But you'll put us on the waiting list?'

'Of course, my darling!'

'It will be so embarrassing, walking down the aisle with a huge belly!'

'Then we'll just do the registry office thing.'

'But I want a Christian wedding! I want God's blessing!'

'Trust me, darling. I will work something out.'

'I *do* trust you. I know I just need to *trust* and everything will be fine.'

Since that conversation, Cassie had become surprisingly sanguine. Once he had expressed his commitment to her, his agreement to marry her, she began to look forward to the future; her attitude being that as long as they loved each other, and the child, it would all somehow work out. She had not yet told Aunt Mathilda… or her parents; the former had not yet, it seemed, become aware of the tightening of her clothes, though she did once remark on the fact that Cassie was putting on weight, smugly attributing this to her own good cooking.

But her classmates were not so naive, and it wasn't long before the pointing and the teasing and the giggling started. And not only her schoolmates noticed. She was summoned to the office of Miss Dewer, the headmistress, who came straight to the point.

'I am so very disappointed in you,' she said. 'A girl with so much promise! You see, this is the reason we are so strict here at BHS. You young girls don't understand; you don't understand that the boys have all the fun, but it's the girls who pay the price. I'm sorry you had to learn the hard way: girls who become pregnant before marriage must leave school. Anything else would be encouraging a lax attitude. I am very sorry, Cassandra, but you must leave us.'

'But… A-levels…'

'Yes, I know. I'm sorry, but these are the rules. I'm afraid you won't be able to sit your exams as a pupil of Bishops' High School.'

Cassie couldn't help it. The tears began to flow, and she couldn't stop them.

'It's all I ever wanted – all I ever did… I worked so hard – want to be a doctor – I… please…' Words stuttered out between sobs as, shoulders heaving, Cassie no longer tried to suppress her distress. Overcome by guilt, shame, regret, she broke down, right there and then in the headmistress' office.

Miss Dewer's features relaxed somewhat. She handed Cassie a handkerchief and waited, as if allowing her to cry herself dry. Occasionally, she whispered, 'I'm sorry. So sorry.'

Cassie finally gulped and pulled herself together. She dried her eyes, gave one or two last sobs, snorted into the handkerchief, and finally looked up to meet Miss Dewer's gaze – a gaze not accusatory, not censorious, but filled with understanding and, yes, compassion.

Once Cassie had regained her composure, the headmistress spoke, calmly, gently.

'I'm so sorry, my dear, and I feel your pain. You're not the first girl this has happened to, and you won't be the last. But, you know, maybe there's a solution. What do you intend to do now? I know your parents live in the Pomeroon. Will you return to them?'

'Y-yes, I suppose so,' Cassie managed to say. 'I've nowhere else to go. The boy promised to marry me, but it will take some time, and until then…'

Miss Dewer nodded. 'I see. Well then, perhaps we can find a compromise?'

Cassie looked up. 'A-a compromise? What do you mean?'

'I've been thinking. Perhaps you could sit your A-levels as an external student, study on your own – we could send you study materials, books, and so on – and still take the exam. You could sit it at the Charity Secondary School.'

'That's a possibility?'

'I don't know. I can't promise anything. I shall have to write to the Board of Education at London University and see if they will allow it.'

'But that would be wonderful, Miss Dewer!'

'Don't rejoice too soon. We haven't got permission yet. And even if they do allow it, you have a very rocky road ahead of you. I'm so disappointed, Cassandra. You have let us all down, let the school down, let your country down.'

'My *country*? How…?'

'Yes, your country. With so many of our brightest stars flying off to a better life overseas we need to nurture local talent, especially our girls, and you have so much potential. How can our country move forward if our young ones don't put their shoulders to the task? If you all become distracted by…' – she struggled for the right word – '…by lust and sweet-talking boys? I would have thought you knew better.'

'Miss Dewer, I…'

But Miss Dewer, looking at her watch, turned suddenly brisk and dismissive. 'That's enough, Cassandra. I will look into the matter and let you know.'

*

Meanwhile, Jitty was struggling with his conscience. Surely, if he really did care for Cassie and their baby – and he was certain that he did – he would stand up for them against Granma. He would be the bigger man, tell Granma he didn't care about her will or her plans to disinherit him – she could go ahead and do what she wanted; he would not see his family so disrespected, his future wife so insulted. He would marry Cassie, and they would find a way together, just as she had suggested. A little cottage in Kitty would be good enough, cheap enough. They didn't need a huge house and the business and shares or whatever prizes Granma cared to dangle before him. That, surely, would be the noble thing, the manly thing.

But then again… And it was here that Jitty struggled. It didn't help that all his friends agreed that he was doing the right thing, because it was *Cassie* who had chosen to have the baby; it was *her* choice, *her* responsibility, and there were other options, but she had said she wanted to have the baby, so very well, let her face the consequences: a ruined reputation, a ruined education, a ruined future.

'It's not your fault, Jitty – she could easily get rid of it. I know a lady up in Berbice…', they said, or '…a lady in Trinidad' or '…a lady in New York'. There seemed to be hundreds of ladies who would help, if only Cassie decided to be sensible, just do away with the problem altogether.

It's her decision, her fault, not yours. She can't make you ruin your life. She can't force you to give up everything. You have it made – why should you sacrifice everything for her, when she could easily not have a baby now? Who knows what the future will bring? You might meet someone else, better than her. You don't need a baby in your life now. You're still so young, boy! Still time to have fun. You can settle down in ten years' time. Don't let her terrorise you. Don't let her make you feel bad. It's not your fault. Send her back to the Pomeroon.

They talked, and Jitty tried not to listen, but he did. And he struggled with his conscience, and won. They were right, these friends: Cassie had made a decision, and he couldn't ruin *his* life for *her* decision.

*

And so, soon after her conversation with Miss Dewer, Cassie confessed to her parents in a letter. They were, as she'd known they'd be, aghast that she had, as her mother described it, 'ruined her life'. That after all that effort, after so much hard work, so much promise, so much potential, Cassie had thrown it all away. And for a boy who would not marry her.

'He will!' Cassie wrote back. 'Just not at the moment!' But Cassie's mother, it seemed, was practical, sensible and loving, and prepared to face the reality that was rather than fret over the reality that could have been.

'Ah, you young girls!' she wrote back. 'When will you ever learn? But what to do? It is as it is. Come home, Cassie. You and your baby will always have a home with us.'

*

'I'm going back to the Pomeroon,' she told Jitty. 'It's best if you make the marriage arrangements and then come up and we get married quietly, up there. Secretly. Then I can come back to Town with you and we can maybe rent a place if your granny doesn't want us in the house.'

Jitty was pleased to hear that she was going home. He teased her: 'Back to behind God's back! Don't forget me out there!'

She frowned. 'I wish you wouldn't call it that. It's so derogatory.'

'Just a joke – it's a metaphor. A metaphor means—'

'I know what a metaphor is. It's still derogatory. It's not like that at all. More like, up there we're...' She thought for a little. '...like we're in the palm of God's hand. If you want to use a metaphor. In paradise.'

And so, Cassie packed her bags, said goodbye to Aunt Mathilda and Uncle Patrick – who were shocked to hear that Jitty had taken advantage of her, but thought she was doing the right thing – and returned to the Pomeroon. Jitty drove her as far as Parika on the Essequibo River, accompanied her on to the bustling dock, carried her little suitcase for her to the water's edge, where boatmen vied for passengers so as to fill up their vessels. He helped her descend into the boat, watched as she settled onto a seat in the covered section, squashed between two women, a buxom older one with a large bundle on the floor between her feet, a young one with a little child on her lap. Cassie gestured at the child as she strapped on her lifejacket, and smiled up at him, a smile redolent with eagerness and joy and trust in him.

He watched as the boat backed away from the dock. Cassie waved to him, and he waved back. Then the boat turned, the engine gathered power, and it sped away, its bow rising high above the water as it raced over the vast brown waters of the Essequibo.

How was he to know that it was the last time he'd ever see her?

Part Two

Coming-of-Age

Chapter Twenty-Three

1986: A Busty Lass

Rita was nearly fifteen when she discovered that Archie Foot was the most evil-looking (evil that year being synonymous with out-of-this-world gorgeous) boy she had ever seen and the only one she'd ever love in all her life. The Foot family had moved into Number Five last July. There had been no logical reason *not* to integrate Archie into the Kaieteur Close Gang, but with a name like Foot, you had to make some extra effort to prove you weren't a drip and Archie hadn't done so, despite the teasing. And it wasn't just the ridiculous name; rumour had it that the Feet (the Foots?) were Returnees from England, Archie's father having been offered a position as Professor of History at the University of Guyana. Whoever returned from London to Georgetown! Only drips and creeps did that, failures, people with names like Foot. Professor Foot! Real people left and never came back! Didn't that prove the Foot boys were unworthy of Kaieteur Close?

At the start of the new school year, Bishops' High School, St Rose's, St Stanislaus, St Joseph's and Queen's College had all simultaneously turned co-educational, which meant that boys were admitted to Bishops', St Joseph's and St Rose's, and girls to Queen's and Saint's. Polly's father insisted that the Saint's science department was obviously better than Bishops' – because Saints had been a boys' school – and made Polly change schools, leaving Rita without a best friend in class.

And all of a sudden Archie was one of three new boys in Rita's class, the only boy from Kaieteur Close at Bishops', which had been the country's elite all-girls' school. Yet another reason for Archie to prove himself...

Girls can be unmerciful. Archie's female classmates shot paper pellets at him with rubber bands. They hid his books. They put a lizard in his desk during break. It was as if he had leprosy; in the classroom, girls cringed away from him, giggling and tittering behind raised hands. The other two boys, ignored by the girls, were Chinese identical twins, the Chans, who had eyes only for each other, so Archie was on his own, friendless and isolated, sitting on his own at a desk directly in front of Rita.

In a way, Rita felt sorry for him, but in another way the fun was too much to resist. She watched, and never said a word, never joined in the verbal needling, keeping a straight face when all the other girls giggled and spluttered. So passive was she in the harassment of Archie that he possibly even thought her a friend; now and then she caught him glancing at her, a half-smile on his lips, and she smiled back kindly and innocently, keeping her betrayal to herself.

For, in fact, Rita was the worst of the lot. Her contribution to the molestation of Archie was silent, and Archie had no inkling of her perfidy. He never saw the notes she scribbled hastily during lessons and at break time, rhyming couplets she passed around the class so that everyone could share the joke. When the note had been read by the whole class – excepting, of course, the Chan boys, who shared a desk in glorious isolation at the front – it returned to Rita, who carefully destroyed it. Over the weeks, the poems had grown bolder as Rita's imagination took wing. Today's was a masterpiece.

Rita grinned to herself as she folded the paper. She glanced up; when Miss Humphries' back was turned, she leaned over, past Archie, and passed the note to the girl sitting diagonally across from her, next to Archie. At that moment Miss Humphries turned,

Rita dropped the note, Archie picked it up, all in the space of an indrawn breath.

'Archibald Foot, bring me that note!'

'What note, Miss?'

'Don't play the fool with me, I saw you pick up a note that girl passed you, now please bring it up here straight away!'

Archie looked genuinely nonplussed. He shuffled his books around as if looking for a note and, finding nothing, looked at Miss Humphries innocently and shrugged his shoulders. 'I don't know anything about a note, Miss.'

Miss Humphries marched forward and stood above Archie, arms akimbo, glaring down at him from her vantage point several feet above. Miss Humphries was enormous at the best of times; fury multiplied her bulk. Her torso was as thick and solid as a sack of flour, with a sharp indentation around the middle of the sack (or, in this case, a polka-dotted cotton dress), where a thin belt hinted at a waistline. Miss Humphries had pale skin. People called her 'white', but in fact it was a well-known fact that she was seven-eighths Portuguese, the name Humphries deriving from an English paternal great-grandfather. That single drop of English blood, however, lent her an authority far exceeding that of all the other teachers put together. Especially when she looked at you like that.

Rita quaked.

Archie Foot, however, looked up at the thundercloud looming above him and said in all confidence, 'You must be mistaken, ma'am, nobody passed me a note.'

Miss Humphries exploded. 'You dare lie to me! You dare! Stand up, you, boy!'

Archie Foot stood up.

'Now, quick-march forward to the blackboard. Go and stand there facing the room. Chop-chop!'

Archie did as he was told.

Miss Humphries, her face set in determined lines, picked up each of Archie's books, one by one, and shook them out. No note fluttered to the floor. She opened his desk; he could, after all, have slipped the note quickly under the flap. But no note lay inside the desk.

To give up now would be an admission of defeat and Miss Humphries never succumbed to defeat. She tramped to the front of the class, grabbed Archie by one ear, pulled him forward and systematically searched him. She began innocently enough, emptying the contents of his trouser pockets and turning them inside out. Nothing there. She peered into his shirt pocket. Nothing there. She made him pull up his cuffs. She made him take off his shoes and searched his socks. Nothing there.

'Take your shirt out of your pants,' she commanded.

Archie did so.

'Now unbuckle your belt!'

At those words a petrified murmur hummed through the classroom. One girl whispered a little too loud, so that everyone heard: 'She's going to make him strip naked!' Some girls opened their desks and hid behind the uptilted lids, others buried their faces in their hands and peeped through their fingers. They shuffled their feet, tittered in embarrassment and glanced nervously at each other. Rita kept her eyes riveted to the tips of her shoes.

But Miss Humphries did not need to strip Archie after all, for the note was tucked inside his trousers, and as he opened his belt, she saw the tell-tale white edge of paper. Triumphantly, she stuck her fingers into Archie's waistband and pulled it out. 'You see! You can't fool me!' she cried in triumph and let out a laugh that positively vibrated with sadism. No one laughed with her.

Miss Humphries opened the note and read it. Slowly, she turned to glare at Rita. 'Rita Maraj, stand up!' Her voice contained a deadly chill. She raised a hand, fist upwards, and in slow motion, uncurled her forefinger so that it pointed towards

Rita and then curled it back into the fist. 'Come here, you,' she said slowly in time to the finger-curling. Rita, still sitting, bit her lip and stared.

'Are you deaf? Stand up!' Rita's chair scraped backwards and she rose to her feet. Her knees trembled; Miss Humphries was renowned for draconian punishments.

'All right. Come here.'

Rita's legs felt too weak even to take one step forward, let alone carry her to the front of the room. She stood immobile, as if nailed to the floor.

'Are you deaf, child? I said, go to the front of the class! Do I have to drag you? Go on, move!' Miss Humphries herself moved her enormous frame and stood menacingly in front of Rita's aisle. Rita could not move, she was frozen. Besides, she would have to squeeze past Miss Humphries, who blocked the narrow aisle with her huge frame, and who seemed not the least inclined to budge. But no, she was coming, moving slowly down the aisle towards Rita, and gave her shoulder a light shove. Rita hastily stumbled backwards. Fearing further manhandling, she scrambled to her feet, almost ran to the end of the aisle and then back up the side of the room to take a position next to Archie.

Rita stepped forward hesitantly. Miss Humphries handed her the note.

'Now read that aloud.'

Rita's voice was thin as she began to read.

Of all the girls who're in my class
I'm Rita Maraj, a busty lass...

Somebody snorted at the word 'busty' and Rita stopped reading.

'Continue!' barked Miss Humphries. Rita swallowed audibly, scratched her head and rattled off, without stopping for breath, her voice almost squeaky with suppressed panic:

I notice how the lonely boy
Archie peeks, but he's very coy.
I wickedly made stealthy trips,
to plant on his cheek my cherry lips
or with my nice reputed…

Rita stopped for a deep breath and the last word shot out much too loud:

…BUST…

More snorts, more laughter. Rita longed to look up, but did not dare. She looked at Miss Humphries. Surely that was enough? Hadn't everyone got the gist of it? But Miss Humphries was merciless.

'Quiet!' she boomed at the class and lashed the desk with her ruler. 'Well? I'm waiting! Repeat that last line and continue!'

…or with my nice reputed bust
nudge his head with a gentle thrust,
but before that derring-do I can
share with the girls my daring plan…

A faint titter of anticipation rippled through the class. Someone smothered a snicker. Rita faltered and looked up at Miss Humphries pleadingly.

'Please, Miss, I can't!' she squeaked.

'Continue!'

Rita read on, her voice now barely audible.

And as they watched I trepid went…

She stopped. She couldn't help it, the laughter swelled within her and if she spoke one more word, she would burst.

'GO ON!' Miss Humphries boomed.

…my bust I thrust, my cherry lips I vent…

The last word went unheard. The entire room exploded. Girls were falling from their desks, rolling on the floor, holding each other up, shaking with resounding laughter. Rita had dropped the note and stood with her head bowed in her hands, quivering soundlessly from head to foot. Archie faced the blackboard and trembled, whether with sobs or laughter, nobody knew.

'DETENTION!' Miss Humphries finally cried. 'Three hours' detention for the whole class. As for you, Miss Maraj, I will speak to the headmistress about you. And you, Mr Foot…' As if for emphasis, Miss Humphries stamped her own foot at this last word, engendering a whole new cascade of laughter so that she never finished her sentence. The class ended in chaos.

By coincidence, Donna deSouza's fifteenth birthday party was that weekend, to be held at her home in Number Four. Archie had not been invited, but the grapevine rippled with stories of Archie's and Rita's budding love affair and everyone – except Rita – insisted that a last-minute invitation be extended to him.

He came.

The jukebox blared like at any other party and they all flung themselves about to the fast music, laughing just like always, and then somebody requested 'Stand By Me' and somebody else turned off the overhead light and without knowing how it had happened, Rita was in Archie Foot's arms, dancing slowly, slowly, ever so slowly, almost not moving, and so embarrassed she thought she'd die, because she had been worse than all the other girls in the harassment of Archie Foot, and the poem, just the thought of it now, made her quiver with abashment. How would she ever live it down? Ever look him in the eye? But here he was, dancing with her. How had that happened? Had he asked her? Had someone pushed them together? She couldn't remember. And now, stealing a sideways upwards glance at him, she saw in the faint rainbow glow of the fairy lights that he was tall and slim and ever so good-looking, with just a trace of soft dark fuzz along his upper lip.

Why hadn't she seen those things before?

Archie hadn't said a word to her since the drama. In the classroom he had avoided her as much as she did him, but now, now, he was holding her in his arms, and it was the most incredible feeling of all. He danced with her till the party was over, not even letting go of her between songs; and she wanted it that way. Talking to him would have been too embarrassing for words, but this, dancing – this was perfect. Just being held in his arms. It was all she wanted.

Because she knew she was in love. She dreamed as she danced, dreamed of her and Archie being a couple and then getting married and living happily ever after, and she buried her nose in his shoulder and closed her eyes and smelled the faint scent of his cologne mingled with sweat, and knew at last what they were all about, those songs and books and films. And plays. This was the real thing! The grown-up thing. Love, with a capital L. Oh, she was made for Love. Born for Love. Love was the summit of all things human, the Treasure at the end of the rainbow. Nothing else would ever be boring, once she had Love. And Archie. And Archie would love her too… She dreamed away as they danced, picturing herself in Archie's arms forever and a day, running barefoot with him along a Barbados beach, he swinging her up into the rolling white surf, her arms round his neck, laughing, laughing, laughing; then stillness, his arms holding her close, outlined against a golden sunset… She dreamed on, a slight smile curling her lips, eyes closed the better to see.

But the party ended and Archie abruptly stepped away without speaking a word. He simply squeezed her hand and disappeared with the other guests streaming out of the gate, without even a by-your-leave.

In the days following the party, the Kaieteur Close youth rearranged themselves. Archie Foot had passed the initiation test. He was one of them. And anyway, he had a wonderful new ping-pong table under the house, and a group of discarded armchairs and a sofa around a scratched wooden table, where you could sit and edge closer to each other and be hugely silly all afternoon. So, the Foot residence became the new hangout.

But all without Rita. Rita simply refused to join the gang. She felt the ball was in his court; he must acknowledge her in some way, take the first step. *Can't let him think I'm after him*, she reasoned. *And what if I turn up there and he ignores me, like he did at the end of the party?* Her heart pounded in panic at the very thought. *If he hates me then I hate him too.*

Had she made a false move at the party? She went through every step once more. Replayed all the songs in her mind, relived every tender feeling, but it only made things worse. He should have said goodbye. He should have pecked me on the cheek. He should have phoned! But he hadn't. Rita's world was crumbling…

Rita wheeled her bicycle out of the Number Seven gate. 'Where are you off to, Rita?' Polly called, leaning out of her gallery window.

'To the Sea Wall.'

'All by yourself? Why?'

Rita put the bike on its stand on the bridge and re-latched the gate. Turned back to the bike, took it off the stand and, glancing up at Polly, shrugged. Wheeled it onto the road.

'I like it there, that's all. Some nice sea breeze.'

'But Archie said we can come over to play ping-pong. That's where I'm going, and Donna and Brian.'

'Go ahead! See you later!' She gave what was supposed to look like a friendly but detached wave and placed a foot on the pedal, prepared to sail away in perfect disdain; but then, out of nowhere, there was Archie Foot, the handlebars firmly in his grip, having dashed out from his own open gate and plonked himself in front of her.

'Wait for me!' he said. 'I'm coming too!'

'Who invited you?'

'I invited myself!' he laughed. 'You don't own the Sea Wall. I've every right to ride along it. Behind you, if you insist.'

Rita tried to suppress a smile. She wrinkled her nose.

'I thought you were all playing ping-pong.'

'They're welcome to use the table if they want to.' He looked up at Polly, who watched with some amusement, and called, 'You heard that, Polly? You can play ping-pong in my yard. Mum won't mind.'

Turning back to Rita, he said, 'So just wait a moment, while I get my bike, OK? And tell Mum where I'm going. Won't be a sec.'

Without waiting for an answer, he dashed away again, back into his yard.

Rita was perplexed. What was the cool thing to do now? Not wait for him, and ride away, her pride intact? Or wait for him, as if she really didn't mind him coming? Let go of her pride?

She looked up at Polly. Polly gave her a big thumbs-up. And she couldn't help it: the smile finally broke through, and a few seconds later, she and Archie rode off together.

'Have a nice afternoon!' Polly yelled. 'Look where you're going, and don't fall off the Sea Wall!'

Chapter Twenty-Four

1986: Green Sponges

'Little sisters. They're the pits,' said Polly and kicked a stone into the gutter.

Secretly, Rita agreed, but she had to stand up for Luisa, her adored little sister. Yet even she had to admit that, at seven, Luisa was no more the adorable toddler who looked up to her and followed her around and for whom she could do no wrong, and whose every peccadillo could be laughed at and excused by squealing: *isn't she cu-u-u-ute!*

Over the past few years a subtle battle had been taking place between Rita and Chandra; never admitted, never with a word or a gesture referred to out loud, but to both of them, quite obvious. And equally obviously, Chandra was winning, hands down. It was the battle for Luisa's allegiance, and, ultimately, for her affection.

The older Luisa grew and the more her irrational toddler ways gave way to the amenable-to-reason behaviour of a growing child, the more interest Chandra began to take in her daughter; this had started from when Luisa was around three. In fact, Luisa was becoming just the image of that perfect little girl Chandra had always dreamed of, a little mini-Chandra, a doll she could mould and form into a perfect reflection of herself.

For a start, Luisa was pretty; the kind of child passing adults would look at and smile and then smile up at the parent to say 'what a beautiful little girl you have there!' The kind of child whose cheeks East Indian mothers and grandmothers would pinch and say, 'Ow, beti! Too too sweet!' With her rosebud lips and little heart-shaped face framed by black curls, tied back with pretty clips, she was practically irresistible. The kind of little girl you could buy pretty frilly dresses for, and furthermore, who loved seeing herself in those pretty frilly dresses, who would twirl in front of the mirror and delight in the admiration of others.

Exactly the kind of daughter Chandra could wean away from Rita. Exactly the kind of child Rita could never understand, because she, with her wild and, according to Chandra, rambunctious ways, was the exact opposite.

So, Luisa leaned more and more towards Chandra, and Rita, who loved Luisa just the same as ever, could only watch in appalled silence as Chandra turned her little darling into an image of herself. All she could do was forgive, forgive, forgive; invite Luisa to share her life as much as ever. Let Luisa know that she could do no wrong. Luisa, perfectly aware of her power over her big sister, abused it to the best of her ability.

'She's not doing any *harm*, though,' Rita maintained now. 'She just wants to tag along.' She stretched out her hand to Luisa, who had stopped outside Number Six to make a face at Carol Coolidge, who was sitting cross-legged on the gutter-bridge, playing jacks with a girl from round the corner.

'She's a pest,' Polly said. 'Always has been. Always hanging on like a leech. She does it on purpose, you know. She knows it annoys us and she likes it. She's a pain in the ass. Why can't she make her own friends like any other kid on the block? That Carol Coolidge, for instance, they're the same age, aren't they? But no, Madame Luisa is much too high and mighty, she has to be with the teenagers. I ask you!'

'Archie won't mind.'

'Who says he won't mind? And even if he doesn't, everybody else does. I don't know why you can't just tell her to buzz off.

Nobody else has their little brothers and sisters hanging on their shirt-tails, only you.'

'It's only for today, I promise. The thing is, she likes his brothers and wants to make friends with them and if she does, then I'll have her off my back. Forever. You know she doesn't like playing with girls.'

'You're all besotted with those bloody Feet, every last one of you.'

Rita lurched towards Polly and covered her mouth with her hand. 'Shhh, not so loud, you idiot, he might hear! We're right outside his house!'

Polly laughed, pulling the hand away. 'Well, it's true, and don't glare at me like that— Hi!'

She waved and called to someone she must have glimpsed in the shadows under Archie's house, and then that person emerged and Rita felt her knees turning to jelly and her heart started to race like crazy, because it was Archie.

Rita spread a grin wide across her face and walked over to where Archie sat on the armrest of the old discarded sofa he'd requisitioned for his friends, along with an odd selection of chairs with broken backrests and unsightly garden furniture. Polly and Archie plonked themselves next to her, and Luisa ran over to join Patrick and Robert Foot, who were climbing up the latticework at the other side of the house. Having reached the top, they carefully reached out for a rafter, caught hold of it, swung a few times to and fro, and jumped to the ground, only to swarm back up the latticework for another swing.

Patrick was eight, Robert six, disdainful of girls and especially of Luisa, who nevertheless craved their recognition and friendship. Seeming not to realise how privileged they were – the only children in Kaieteur Close Luisa deigned to acknowledge – these two scathingly ignored her cries of 'I can do that too!'

Luisa stood pouting, watching, longing to join in, yet lacking the courage to do so unassisted. 'Let me come up too!' she cried, and stamped her little foot. Patrick and Robert pretended not to hear; they were counting the number of times they could swing before having to let go. Patrick managed seven, Robert only four. 'I can do that better than you!' Luisa called at the top of her voice. 'I can swing ten times, I can too, I can too!' And she grabbed hold of the latticework and began to climb up.

'Oh, get lost, little brat!' said Patrick as he jumped to the ground. 'And don't you dare climb up there!'

'I can, I can, I'm going to show you!'

Luisa was scrambling up with remarkable speed.

'Come down, you little idiot!'

'I'll get her!' called Robert, who was up at the top. He climbed down a little way and fought Luisa's hands with his feet; whenever the girl tried to get hold of a lath, Robert kicked her fingers away. At the same time, Patrick pulled on her legs from below, but neither he nor his brother had reckoned with Luisa's stubbornness and need to conquer. The more they fought her, the more she struggled; her hands were quick, they clung to the wood with the tenacity and sheer power of a monkey to a branch, and kicked at Patrick with a viciousness he had not expected. She caught him in the eye with her heel; he cried out and briefly let go, then returned with a vengeance, this time swarming up the latticework himself and catching hold of her round the waist.

Rita, Polly and Archie couldn't help but notice the commotion; and as Patrick and Luisa fell to the ground, intertwined and squirming, Rita and Archie dashed across to intervene.

'Luisa, it serves you right, you should have left them alone!' Rita scolded, giving her bawling sister a hand and pulling her to her feet. She wasn't hurt; Patrick had broken her fall, and her cries were cries of rage and not of pain. Rita knew the difference, knew how to recognise the peeved screeching of wounded conceit, but also knew that if it wasn't quickly soothed it would burst all boundaries and the result would be a tantrum. She couldn't face a tantrum now.

So, when Luisa flung her arms round Rita's waist and buried her face in her belly and sobbed bitterly, Rita stroked her black curls and said, her voice as gently genuine as she could make it, 'It's all right, dear, calm down, Patrick didn't mean to hurt you. Don't cry, darling, it's all right.'

Archie, meanwhile, was dealing with his brother. 'How could you pull that little girl down like that! The poor child could have hurt herself badly. What's the matter with you? And you too, Robert. If you want to fight, why don't you pick on boys your own age?' He swung out and boxed each boy on the shoulder.

Patrick shouted back at him, 'She's just a little pesky brat, always hanging around here an' trying to barge in! What's she doing here at all? She should find friends her own age. Why do we have to play with a baby like that? Who invited her to come here? We don't play with girls and we don't play with babies!'

Robert yelled, 'She's always hanging around at the gate peeping in and we hate her and we weren't fighting her, but she can't climb up with us, girls can't do that, and she tried to climb up and it's dangerous for girls!'

At those words, Luisa yelled: 'I can, I can too! I can climb up there and swing, I've done it a hundred million billion times and I hate you, I hate you, I hate you! I want to go home, Rita. Take me home, I hate those boys and I'm never coming back here. I hate all of you, nasty mean bloody Feet, and my mummy says your mother is an old bag, she's all fat and ugly and her bum wobbles when she walks and her bosom looks as if she filled it with two buckets of Jello, so there!'

Rita gasped aloud, and before she could stop herself, looked up at Archie. She met his eyes, saw her own mortification reflected there in the second before they both looked away. Rita knew she couldn't possibly let that pass; she leaned over and landed Luisa a hot slap on her cheek. Luisa wailed. She threw herself onto the concrete ground and yelled for all she was worth, squirming with rage, kicking and squirming so that her dress twisted up around her waist.

For a moment Rita stood staring at her hand. She'd never done that before, never slapped Luisa, though she'd often been tempted. Guilt swept through her but there was no time to deal with guilt right now for Luisa was having a full-on tantrum.

Rita bent over and picked her sister up. She knew exactly how and where to hold the squirming, squealing Luisa. She'd be black and blue from the kicks by the time she got home, there'd be a few scratches on arms and face, but enough was enough.

'Come,' she said firmly, 'let's go home.'

'I don't want to go home, I want to climb, I want to stay here!'

'You can't, we're going home.' Arms tightly round the struggling child, Rita turned towards the gate.

'I hate you, I hate you, I hate you and you're an old bag too, and I saw you stuffing your bra full of green sponges, I did, I did, and I'll show everyone, and...'

Before Rita could stop her, Luisa had torn open her blouse and pulled the green sponges out of her bra. There they lay, scattered on the concrete for everyone to see. Green sponges. Some of them painstakingly cut to fit the contours of the bra she had so carefully chosen with Polly at Fogarty's lingerie department just a week ago, her very first bra, giving her the bust she was so proud of, the very bust that had inspired her poem to Archie Foot. And now the green sponge filling lay as an offering at Archie's feet.

Rita didn't wait to hear them all laugh. She let go of Luisa's waist, grabbed her by the wrist, and dragged her towards the gate. She opened the gate and hauled Luisa out into the street.

Luisa screamed and pulled and twisted but Rita's grasp was like iron. Rita lugged her all the way home, and only when they were safely inside the gate of Number Seven, safely out of hearing and out of sight of Archie, Polly, Brian, Donna, and everyone else, only then did Rita turn on her sister.

'How dare you, how dare you!' Her voice was icy cold, the words pressed out between teeth gritted together in the effort not to explode. A primitive rage screamed inside her. She balled her fists, fighting the urge to pummel the child from top to bottom.

'You're a wicked, wicked little devil!' She growled the words in a low, slow voice, dangerously toneless, for she could not trust what would come out if she once let go. 'I'll never take you anywhere again! That's the last time, the very last time. You're a devil, devil, devil and you've ruined my whole life!'

She looked around her for a weapon – a stick, a cricket bat, a twig, anything. Finding nothing, she raised her right hand, her left one still holding the petrified child as in a vice, fingers digging into her skinny upper arm. The right hand hovered above Luisa's head, gathering force and momentum for a swift and painful descent, for the second blow of the day.

Luisa, who till now had been frozen stiff by the chill of Rita's voice and the unaccustomed finality of her words, looked up at the hand hovering above her, opened her mouth and let out a piercing scream, the scream of a torture victim before the final onslaught, squirming to free herself from Rita's grasp.

Chandra came clattering down the front stairs. 'Luisa, what happened? Oh, my baby, my poor baby, did she hit you? Did that bad girl hit you? Come to Mummy, darling, come, oh baby darling, don't cry. Mummy's darling girl. Heavens, look at your face, what did she do to you? Come to Mummy…'

Rita stood watching. She had let go of Luisa the moment Chandra appeared, and the passion that had filled her a moment ago with the urge to strike, to hurt, to maim, left her as quickly as it had risen. She simply stood and stared as Luisa ran to her mother and buried her face in her skirt, blubbering indistinguishable words between the desperate sobs. Chandra crouched down to enfold the girl in her arms, stroking the curly-mopped head and the heaving back. She raised her head for a moment to throw Rita a stare in which threat, accusation, antipathy and triumph mingled and fought for ascendancy.

Rita bowed her head and walked away. The primitive rage had evaporated. All that remained was guilt, and deep embarrassment. She had slapped her sister. Luisa had made a fool of her. Everyone, the whole gang, was laughing at her.

That evening, when Rita went to bed she found it already occupied.

'Luisa!'

Luisa looked up at her, huge sleepy eyes blinking. 'Can I sleep here with you?'

'Why don't you go to your mother?'

'Don't like Mummy, she's mean! Rita!'

Rita had turned away to undress, and didn't answer. She was still burning inside with shame and anger; she'd never in her whole life be able to face Archie again, nor any of her friends.

Her whole life was ruined.

'Rita!' Luisa's voice was soft and coaxing. Grudgingly, Rita turned round to look at the little girl, who had drawn the sheet up beneath her chin. She hugged a tattered teddy bear. Her features were soft and languid with sleepiness, and her smile was innocent and apologetic and heartbreakingly sweet. When Rita looked at her, she stretched up her little arms, and wiggled her fingers in impatience.

'Rita, I'm sorry, I'm so sorry I was bad. Sorry I pulled out your green sponges. Please, please don't be vex with me. I can't bear it when you get vex with me, Rita, I love you so much. Please, let's be friends again. It hurts so bad when you don't like me and you didn't give me a goodnight kiss and I couldn't sleep and I can't never sleep again if you don't give me a kiss.'

Rita looked sternly down at the little girl, unsmiling, ignoring the wiggling fingers and the outstretched arms.

'What you did was just terrible.'

'I know, Rita, and I'm so sorry and if you like, I'll go over there tomorrow an' 'pologise. Promise. An' I'm goin' to be good for ever and ever after, I promise, Rita, please don't hate me!'

'I don't hate you.'

'But you vex with me! Oh, Rita, please don't be vex with me any more, otherwise I goin' to cry!'

And sure enough, the big black eyes moistened, looking like glimmering pools above the smooth honey-golden cheeks. The child gazed up at Rita with such abject misery she couldn't bear to look into them so she turned away and busied herself with the bookshelf.

'I don't care if you cry, just don't do it here. Go back to your room and cry there or go to your mummy and cry on her lap.'

Her back still turned, she took her time selecting a book. Luisa did not speak again, so Rita walked over to the window, a book in her hand, and drew the curtains. She glanced at the bed. Luisa had drawn the sheet up over her head. The tiny white hump quivered. Rita strode over to the bed and whipped the sheet away.

'Come on now, none of that! Get out, go over to your own room.'

Luisa lay on her stomach, her face buried in Rita's pillow. Her back heaved with repressed sobs, which at Rita's callous words now burst their boundaries and escaped in a blustering, blubbering fountain.

Rita sat on the edge of the bed. Tentatively, she stretched out a hand and placed it on the mop of silky curls.

'OK, Luisa, that's enough. Now calm down and go back to bed.' She tried to keep her voice dispassionate. The sobs increased.

'Luisa, that's enough! Come on, I want to go to bed and you're tired too. Stop that bawling and go to bed!'

But Luisa could not hear above the din of her own sobs, and besides, Rita's words were unconvincing even to herself, and it was her fingers, now gently massaging the back of Luisa's head, that told the truth, and to which Luisa now responded. In one hefty motion she flung herself from her prone and helpless position across the bed and into Rita's lap, her arms flailing out and locking behind Rita's neck. The sobs, loud up to now but nevertheless muffled by the pillow, were a clamouring barrage of snivelling howls.

Luisa was the best apologiser in the world. She could break a sister's heart with contrition. But there had never been a tiff as bad as this. This was serious; Rita's whole life lay in splinters under Archie Foot's house.

Green sponges! The more she tried not to think of them, the greater they loomed into her consciousness. How could she ever, ever face Archie again? Face any of them, but especially the boys? Even now, her cheeks burned at the memory and yet Luisa's sobbing was irresistible.

Involuntarily, Rita's arms closed round the little girl's body, giving reluctant comfort even as her inner voice argued with a better knowledge. And just as Rita's arms wrapped round the little girl, so too did the little girl wrap herself round Rita's little finger.

She's only a child. Only a baby. She doesn't know any better. She doesn't understand, can't understand. She didn't do it on purpose. She didn't mean to embarrass you in front of Archie, she doesn't even know you love him. She's your baby, she loves you, she needs you. She can't help it if she has problems, after all she's been through. You have to forgive her. Poor thing. Poor little baby, who does she have but you? You've got to love her even when she does those bad things, because you caused her to be that way. She needs you. Look at the way she's crying, poor little thing. If you don't love her, who else will? Come on, don't be heartless.

And so, Rita's arms grew tighter and her hands spoke in gentle caresses to the little girl, and she fell back onto the bed and drew the sheet up over both of them, and Luisa sobbed herself to sleep in Rita's arms without another word spoken.

*

Luisa kept her promise. The next day she went to Archie's house, all by herself, and apologised sweetly to him, charming him with her big black eyes and a bunch of white roses stolen from Chandra's favourite bush.

And then it was Rita's turn. For a whole week, Luisa spoiled her. Every day when Rita returned from school there was a bunch of flowers in a jar on her desk. There were cute little paintings on the pillow. Luisa danced attendance on her; she brought Rita glasses of juice, squares of fudge (stolen from the biscuit tin). She peeled tangerines and split them into segments, laid them out prettily on a plate that she presented to Rita with smiles and curtseys. She polished Rita's bicycle until it glowed. She sat Rita down on a chair and danced for her to her favourite tape, twirling and swirling and leaping on her toes so that Rita couldn't help but smile.

Rita wouldn't so much as glance at Archie. She walked past his house with her head turned away. At school, she changed desks so that she was at the other side of the classroom. Whenever she saw him coming, she turned and walked in the other direction. She vowed never to look at him or speak a word to him again in her whole life. She contemplated running away from Kaieteur Close.

Then it was Archie's turn.

Rita picked up the ringing telephone. 'Hello?'

'Hi there it's me, Archie.'

Immediately, her cheeks began to burn.

'Oh. Hi.'

A deep, seemingly unbreakable silence descended between them. Then Archie broke it.

'I was wondering,' he said, 'if you'd like to go with me to see the rerun of *Love Story*? It's on at the Metropole.'

'Oh!' said Rita. And then she said, 'Yes! Yes, I'd love to!'

Archie picked her up punctually at three and side by side in embarrassed silence they rode their bicycles into town. They still hadn't spoken a word to each other when they took their seats in the cool darkness of the balcony. Rita was so busy thinking about green sponges she couldn't follow the film; she still had not so much as glanced at Archie.

In the middle of the film Archie reached over, grabbed Rita's hand, and held it for the rest of the film. Rita felt his hand round hers, stared at the cinema screen, and saw only bosoms filled with green sponges.

Her own bosom was as flat as it was before the green sponge episode. She hoped it would always stay that way. She loved Archie. She hated him. She would never, ever live this down. Green sponges would haunt her all her life.

When Archie brought her safely home again, he gave her a quick peck on the cheek and said, 'Thanks, er, it was lovely.'

'Yes, thanks, er, it was very nice.'

'You really enjoyed it?'

'Um, er, yes, thanks a lot.'

'Um, would you, I mean, I thought… well, if you like we could – um – ride to school together?'

Rita nodded, without looking at him, of course.

On Monday morning, he was waiting for her. They spoke first in monosyllables, then in three-word sentences. Finally, they were a couple: officially 'going around', in the lingo of the day.

But then, as the term drew to an end: disaster.

She and Archie were sitting on the old sofa when Archie said, 'I have something to tell you, Rita. It's bad news.'

'Oh, gosh! Don't tell me then.'

'But I have to. It's just that – that I'm leaving. We're all leaving.'

'What? Who? What you mean?'

'Daddy got a new job, back in England. We're moving back, all of us. Daddy got a job at Bristol University and that's where we're going. He doesn't like it here and the pay is terrible.'

'Oh!'

'Yes. I'm sorry. Really sorry. But we could be pen-pals?'

'Archie! It's not the same, being pen-pals!'

'I know it's not the same.'

'You'll forget me, I know you will!'

'I won't, I promise! I could never forget you.'

'But you will, I just know it. But I'll never, ever forget you!'

It was the most heartbreaking scene imaginable, as good as anything she'd ever seen on the big screen. Rita cried, Archie cried. Rita howled, Archie howled. He wiped her tears away, she his.

'When – when are you leaving?'

'Tomorrow.'

'Tomorrow! But – but that's... that's *tomorrow!*'

'Yes, I know,' he sobbed. 'It's all happening so quickly!'

'Archie Foot, how long have you known this? That you're leaving *tomorrow?*'

'Um... ah – about a week?'

'So, you've known all this time, and only now you tell me? All this time you were pretending that nothing's wrong, and then you break it to me and – and you even *cry?*'

'I didn't want to hurt you.'

'Archie Foot, you are one big fake of a boyfriend, and I'm never going to speak to you again!'

She stalked off, straight over to Polly's.

'*Boys!*' she declared as she burst into Polly's room. 'What's *wrong* with them?'

Chapter Twenty-Five

1986: An Older Man

The Older Man was an American. An American family, a middle-aged couple called the Reynolds, had moved in when the Isaacs moved out the previous month, to Number Eight, next door to Rita, and opposite Polly, and the Older Man was their son who had come for the August holidays.

Rita wrote in her diary,

> He's sooooo handsome. He's got blond hair that hangs over his forehead almost covering his eyes, but short at the back, and freckles, and he's tall, and blond, the kind of All-American hero, a bit like Robert Redford. The trouble is he's at least twenty. Why would a twenty-year-old notice silly little me, with my stupid big mouth and gap-tooth grin and a body that's all out of proportion? Booby too small, legs too long and skinny, hair wild and kinky. On the attainability scale, he must be the equivalent of Mount Everest. His name's Ross. I found that through chatting with the servants. What's more, he has lots of friends, probably the sons of other Americans from the Chase Manhattan Bank or the American Embassy or that big new computer store on Water Street, Compu Tech. And all these white boys, they all gather at Number Eight and play ping-pong under the house or swim in

the pool at the back of the garden. And they are all <u>so</u> dishy! And <u>so</u> out of reach.

I wish I was five years older and looked like a movie star. Not even blond! Maybe like Cher – she's got dark hair but even if I straightened mine and wore make-up and all that, I'd never look like her.

Sigh. Rita

All the Kaieteur Close girls thought the boys at Number Eight were *evil.*

'I like the dark one best!' said Donna, hugging herself. 'He's so eeee-vil!'

'No, Ross is by far the best!' That was, of course, Rita. 'But you can't have him, he's mine!'

'Can you find out his name for me?'

'I'll try. Their maid chats with Saraswati sometimes, so I could ask.'

'But discreetly! I don't want him to know it's me!'

'Of course!' She turned to Polly. 'Which one's yours?'

'Oh, I'd take any of them! Blond, dark, redhead, tall, short… maybe the redhead, since none of you want him. I bet he's rich!'

They all giggled. 'They're American, they're bound to be rich.'

'Imagine you could catch one and marry him! He'd whisk you off to America and you could live in a mansion like they have in the films, and ride horses and travel around in limousines.'

Thus, they talked and dreamed. They were all evil, but Ross was the most evil and he was Rita's; that was established from the beginning. They acted out scenarios:

'Oh, Rita!' said Polly, in a bad American accent, 'hey there! I'm Ross, and I've been watching you from my window all this time! Say, you're quite a beaut, aren't you? Wanna go for a date? I really like that slinky dress you're wearing!'

Rita put on an exaggerated pose, one leg slightly bent in front of the other, one hand on hip, the other holding an imaginary glass. In what she believed was a posh British accent, she said, 'Oh, good afternoon, Ross, my name is actually Amanda. Could you pour me some more champagne, please? And I shall consult my diary to see when I'm free and can fit you in.'

They took their dreams to bed with them and fell asleep smiling, and then they'd wake up next morning and put on their school uniforms and reality would crash into their lives.

Life was difficult when you were only fifteen and in love with Older Men.

But Rita was not Jitty's daughter for nothing. She had imagination, and wiles.

One afternoon after school, when Polly's mother was out and her father at work as well as Ross's parents – they both drove over to the American Embassy, though it was only a few blocks away – the girls gathered behind lowered shades with a splendid view of the house across the road, which had a gallery fronted by an unbroken row of curtainless windows, all of which stood open, so you could see clearly across the gallery and the living room and into the inner recesses of the house, and you could see exactly what the Older Men were doing at all times.

Right now, they were sitting round the table eating. But the telephone rang and one of them – Polly's redhead – got up to answer it.

Across the road, at Number Six, there was a minor scuffle as Polly and Rita fought for the telephone receiver, but luckily, Rita's hand, wet with the sweat of excitement, was firmly clasped over the mouthpiece so the redhead couldn't hear the giggles. Rita won the fight and turned away from Donna and Polly the better to keep her face – and even more important, her vocal cords – frozen into seriousness.

'Hello? Who is this speaking?' she said, her voice soft and sultry.

'This is Tom, who's that?' said the voice at the other end.

'Oh, Tom... Well, Tom, I must tell you that a friend of mine is quite smitten by you. And she's wondering... aaam... Well, as a matter of fact, I'm a great admirer of yours too, you know— Where we saw you? Oh, we saw you at the bank the other day. We both work at the bank, you know... We saw you fellows there and...'

Rita felt a poke in her ribs and made an impatient gesture with her free hand, not looking. Another poke, and then Polly's face appeared before her, mouthing excited words and pointing behind her back. Rita turned and peered through the laths of the Venetian blinds. The other two boys had left the table and now all three were gathered around the telephone – just like the three of them.

Rita cleared her throat and put on her most expensive voice.

'Ahem... well, Tom, we saw all three of you fellows and we think you're just our types. Only thing is, we don't know which of you is which. Or rather, who is who. So tell me now: who is that tall dark handsome one? Oh, Ross. Now listen, Ross is the one I like best. Could you give me Ross, please? Hi, is that Ross? May I call you Ross? My name is... is... Amanda. I saw you the other day at the Chase Manhattan Bank and I was really admiring you. I'm sure you saw me. You couldn't have missed me. I'm tall and dark and very beautiful, if I do say so myself. My lips are red like wild cherries. Everybody says so. Even now, they twitch to touch yours... Hey, what are you laughing about? This is serious. Now, listen, Ross, you have a nice blond friend there, don't you? What's his name?' She paused, rolling her eyes at Donna. 'Oh, Bill. Thanks. I'd forgotten. I did check your records at the bank, but I was a bit confused. Well, I just want to say we know all about you guys. We have our spies. Anyway, my friend, who is an evil busty Indian lady, is just dying to talk to him. Here she is, so let her talk to Bill, all right? Bye, Ross, see you soon...'

Donna grabbed the receiver from Rita but instead of talking she pressed the mouthpiece to her breast and, bent over double, exploded in helpless giggles. Polly, too, seemed incapable of speaking a serious word so Rita took back the receiver.

'Sorry about that, Ross— Oh, sorry, Bill! Well, Bill, my friend Genevieve really adores you but she can't speak right now, she's too full of emotion. Anyway, we're three really lovely, lonely girls and we're dying to meet you fellows soon. How about it? Where? Well, let me think a moment, where would be a good place? Let me ask my friends.'

Polly was again desperately mouthing some message. Rita looked at her, understood, and spoke into the receiver: 'Listen, Bill, what about the Pegasus Hotel? It's great there. We'll meet at the pool, OK? Saturday afternoon? Four o'clock? Oh, wonderful. Fantastic. I'm really looking forward to it. Don't forget our names: ask for Amanda, Genevieve, and… and… Carmen. See you then. Saturday. Give my love to the boys. Bye!' Rita made some final kissing sounds and replaced the receiver. The girls collapsed into a heap of giggles.

'We have to go! We really have to go on Saturday!'

'No way! They'll know it's us. Three girls…'

'They won't be expecting girls our age. We could just walk in and order Cokes or something.'

'They'd know, trust me. I for one wouldn't be able to stop peeping over to them. And I couldn't keep a straight face.'

'Maybe they won't even go. Maybe they know it was just a joke.'

'Well, we'll soon find out, won't we?'

But on Saturday, at a quarter to four, the girls watched as Ross, in his parents' car, pulled out of the Number Eight drive and turned out of the close.

'He's going! They're really going!'

'Come on, Rita, let's go and watch!'

'No. No way! They'll know it's us. It'll be too embarrassing for words.'

It was Luisa who finally brought Rita and Ross together.

Luisa, riding her bicycle up and down Kaieteur Close, swerved when a cat ran across the road, and fell, hurting her knee. She dropped her little bike and ran screaming into the house, where the knee was tended by rather too many concerned adults. Luisa recovered quickly from the shock and the pain and disappeared into her room to listen to a cassette on her stereo, forgetting the bike.

Rita was on the phone with Polly when the doorbell rang. She hung up and went to open it, and nearly fell over flat when she found herself facing a sheepish-faced Ross.

Shocked, speechless, she could only stare, but Ross was too apologetic to notice her confusion.

'Look, I'm real sorry, but – well, look what I've done!' he said, and held up a twisted knot of metal. Rita recognised Luisa's bike and pulled herself together. Ross had not come to confront her, had not come to force her into admitting that she was the mysterious 'Amanda' who had been calling him up with seductive messages every single day for the past week. Who had apologised profusely for standing him up at the Pegasus pool the previous week, and since then had been entertaining him every afternoon with anecdotes and jokes and invariably reducing him to tears of laughter. Depending on the circumstances – whether there were adults around – she called sometimes from her own home, sometimes from Polly's, where she could peer through the blinds and watch his reactions.

She had discovered a new power: the power to make a man laugh, and it was intoxicating – but she knew that meeting him would be the end of it. And now, here he was, face to face with her on her doorstep.

She gulped and tried to pay attention to what he was saying.

'…I didn't look, you see. It was lying on the road behind my car and I just got in and reversed into the road, and the next thing

I knew there was this crunching sound and… it was this thing. I've seen that kid, she's your sister, isn't she? I thought so. Couldn't be quite sure, so many kids on this road. Anyway, of course I'll buy her a new one, no question. You got to be careful on a road like this with so many kids, always look behind you. Lucky there wasn't a kid sitting on it at the time… I mean, I'd have seen a kid riding a bike but because it was flat on the road…'

'It's all right.' Rita's voice emerged as a squeak in her attempt to disguise it. And then Luisa came prancing down the stairs and saw the bike and promptly burst into tears.

'It's all right, it's OK, honey. I'll buy you another, I'm sorry. Look, you'll get a real nice bike, OK?'

'When?'

Ross's eyes met Rita's above Luisa's curly mop.

'Well, how about… now?'

Before she knew it, they were in Ross's car, driving into town, Luisa bouncing about in the back, Rita in the passenger seat next to Ross, not daring to say a word just in case he recognised her voice. She needn't have bothered.

'Rita knows another boy called Ross,' Luisa piped up.

'Is that true?' said Ross, and turned to grin at Rita. 'It's not such a common name over here, is it?'

'He's her boyfriend. She's in love with him and she draws hearts all over her exercise book and writes his name and hers in it. And sometimes she talks to him on the phone and puts on this stupid drooly voice. "Ross, dahlin' … Ooh, Ross, sweetheart." I heard her myself.'

Rita wasn't sure which magical power she would rather have: the power to shoot Luisa off to the moon never to return, or the power to evaporate and never return herself. Both would be better than dissolving into soup and dripping into the footwell of Ross's car.

All the way to Persaud's Bicycles she kept her burning face turned towards the window, her body slouched back into the seat as if willing it to melt into the upholstery. Ross did not speak for five minutes but she felt his glance scorching through the back of her head. She felt his anger – in a minute, he'd stop the car and throw her and Luisa out head first and then she'd *really* shoot Luisa to the moon.

So, when she heard the first chuckle, she didn't quite trust her ears. The second chuckle was louder and longer, more in the nature of a small explosion, and she glanced suspiciously out of the corner of her eye, but all she could see was Ross's profile with a wide grin spread all over it. And then, suddenly, Ross swerved to the roadside, stopped the car, slumped forward over the steering wheel, and collapsed in an avalanche of helpless, uncontrolled laughter. Rita, still paralysed by embarrassment, considered opening the passenger door and making good her escape. But then Ross stretched out one long tanned arm, turned to her with a lobster-red, tear-streaked face, twisted her round to face him, and held her in his arms, burying his face in her shoulder till at last she, too, collapsed with mirth, letting the laughter peal out.

'What are you laughing about?' cried Luisa, bouncing furiously in the back seat. 'What's the joke? Tell me! And what about my bike? I want my new bike! Stop laughing, I tell you, and go and get my bike!'

But for once, nobody obeyed her.

Dear Diary,

I just discovered that his bedroom is next to the mango tree. I climbed the tree and looked in. He doesn't have any curtains at the window and I saw him without his shirt on. He had his back to me, standing at the mirror, but once he turned around and walked over to get something and I saw he has a hairy chest. He was shaving and I watched him for a long time and then I climbed back down again. If he knew I could climb trees, he'd be even less impressed. Grown-up women don't climb trees. Gosh, I wish I was a grown-up woman at last and didn't climb trees and knew more about men and how to make them like you.

Chapter Twenty-Six

Bamboo Gardens

Dear Diary,

Luisa has started ballet lessons and really loves it. Her ballet teacher says she's a natural. And now all she does is put on that silly little skirt and twirl around the place. She even came over to Ross's when I was there because that's where me and Polly and Donna hang out now, playing ping-pong and listening to music, and they invited us even to swim in the pool but I don't want to because of the green sponges. I can't keep my eyes off Ross, I wonder if he noticed?

He's so funny. He likes to tell movie jokes, about things you didn't know if you didn't go to the movies.

Anyway, Luisa came over yesterday and started showing off, spinning on her toes and kicking up her legs and even flirting with him. I tell you. At eight years old! At eight, I was still playing with tadpoles from the gutter!

And he even noticed her and was impressed by her. 'She's going to be a real looker, that little sister of yours,' he said to me. 'She'll have the guys beating a path to your door in a few years. I'd better stick around!' Vomit, vomit.

She wished she was five years older and looked like an elegant, sophisticated film star, graceful and elegant, and had a soft purring voice, and waved a cigarette nonchalantly about while stylishly puffing out slinky tendrils of smoke from between red lips. And wore slinky black dresses and high heels. And could talk elegantly and cleverly so that people listened, and tell jokes that everyone laughed at, and have lovely porcelain white skin and soft silky blond hair hanging over her shoulders and swishing when she moved.

Instead, she hated her body. Her legs were too long and skinny and pencil-straight, and she had that stupid gap between her front teeth, and her mouth was too big.

Dear Diary,

Ross has asked me out on a date!!!! I can't believe it!
What am I going to wear??????

She felt awkward, slipping onto the passenger seat of Ross's car. She had bought a new dress, a ready-made minidress from Fogarty's (where her family had a permanent discount, due to Chandra), with a low-cut neckline. Nothing special; it was red, though, and shiny, and she'd never worn anything this revealing before. She'd had to beg Jitty for some money, which he had willingly enough handed over. 'Hot date, yes?' he'd said with a wink, which was terribly embarrassing. 'Just going out for dinner,' she said. 'It's nothing.'

'With a boy?' She nodded. Hopefully he wouldn't ask *which* boy. Jitty wouldn't approve of an older man. At least him living next door meant that to pick her up, he merely had to ring the bell at the gate and she'd come down to meet him there, so he wouldn't have to face her father.

'Well, remember, home by ten thirty.' She nodded. Jitty, now that she had reached adolescence, had started to keep a watchful eye on her, remembering his own wild youth and what he called 'the ways of boys'.

*

'You look beautiful!' said Ross in his devastatingly seductive American accent. His gaze wandering over her body made her feel just like one of those film stars she wished she looked like. Grown up; no longer an awkward teenager on her first proper date.

Ross drove to Bamboo Gardens, where he'd reserved a table, just like in the movies. Without asking, he ordered rum and Coke for them both. Rita pretended this was perfectly normal for her. Of course, she wasn't allowed to drink – another of Jitty's rules – but how could she be such a baby and refuse? What would he think? Ross, after she'd confessed that she wasn't the devastatingly sophisticated Amanda, had asked her age, and she'd said sixteen. That was still too young to drink, but he didn't seem to care. They weren't supposed to serve people her age either, but the waiter was black and impossibly fawning to Ross; Ross could have told him to stand on his head and he would have done so. *White skin has that effect on serving staff*, Rita thought. *It's the ultimate power.* But she said nothing.

It was a lovely evening, out there on the Bamboo Gardens roof terrace. He recommended a fish curry, which she ordered, and conversation, led by him, flowed easily; he told her all about himself, and all she had to do was listen. She was glad. She could not possibly live up to the role of Amanda in real life, anecdotes and jokes rolling off her tongue, not in the presence of those brilliant blue eyes, fixed on her. Not when she could actually see him, see his movie-star good looks. The lights were dim and the music was soft and, as each second passed, the more Rita relaxed, the more she fell in love. The rum and Coke was a great help.

She gazed into his eyes and he smiled back lovingly; at least, she *thought* it was loving. But mostly, she was looking forward to when he brought her home because she just *knew* he would kiss her goodbye.

At last, that moment came.

'Come on, let's go,' said Ross, and Rita breathed a sigh of relief. She was looking forward to that goodnight kiss, because it would mean they would be boyfriend and girlfriend. And they would go to parties and dance, close and cuddly. Images of their future crowded her mind, and she felt all soft and pliable; the rum went some way to helping; she even imagined they would be in love forever, and one day marry and have children and go off to America. She imagined her married name: Rita Reynolds. Ross and Rita Reynolds. Even their names matched, fitted beautifully, alliteratively, together.

But instead of heading home, he drove to the Sea Wall and parked there. Rita felt quite nervous; she could see all the other cars parked along the wall, darkened cars.

Everyone knew why cars parked along the Sea Wall at night. Everyone knew what went on in those cars.

'Why did you come here?' she asked. 'It's not a good place.'

'Just for a moment, to enjoy the fresh air,' Ross replied, parking in a gap between two other cars.

'No,' said Rita. A wave of clarity swept through her, overcoming the rum-induced daze she'd been in. 'I don't really want to be here, Ross. Please take me home.'

Not rudely, not aggressively – she'd said please, after all – but firmly.

'Sure,' said Ross, 'but let's have some fun first.' He turned off the car headlights. The car became just another of those dark silent beasts lined up against the wall. For the first time, fear gripped her.

Ross reached over and pulled her towards him. Shocked, she struggled a bit; he laughed.

'Come on, babe, you know you want it, you've been flirting with me all week, and all night!'

It was true, Rita thought; she had been flirting, but that didn't mean she wanted to come and park along the notorious Sea Wall

at night, alone with him. Surely it didn't mean that! And all at
once she was unsure. Maybe it *did* mean that. Maybe there was
some unspoken rule, that if you flirted with a boy – a man! – for a
week, it meant he could take you to the Sea Wall for a bit of fun.
A rule she didn't know.

So, maybe, she thought, OK, just one kiss, because she *had*
wanted to kiss him. She let him. But it was horrible, all wet and
slimy, and he began to breathe heavily, and his hand wandered up
to her breast and squeezed, and then down to her thigh, under the
hem of her tight dress, and squeezed there.

'C'mon, baby, let's go on the back seat,' he moaned.

Rita pulled away, pushed his hand from his thigh. 'No!' she
cried. 'Ross, take me home, now! Please!'

But Ross only laughed and moved in again, face and hands all
over her. He was big, and strong, and never had she felt so frail,
so unable to defend herself.

And then it turned bad. *Really bad.* Ross grabbed at her, pushed
his hand down below her neckline and beneath the fabric of her
bra. Pulled out the green sponges – and laughed.

'What! I thought they were real!' he said. His hand probed up
beneath her dress hem as she struggled.

'No, Ross, no! Stop it, please!' cried Rita, struggling against his
grip, but he would not stop. That was when she punched him. In
his crotch. Really, really, hard.

Ross yelped in pain and pulled away, hands on his privates.

'You bitch!' he yelled. He pulled away, back into the driver's
seat, left hand still cradling his crotch. A torrent of abuse followed,
snarled at her as he sat doubled up in agony over the steering wheel.

'You little slut, cock-teaser! Little whore, leading me on all
week! You think I play games, or what? Who do you think I am!
Fuck you, you little slut!'

Rita cowered against the passenger door. Ross gave a howl of
anger, which seemed to mitigate his pain for he turned and hurled

himself at her, grabbing her arm. But with her other hand she crunched down on the door handle; it opened. She flung herself out of the door, landing on all fours on the road. She quickly righted herself and began to run. Run, run, run! Along the Seawall Road, along the line of darkened parked cars, past the Promenade and the bandstand, crying as she ran and, finally, panting as she turned into Barrack Street and then, at last, into Kaieteur Close.

Dear Diary,

And I just want to die.
I hate myself. I hate my skin and my hair and my skinny legs and I hate growing up and I hate Ross. But most of all, I hate myself.
I hate being a stupid girl. <u>I hate boys.</u>

<u>Love Rita</u>

The news that buzzed through the Kaieteur Close Kids grapevine just two days later was that Ross Reynolds had gone. Gone back to America, never to return.

Chapter Twenty-Seven

Home Life

Jitty, meanwhile, had reached an impasse, professionally as well as personally. He had received the shock of his life back in 1980, when his hero, Walter Rodney, the intellectual giant slated to lead the country into a new era of ethical politics and interracial integration, got into a car rigged with a bomb. It blew up and killed him. There was no doubt it was a political assassination, and all fingers pointed to the party in power, the PNC, and its leader, Forbes Burnham. Since then the political situation in Guyana had only deteriorated.

Burnham himself had died of a heart attack on the operating table in 1985 – minor throat surgery that had gone wrong – and half the country had rejoiced. His successor as Executive President was his second-in-command, Desmond Hoyte, and hopes had been high that Hoyte would restore honesty and order and bring prosperity to the country, especially when he began courting foreign investors and making peace with the International Monetary Fund in order to relieve society's endemic poverty and the crippling national debt.

But things were moving too slowly for Jitty. 'We're in a swamp!' he complained to all who'd listen. 'A swamp of inefficiency and corruption. No wonder so many Guyanese fleeing the country!'

That was indeed happening. Guyanese were leaving like rats from a sinking ship. The brain drain was a national embarrassment – it seemed that the brightest and best were escaping. The country was divided into Leavers and Remainers, and the Remainers were the dregs, which didn't sit well with Chandra's pride or Jitty's sense of professional and personal failure. Not one of his brilliantly composed articles giving advice on how the country could stand on its own two feet had been taken seriously. A contagion of complacency had settled in – a sickness spreading to businesses and public services and government agencies. Being one of the Remainers did not sit well with Jitty's self-esteem, or his ambition.

Of course, for years now Chandra had been nagging him about moving to Canada. By now, almost all of her many Jha relatives had made the leap and were settled in Canada; apart from two spinster aunts in a rickety old house in Waterloo Street she was the last still in Guyana. She had, in fact, no one left. Her mother had died of cancer in 1980, and subsequently her father, a Jha, had also absconded to Toronto. It stung, to be the last of the young generation, left behind in a dying country. She prodded and poked Jitty to leave. She had visited her Toronto cousin twice, by now, and couldn't stop raving about the city. But even she admitted it would be hard to emigrate there: a family of four could not just arrive at a relative's home. Immigration was never easy at the best of times; for a whole family, it was even worse.

'If it were just the three of us, it would be easy,' she told Jitty. They were in the office, for privacy, but Rita sat outside on the kitchen steps eating chow-chow. Listening.

'What do you mean?'

'Well, you, me and Luisa,' said Chandra. 'I mean, Rita has other relatives here, doesn't she? That old lady in Peter Rose Street who keeps ringing and sending gifts and cards. And the people up there behind God's back. She could go there. To them. It would be easier for just the three of us.'

'You mean, you want me to abandon my daughter? Go away and just leave her here?' Jitty's voice rose in chilled fury and Rita grinned to herself. *Good old Daddy, he was beginning to see the ugliness…*

Chandra stepped back now. 'Well, what about your Aunt Mary? She has that big house in London, and it's just her and her husband.

I wonder exactly how big the house is. Surely she could put us up for a few weeks, just until we found our feet and our own place? I mean, all four of us.'

'What about *your* relatives?' was Jitty's reply. 'Don't you have an English grandmother still alive? Maybe she has a big house too.'

'Well, yes. But I don't actually know her. She used to send me cards when Grandad was alive, but that stopped ages ago. It would be awkward. You know what white people are like. I can't very well…'

'Well, I'm certainly not going begging to Aunt Mary,' said Jitty, and that was that. Rita was a bit disappointed. She longed for a bit of adventure, a change of scene. Most of her friends had also left for greener pastures; Polly was the only one remaining on Kaieteur Close, and one day, Polly too would leave and she'd be the only one left. England, or America: that would be an adventure. Instead, they were stuck here, in this backwater of a country. She wished Daddy would, indeed, approach Aunt Mary. Maybe she, Rita, should write to Aunt Mary, introduce herself, try to make friends – they could, perhaps, go for a visit, at least, and check out the possibilities…

Canada, for Rita, was completely out of the question. Those Jhas…

But then, out of the blue, an adventure deposited itself onto her lap. And it was neither England nor America that called…

Chapter Twenty-Eight

Aunt Penny

One afternoon, soon after Ross's departure, Rita was just parking her bike outside Bookers' after school when a woman came up to her and said, 'Excuse me, Rita. Can I have a word with you?'

Rita looked up and frowned. The woman looked vaguely familiar, but she couldn't place her.

'What is it?' she asked, rather curtly.

'I'm your Aunty Penny,' said the woman. 'I just thought we could talk for a while.'

Rita looked at Polly, who had already locked her bike and was waiting for her. As usual, they had been planning to make a beeline for the snack bar and sit around there eating hot dogs or hamburgers and drinking milkshakes and waiting for the boys of St Stanislaus and Queen's College to join them. Bishops' was by far the nearest school to Bookers', so they were always the first to arrive after school.

She frowned. 'What's it about?'

A flicker of annoyance passed over the woman's face, but it was gone in a wink.

'I'm your aunty,' she said. 'Your mother's sister, and you don't even know me. Don't you think we should put that right? I'm not often in Town, but now I'm here, I thought we should meet.'

'How did you even find me? Know what I look like?'

'I been coming here a few days after school and asked around. A girl about your age pointed you out.'

'Did you ask Daddy?'

'I don't need your father's permission to meet my own niece!' The woman's voice, now, held more than a twinge of annoyance. But again, it was gone with her next words: 'Please, Rita. I'd love to get to know you.'

'Well, all right, but not now. My friends are waiting. Maybe tomorrow, after school.'

She supposed she could miss one afternoon of hanging out at the snack bar. It was annoying, but it was just one afternoon. If it would mean getting rid of the woman now, then why not?

'I'm going back to the Pomeroon tomorrow,' said Aunty Penny. 'It has to be today.'

Why does it have to be any day at all? thought Rita. *Such a nuisance.* But then, a thought occurred to her: *Aunty Penny would know. Aunty Penny would definitely know.* Definitely have the answers to all those questions that had plagued her, Rita, since she was a child. True, of late they had slipped to the background as other important matters – namely, boys and parties – took over her life. But they still remained, unanswered.

It hit her like a thunderbolt. *Why?* Why had it never, never once, occurred to her to seek out all those aunts and uncles, that Granpa and Granma, the senders of all those dolls and cards and, in the last few years, books, and ask them? If Daddy wouldn't talk, surely they would?

'Well – OK, then.'

'There's a little cafe on Main Street. Let's go there. We can walk down, you can wheel your bike.'

An awkward silence fell between them as they walked. Not that Rita herself ever felt silence to be awkward, but she knew adults couldn't deal with it, and that, having nothing to say, she was being difficult again. But surely it was up to Aunty Penny, she being the one so eager to talk? One of them had to break the ice, and Rita was terrible at small talk. She could hardly, while walking down the avenue, just barge in with, 'Tell me about my mother, how she died, I want to know the whole story'. There had to be a warm-up, and that's what was causing the problem. Luckily, though, Aunty Penny was neither embarrassed by silence nor lost for small-talk conversation.

'So how you getting on at school?'

Rita shrugged. 'So-so.'

'You know what you want to do afterwards? More studies, or get a job?'

'I'm not sure, actually.'

'You got a boyfriend?'

'No.' At least that was a definitive answer. They reached the cafe. Rita parked and locked the bike and they entered. Aunty Penny chose a table near the window. 'What would you like?'

'Just a Coke.'

Aunty Penny nodded and walked to the counter to order, then returned and pulled out the chair opposite to Rita.

'Aunt Mathilda sends her love.'

Rita shrugged. 'OK.'

'She wants to know if you enjoyed the books she sent for your last few birthdays.'

Rita nodded, and said, 'Yes.' Another definite answer. She could have said more, at this point, but Aunty Penny was virtually a stranger, and Rita wasn't about to discuss books with her. But for a stranger, Aunty Penny didn't pull any punches.

'Why did you never reply to any of your granny's letters?'

Rita stared as if punched in the gut.

'Letters? What letters? You mean Christmas cards? Birthday cards?'

'No. Proper letters. I helped her write them. Wrote you a few myself. You never got them? None at all?'

'No!' Rita cried. 'She wrote to me? How often? Why didn't I get them?'

'Well, obviously, your daddy didn't pass them to you.'

'But why not? Why?'

A waiter brought her Coke and a ginger ale for Aunty Penny, who thanked him and poured it into the glass provided, then started to sip. Rita waited impatiently for Aunty Penny to respond. At last, she said: 'You need to ask him, don't you? Ask him why. *Why* he didn't give them to you.'

'He's not going to tell me, obviously!'

'Well, I suppose he was afraid your granny would tell you things he don't want you to know.'

'Well, I've figured *that* out!' It came out rather rudely, and even Rita realised it. She said: 'Sorry, but it's just so damned frustrating! Now I know there were letters, and a granny, and secrets he doesn't want me to find out, and… it's maddening!'

'He really never told you?'

She shook her head.

'No.'

'Nothing at all? Not one blessed thing?'

'Nothing.'

'You mean, he just left you in total ignorance?'

'Ignorance of *what*? But, yes, total ignorance.' Aunty Penny shook her head slowly, as if in complete bafflement.

'What do you remember, of before you came to Town?'

'Nothing.'

'Nothing at all? You don't remember your daddy coming and tearing you from the arms of your granny? You screaming your head off? Your granny in hysterics? You fighting your daddy to run back to her, struggling and screaming? Your granny running behind you?'

Tears pricked Rita's eyes, but she took a deep breath and forced them away.

'No. Nothing. Did – did that really happen?'

'Of course. But then, you were only five so I suppose it's possible to forget. I thought something like that, with screaming and such, would make an impression. Maybe you erased it from your mind, as a protection. Blanked it all out, the whole trauma.'

'But why? Why did he come and take me? I don't, I don't understand. I don't... He doesn't tell me *anything!* Nothing! I asked him so many times, so many questions, about her, and about how she died, but he never tells me anything! Just silly stuff like what music she liked and what birds. Nothing serious like what she died of. It's just, *no point bringing up the past, let's look forwards not backwards*, and all that shit.' She mimicked Jitty's sing-song, dismissive voice.

And there they were: the tears. She hadn't cried for her mother in years, yet the tears were still there, just waiting for a reason to flow. She could feel them trickling down her cheeks, and she swiped at them with the back of her hand. Aunty Penny fished in her handbag and produced a hanky. It was a white one, nicely ironed and folded, with an embroidered edge. The kind of hanky old ladies carried around in their handbags. Rita patted her eyes and cheeks and handed it back.

'Well, Rita, that kind of seals it. I actually came to invite you to come back with me to the Pomeroon, tomorrow. I know school holidays start on Monday. Come and meet your granny and granpa – it seems you've forgotten them completely, but they haven't forgotten you. They think of you all the time – we all do. We were wondering why you never replied to the letters. Granny suspected you didn't get them, and she was right. Your daddy didn't even want you to meet me, when you were a little girl. Afraid I'd talk, I suppose. So, we waited. Waited till you were big enough to decide for yourself, old enough to override any objection he might have. You're old enough now. So, come back with me, Rita. Come with me tomorrow. Meet your family. Grandparents, your

Uncle Douglas, your cousins; you have three cousins, you know! Everyone's dying to meet you!'

And before she had time to think, before she had time to even digest what Aunty Penny had said, Rita found herself nodding, and a very small, humble 'OK' left her lips.

Rita found her voice just fine, that afternoon, when Polly came over to help pack.

'I don't know why I agreed!' said Rita, flinging clothes into a suitcase. 'It's really behind God's back. Over there, you know what they have?'

'What?'

'Trees. And water. And that's about it.' She sat on the bed and began to count off on her fingers.

'No radio. No telephone. No cars. No bicycles, even. No cinema. No friends. No you. No boys.'

'I thought there were two boys up there, your cousins?' Rita rolled her eyes. 'But what *sort* of boys, living in the back of beyond? Boring as hell! And anyway, cousins. What use are boy-cousins? They have a girl but she's just a child. So, no friends. No bloody *nothing!* I'm going to die of boredom! I'm going to go utterly crazy up there!'

'And for two whole weeks! I don't envy you!'

'She said it's such a long journey, it's not worth it, going for just a few days. And I would have so much to talk about. But I won't! I'll go mad! Completely and utterly mad!'

'Why did you say yes, then?'

'Well, I have to go, don't I? There's a whole slice of my life missing and they have the answers. My mother – somehow, she's there. I'll find her there. I've got to stick out the boredom.'

'You need to take lots of cassettes.'

'And lots of batteries as well! They don't even have electricity! How do these people even *live?* They're like – like from the Stone Age!'

'Rita, don't talk about them like that! They're your grandparents! You should take lots of books as well.'

'I am.' She pointed to a bulky duffel bag, on the floor. 'I already packed my books. Luckily, I just borrowed a few from the library, because the library is closed now so I can't even restock. I'm taking lots of my old books, though. I can read them all again.'

'That one you love so much!'

'*My Friend Flicka*. Yes, that, of course.' Aunt Mathilda had followed Daddy's instructions to the letter; the dolls had stopped arriving, and now there were books for her birthday, animal books, as Rita had requested. *Cleopatra the Turtle Girl*. *Tarka the Otter*. *Black Beauty*. And then, like manna from heaven, *My Friend Flicka*. Daddy had come home from work one afternoon to find Rita dissolved in tears on the back stairs.

'What's the matter, darling?' She'd pointed to the book beside her on the stair. 'It's so sad! It broke my heart! I can't stop crying!'

'What's it about?'

'About a boy, and he's clumsy and failing at school and every-thing, and all he wants is a horse. And he lives on a ranch in Wyoming and his dad has lots of horses but won't give him one because he's so angry, but then he *does* give him one, a beautiful filly, and it all – it all goes wrong, the boy falls in love with the filly but she… but she's too wild and – oh, Daddy! It broke my heart! He loved her so much!'

'Did she die, in the end?'

'I'm not telling you! You have to read it yourself! Please, Daddy, please, please read it! For my sake, so we can talk about it!'

'All right, I will.'

'You promise?'

'I promise.'

But Daddy never did read it, so Rita had read it again and again, and each time she'd discovered something new about it. For her next two birthdays, following a glowing report from Daddy, Aunt Mathilda sent the two sequels to *My Friend Flicka*.

'Bookers' Book Shop didn't have them – she had them sent all the way from England! Uncle Patrick had his sister buy them in London and send them. They're the best books I'll ever read!' Rita had said then. 'And when I grow up, I'm going to live in Wyoming, on a ranch.'

But instead, there was this: she was off to the Pomeroon, in a far-off corner of Essequibo District. And she knew very well why she'd said yes to this trip, despite all the objections she'd listed, all the complaints she'd made to Polly, all the resistance, all the rebellion suddenly rising up within her, all the reasons not to go.

She knew it very well: *It's Mummy's place. Mummy will be there. Her spirit will be there. I will find her there, at last.* No radio, phone, parties, friends, boys: what did all that matter? What mattered was this: she'd find out the secret Daddy was hiding from her. It was as plain as day that Granny knew it, and that Granny was the key to everything.

Chapter Twenty-Nine

Two Long Empty Hands

'You can't just go with your two long empty hands,' said Chandra, later that evening. Rita had announced the news of her departure at the dinner table. Jitty had been speechless with shock, stuttering a useless protest. Chandra had been pleased: 'Oh, how nice for you! Finally getting to meet your people!' The words *your people* said with blatant scorn. Rita had bristled, but said nothing, only nodded and glared at Jitty, daring him to object. He didn't. But he didn't meet her eyes, either.

'So, you better take this with you,' Chandra said now.

Rita looked sceptically at the box on the kitchen table. She had seen it before. It was the electric Mixmaster Chandra had been sent two Christmases ago from her aunt in Canada, the very latest kitchen gadget. Chandra had sucked her teeth at the time and said: 'What's she thinking of? She thinks we're so backward here, or what? She don't know I got one of these things already? I tell you, she's just showing off because she lives in Canada. Anyway, I suppose I could pass it on – save me having to buy somebody a present.'

She had passed it on to a cousin, who had promptly returned it. 'It don't work,' the cousin said. 'You better take it back to the shop and get it repaired. You must have a guarantee?'

But Chandra didn't have a guarantee, and anyway, it had been bought in Canada, and so the box had sat there at the back of a kitchen cupboard for two years.

'It doesn't work, I thought,' said Rita now.

'Yes, but it's the *thought* that counts,' said Chandra. 'You can't go with your two long empty hands, you got to bring something from Town. Something they wouldn't have up there.'

'But Aunty Penny says they don't have electricity! It would be useless anyway, even if it did work!'

'I know these country people. She will be very happy with a nice modern electric gadget, you can't get those up there. At least it's new! When they find out it doesn't work you can apologise and offer to have it fixed. But they won't find out because they don't have current. Even if they find out, it's the thought that counts,' Chandra said again. 'You think they'll bother to send it down to Town and back? When they hardly ever come to Town anyway? And anyway, they can pass it on to someone else if they don't like it. That's what everybody does.'

'Why don't we just buy something new? Something that works?'

'You think we made of money, or what? What you're complaining about? They'll be glad to have a thing like this up there! I bet they're the only people to have one! I bet they never even see one of these before, up there in the bush! Look, here's a bag, let's see if it fits inside – yes, perfect.'

'But…'

'But but but… Child, you made up of buts. Every other word you say is but. If you go through life like that, you going to turn into a goat!'

Chandra zippered up the bag and lifted it up by the handles, testing its weight.

'And it's not too heavy. You haven't got too much luggage anyway so you can easily carry it. And don't forget—'

'Mummy, let me go with Rita. Please let me go!' Luisa interrupted.

'No, darling, of course you can't go. Rita is going to see her granny and granpa and you wouldn't be happy there.'

'But I don't want Rita to go! I want her to stay with me! Who's going to tell me stories at night?'

'I will, darling. I'm your mummy, after all!'

'But you can't make up nice stories like Rita can, all you can do is read those boring ones from a book! I want to go with Rita! Rita, please let me go! Please please please!'

Luisa flung herself at Rita and clung to her, looking up with eyes brimming with unshed tears, eyes in whose depths a dangerous gleam hovered in anticipation of refusal. Rita recognised that gleam: a tantrum was brewing. And the last thing she wanted to deal with on the eve of her journey was a tantrum.

'Darling, I'd love to take you but think of your ballet classes. You'd miss two whole weeks of ballet. You wouldn't like that, would you?'

Luisa stopped sobbing for a moment and frowned. Rita could clearly see the little mind working behind the ruffled brow, thrusting out for a new ploy. 'Let me come' was thwarted – wild horses couldn't keep Luisa from her ballet – but 'you stay with me' would certainly come next.

'I've got a fantastic new story for you,' said Rita quickly. 'It's just waiting to jump out at you. You'd better run upstairs quickly and hop into bed before I lose it!'

Luisa's face lit up with a broad beam, slyness evaporated, and all she was was a child filled with delight: 'A scary story?'

'So scary all your hair will drop out and your skin will turn green and your teeth will start to quiver!'

'IIIEEEEEEE!' yelled Luisa and scampered off. Rita breathed again.

That night, Jitty came to Rita's room and handed her an envelope. There was a certain slyness in his face, an evasiveness. Embarrassment.

'Give this to your granny,' he said. 'It's important.'

'Can I read it?'

'No! Absolutely not. It's private.'

Rita glared at him again the way she had at the dinner table. Again, he could not meet her eyes. She held it in her hand, waving it, as she deliberated. And then she stood up, jumped out of bed, fetched a nail file, slit the envelope open. Jitty leapt to grab it, but she was quicker than he was and he missed, grabbing only air, knocking his hand against the headrest.

'No, Daddy. I'm going to read this one. Just like you probably read all of mine.'

'What – what you mean? I didn't…'

'Don't lie, Daddy! I know you did! I know they wrote me all those letters and you never let me read them, not a single one! So, I have the damn right to read this one.'

He stuttered a few incoherent words but Rita had already removed the single page, unfolded it. So, he just muttered, 'Good night then, darling. Have a good trip.'

She looked up, glanced at him as he slunk out the door.

'Sure. Good night, see you in two weeks.' But she hardly saw him leave; she was already reading:

Dear Mrs Gomes, Rita doesn't know about Cassie and she's not ready. She's still too young and it would devastate her. She might appear tough on the outside but she's very sensitive inside. So please don't tell her, for her own good. I will, when the time is right. I trust that you will honour this request, as we agreed back then.

Sincerely, Jitendra Maraj

Chapter Thirty

The Back of Beyond

The house was fast asleep when Aunty Penny came to collect Rita in a taxi early next morning. Her packed bag was waiting for her by the front door, and next to it, Chandra had placed the black cloth bag containing the Mixmaster in its box. Rita considered simply leaving it there. Why should she insult her grandparents by bringing them a broken, if brand-new, Mixmaster? But then she shrugged, picked it up and slipped out the front door. She'd hand it over dutifully and then explain it didn't work, apologise for the insult, and let that be an example of how despicable Chandra was.

It was a long trip. The taxi took them to Stabroek Market, where they squeezed themselves into a packed minibus, their luggage shoved between the rows of seats so that there was no room for their feet; they sat with their feet perched on top of their bags. Aunty Penny said it was always this way. 'We gon' to be lucky to get to Charity alive,' she warned.

The bus was driven by a large black man with a multicoloured cap of knitted synthetic yarn, pulled down over an enormous pile of dreadlocked hair. Reggae blared from the loudspeakers, deafening music that condemned the passengers, a more or less equal mixture of Indian and African men and women, to silence for the entire journey.

The minibus raced off, swerved hell-bent through Georgetown's early morning traffic and the outskirts of Town. When they reached the Demerara River, the swaying pontoon bridge over it forced the driver into a more sedate pace, but once across the river he sped off again at an even more breakneck speed.

They arrived at Parika in one piece, even if that piece was stiff and aching. Aunty Penny said, 'Come, dear,' and picked up her own bag and one of Rita's – the black one with the mixer – and ploughed into a chaotic mass of people, some streaming towards the dock, laden with luggage or goods, avoiding others streaming away from the dock.

Rita gripped her bag, slung the strap over her shoulder, and followed. Aunty Penny led her to a long wooden wharf jutting out onto the Essequibo River.

At the wharf there were several long covered boats waiting for passengers. The boatmen and their agents on the wharf were furiously screaming at each other; a few of them seemed poised to lunge at each other's throats. Aunty Penny, immediately recognised as a new victim, became almost the centre of a little brawl:

'Come here, lady, room for two, room for two. Just get it. Come, come, sit here. I got room for you. Just come, come on…' They surrounded her like yelping dogs; one tried to grab her bags away, but she swung her handbag at him and then at them all, clearing a space for her and Rita.

Aunty Penny screwed her face into a disdainful sneer and cast her eyes contemptuously over the boats and their drivers.

'Where's Errol? I want to go with Errol.'

'Errol not here, madam, he over the river, in Supenaam.'

The Essequibo was one of the many rivers that gave Guyana its name: the word meant Land of Many Waters. Three of those rivers, the Berbice, the Demerara and the Essequibo, were mighty waterways that divided the country into its three counties, and gave those counties its name. Georgetown, the capital, was in Demerara, the middle county. The Essequibo – the river and the county – was to the west, next to Venezuela; Parika was the river port on the Demerara side, and Supenaam on the opposite river bank.

'Then Harold… I'll go with Harold.'

'Harold not here either,' said one of the loudest men, a giant in red shorts. 'Come with me, I nearly full, just need two people and then we're off.'

His boat was indeed almost full. There were at least twenty passengers sitting quietly side by side on the rows of seats, bright orange lifejackets covering their upper bodies, their features fixed into expressions of stoic indifference.

'Well, we not going with you for sure. You full up already. You lucky if you don't sink with that load of passengers. Hey, you – YOU!'

She pointed to a thin Indian man in the next boat, whose back was turned. Hearing her shouts, he looked over his shoulder and then came towards her, grinning broadly. 'Yes, ma'am, you want go Supenaam?'

'Yes. Two, me and this girl. Here, take this bag. And let the girl go in first. Come, darlin', step in carefully. Give she a hand – there. Good!'

Aunty Penny got in after Rita and handed her a lifejacket. This boat was almost empty, but it was filling up quickly, and minutes later, they were on the river, the boat's bow pointed to the tree-lined horizon on the far bank, the scrawny boatman at the helm tending to the motor. The boat gathered speed; its bow rose high above the water's surface. Soon it seemed as if they were out at sea; to their right, in fact, the brown Atlantic spread out into the shoreless East, while straight ahead, the line of trees at the horizon seemed as distant as ever. The water beneath them swelled and sank, sometimes rising to meet the boat's bow, sometimes falling away in a trough, the bow falling into it with a sickening thud.

'You not frightened, chile?' asked Aunty Penny as Rita took her hand.

'I didn't know the Essequibo was so *enormous!*' Rita admitted. Somehow, along the way, she had found her voice as well as a certain rapport with Aunty Penny. She couldn't explain it. It just happened that way; with Aunty Penny her defences, the prickly hedge in which she enclosed herself, had fallen away. She pointed to the land visible in the distance. 'It looks so far – how long will it take?'

'Oh, those are only islands,' said Aunty Penny smugly. 'In the middle of the river. Supenaam is about three hours in a speedboat from Parika. The Essequibo is twenty-one miles across here at the mouth. That island there – it's bigger than Barbados. But don't worry, girl, it's perfectly safe. They hardly ever have accidents, only when there's a storm. And anyway, you got your lifejacket. You can swim?'

Rita nodded, blanching.

After what seemed half a day, they arrived at Supenaam, where a crowd of loud-mouthed taxi drivers almost came to blows over the disembarking passengers. Aunty Penny ignored the squabbles and hands grasping for their luggage, swatting them away impatiently as if they were flies. She walked over to one of the waiting cars, plonked the luggage on the ground so the driver could stow it in the boot, and gestured for Rita to get in. The driver, his round face gleaming with sweat like polished mahogany, picked them up.

'Where to?'

'Charity,' said Aunty Penny curtly. And to Rita: 'Is not far now. Only a couple more hours.' Rita sank into the back seat, Aunty Penny got into the front passenger seat; but the driver had disappeared. He reappeared a moment later with three more passengers, two fat women and a man, opened a back door, and almost pushed them in. 'Come on, girl, move down, make space!'

'But… but…' Rita began to protest but already one of the fat women was squeezing her against the door. The man climbed in after her, and then the other woman tried to squeeze herself in. The door wouldn't close.

'Come, lady, you go in front and the lady in front, she can get in the back next to she daughter.'

'She's not my…' Rita began, but nobody listened because they were all talking at once, the fat woman standing at the front passenger seat yelling at Aunty Penny, Aunty Penny refusing to get out, the driver trying to persuade her to do just that.

'You daughter can sit on you lap!' he shouted. 'Everybody got space!'

'I'm not her…' Rita tried again, but again, nobody was listening. Finally, Aunty Penny all but threw herself out of the car, furiously swung open Rita's door, and pulled her out.

'Come, girl, me in't able with this nonsense. We gon' find another car.' And they did, one with a woman and four children, who all managed to arrange themselves nicely on the back seat, including on their mother's lap. The car, a green Vauxhall with broken side-mirrors, a smashed headlamp, rusting fenders, and one broken window repaired with cardboard and Sellotape, sped off along the coastal road of Essequibo county; at least, sped is what they would have done had the road not been narrow and potholed, had there not been dray-carts plodding along before them, impossible to overtake, or the occasional cow or goat or herd of sheep, or dogs randomly crossing in the villages, never stopping to look for traffic.

The higgledy-piggledy villages themselves had such random names, names so mysteriously creative that Rita was entertained just wondering what had inspired them. Some seemed to have stories behind them, such as Good Hope and Makeshift, Adventure and

Three Friends. Some hinted at nostalgia for Good Old England: Richmond and Exmouth, Middlesex and Somerset. Others seemed to be punching above their weight, aspiring towards grandeur: Hampton Court, Windsor Castle, Devonshire Castle. Others were clearly religiously inspired: Paradise, Fear Not and Land of Plenty. And there were villages with Dutch or French names, Onderneeming and Zorg en Vlygt, La Belle Alliance and La Resource.

The villages seemed almost identical, collections of little wooden edifices high on stilts, clustered on both sides of the dusty road, behind rotting bridges and overgrown grass verges and front yards where a cow might graze or a donkey might be tethered. Occasionally, beyond the villages, they passed a grander house, two-storeyed, perhaps, and freshly painted, the gardens well-tended and bursting with colour, the house itself perched on tall solid columns. But everywhere, the sheer greenness overwhelmed: wild-growing bushes, flowering shrubs, trees hung with fruit. Coconut groves and rice fields, wild cane and banana orchards. And all this against the backdrop of blaring reggae pouring from the car's loudspeakers. But finally, they arrived at Charity.

Another wharf, more boatmen vying for customers, river taxis, with smaller boats this time. Aunty Penny seemed to know them all, chose the one they liked best, and helped Rita down a rickety ladder and into another orange lifejacket. It was just the two of them this time; off they sped, the boat slicing almost upright through the brown water of the Pomeroon River, creating cascading walls of clear water on both sides of the hull. They headed south, at first crossing the river and then heading inland close to the western shore, a wall of rainforest interspersed with clearings in which nestled little wooden cottages on stilts, set back from the river and connected to it by long wooden jetties, boats bobbing beside them.

The journey seemed interminable, but finally, the boat turned westward into an inlet, and slowed down. This was the Jo Ana Creek, Aunty Penny explained, and home was now only a half-hour away. 'Jo Ana: it's Warau for Blackwater,' said Aunty Penny. 'It looks black, but it's as clear as glass!'

On and on they chugged, the boat sliding through shiny black water that seemed as still as a mirror, reflecting the trees high above, as well as the mangroves that covered both banks, pushing long bare stems down into the watery depths. With every minute Rita became more aware of the stillness, of just how remote her grandmother's home was, how isolated and cut off from the rest of the world. It was a notion that at once exhilarated and scared her.

Nobody spoke, now, and that made it worse. A great silence engulfed her, pulled her in, overwhelmed her. She wanted to scream, shout, no, no, no: this is not my world, not my place! Hustle back to Georgetown, to the familiar sounds and sights, to people and places she knew, to the chaos and madness of town life. Already this place was cutting her off from everything she'd known before, and she wasn't even there yet.

She was being jettisoned from herself, and that was the last thing she'd expected, the last thing she wanted. The jungle trees, that green canopy through which the creek drew just a narrow path of sky, seemed to reach out to her, suck her in, and she was helpless against it. But there was nothing she could do, and presently the boatman cut the engine and let the boat just drift forward because there, just after a bend in the creek, was her grandmother's pier.

They disembarked, up a rickety ladder onto the jetty, and the river taxi turned round to return to Charity. Rita, stiff from the hours of sitting still on the boat, stretched arms and legs and walked up the wooden jetty behind Aunty Penny and onto the land.

Up a sandy path they walked, lined with the familiar flowering trees and bushes she knew from home, her own garden – frangipani, oleander, ixora, hibiscus, all well-tended and in full flower. The sand spread over the front yard was pink. She could tell that it was made up of ground shells, flaky, like Quaker Oats, but hard and crunchy under her feet. Later, she was to learn it had been brought here in boatloads from Shell Beach on the Atlantic coast.

In the background, tall coconut palms were silhouetted against the sky; further back yet, more trees, more green; and in the centre of it all, framed by the palms, the house itself: two storeys, balanced on tall thick pillars with a staircase leading up to the front door; the typical jutting gallery with a long veranda, wooden shutters, Demerara windows. Much bigger than Rita had expected; she had been thinking more in terms of a cramped wooden cottage on rickety stilts, like in the villages they'd driven through. She knew that her grandparents were farmers, but she'd always associated farming with poverty, and this house would not have been out of place in Town – though its wooden boards could do with a coat of white paint. A friendly house, inviting, and now, movement from the house; they appeared from nowhere, two nondescript mongrels, one black, one brown, throwing themselves at her with yelps of delight, jumping up at her with long tongues hanging out, aiming at her face, beside themselves with adoration; she grinning, patting, soothing, stroking, bending low to greet them, finally kneeling on the pink shells. She offered her face to be licked. She placed her arms round them and drew them close, and they were quiet.

And there, too, was Granny herself, hurrying, almost stumbling, down the stairs from the front door, grasping the banister with one hand, waving with the other, and calling excitedly. And then her grandmother's arms closed in round her. And as if by magic, all her fears melted away, and she was a five-year-old child again, and it all came flooding back, a vanished memory, a forgotten sense, the sense of home and comfort and security. And Granny's voice, suddenly familiar, as if she'd heard it all her life, speaking precious words over and over and over again:

'My baby come home! My baby come back home!'

Chapter Thirty-One

It's the Thought that Counts

Granny was short, but stockily built, and, as it turned out when she sprinted back up the steep staircase leading to the house's front door, agile as a child, and strong as an ox. Her hair was black, shiny, long and dead straight, caught at the nape of her neck in a plastic clasp and hanging down her back in wispy tendrils. Her skin was a glowing dun colour, like very milky coffee. Aunty Penny was dark – sapodilla-brown, as it was called here – and, as Rita knew from the one tiny photo she had of her mother, Cassie had been just like her.

The darkness, she discovered, came from Granpa, whom she found in a rocking chair in the gallery.

'He can't walk no more,' Granny explained. 'Arthritis too bad.'

'Come here, chile, let me look at you,' Granpa said. Rita kneeled beside the chair and the old black man with the white hair tilted up her face at the chin and stroked her cheek and ran his fingers through her hair. To her utmost embarrassment he placed his palms on her cheeks and drew her face up to his and kissed it all over, weeping profusely. He moved his hands to her back and drew her closer, hugging her so tightly she could hardly breathe.

Finally, he covered his own face with his hands and wept some more, sobbing loudly and shedding tears, which Granny mopped away with a corner of her apron. His crying was infectious; Granny wept too, all over again, and so did Aunty Penny, both kneeling beside her and hugging her, and Rita couldn't help it: she cried too. It was overwhelming, releasing swirls of emotion she was quite unprepared for, and incapable of dealing with. She wanted to run away, back to Town and the familiarity of friends who knew her and liked her; because being *liked* was one thing, but being *loved*, and so forthrightly, so artlessly, so without subterfuge or masks or coyness, was a different dimension altogether, unknown territory, and she had no idea how to navigate it, and if she had known, she would never have come, and if she'd had a choice, now that she was here, she would have turned and run. But there was nowhere to run. She was here, and that was that – she'd have to stick it out.

It was the first time in her life she had ever been the focus of emotion of this kind. It was embarrassing. And yet… so good. Delicious. Weightless. As if a layer of cloud covering the sky with greyness was slowly drawing back.

'My baby, my li'l baby girl,' Granpa kept saying, over and over again, just as Granny had done, between sobs. Rita wanted to remind him that she wasn't a baby girl any more, but then he said, 'My Cassie. My baby Cassie, my first-born! You is all we got left of Cassie!' and she realised then that all the tears, all the emotion, weren't just for her and her return to her grandparents' home: they were for her mother, their child, Aunty Penny's sister. For Cassie. Which felt slightly disappointing, and even slightly insulting, until Granpa said, 'You was my li'l baby girl too! My li'l Rita-girl! So long, so long. Why you didn't come back to see you old granny and granpa? Why you daddy keep you in Town, why you didn't write we no letters?'

'I… I didn't know… nobody ever—' Rita began, but Granny interrupted.

'Hush, Rudolf, don't be so rude to the child, is not she fault, she didn't know…'

'She look just like she mother, eh?' said Granny to Granpa.

Granpa pulled her close one more time and hugged her so hard, she thought he'd squeeze the life out of her. Aunty Penny came to the rescue.

'Now, Daddy, let her go. You hurtin' her. She's hungry and tired. Let me see what food we have for her, and then she can lie down and have a rest and afterwards we can show her the place. And you can meet your cousins, George, Pete and Kathy. They went fishing with Dutch, comin' home any minute now. Kathy can't wait to meet you!'

And Rita ate a delicious meal of pepper-pot, and then Aunty Penny had led her upstairs to the room allocated to her; it had once been her mother's room, Aunty said, and it still had the faded posters Cassie had pinned to the wall, of the Beatles and various other sixties groups Rita didn't recognise. She lay down on the bed – Cassie's old bed, Aunty Penny informed her – but she was far too restless to sleep. The journey had been endless, but her body felt stiff and fidgety from the hours of sitting – she needed to *move*.

'I'm going for a swim!' she declared, and without waiting for a reply, ran out of the house and down to the jetty. She tore off her T-shirt and was just about to dive into the clear but brown-stained water when Aunty Penny hurried up behind her.

'Be careful, Rita,' she said calmly. 'There are piranha in the water.'

Rita stopped and looked back at her aunt, who threw back her head and laughed.

'Don't worry,' she said, 'it's safe in the wet season – they have plenty of food. It's in the dry season you have to avoid the water. But I just wanted to warn you – you're in the rainforest. There are dangers you need to be aware of. Always ask before you do anything, go anywhere. Why not wait till the boys and Kathy come home, and swim with them?'

Rita sighed and pulled her T-shirt back on. 'I just feel so – so kind of rusty from all that sitting, all day. I need to go for a walk or something.'

Aunty Penny held out a hand. 'Come with me, I'll show you around. Show you the farm. That'll help settle you.'

Chapter Thirty-Two

Kathy

Behind the main house was a smaller cottage, where Aunty Penny and Uncle Douglas lived with their two boys. The youngest child, Kathy, Aunty Penny told her now, lived with Granny and Grandpa, as the cottage had only two small bedrooms.

'Kathy can't wait to meet you,' she said as they walked past the cottage to the vegetable plots behind the buildings. 'She's so excited! She's heard so much about you!'

'But how? None of you knew me!'

'Ah, but you've always been a part of the family. Just like your mother was. Cassie. And Kathy looks so much like both of you! She could be your sister.' She paused. 'You might find her a bit of a nuisance. She can't wait to have a big girl cousin around. She's quite the chatterbox, so if you need peace and quiet, just send her away!'

The last thing she needed was peace and quiet, Rita thought; that was surely the last thing she'd be missing. What she wanted was a bit of action. Already, the backdrop of still greenness, still water, endless sky was beginning to get to her. Unnerving.

'I won't mind her chatter,' said Rita. 'And I'm used to having a little girl hanging onto me – my stepsister, Luisa. She won't leave me alone! She even wanted to come here with me!'

'Another time, maybe. This time, we need you to ourselves. Look, here's where we plant the root provisions – cassava, yam, sweet potato, eddoes. And behind that, the bora beans and the boulanger. Once a week, we take the produce to market in Charity.'

'And – and you can sell enough to live on?' Rita did not want to appear nosy, but it did seem so little.

'Oh, this isn't everything. We have a coconut plantation near Charity and a man looking after that, selling copra. There's a good export market. And we have some more land beyond Charity. Douglas wants to start growing coffee. There's a big market for coffee. And maybe cocoa. Passion fruit. One thing Guyana has an abundance of, it's land, cheap land. Or you can lease it. We have acres and acres leased behind Charity, lying fallow, waiting their turn. Right now, it's just vegetables and coconuts. And of course, oranges and grapefruit. And limes. Look, this is the orchard...'

As they walked through the land, Aunty Penny pointing out this and that, mango trees and avocado and plump ripe bananas yellowing in huge heavy clusters hanging from their trees, Rita slowly relaxed. To her surprise, she found Aunty Penny's descriptions and explanations not boring but, for some reason, exhilarating. She listened, and asked questions, and by the time they turned to return to the house, she already felt much of her tension had left her.

Just then, a cry interrupted the conversation. Aunty Penny smiled.

'That's Kathy! And here she comes!'

A young girl was running towards them, pigtails flying, long brown legs flashing, arms waving.

'Rita! Rita!' she called, and as she joined them, flung herself at her cousin, wrapping her arms round her. 'I'm so glad you came! I wanted to meet you all my life! I wanted Mummy to take me to Town! So many times I begged, but she never did, and now you're here! I can't believe it!'

'See what I mean?' Aunty Penny smiled at Rita. 'She won't stop. Kathy, you have to let your cousin settle in and don't bombard her with questions. She wanted to go swimming earlier – you think that's a good idea, or is it too late?'

'It's never too late to go swimming! Come, come with me!'

Kathy grabbed Rita's hand and was about to charge back towards the house, pulling her along, but Aunty Penny snatched her by the arm.

'Kathy! I said take it slowly! You don't have to run everywhere! Rita, if you still want to swim…'

'I do… It's all right, Aunty Penny. I can manage.'

And side by side, Rita and Kathy walked back towards the house, the jetty and the creek. And for the first time, Rita felt she might just like it here.

Granny was delighted with the Mixmaster. She laughed with glee as she unpacked it later that evening, and then placed it proudly on the sideboard, moving a vase of artificial flowers and a faded wedding photo in a plastic frame aside to make room for it.

'Thank you, darling, it's lovely!'

'Well – it's not from me. It's from Chandra actually. And it doesn't work… I told her to—'

'It don't matter if it don't work, we don't have electric current anyway. But it look so nice and new. We don't get too many new things like that up here. It look so nice up there on the sideboard.'

'But… I could take it back, you know. She only did it to insult you.'

'How you could say such mean things about your stepmother, girl? It's a very kind, generous gift. I have to write her a thank-you letter. You must help me, my spelling in't so good, you know. I not used to writing letters. Aunty Penny helped me write a few letters but I hear he never pass on the letters to you. So, you must help me with the thank-you.'

'But you shouldn't—' Rita stopped abruptly, as if by an instinct of respect. Who was she to lecture her own grandmother? Granny had taken the mixer into her arms and was looking down at it in admiration, stroking it and, it seemed, almost cooing to it.

On her face was an expression of tenderness. She looked up at Rita. 'You got to say thank you when somebody give you a gift,' she said. 'Even if you don't like the gift. I hear that you never said thank you to Aunt Mathilda. Never went around to visit her. She was so kind to you! Sent you birthday presents every year!'

'I don't even know her!'

'You don't know her, but she sent you gifts. So, you shoulda say thank you, and gone to visit with a bunch of flowers. That's being polite. Aunt Mathilda is a sweet lady, shy and humble. It woulda make her so happy!'

'Well, I…'

'She'll forgive you, Rita; she won't even think there's anything to forgive! And we, we sent you cards, birthday and Christmas cards. I know you got those. But never a card from you, never a thank-you!'

'I…'

'Penny tell me you very rude. Never say please or thank you. Don't return greetings, just stare. You slammed the door in Penny's face first time she visit. It's rude, Rita, very rude.'

'But…'

Granny patted her on the back. 'Is not your fault, though. Is your daddy fault. He should teach you manners. And when you get a gift, you don't grumble about it. It's the thought that counts.'

She stroked the mixer again, and her features turned from stern to soft. It was almost the same expression of tenderness Granny had shown when she had first arrived, and Granny had cried with emotion, her wizened little face, the skin like soft pale leather laid in tiny folds, wet with tears and her eyes shining with love. Rita had never known anything like it in all her life.

Rita had hoped to show up her stepmother by presenting Granny with the Mixmaster, and letting her know just what a horrible old cow Chandra was. But the ploy had backfired. The gadget might have been given in bad faith, but it was received with gratitude and even joy, and Chandra had been proven right: it was, indeed, the thought that counted; and even if the thought had been misinterpreted, Granny had come out on top. Her open delight at the gift, and her defence of Chandra, put paid to Rita's plan to discredit her nemesis. So very frustrating.

That first night, after she had gone to bed, Granny came into her room, a kerosene lantern swaying in her hand.

'I just came to say goodnight. If you not too sleepy, we can have a li'l chat? Jus' you and me,' she said. 'Let me get in with you.' And she set the lantern on a table, lifted the mosquito net and climbed into the bed, and she and Rita sat cross-legged facing each other, like two schoolgirls in a ghostly tent, lit only by the flickering flame of the lamp casting eerie shadows on the walls and across their faces.

'You had a good swim?' Granny asked.

Rita smiled. 'It was wonderful!'

Kathy had dragged her back to the cottage, where they'd picked up Pete and George. Short introductions, then all four had run down to the jetty, stripping off their outer clothing as they ran, and plunged straight in. It had been a glorious half-hour of splashing and swimming, diving and laughing. And ruthless teasing. George and Pete swimming up beneath her and pinching her legs. Yelling: 'Piranhas! Watch out!' and laughing at her alarm.

And then they had dried off with towels and sat on the jetty while dusk approached, her cousins telling her about the past day's fishing with someone called Dutch who had a motorboat, and they'd go fishing again tomorrow, and they'd caught fish for dinner, and Dutch was their cousin and would take her everywhere, just everywhere, because he knew the creeks like the back of his hand.

'Dutch is my favourite, favourite cousin!' declared Kathy, then amended her statement: 'Except for you, of course, because you're a girl too, and my age. But Dutch is my favourite *boy* cousin. He's a lot nicer than my own brothers, you'll see! He's coming again tomorrow!'

And that, it seemed, was something to look forward to.

But then the first mosquitoes had floated in for the attack, and it was time to go indoors, and they all walked with her back to the house. After a hearty meal of fried fish – fresh from the creek – and bread, her cousins chattering away and making plans for the week, a cloak of exhaustion quite suddenly descended on Rita, an exhaustion that was perhaps more mental than physical. She had yawned and taken leave of them all, and retired to bed. And then Granny had come, bearing her lantern.

'Granny?' she said now, in the intimacy of the mosquito-net tent. Granny's welcome had been overwhelming in its warmth, and Rita felt grateful for being received with this abundance of love, but it was all a bit too much; she had come here to the Pomeroon for one thing, and one thing only. 'Can you tell me about Mummy?'

Granny sighed. 'Too much, too much to tell. What you want to know?'

'Everything. What she was like. And most of all, how she died.'

Granny stiffened, and her face turned hard. 'That's for your daddy to tell, not me.'

'I asked him a million times but he says I'm not old enough. And I know he wrote it, in his letter, not to tell me anything. I know that's what he meant.'

'So, you read his letter? You know that's a bad thing, to read other people's letters. It's prying.'

Rita laughed. 'I read it right in front of him! Because he had stolen my letters, from you! So he deserved it. It wasn't prying because he knew I was doing it. He deserved it.'

Granny chuckled. 'In that case, if you did it openly, it wasn't prying at all. But it was presumptuous.'

Rita ignored the mild rebuke.

'He deserved it,' she repeated. 'He's always going on about karma. Well, that was karma. Anyway, he meant about how she died, didn't he? In the letter? Why can't I know?'

'If you read it, you know why. He say the time not right.'

'Why not?'

'You got to ask him.'

'I'm asking you, Granny. He says you know. So tell me!'

'He said don't tell you. You read it.'

'But why?'

Granny sucked her teeth. In fact, every time Rita mentioned Jitty, she sucked her teeth, or frowned, or made some disparaging remark. Like now.

'That boy! Born a rascal.'

'Why you hate him so much, Granny?'

'I don't hate him. I don't hate nobody. I'm a Christian. But I vex, I vex bad.'

'Why, though? What did he do? How did she die? Why is it such a big secret?'

'No, Rita. It's not just about that one night. It's about what went before, and that's not my story to tell. You have to ask your daddy and when he's ready, he'll tell you. I know you miss her, but she is with you all the time.'

'But I need to know! I know there's some bad thing happened and nobody will tell me!'

Granny nodded slowly. 'Yes,' she said. 'Yes. A bad thing happened. A very bad thing. But it's not my place to tell. You have to talk to your daddy. It's important, Rita. He must be the one to tell you.'

'But he won't!'

'He will, eventually. Because it's the only way he gon' find healing. Because, Rita, he hurting too. Just like you. And he got to heal himself.'

'I want to know what bad thing he did!'

'He'll tell you when you ready. Your daddy not really a bad man. But he did a bad thing. An' he need to tell you, and he will. He need to make confession, like them Catholics. But confession to you as well as to God.'

'Confess what?'

'Is for him to say. He got to do it himself. Is not for me to confess on his behalf.'

'But, Granny…' But she was adamant. Rita sighed.

'Do you at least have a photo of her I could have?'

'Your daddy didn't give you a photo?'

'Just a group photo of her class at Bishops'. Her face is so small in it!'

'Wait a minute.' Granny got up and walked away, returning a few minutes later. She climbed back into the net and placed a Polaroid photo in Rita's hand. Rita stared. The photo was of two women. One was a much younger Granny. The other was…

'Mummy! And is that… is that…?'

'You. As a baby. A newborn.' It was a close-up of two women, their faces bathed in joy, smiling, bright-eyed with a love that simply glowed from the photo. The younger woman's hair was dishevelled, but her face was lit with a beauty that was almost ethereal, sublime. Rita looked up at Granny, a broad grin across her face.

'Then she *didn't* die in childbirth! Donna deSouza told me she died in childbirth but I *knew* it wasn't true! I *knew* she knew me, loved me! I felt it, all along!'

'So, it's not true that you didn't know how she died? You thought she died in childbirth?'

'Donna told me that, but I never believed her. Long ago. She told me I killed her. She said I exploded Mummy's tummy, and that's how she died. Obviously, I know that's silly, now, and I didn't even believe it back then. Not really. But I thought… I thought maybe it's *partly* true. That I killed her in childbirth.

Maybe it was just nasty gossip, but there must be some truth to it, I thought.'

'How did she hear such gossip?'

'She said she has an aunty who lives in the Pomeroon, who told her.'

'People like to talk too much. You should not listen to rumours. Find out the truth and stick to that.'

'Well, tell me the truth, then. How exactly did she die?' But Granny would not be tricked into telling.

'Ask your father.' Her tone had changed from soft and embracing; now there was something hard, brittle about it. Something unrelenting. Grim, even. She climbed out of the net, walked over to the table to pick up the lamp. Holding it, she stopped for a moment before opening the door. The lantern's light flickered against her, so that her face appeared and disappeared again between light and shadow.

'Is not so much *how* she died, Rita. Is *why* she died. I don't even know that myself. You got to ask him, because he's the only person that know.'

Chapter Thirty-Three

Dutch

Dear Diary,

Today was probably the best day in my life. I got up early, even before dawn, because Kathy came to get me. I like Kathy. She feels almost like a little sister, like Luisa used to be, but different, because she's not like Luisa. Not at all. She's more like me. Anyway, she dragged me out of bed and said we had to go swimming again. At first, I groaned because I wanted to sleep but then I got up and went out and we all went swimming and diving again, and it was wonderful!

The water looks so black but it is pure and clean and cool and it woke me up completely to dive in from the jetty and we had loads of fun. George and Pete like to play they are piranhas nibbling at my legs! But I kick them away and know it's not true – piranhas only come in the dry season.

And then they took me in Granny's canoe for a ride up the creek and taught me to paddle it myself.

A canoe is different from a speedboat! It is slow and quiet and <u>much</u> nicer. It just kind of glides on the water, cutting through it like a razor-blade. And the creek is dark and mysterious and even the air is green because all around it is rainforest, and the air is filled with moist greenness, which feels so <u>good</u>. I never knew you could feel colours before! It's all sunlight and shadows and everything is tinted green, even the black, black water, all smooth and silky.

It is just like a black mirror, perfectly unbroken, and the trees reflect perfectly on it, and now and then, the sun, shining and glittering through the trees and making patterns of light and dark on the mirror and golden in the sky if you look up through the leaves, and perfectly round in the water, as clear as the one up above, but cool because the water is cool.

Love Rita

Further up the creek, the mangroves reached out across the water and Rita, holding out her hands, found she could almost touch from both sides. The canoe just slid along silently, and nobody spoke, not even Kathy, as if she, too, was under a spell. They all were. A silence broken only by the regular gurgle of Pete's oar in the water, or the squawk of a parrot or the crashing of its wings as it plunged through the rainforest, or the occasional chattering of monkeys.

But behind those sounds was yet more silence; they were mere superimpositions on that background of deep, absorbing stillness.

It's so weird, she wrote in her diary that evening;

there are fifty million insects and bugs and birds twittering and cheeping in the silence, just like in the darkness of night but in a deeper, more profound kind of way, cavernous sort of as if it is calling you in and forcing you to listen, and you yourself grow still and silent so as to listen better, and it kind of absorbs you, draws you in, and makes you feel this wonderful deep contentment, something I never knew before. And I felt so happy, happier than ever in my life and that wasn't even the best thing of the day!

For Rita, the best thing that day was when they got back home.

'Dutch!' cried Kathy when she saw a motorboat moored at the jetty. She scrambled up to the jetty and would have raced off, but then she remembered Rita and stopped.

'Come, Rita! Come and meet Dutch!' Rita climbed up beside her and Kathy raced off towards the house. Rita had no option but to run behind her.

There he was, sitting on the front steps, fondling the dogs. 'Dutch! Dutch!' Kathy cried. 'This is my cousin Rita I told you about! Rita, this is my cousin Dutch!'

He stood up. They smiled at each other. Rita, realising she was still in her swimsuit, felt suddenly awkward, self-conscious. She wished she'd stopped to at least pull on her shorts and T-shirt, but she brushed her hair off her face and tried to look bright as she said,

'Hello Dutch!'

'Hello Rita!'

Dutch was a good bit older than her, about nineteen or twenty, Rita reckoned. His skin was chocolate brown and gleaming as if polished beneath a rather tattered singlet that showed toned muscles on sinewed rowing arms. He wore cut-off jeans, frayed at the knees and also slightly tattered, revealing strong long calves, and old tennis shoes with the toes cut out. But the best thing about Dutch, Rita found, was his eyes. They too were chocolate brown, a darker shade than his skin, this time melting chocolate, reflecting a smile that made her feel – she struggled to figure out how, exactly, she felt. Warm, and accepted, but not in the exuberant way of her grandparents and not in the excited way of Kathy and not in the uncomfortable lusting way of boys from Town. In a way that was simply in tune with everything she had felt that morning: with the water and the trees and the parrots and the insects and the monkeys, as if it was all one big round circle and she was a part of it. Embracing.

He shook her hand as he smiled and his grip was firm and confident.

'Welcome to the Pomeroon!' he said, and his voice was warm and resonant and for some reason Rita now felt shy and self-conscious, but managed to whisper a few words of thanks.

Dutch had wild black hair that was, by Town standards, much too long, too unkempt, wiry rather than curly, and falling over his forehead and touching his bronze shoulders. His hair, she thought, that was not unlike her own, a result of the mixing of races going back several generations. We are of a kind, she thought. We're a new breed, more than hybrid, a fusion of types and he is the result – he's beautiful, a word she had only, till now, associated with women. She found herself staring, and looked away, embarrassed, but Dutch had not noticed; he was being beleaguered by Kathy on what to do that day for Rita's entertainment.

'Shell Beach!' Kathy cried. 'Please, please let's go to Shell Beach!' She turned to Rita. 'Shell Beach is where the turtles come to nest,' she said. 'I've heard so much about it. Dutch has a friend there and he's been promising to take me but he never has the time!'

'Turtles! Marine turtles?' Rita said. She'd read about turtles, and how vital they were to the ecosystem of the oceans.

'Yes,' said Dutch. 'Leatherbacks, the largest of all sea turtles.'

'They're *enormous!*' interjected Kathy. 'I read a book all about them, with pictures. Aunt Mathilda sent it to me for my birthday!'

'I think she sent me that book, too!' said Rita. 'It's about the Shell Beach turtles, isn't it? I didn't know Shell Beach was near here!'

'Not exactly near here,' said Dutch, 'but a lot nearer than from Georgetown. But – I can't do it today, sorry. It needs a bit of planning. I have to find someone for Granma.'

He turned to Rita. 'My great-grandmother, I look after her. She lives on the main river, towards Charity.'

'You always say that!' pouted Kathy. 'Always make excuses!'

'But it's true! We'd have to go overnight, and I can't leave her on her own.'

'You promised!'

'I know. And I always keep my promises. I'll figure it out.' Dutch held up two fingers as in an oath. He turned to Rita again.

'There was an article in the papers the other day,' he said. 'About leatherbacks. About Peter Pritchard; he's the author of that book. He was here last month and they interviewed him in the *Chronicle*. You didn't read the article?'

'No,' she replied, and felt obliged to add, 'My dad works at the *Graphic*, so we don't get the *Chronicle* at home.'

'Pity. I got a copy at home, I'll bring it nex' time. He talks about the conservation programme for turtles. Shell Beach is the nesting place for them and he launched the programme to protect them and their eggs. It's the most important turtle conservation programme in the world. Dr Pritchard – a good man. We call him the Turtle Man up here – he don't mind! Every now and then he comes with his wife – she is Guyanese. Anyway…' He turned back to Kathy. 'We still haven't figured out what to do today. Any other suggestions?'

The question was directed at Kathy. She scrunched up her face as she considered.

'Well, we could go fishing, but we did that yesterday. What about – Parrot Creek?'

'Good idea!' said Dutch. 'We'll do that. Go and get yourself ready. We'll take a picnic. Maybe George and Pete want to come too?'

George and Pete didn't. Aunty Penny had brought some new videos up from Town, and they wanted to go to Charity to watch them.

'But I don't know anyone, even in Town, with a TV!'

'Of course not. There's no TV station in Guyana yet. But a friend of theirs in Charity has a video player and some of the teenagers like to hang out there. It's like a Charity Video Club! Mostly boys, mostly this kind of action-type stuff – what they call them? Blockbusters? But mostly they just re-watch the old ones. *Star Wars* and *Rambo*, that kind of thing. We don't have a cinema up here so Aunty Penny lets them go, as long as they do their chores. They know those old films off by heart. George and Pete – they much too modern for this place. Kathy is different. Kathy is… she's an animal girl. A nature child.'

'I was an animal girl too,' said Rita. 'Or used to be, when I was small.'

Aunty Penny sighed. 'Yes. You probably don't remember. You were five, and Kathy was nearly three, back then. She adored you; like a big sister. And you showed her all the animals you knew. The two of you were always up to something with animals or insects. It broke her heart when your daddy took you away.'

'I don't remember,' said Rita miserably. 'Not a thing.'

'Well, she's remembered! She's talked about you all the time, ever since. That's why she was so excited to see you. You looked after her from when she was a baby, even though you were only three.'

'Oh! That's just like when Luisa was born, my little sister!'

'Maybe Luisa reminded you of Kathy.'

'But she's so different to Kathy! So different to me. I mean, I still love her but we don't like the same things at all. She loves pink frilly dresses for instance and I always hated them. And she hates animals. We still get on, but I think she takes after her mother and *she* hates me.'

'I'm sure that's not true.'

'It's true. And she used to be glad, when Luisa was small and a nuisance, that I took care of her but now, well, now she's like a doll Chandra likes to dress up. Both love it, and I hate it. And her. Chandra, I mean, not Luisa.'

'You know what, Rita? You use the word *hate* too much. It's a bit extreme. You shouldn't be hating anyone.'

'Well, I do.'

But Aunty Penny only shrugged, and changed the subject.

Dear Diary,

Today, Dutch took Kathy and me to a place called Parrot Creek about an hour away. The forest here is just bursting with parrots! You wouldn't believe it! The trees full of them, all squawking at the tops of their voices! Thousands and thousands of them! And we went for a walk into the forest. I was scared at first because the trees were so close and they all seemed alive, as if they all were living beings just like humans, except rooted to the spot, and talking to each other and we were the interlopers. But Dutch was so at home in there, he definitely wasn't an interloper. It was as if he and the trees were all one. And every now and then he would point up to the canopy and say, there's a rufous crab hawk, or a blood coloured woodpecker or he'd stop talking and say, listen! That's a red cotinga! and I'd listen as intently as I could but I never heard what he heard or saw what he saw.

It was extraordinary, as if he has extra-sharp eyes and ears and sees and hears things beyond my own senses. Or else maybe my own senses are just too dull to see and hear these things, because I live in Georgetown and the city noise has blunted me and that's why.

I like it here in the Pomeroon, though it's sometimes a bit scary. At night you hear the howler monkeys, they have this really eerie cry, like phantoms. And bats fly in through the windows. Vampire bats! Granny says to keep my feet well away from the mosquito net when I sleep because they come and bite and lick the blood. But how can I do that, if I'm asleep? It's a mystery! And

I definitely don't like mosquitoes. And you have to be careful because there are scorpions and snakes. But I like living with danger!

Dutch is so clever! He knows all about the animals and birds who live here, everything! And he tells me so much, I can't even retain it to tell you about it. He asked me about myself but I didn't want to talk about my stupid life at home so I asked him about himself instead.

Tomorrow we're going to an Amerindian reservation called Wakapoa, to meet some of Dutch's relatives. His mother is pure Amerindian, just like Granny, and some of her friends live there and some of my distant relatives. And the day after that I hope we get to go to Shell Beach at last. I can't wait!

Love Rita

Parrot Creek led to a lake with white sand beaches, where they sat on a sandbank to have their picnic. Rita had lost her shyness by now, and chatted easily and freely with Dutch. She was curious about one thing:

'Why are you called Dutch, instead of a proper name?'

'It's just a nickname, a call-name. It's because my ancestors were Dutch slave-owners,' he replied. 'My surname is Van der Zee, which means "from the sea", and my first name is David but nobody calls me that.'

'That's my name too!' Kathy said. 'I'm from the sea too!'

But Rita had picked up something else, another word.

'*Slave-owners?* Really?' She was horrified.

'Of course. And it's the same with you, Rita. Your grandpa is mixed-race, black and white. Everyone says the mixed-race black people are descended from slaves, but we're also descended from slave-owners: white people, British or Dutch, who first came here and ran the plantations. It's horrible but true. Those people kept slaves and they must have raped the women and had babies and it all ended up with people like your granpa and you and me. Everyone here with African blood, we came from slaves. And if we're mixed, it's because the slave-owners just grabbed any woman they wanted.'

'I never thought about that before,' said Rita. 'It's awful!'

'Yes,' said Dutch. 'And it's said the Dutch were the cruellest slave-masters of all.'

'But why you call yourself Dutch, then? You like to be reminded of that?'

He laughed. 'I didn't give myself the name. Up here, they give everyone a call-name, and because I got a Dutch last name, they call me Dutch. No matter! It's all in the past and we're here now and no need to harbour grudges and resentment, because we're all fine these days. We're lucky to be born here in such a rich country, no matter how awful the history! Look at all the magnificent animals! I'm glad I'm here, born here!'

Kathy put in: 'They could-a call George and Pete Dutch too, or Dutch's brothers, but Dutch is the eldest so he got to be called that!'

'Yep. We're a big family, and I'm the eldest. I've got four younger brothers and one sister, all in Town.'

Dutch's mother, he explained, was pure Amerindian, and she had taught him all she knew about birds and animals, their habits and how to recognise them by their tracks and their calls, and all about plants, and the healing properties of some herbs and leaves and roots.

'She and my dad live in Georgetown. My dad used to be a boatbuilder and a mechanic of outboard motors. He set up a business in Georgetown, importing and selling and repairing boat engines, and it really took off. So that's where most of the family lives. I stayed here. I live halfway between here and Charity, looking after my old great-grandmother. I'm the only one left after my parents moved to Town with all my brothers and sisters – I'm the eldest. So, it's me left to care for the old lady and look after her farm. The only relatives I have left here are Uncle Douglas, Aunty Penny's husband – he's my dad's brother, my uncle – and of course my cousins. Kathy, George and Pete. Everybody else, they just skedaddled.'

'Don't you want to move to Town too?'

He shook his head. 'Not really.'

'So, you're just going to live here forever?'

He laughed. 'Hopefully not! What I really want to do is be a pilot and fly all over Guyana, but I can't because, well, I have to look after Granny.'

'So, you'll just stay here until she dies? That could be ages! Years!'

He shrugged. 'Granny's ninety-six, so probably not too much time left. But anyway, that's life, isn't it? Somebody has to do it, and it turns out to be me. Life is still good, and I like it here. We'll see what happens. No hurry. What's a year or two or three?'

That night, Rita wrote down the conversation with Dutch in her diary. She wrote down everything else she'd done that day, everything she'd learned:

> Dutch knows all about animals. Everything there is to know about them, he knows it. He's like an animal king in my eyes! He told me about jaguars and birds and snakes. And turtles, mother turtles who come to lay their eggs on Shell Beach. He's promised to take Kathy and me to Shell Beach and maybe we'll be able to see mother turtles nesting, or baby turtles hatching.
>
> Shell Beach is a special place, really isolated and far away from everywhere. But it's not safe for turtles. Years ago, the local communities used to kill the nesting turtles

for their meat, after they had laid their eggs, and then ate the eggs too. So, the turtle population was diminishing.

Then this man called Dr Pritchard came. He's like a turtle saviour. He's a British zoologist from the University of Florida. He and Dutch's friend Ronald decided to involve the local communities to help preserve the turtles so they helped them establish chicken farms for meat and got them to help patrol the beaches to stop people digging up the eggs. They also needed ways to make money, and that seemed to be in the market for copra, from coconuts.

And now the Shell Beach turtle conservation programme is the most important in the world! Kathy and I asked him to take us to Shell Beach, but he doesn't have the time, because we have to spend the night and he has to look after his old granny. She loves animals just the same as I do. She's like a little sister, but just like me, not like Luisa, who likes everything I don't. She's so lucky to live up here surrounded by all these wild animals! She wants to be a zoologist, like Dr Pritchard. Maybe I want to be that too, then we could work together and live together.

And Dutch – well, he's like a teacher, but not really, because he's not bossy and scary like a teacher, he's nice and I could listen to him all day. He can whistle every single bird call. You'd think it's a real bird. Kathy says the birds think it's a real bird too and reply to him. He's going to take us birding one night, if Granny allows it. There's so much to look forward to, I don't even know if two weeks is long enough.

I'm not sure about Granny, though. I like her but it's kind of weird how she looks at me as if she wants to eat me up! She makes me a bit nervous. But I like Dutch, a lot. He's the kind of man I'd like to marry. One day.

I wish I were a few years older, then I could marry him
now! I wish all men were like him, not like those idiots
Archie Foot and Ross.

It was the longest diary entry for months; she felt she had to
record every detail of the day, every word Dutch had spoken, every
twinkle in Kathy's eye. She wrote until her eyes grew heavy with
exhaustion, and the light from her torch grew dim as the battery
ran out. She wrote, 'good night, dear Diary', slipped the book
and the torch under her pillow, turned over and was asleep in less
than ten seconds.

Chapter Thirty-Four

Shell Beach

And then, at last. Shell Beach.

Early that morning, Dutch arrived with his motorboat. The four young people sat on the jetty after their swim, waiting.

'I hear him!' cried Kathy, and George and Pete agreed. Rita heard nothing; it seemed that everyone here except her had super-hearing. It was a good five minutes before she too heard a gentle chugging, and another five before the little boat rounded the corner and became visible, then drew near. Dutch turned off the motor and the boat sidled up to the jetty.

Sitting in the middle of it, in an orange lifejacket, was a little old lady, wizened as an elf, but straight-backed and with eyes that were alert and lively.

'Hello Granny Minnie!' called Kathy. George and Pete called out similar greetings, caught the rope Dutch threw them and tethered the boat. Dutch moved forward, lifted the old lady into his arms as if she were light as a feather, while George climbed halfway down the ladder; Dutch handed him Granny Minnie, and he gently laid her over his shoulder and climbed carefully back up, Dutch behind him. Once on the jetty, Dutch reached out and took his great-grandmother into his arms; after which he strode off to the cottage to hand her over to Aunty Penny, her granddaughter-in-law.

In the end the solution had been simple; Granny Minnie, as they all called the old lady, would stay overnight with Aunty Penny, who would look after her. Dutch was free to take them all to Shell Beach. Except that 'all' turned out to be only the two girls, Kathy and Rita.

George came over with a basket of provisions packed by Aunty Penny and, shuffling on his feet, said somewhat ashamedly, 'Pete and I've decided not to come. Aunty Penny brought those new videos…'

'We watched *Raiders of the Lost Ark*,' said Pete, voice raised in excitement. 'We're going to Charity to watch *The Empire Strikes Back*.'

'We're not *that* interested in turtles,' added George.

Dutch laughed. 'I get it. We're a bunch of turtle weirdos. Right, girls?'

'Dutch, I put you in charge, right? Look after the girls,' said Granny sternly. She opened a cupboard and removed two jars. 'Here, take some pepper sauce and tamarind balls to give Ronald's mother. And some coconut cake for Ronald and a nice big pineapple.'

She tucked the items into Aunty Penny's basket, handed it to Dutch and rumpled his hair fondly. He grinned. 'I'll guard them with my life!'

At last they were all ready. Rita and Kathy climbed down into the boat and sat themselves down on the middle row. Dutch threw them their lifejackets. Granny, who had come to see them off, unhitched the mooring rope and threw it into the boat. Dutch, at the back next to the outboard motor, pulled at the starter cord. The motor spluttered. He yanked again; a little cough. A third yank: cough, cough, caught. The motor chugged comfortably, confidently, and they were off. The boat made a smooth circle in the creek to head back to the river. Rita waved at Granny, standing on the jetty, and her heart gave a little lurch of excitement as the boat zoomed off, its bow rising up as it gathered speed, pointing to the sky; and the water parted for them, curving away from the bow like huge wet wings; and Rita, too, felt as if she were flying, a bird rising up on wings of joy.

The boat raced down the creek, turned left, northwards, into the brown Pomeroon and sped on towards the estuary at the Atlantic Ocean. The wind lashed her face with tiny prickles of water, pinpricks of spray that tickled her skin and left it wet, and tossed and tangled her hair so that she reached up and clasped it to her head, and threw her head back in exhilaration. The cooling wind vied with the warmth of the sun, now at its zenith, high above, in a cobalt blue sky without a single cloud. She glanced at Kathy in glee; Kathy was grinning into the wind, her hair, too, whipped in all directions; their eyes met, and spontaneously, their hands reached out and met and clasped.

Now and then they passed other boats, speeding in the opposite direction; the occupants of both boats waved at each other in passing, yelled words instantly whipped away by the wind. They passed canoes, too, entire Amerindian families placidly rowing their way downstream, a mother with her children, sometimes even a child alone. These were river folk; water and boats and fishing were their world, and it seemed now, to Rita, a good way to live; a happy way to live.

The river spread wider and wider; they passed Charity, passed more and more riverbank settlements, more boats, more people, and then, all of a sudden, there it was, stretched out before her, rippling gently and sparkling in the sunshine, a vast expanse reaching out to the horizon: the Atlantic.

The boat slowed down slightly, went out a little way, then turned westwards and onwards, following the coastline until after what seemed like hours they came to Shell Beach. Dutch brought the boat into shallow waters, then the girls climbed out and helped pull it up onto the shore. Rita looked around in awe as she stepped out, dipping bare feet into the lapping tide.

'It's *huge!*' she exclaimed.

'Yes – it goes right up to Venezuela,' said Dutch, now dragging the boat out of the water and up the shore. 'About ninety miles long!'

'And *wide* – and, and just *shells!* Oh, my!' she gasped.

Dutch laughed. 'There's a reason they called it Shell Beach!'

Indeed; this was not a beach of sand, but entirely of shells, some whole, some crushed. Shells of all shades from cream to white to black and brown, shells that crunched beneath her feet as she walked up towards the shore.

They unloaded the bags and baskets from the boat and, thus laden, walked across the expanse of shells to a little house behind the beach, where they were welcomed by a smiling couple who introduced themselves as Uncle Errol and Aunt Mavis.

'And this is our son, Ronald,' said Aunt Mavis, as a young man stepped forward.

'Welcome to Shell Beach, Rita and Kathy! Ronald will show you over to the camp.'

Later, Ronald showed them the hatchery where the rescued turtle eggs were kept, protected from predators, both animal and human, until ready to hatch.

'These are all leatherback turtle eggs,' said Ronald. 'Four kinds of sea turtles come here to hatch: the green, hawksbill, leatherback and the olive ridley, but the leatherback is the biggest. They're all endangered, so Dr Pritchard founded the Guyana Marine Turtle Conservation Society to protect them. He and I, we worked together to make the locals aware that they, too, need to protect the eggs. They used to eat turtle meat, but we helped them to raise chickens instead. And we collect the eggs and bring them to the hatchery; and when they hatch, the turtle babies all run back down the beach to the sea – it's an incredible sight!'

'Oh! I'd love to see that! Will it happen when I'm here?'

Ronald shook his head. 'No, they're not ready. But we'll sit out tonight on the beach and if you're lucky, you'll get to see something just as good.'

'What?' But Ronald only smiled and shook his head. 'You'll see!'

He told me all about the turtles as we sat there in the sand. It was a dark night because the moon had not yet risen so we sat there in the darkness, just the four of us, me and Kathy, Ronald and Dutch, and the breeze was so cool as it wafted around us, and the tide was in and the water moved slowly back and forth, and it crept forward and lapped gently at the beach making the sweetest frothing and slurping and slapping sounds and then retreated again, sucking backwards, and it was absolutely GORGEOUS.

And that's not a word I use lightly, diary, or would use about any other night at all but it was just that, gorgeous. Heavenly. As if God was smiling down on us and nodding.

And the biggest thing <u>still</u> hadn't happened yet, and yet I was even <u>happier</u> than I had been in the creek and the boat. The happiness just kept growing bigger and bigger, filling me up more and more! And I wanted to get up and dance with joy right there on the beach, on the cracked shell Quaker Oats beach! And we sat on the shells and waited in the darkness, talking quietly, and I listened to the lapping of the water as it moved back and forth with the tide, and we all just waited, and the cool breeze wafted by, and brushed gently against my skin, and the moon rose and it was almost full and shining up in the sky like a gleaming yellow ball, and oh, it was just magical and I'll never, ever forget that night.

But the real magic was when she came.

She lumbered out of the sea, like a prehistoric beast. 'She's ENORMOUS!' whispered Kathy. Rita could only gasp, her hands flying to cover her mouth, eyes opening wide. She held her breath, then as she stared, stunned into silence. There she was, the mother turtle. A gigantic beast, emerging from the sea, otherworldly as she lumbered up the beach, her flippers seemingly much too small for the burden of hauling that huge body slowly across the sand. Ponderous, but with fierce determination, she crawled up across the shore. Rita could hardly breathe. She had never felt this before: pure and unadulterated awe. A sense of something almost magical filling every fibre of her body. She stared as if under a spell.

On and on the turtle crawled, away from the water. Excruciatingly slow, she carried the cumbersome load of her body staunchly to safety. The moon was now high in the sky, and bright, and it cast a benign glow on the scene; to their right, the ocean gently undulating with a quicksilver glow on its surface of silk, to their left, tall coconut palms silhouetted against the cobalt sky, and between the two, this miracle of gestation: a mother seeking safety for her offspring, nature's interpretation of love.

Finally, beyond the reach of the tide, she found her place and stopped crawling. She began to dig, scratching at the oatmeal sand with her front flippers.

'What's happening?' Rita whispered, momentarily released from her paralysis of awe.

'She's digging a hole for her eggs,' Dutch replied. 'Just wait. Let's not scare her.'

And so they watched and waited. The digging of the nest was another laborious undertaking, carried out with ruthless tenacity. Sand flew backwards as she dug, deeper and deeper. And then at last it was over. The turtle positioned herself above the hole.

Dutch said 'Come!' and held out both hands and pulled Rita and Kathy to their feet. They walked forward across the moonlit beach lit only by stars until they were right next to the turtle. She ignored them, now quite still, making strange wheezing noises, breathing heavily as the eggs plopped into the nest, three or four at a time.

Dutch leaned forward and raised one of her back flippers and there they were: the eggs! Round as a ball and shiny, gleaming white. Dutch reached down and put one each into Rita's hand and Kathy's. Rita's fingers closed around it, gently feeling: it was soft-shelled, not hard like a hen's egg. Dutch replaced the eggs. The girls both leaned forward and stroked the turtle's shell; it was hard and black and ridged, slightly rubbery, like a huge truck tyre, and scattered with white spots. Her head was as big as a football, and a liquid ran from her eyes.

'She's crying!' exclaimed Kathy, and Dutch laughed.

Indeed, tears dripped down her ancient face and her eyes pulled backwards into her head every time she blinked; and her front legs looked like paddles, with no fingers or toes, and Rita felt her own eyes welling with tears.

Dutch must have noticed the emotion welling up within her; or maybe he felt the same. He placed his arm round her, and pulled her close; and it was a gesture of infinite warmth, eloquent in its simplicity. She did the same, and so did Kathy, from the other side of Dutch, and together they stood there, unified in the sense of wonder at what they were witnessing.

The turtle finished laying. She turned and scratched at the beach, covering the eggs until they were completely buried to the turtle's satisfaction. Her eggs safely underground, she continued to scratch at the sand, scattering it all over the place. The three of them backed away from the wildly scattering sand. On and on the turtle scratched, flinging sand about, until the eggs were not only buried, their sandy surroundings so disturbed no predator could find them.

At last she was satisfied. She turned and lumbered back towards the ocean and disappeared under the waves.

Rita wrote the next day, once safely back at Granny's: And the moon was high above us, and the night glowed silver and even the stars seemed to be singing and once more I just wanted to dance with joy, but I didn't. I was just overflowing with gladness and gratitude and I couldn't help it, I was crying and I flung myself at Dutch and said thank you, thank you, a million times, and he seemed to understand for he gave me another big hug, and then I hugged Kathy too and she hugged Dutch and Kathy was almost crying and Dutch was laughing, but I think he was just as moved as we were. And we all went back to the camp and the moment I lay down, I fell asleep.

And, dear Diary, here's my big, big secret: I have a big, big crush on Dutch. More than it ever was for Archie Foot or Ross. More than anything, ever. But I'm not letting it take over. I won't let him know, not with a single word. It's between you and me. He's too old for me anyway, a man more than a boy. Five whole years older! An older man, and they're all the same, boys and men. Losing your heart to them only leads to the worst pain in the world – you feel terrible afterwards when you find out that you cared and they didn't. Archie was so horrible in the end and Ross was nasty. I'm scared that Dutch might turn out to be horrible too, if I let him think I like him. Why do they do that, take a girl's heart and break it as if it were nothing? I won't let that happen, not this time. I'm going to guard my heart, put it under lock and key. You're the only person to know. I won't even tell Polly.

I'm only afraid it might show in my eyes. They say that eyes are a window to the heart. What if I can't close that window? What if I can't pull down the blinds?

Love Rita

Chapter Thirty-Five

Granny

The more time Rita spent with Granny, the more her admiration grew. Granny seemed to be the axis on which the whole household turned; she was the dynamo at its centre, from whom everyone else drew their energy, strength and sense of direction. She was up before dawn, sweeping the yard, feeding the chickens and letting them out, lighting the wooden fire in the kitchen, fighting with the smoke it emitted, fetching bucketfuls of water from the river. Aunty Penny and the boys – and from that day onwards, Rita – helped, but it was perfectly clear that Granny was the earth in whom they were all solidly planted; the sun around whom their lives revolved.

At breakfast, Granny slipped a plate with two bakes and pumpkin stew in front of her with the words 'Eat up, darlin'!' and from that moment on, Rita felt as if she was attached to some invisible powerhouse that over the rest of her two-week holiday was imperceptibly and constantly filling an underground battery in her body with nourishment and strength. Granny's face, the colour of creamy coffee and perfectly smooth in spite of her age, which, Rita, calculated, must be nearing sixty, sometimes frowning, sometimes laughing, sometimes stubborn, sometimes pensive, drew her like a magnet.

When Granny spoke, everyone listened; what she said, and how she said it, seemed sometimes as naive as the utterings of a child and yet her every word possessed a basic truth. Granny got straight to the heart of things, and what at first appeared naive turned out, finally, to have a wisdom of its own. Rita had hoped to find an ally in her silent battle of wills against Chandra, but Granny was having none of it; Granny refused to comfort and console her, refused to confirm Chandra as the villain of the story.

'Stop complainin'!' Granny said whenever Rita started once again on her litany of grievances against Chandra. 'She's your stepmother! Is her house. You got to behave yourself.'

Granny had no time for self-pity, and brooked no nonsense in her own home; she had her rules, and insisted on good behaviour.

To Granny, good behaviour meant knuckling down to help on the farm, and no child was excused, not even a spoilt fifteen-year-old who had never lifted a finger for a chore in her life – or at least, not since she had first left Granny's care.

In the time between meals Rita was expected to help on the farm. Yes, she could go out with Kathy and Dutch on expeditions here and there, but when she was home, work was expected. And yet, somehow, Rita didn't mind, and found she even enjoyed being a part of farm life.

Granny grew avocados on the farm, on ten trees that produced pear-shaped fruit bigger than Rita's hands, their soft flesh yellow and succulent. Granny's pineapples were the most delicious ones Rita had ever tasted, and the passionfruit juice she made from the rows of vines at the back of the farmyard was, well, *divine* was the word Rita used, and Granny laughed and said, 'All of God's fruits are divine!'

Vegetables too, grew in abundance and Rita found that working on the earth, *with* the earth, her hands working the soft black soil, seemed to deepen and solidify and clarify feelings long buried.

Chapter Thirty-Six

The Wound

Rita's time in the Pomeroon – well, there was no other word for it but 'magnificent'.

The night before she was to return home Granny came into her room, climbed under the net and sat cross-legged at the end of her bed in the darkness, just as she'd done that first night. In the half-light of the moon – no lantern needed this time – shining through the open window, she looked ghostlike, ephemeral. Rita sat up, facing Granny on the bed. In the darkness she saw little more than Granny's dark profile, and the gleaming whites of her eyes. But Granny's features were imprinted on her mind and she knew in her heart that those eyes would be like open windows, and closing her own eyes she felt, without looking, the strong love shining there.

She bent over and kissed Rita's forehead, and made to get up and go, but Rita clung to her hand, pulled her back.

'Granny,' she whispered, 'what was she like?'

Granny knew exactly who 'she' was.

'She was wonderful,' came the whisper. 'A darling girl, a fine woman – though she was hardly even a woman when you was born. Just turned eighteen. And so clever and so good. Good at everything. Good at school, good at sports, good at singing. And dancing! Oh, how she loved to dance! When she was a li'l girl, she would sing loud and grab the dog we had by the front paws, and dance, dance, dance. She used to say she would be a dancer when she grew up. She could sing and dance real good. She was just good, at everything. Good at being human.'

Granny sighed and placed an arm round her, pulled her close.

'She was such a bright girl. The cleverest in the region – we was so proud of her. She was desperate to go to Town, to go to Bishops'. She wanted to be a teacher, or a doctor. She said once she was a teacher, she would come back here to the Pomeroon and set up a school for rural children, further up from Charity so they wouldn't have those long boat rides. A free school and free transportation and free lunch. And then, later, when she was at Bishops' and got more confident, she said she was going to be a doctor, and build a hospital in Charity. I used to ask her where she would get the money from but she said she would force government to provide. Because government has a duty to provide for everyone, even us up in the country.

'She got into Bishops', easy. She was so bright, Rita, in all subjects! She stayed with Mathilda in Peter Rose Street, and rode her bike to school every day, and got top marks – always in the top set at Bishops'. She got seven O-levels and went on to sixth form. But you know, a person can be bright up here…' she tapped Rita's forehead… 'but foolish down here.' She tapped Rita's chest.

'Cassie was foolish. Naive. She had no experience. She had only known good, kind country people and she thought everyone was like that. So much love was in your mummy's heart, baby! She loved you so much! But she didn't know of the ways of men. Your daddy, now…'

'He's not a bad man, Granny!'

'No, he's not bad, but he's a *man*. A jackass. But he got this charm – I met him, you know! A charming man full of smiles and sweet-talk. That's how he caught her. With charm. She di'n't know no better. She used to write home, what a wonderful man he was. So in love with her! She thought that. She thought sweet-talk and attention and presents was love.

'And maybe he did in a small way, but men like that, they don't know what love is. Not real love. Is all about the pants. What they feel in the pants, but that not love at all. What they can *get*, not what they can *give*. But at that age, they think is love. Now Cassie, she *did* know about love. The heart kind. The real kind. And she gave it all to him – she was a giving kind of girl. And men like that, they happy to take. They don't know how to give, how to care for a woman's heart. They take the body and throw away the heart as if is just a snack they couldn't finish eating.' She sighed and shook her head. 'Cassie made mistakes, and you are the result. But in the end, you wasn't a mistake. She always wanted you, love you before you were born. "If it's a girl, I'll call her Rita," she said. 'That's how you got your name. She name you after Rita Hayworth, that actress who used to dance in those films with Fred Astaire. She had seen some film with her dancing down in Town.'

'And *her* name? Why did you call her Cassandra? It's such a rare name – from Shakespeare, right?'

Rita doubted that Granny read Shakespeare. She read little more than *Woman's Own*, the Bible, the *Daily Word*, and the occasional newspaper that made its way to Blackwater Creek.

Granny laughed. 'When I was pregnant with Penny, somebody gave me a *Woman's Own* because it had an article in it about baby names. It said that the baby name revealed its future and it would be good to give a baby a positive name, and it said that posh names were now in fashion and gave a list of posh names. So, I chose Penelope.'

Granny pronounced it Penny-lope, but Rita didn't correct her. Granny continued: 'It's a Greek name, the article said, and it listed other Greek names, and names from Shakespeare, and Biblical names. I kept the magazine and when I was pregnant with Cassie, I looked at it again and picked that name. I just liked it.'

'There's a singer called Mama Cass,' said Rita. 'My favourite singer! I used to listen to her and think it was my mummy singing, and even pray to her. Listen!'

She ran off to fetch her cassette recorder, pushed a button, wound the tape back and forth until she found the place she was looking for: 'Dream a Little Dream of Me'.

'Listen to the words, Granny!' Rita said. 'I used to do that: every night before I went to sleep, I would promise myself to dream of Mummy. Mama Cassie, I used to call her, and imagine she was watching over me, coming to me in my dreams, singing that song. Daddy said it was one of her favourites. And I used to cry, sometimes, because I missed her so badly.'

Her eyes filled with tears now, and Granny, whose own eyes grew moist, wiped a leaked tear away with a corner of her apron.

Rita whispered: 'Please tell me, Granny. How did she die? I know you said you wouldn't, because Daddy told you not to. But—'

Granny took Rita's hands in hers, caught her granddaughter's gaze. 'It's in the past, sweetheart. One day you'll know. Your daddy will tell you, and it will help *him* to tell you. But, it won't help *you*. Knowing those things ain't going to heal you.' She paused, as if making a decision. Rita waited. Granny spoke again:

'You got another wound in your heart. A deep, deep wound you can't even see yet. I know it, I can see it, but you can't. It don't have nothing to do with your mummy's death.'

'Then what?'

But Granny only shook her head. 'You got to find it out by yourself. You can't heal that wound if I tell you. You got to *feel* it, feel it until your whole body shake with tears, good tears. And then you will be healed, I promise. The tears will heal you. Good tears heal.'

She leaned forward, and kissed Rita on the forehead.

'Night-night, sweetheart. Think about it.'

When Granny had gone, Rita reached under her pillow for her diary, her pen and her torch.

Dear Diary, this is goodbye, forever. Somehow, it's over, me and you. I haven't even written in you again, since that wonderful night at Shell Beach, and you know, I think it's because I don't need you any more?

And that's not a bad thing. It's as if there are two me's, a sad, confused, turbulent me, and <u>another</u> me that is whole and healed and comfortable, but hidden; and you were the first me, and the whole time the first me was reaching out to that <u>other</u> me by writing to you and telling you everything so that you could help. And you did help. You helped right up to that night, and that night on the beach when the mother turtle came out of the sea to lay her eggs, and I thought of her making that long, long journey across the ocean just to lay her eggs where she herself was born – it's such a miracle, isn't it? And I was born here, too, and I came back, and coming back helped me so much. Helped me, but didn't heal me. I've got a long way to go now. Granny says there's a wound deep inside and I need to heal that too. Granny talks in such riddles sometimes, but I think she's right. I think she sees something I can't see. She knows something I don't know and it's not just about Mummy's death.

I wish Mummy hadn't died. I wish nobody would dig up turtle eggs and eat them. I wish I had known Mummy. I wish I could talk to that mother turtle, sing to her, dance with her. I wish so many things, but like Granny says, so many things we wish for and we can't have, but we can always dream, and we can always be happy, even when the things we want are impossible. Because Granny says it's not about <u>getting</u> happiness, it's about <u>being</u> happiness, and I felt it that night on the beach, with the turtle. And that's going to be my motto from now on and even for evermore (that's from some prayer I once learned, funny how it came out like that!). And from now on I'm going to be talking to Mummy in my heart, because I found her there, and she is listening.

And I promise to try harder at school and with Chandra and with Daddy and be tidier at home and nicer to my friends. I promise to be a better person. I promise to be the person you taught me to be, Granny taught me to be, Dutch taught me to be (yes, I still have a crush on him but he'll never know and he's much too old anyway).

And even the mother turtle taught me how to be a better person. All that effort she made, to come all that way and lay her eggs! I will never forget her. And I will come back, when I'm a better person. I'm going to miss them all, Granny and Aunty Penny and Kathy, and Grandpa and Uncle Douglas and Pete and George. And, of course, Dutch. The French word for goodbye is <u>au revoir</u>. The Spanish is <u>hasta la vista</u>. The German is <u>auf Wiedersehen</u>. They all mean, <u>until we meet again</u>, and that's how I feel.

But to you, dear Diary, this is goodbye, forever. But I will keep you, and one day when I'm old, I'll read you again and remember.

Thank you.
Love Rita

Chapter Thirty-Seven

The Few Good Ones

Jitty knocked and without waiting for an answer, popped his head round the door. Rita was already in bed. Her suitcase still lay on the floor, half unpacked; her bedside lamp was on, and she was reading: *My Friend Flicka*, which she had not once picked up while in the Pomeroon.

'Well,' he said, 'welcome home, stranger!'

'Hi Daddy!'

He came in and sat on her bedside. They spoke through the mosquito net.

'Bet you're glad to be back in civilisation! How were all the trees?'

'Don't joke about it, Daddy! I had a good time!'

'You liked your granny? Got on well with her?'

'Of course. She's nice.'

'What did you do? Didn't you miss Town? Your friends?'

'Not at all. I met some nice people.'

'Really?'

'Yes, really.'

She didn't feel at all like chatting, but he wasn't getting the message.

His eyes fell on a photo on her side table, leaning against the lamp. She'd have to buy a frame for it, one day soon. He picked it up.

'Where did you get this?'

'Granny gave it to me.'

He put it back, saying nothing. Rita dropped her eyes back to the book. Jitty sat for a while, saying nothing, and then he said, 'Did she tell you?'

'Tell me what?'

'You know. About your mother.'

'Oh, that. No, she said it's your story to tell.'

'Oh! She did?'

'Yes.' Suddenly Rita clapped the book closed and sat up straight in bed.

'So, tell me. Now. It's a great time.'

'Now? Look, darling, it's a long story and you're tired and I just came back from work. It's really a bad time. I just came to say good night.'

'Well, good night then.'

She slipped back under the sheet, picked up her book again. She even managed a yawn as she looked down at the page.

'Don't be like that, darling! It's not exactly a story I can tell in five minutes!'

'Look, Daddy, I'm beginning to lose interest in this whole bloody game. This whole secret drama, like some Sherlock Holmes' mission and I have to investigate. Let's just drop the whole thing if you're not going to come out with it.'

'It's not that, darling. I'll tell you, I really will, but it has to be the right time, and…'

'All this secrecy! And I really don't care all that much any more. The only thing I cared about really is that I didn't kill her when I was born, like Donna deSouza said.'

'That stupid story again! You never believed it, did you?'

'I didn't, but in a way, I did. Deep inside, I wondered. But now…'

Through the net, she pointed at the photo. 'Now I know. Because of that. That was after the birth. It's Mum and Granny and me, so I obviously didn't kill her, and that's all that matters.

Because thinking I killed her was killing me! But since the photo, it's OK. She died, and it's in the past, and whatever quarrel you and Granny had, and I know you had some quarrel, because she can't stand you, well, it sounds to me like some teenage melodrama. I just don't care— Daddy! What's wrong?'

Jitty had buried his face in his hands and his shoulders heaved with sobs. Rita moved forward, pulled back the net and hugged him.

'Daddy, what's the matter? Tell me!'

'I can't, I just can't. I will tell you, I promise. Just not now.'

Rita pulled away from him and crawled under the net again, under her sheet.

'When, then?'

'When you're eighteen.'

'Oh really? So, I have three years to look forward to it. It better be good, Daddy.' She yawned again. 'Look, I'm tired. I'll see you in the morning. Good night.'

Jitty leaned forward and kissed her through the net. As he walked towards the door, Rita called out: 'And you never keep your promises anyway.'

She switched off the light before he'd even opened the door.

She was back home, and overnight, it seemed the world had become a different place. As if Granny had given her a magic formula, and everything dark and gloomy had changed to light; but she knew that in fact nothing had changed, *she* had changed. The sense of worthlessness that had followed her like a shadow all her life had miraculously vanished into nothing.

A certain inner verve lit her from within, and now even Chandra was nicer to her, welcoming her home with a big smile, as if she was actually *pleased* to see her. And Luisa had jumped into her arms and proclaimed: 'I missed you, I missed you, I missed you! You shouldn't ever go away again!'

And over the next few days Jitty paid her more attention, and the popularity she'd had as a child – it all came flooding back, as well as the naughty spark that had once simultaneously exasperated and entertained others.

Rita, everyone said, was a *character* – eccentric to the tips of her fingers. And they rolled their eyes upwards and smiled knowingly, fondly, to each other.

They invited her to parties, to their homes; all the girls wanted to be her friend, but Polly was still her closest confidante, and it was with Polly she could share her heart and it was with Polly she could laugh and, sometimes, cry.

As far as boys were concerned, Rita had learned two important lessons. One was from Ross, and it was Keep Your Bloody Hands Off Me. The other was from Dutch. Dutch, far off in the Pomeroon, attained a place on a pedestal. He remained etched in her memory as a young god, a dark, mobile David of sorts, one who had done no wrong, but brought joy and life and substance to her life, and had done so in only two weeks. Dutch might be unattainable: too old, too wonderful, too wise, too utterly *divine*, and he'd probably find some goddess to marry because she, Rita, was just a silly girl who had said silly things about dancing on the beach, and why would he ever remember her?

But Dutch had given her a gold standard. Compared to him, all these Town boys were just that – boys, who knew nothing of any consequence and talked only of motorbikes and Rambo and huddled at parties, eyeing up girls and had straying hands.

Polly laughed at her devotion. 'He can't be *that* perfect – no boy is!'

'Well, he's as near perfect as a boy can be, and nobody else can live up to him.'

'So, what then, if you can't get him because he's a god and you are only human? You're going to stay a spinster forever?'

Rita crumpled. 'I don't know, I just don't know. It's just that, well, after Ross, and then after Dutch, they just all seem so, so, I don't know. I just don't like anyone that much any more.'

Polly sighed. 'I wish I could be that complacent. I wish...'

Rita listened, for the first time, as Polly poured out her own heart, listened as she had never really listened before, so absorbed had she been in her own problems and heartbreaks, so oblivious to Polly's own inner frailty.

Polly, it turned out, was still desperately in love with Bobby Fung of Fung's Funeral parlour, who was pestering her to 'do it' with him, but she didn't really want to; and it was a secret because her father would kill her and him if he found out that they planned to marry, because her father had other, higher plans for her, and she wasn't sure if she wanted to be a micro-biologist any more, and she could well see herself as the wife of someone who worked at a funeral parlour, even if it *was* a bit creepy, and what did education *matter* anyway? Surely the most important thing in life was love? And pleasing the one you loved? Being kind to him and giving him what he asked for, even if you didn't really want to? Because if she *didn't*, he'd break up with her, and...

'Then he's not worthy of you!' said Rita right away; and saying that opened a door to a dozen new insights concerning boys, and together, they worked out the best words to say, the best strategies that would keep Polly's dignity intact and her heart from being broken; and what to do about Brian Coolidge, who was pestering Rita to go steady with him but she couldn't, because now there was Dutch, and Brian wasn't fit to tie Dutch's shoelaces. And it was she and Polly against the world.

'I hate men!' said Polly. Polly was furious with her father; the highly respected Dr Wong, had left Aunty Jenny for a young nurse and a divorce was pending. It had hit Polly hard. Aunty Jenny, however, had quickly pulled herself together and now that the children were older was working as a dentist.

'They're not *all* bad,' said Rita, thinking of Dutch. 'We just have to find the few good ones. Sort out the wolves and discard them.'

At school, Rita remembered Granny's words and listened: listened to her mother's voice from within. In all subjects, she improved, drastically so – but it was in English that she shone, and in English, that she most exasperated. There were days when she would suddenly snap into life and start writing furiously, right there in class, stopping only for seconds to chew her pen, scratch her head, before scribbling away again.

It was Miss King who finally found the red exercise book. It was filled with poems, dedicated to her teachers.

> *Our Miss Norse should change her name.*
> *Her pupils twist it: such a shame!*
> *When walking fast she's in a canter,*
> *and pupils laugh in horsey banter.*
> *When Mr Baichoo he did sneeze,*
> *he made a loud and awful breeze*
> *that rolled the chalk onto the floor,*
> *which had us laughing all the more.*
> *Mrs McIntyre we all love,*
> *she's overinflated, waist above.*
> *I wondered if a pin I stick,*
> *will she deflate by simple prick?*
> *Mr Currie's a friendly fellow*
> *but vex him and he starts to bellow.*
> *Homework we do fear to mention:*
> *quickly puts you in detention.*

Rumour had it that the exercise book was passed around the staffroom and had the teachers in stitches. The guilty author was called to Mrs Clark's room.

'Rita!' said the headmistress, shaking her head slowly. 'What are we going to do with you? You really should put your talent to better use. I *should* suspend you – but you've improved so much, I'll let you off this time.'

'No! Oh, please suspend me! For a week! So I can go and see my granny!'

But Rita's punishment was detention, and to write an essay on the school motto, *Labor Omnia Vincit*.

She was ordered to stay after school on a Friday, sit alone with nothing on her desk but an exercise book and a pen, watched over by a teacher. She sat for ten minutes with a blank mind, and an hour's time to write.

She could not think of a single word.

She looked at the essay title. The first word. *Labor*. Work. But also labour. The female kind. The birthing kind. The kind that brings every human creature into the world... every mammal...

She put pen to paper and wrote: 'I have never known my mother; she died when I was a baby. But she gave birth to me, and held me in her arms; and a photo of her holding me is all I have of her. She gave me life through labour, through the miracle of birth, and I will always remember her.

'But last week I witnessed a mother giving life in a different way, a different kind of labour: a leatherback turtle laying her eggs. And witnessing that labour not only healed me but made me fall in love with this magnificent creature...'

From then on it was easy. She wrote in rhapsody about the turtle, its life in the sea, the thousands of miles it swims to return to the beach of its birth; about the eggs that need protection and the hatchlings running back to the ocean...

At the end of the hour she hadn't finished, but had to hand in what she had written. That weekend, she finished the essay and handed it in on Monday.

On Tuesday, she was once again summoned to Mrs Clark's office, and this time she was greeted by an all-embracing smile.

'Rita, this is a magnificent essay, the best you've ever written,' said Mrs Clark. 'I'd like your permission to send it in to the *Chronicle*.'

The *Chronicle* published it in their *Weekend Family* supplement, on the Youth page, and Jitty was beside himself with pride. 'Another writer in the family!' he said. 'I always knew you were clever!'

Rita only shrugged, hiding her own pride behind a mask of indifference. This was the beginning. Next year there were exams to sit, and that would be the test.

'You can do it!' said Mrs Clark.

'You can do it!' said Jitty.

'I can do it!' Rita told herself and buried herself in books.

And buried in books, slowly, slowly, the memory of the Pomeroon, of those glorious two weeks spent on Blackwater Creek, faded. All that remained were the letters: letters to Kathy, her new little sister, flew back and forth with monthly regularity, her last link to the place she called heaven, the place where she was closest to her mother. But gradually, the memory of Granny, Aunty Penny, of Dutch and even of Kathy grew dim.

They were all so far away, living in a different world. They attained a dreamlike quality, an unattainable perfection far from her daily reality; the time spent with them a single shining jewel that, as the weeks passed and the months and finally the year, grew so dull as to be lost among the detritus of everyday life, amid the demands of schoolwork and the goal she had set herself.

She would never be an egghead, would never find satisfaction in academia. But exams were the next reality, a test of herself. She determined to do well, for Cassie's sake. To overcome her inherent laziness and disinterest when it came to schoolwork, leading to poor results. The article's success gave her new confidence, new motivation, new energy. She reached out to her mother, spoke to her constantly, asked for help and guidance, and as if Cassie, somewhere, had heard, and was whispering to her, she mastered school.

Guyana's educational system had changed in the last few years, from a British one to a Caribbean one, the Caribbean Secondary Education Certificate exams, known as the CXC, the equivalent of O-levels.

To her astonishment and delight, Rita not only passed well but achieved distinctions in English, French and Spanish. Up to now, she'd convinced herself of poor results, and made up her mind to leave school after CXC. With these results, though, she could defer leaving for a further two years, and sit the Caribbean Advanced Proficiency Examination – CAPE – exams, which had replaced A-levels.

'But,' she warned Jitty, 'I am not going to university. You got that? I am not going to university!'

Chapter Thirty-Eight

Tooting

Aunt Mary's letter slipped into the letterbox and everything changed in the blink of an eye.

My dear Jitty,

I do hope you and your family are well. I was so happy to receive a letter from your daughter Rita a few years ago – I did reply, but didn't hear from her again – I wonder if my letter arrived? It made me happy, and a bit homesick, to reconnect with family. Family is indeed everything, is it not?

The older I get, the more I think of you all, and today I come with a request that I hope you will grant. I am quite desperate. I know you are not the best letter-writer, and neither have I been. I do wish we had kept more in contact with each other, but only now I realise that it's my fault. You were my last living relative and I neglected you as a child and instead ran away to England at the first opportunity. I feel we should breach that distance, repair the relationship. I am so sorry.

Roland was a good husband and I have no complaints. He looked after me in every way, right up to his death last year, but quite honestly, he's not really family, and he's English, and he could never understand. I have been homesick for many years and since his death thought of coming home to spend the evening of my life – I know I will always be welcomed back in Kaieteur Close, which is my home as well as yours. You were always a good nephew to me, even with your wildness. You were fond of me, weren't you? As I was of you.

Jitty paused in the reading – they were all at the dinner table – and cried, 'Good Lord! Aunt Mary wants to come home! To live with us!'

'Over my dead body!' said Chandra.

Jitty returned to his letter.

However, it is not to be. I have been diagnosed with cancer and I don't have long to live, the doctor says. Of course it is terrible news for me and I am all alone in this country. I have no relatives and have made few friends – it is hard to make friends in a new country and of course the attitude towards immigrants is not very welcoming. So here am I rattling around in this big house in Tooting with nobody to talk to. The evening of my life to be spent in utter loneliness.

Coming back home is out of the question. My treatment under the NHS will be excellent. I'll be in and out of hospital and even have home care, if and when needed. I am so lucky to be in the best medical hands, here in London, but it's family I want more than anything, and you are my only family.

So, it is only now that I realise my faults and how negligent I have been – can we not put this right? The one good thing I did for you was to have you baptised after your parents died. But I should have been a better godmother, closer to you.

Can you not come, Jitty, and visit me? I know you have your job, but if you came for just a month or two, if that is possible, it would make a world of difference!

That is all I have to say now, though I should mention that I will of course pay for your travel and all expenses. I do have quite a bit of savings – we have lived modestly – and of course this house will come to you when I pass on.

Please, please, Jitty, please come! You can bring your family too, if you'd like – I'd love to meet them all, especially Rita! Such a kind girl, to write to an old aunty! You are all welcome. All the more company for me!

'Oh, my dear, you must go!' cried Chandra. 'The poor thing! You must go as soon as possible!'

'That's what I was thinking,' Jitty said, replacing the letter in its envelope. 'It's my duty. I can't leave her alone at this time.' He turned to Rita. 'I didn't know you had written to her. When was that?'

Rita shrugged. 'Oh, years ago. She did write back, but I kind of forgot to write again.' She felt a twinge of guilt – Granny would definitely disapprove.

Chandra said: 'She didn't say how long she has to live, did she?'

'No, no mention. "Not long" could mean anything from a few weeks to a few months to a year or two. I wish she'd been clearer.'

'She does seem in a hurry to get me over,' said Jitty, 'and that last mention of the house…'

'Jitty, this might be our chance! You know…'

They looked at each other across the table, each knowing what the other was thinking, but not speaking it out loud. There had been talk of emigration for some time now. Canada, where Chandra had relatives, or England, where Jitty had Aunt Mary. There was talk of needing a sponsor, and the visa problems, and a place to stay – but surely those were problems that could be solved. And now, here, the last and most serious of those problems had been solved, just like that.

It must be Destiny.

Jitty slapped his hand down on the table.

'We must all go!' he said. 'Poor Aunt Mary – I was always fond of her as a child. And she's never met any of you. We must go and be by her side!'

'She did say she has a big house. Rattling around, she said. So, there must be room, if she can invite all of us like that.'

'Yes, that's what it sounds like. A big house. And we are all welcome.'

'She'll even pay for our plane tickets! Isn't that what she meant? Not just yours, all of our expenses?'

Jitty scanned the letter again. 'It's not clear – she first invited me alone, and offered to cover everything, but then at the end she says we must all come…'

'I'm sure she wants us all with her. An old lady like that, child-less – of course she'll want to meet the kids. Her last living relatives. She says she has savings – it means she wants to pay.'

'Yes, that's the message I'm getting. She wants us to be with her. She can afford it. I understand her husband was quite wealthy. And they had no children, so…'

'Let's go, Jitty. And not just for a visit. For good!'

And just like that, Jitty and his family attained the privileged status of Leavers.

'It's the opening of a door!' Jitty said, later. 'I'm sure I can get a job working for one of the big British newspapers. Chandra, you'll love London: the fashion capital of the world, after Paris! And you girls: Rita, you can finish your education and then go on to a British university, imagine! And we can put Luisa in a good private school. Of course we must all go!'

Rita had promised Granny and Kathy that she would return to the Pomeroon that year, and now felt guilt at her disloyalty: they would both be so disappointed – and of course she, too, would have loved to return – but the world of rivers and trees, of fish and turtles, had slipped far away from her grasp.

And really, what an opportunity: LONDON! Who wouldn't choose London over the Pomeroon and a dreary future with, at best, a University of Guyana degree or a job at the *Graphic*? It was what they called, these days, a no-brainer. As for Dutch: he'd anyway been an impossible dream. She'd meet better men in London, for sure. And she'd miss having a best friend, a Polly to share her life with. But London! *London, here I come*, her heart sang.

The plans to emigrate brought the family together as never before. Chandra took both girls shopping for new clothes: Rita got a pair of Levi jeans, to her great delight, and Luisa three ready-made dresses from Fogarty's.

Jitty considered burning down the last bridge and selling the Kaieteur Close house, but at the last moment changed his mind; the house was, after all, his history, and who knew, maybe one day Guyana would take off; oil would be discovered or something and there'd be an economic boom and then they could all come back. He rented it to a single male colleague of his.

As was usual, the entire family came to the airport to see them off. The entire family meaning Chandra's family, as Jitty had nobody except Rita, and Rita had nobody except Granny, Granpa and Aunty Penny, none of whom could come down from the Pomeroon. And so it was just all the Jhas who came. Some came all the way from Berbice, all in their Sunday best, as one did when a relative took off for the great Abroad.

There was much weeping and hugging and more hugging and more weeping – all for Chandra and Luisa – and then waving, as the Leaving party walked across the tarmac to the BOAC jet, and the Remaining party waved frantically from the viewing balcony; more waving as they stood on the steps to the cabin; and then they were in the plane, and Chandra had another weeping fit; and then they were off, in the air, on their way to a brilliant new life.

*

They took a taxi straight from Heathrow to the house in Tooting (Luisa was having lots of fun with that name: *I'm going to be tweeting in Twooting!* she kept saying, and everyone laughed to humour her). The car turned into a street lined on both sides with terraced houses, cars parked along both sides of the road. There was no space to park, so the taxi stopped on the road and they all piled out; luckily, there was little traffic and so there was not much of a hold-up, though the taxi driver did seem keen to get rid of them all, plonking their luggage on the street, taking his money, and slamming the door with unnecessary verve.

'Did he just say bloody immigrants?' Jitty said to Chandra, but she was busy looking at the house beyond the pavement – really, just a door in the wall, with a number above it, as you couldn't tell where one house ended and the next began.

'A *big* house, the letter said!' she muttered, but Jitty had already grabbed two suitcases and was walking up the steps leading to the door. He rang the bell, and it opened.

A buxom black woman in a white uniform opened the door.

'You must be the Maraj family!' she said in a strong Barbadian accent. 'Welcome to London! Your aunty can't wait to see you!'

They all entered, one by one, lined up in a narrow hallway smelling slightly of boiled cabbage and Dettol, with a slight tinge of what could only be some unmentionable human waste. The overall smell was of sickness. Aunt Mary's living room had been turned into a sickroom, and that was where she lay, in a hospital bed. She held out her arms to Jitty, who, a big smile plastered across his face, leaned down to kiss her on both withered cheeks. This was not the Aunt Mary of his memory, and he drew away quickly to make room for Chandra, Rita and Luisa, who all received their welcome hugs in turn, all pulling away as quickly as they could.

Aunt Mary was so overjoyed, she died the very next day.

The house, it turned out, far from being the mansion in Belgravia of Chandra's imagination (which was how she interpreted 'big'), turned out to be a two-up, two-down, cramped, narrow mid-terrace, sadly in need of renovation, with ancient brightly patterned but worn red carpets, a badly cracked olive-coloured bathtub, a handkerchief backyard and three cats, plus a noisy road outside.

Rita and Luisa were forced to share a room for the first time in their lives; not an easy arrangement as the sisters had grown even further apart since Rita's Pomeroon trip. Luisa was now quite blatantly on Chandra's side and followed Chandra's lead in every way; which meant, now, disgruntlement and constant complaints and comparisons. They all made complaints and comparisons, and the Tooting house was simply not up to scratch. The cold water was too cold and the hot too hot and they all missed their daily showers (why sit in your own dirty water, they wondered?). Under the circumstances, it was Number Seven that seemed palatial in comparison.

There were other problems. Aunt Mary's savings didn't allow for a private school for Luisa and she didn't adjust to the local primary. Rita went to enrol in the local college, and was called in for an advisory interview. She had planned to start A-level courses in English, Spanish and French; the college also offered a course in Journalism, and Rita was tempted. So many opportunities, here in London! But the student adviser, a fortyish woman with cat-eye glasses, enthusiastically pointed her in another direction: 'You have to think ahead!' she said. 'Of your career opportunities! Everybody wants to be a journalist – they think it's glamorous, but it's hard to get work.'

Rita thought of Jitty's struggles finding work, and nodded. The adviser continued: 'You should definitely look to Computer Science. Computers are the future. A whole new world is going to open up in a few years, and you'll be right on the spot!'

So, Rita took that advice and started a course in Computer Science. She hated it from the start. She hated college from the start. It surprised her, because most of the pupils were dark-skinned, like her, this being an area of high immigration, especially from the Caribbean. But nobody spoke to her at all for the first few days; everyone had their own friends and nobody was even mildly curious about her, the newcomer. How different to back home, where every newcomer was immediately pounced on, immediately overwhelmed with invitations and questioning, often too much to handle!

On the fourth day, however, at the college canteen, a tall black girl slipped into the chair next to her and said hello. And smiled.

'Hello,' said Rita. The girl picked up knife and fork and began to eat. 'You're new, aren't you? New to the area, too?'

'New to the country,' said Rita.

'Welcome, then. I'm Tonia!'

Tonia, it turned out, was second-generation Trinidadian, born and bred in Balham. She was also an outspoken activist for black rights. Discovering Rita's vaguely apolitical stance, she set about winning her to the cause. The very next day she brought a book and put it into Rita's hands: 'This will tell you all you need to know!'

Rita looked at the cover: *The Autobiography of Malcolm X*. She flipped through the pages.

'I'll read it,' said Rita. 'You know something? It'll be the very first book I ever read by a black author, or with black characters.'

'There you have it!' said Tonia.

But apart from her friendship with Tonia, Rita felt more than ever that she was a stranger in a strange land, unable to find her place in this city that cared not a whit for her.

It was the same for all of them.

Jitty, though armed with newspaper clippings of his features about and interviews with Mahalia Jackson, Muhammad Ali, Fidel Castro, Stokely Carmichael and Miriam Makeba, couldn't get a job at any newspaper, big or small. He lacked local knowledge, they said, and the competition was strong.

In the end he found a job as part-time proofreader for a local rag, and another job at a nearby shop selling Caribbean and Indian goods.

'Why don't you try to contact your English grandmother?' he said to Chandra after the fourth rejection. 'She might have other ideas.'

'But I never met her! And – she's old! What can she do? And I'm a bit nervous about those Fogartys. You never know with white people.'

'Let's at least try. Where does she live? Not in London, you said. But where? Maybe another city. I heard there are lots of Indians in Birmingham.'

Chandra fetched her address book, opened it.

'Cork,' she said. 'She lives in Cork.'

'Cork! That's in Ireland! I'm not going to Ireland! You know the troubles they're having over there?'

'How should I know where Cork is? You're the geography expert. Anyway, it's all one, isn't it, England, Scotland, Wales, Ireland? I do know my grandparents were English, though, and because of that, I have the right to British nationality.'

'Maybe you should write to her anyway. We can't possibly move to Ireland, but we might need some documents for you if we stay here.'

'Well, we can try. But those Fogartys – I don't know. There was an awful fuss when Mummy married an Indian. They didn't like it. Grandad came round in the end but who knows what his wife thinks. And the rest of the family – to them, I'm just a bloody half-caste.'

Rita, on hearing that word, turned away to suppress a chuckle, remembering the half-caste debacle years ago. It was good to see the shoe on Chandra's other foot.

'Write to her,' Jitty said firmly.

She did, and received a reply saying that Grandmother was in a nursing home and *absolutely* unable to help. The letter made it abundantly clear, in charmingly polite language, that none of the other Fogartys wanted anything to do with Chandra.

Chandra was dissatisfied on another account: what good was the latest London fashion, she thought, when you had nowhere to go where you could show it off, no friends, no parties, no invitations? Once a boy cornered Rita in an empty hallway at college, and groped her. She managed to fight her way free. They didn't have a car. Nobody knew them. One night, six months after they first arrived, when Jitty was walking home from a late shift, a bunch of drunk white teenagers chased him, outran him, wrestled him to the pavement, called him Paki, and beat him up. He came home bleeding from his forehead and said, with finality, 'That's it. We're going home.'

They were all back in Guyana by the end of the year, travelling this time by sea, a passenger ship called the *Columbie*; Aunt Mary's savings had been mostly spent and there wasn't enough for flights. Better to be a big fish in a small pond, Jitty said, than a small, insignificant, ignored, maligned one in a shark-infested ocean.

'Too many white people,' Jitty said, 'and they don't like us.'

As the ship approached the South American shoreline, all the Guyanese on board – and it was practically all Guyanese by now, several passengers having left the ship at Kingston and Port of Spain – gathered at the rails. Somebody began to sing, and everybody joined in:

> When your ship has passed the islands
> and the blue sea turns to brown,
> And the leadsman calls 'Five Fathoms'
> when he casts the lead line down,
> And you see a long flat coastland and
> a smokeless wooden town,
> You can know that you are nearing Demerara.
> Demerara, Demerara, you can know
> that you are nearing Demerara.

*

A lump rose in Rita's throat. This was home. She'd never thought of herself as patriotic, but she loved this corner of the world. It was hers; it had nourished her, like a mother. She sang as loudly as all the others, embracing the corny nostalgia folding in around her. Home again.

Jitty turned out the colleague renting Number Seven and returned to his old job at the *Graphic*; they were happy to have him back. Chandra showed off her newly acquired London fashions to the envy of her old friends, Rita returned to Bishops' for her two-year CAPE course, Luisa, now eight, returned to St Margaret's Primary, and life returned to normal, missing hardly a beat.

They were neither Leavers nor Remainers; they were Returnees; but relieved and happy Returnees, more appreciative than ever of the serene grandeur of Number Seven and the friends who closed in around them in welcome.

Chapter Thirty-Nine

Cornrows

The one thing, or rather, person, Rita missed about London was Tonia. Tonia had the makings of a good friend, as close as Polly, yet different. Whereas Polly was a sobering influence, a girl who walked the straight and narrow, who made sensible decisions and encouraged Rita to do the same, and for that reason would always come out on top, Tonia was a rebel. She broke the rules and surged forwards into new territory, and for that reason alone earned Rita's admiration and respect.

Tonia woke Rita up to an aspect of her life she had completely ignored up to now. Growing up in Guyana, a country that prided itself on its six races, a nation that liked to pretend that those six races all lived together in perfect harmony, Rita knew that it was not so. It was all very well growing up in Kaieteur Close with its closed community of rainbow families; outside, in the streets, in the villages, in the ghetto of Tiger Bay and the halls of power and the voting booths – and, of course, written down in black and white in her own father's editorials – Rita knew that the country was terribly, horribly divided. She knew of the infighting and the name-calling and the voting-by-race that pulled the very fabric of society apart. Until now she had stayed out of the fray. But Tonia had told her this was wrong, utterly wrong. She needed, urgently, to uncover, and take pride in, her identity. As *black*.

'But I'm not, not really!' Rita had protested, at first. 'I'm half Indian; my grandmother is Amerindian. Only my grandfather was black, and even that was diluted. With Portuguese.'

Tonia waved her objections away. 'Ever heard of the One Drop Rule? It's what defined racism, back in the day. If they discovered just one black African ancestor, no matter how far back, you counted as black. Watch Harry Belafonte in *Island in the Sun*. A good movie, tells all. They used it to reinforce racism. We use it to reinforce pride.'

She held up a strand of Rita's hair, a crispy black spiral. 'You're black, sweetheart. Own it. Your hair gives you away: nothing Indian about your hair! No long black silky tresses! Black is your strength. It's your secret power. It's your heritage. Stand up for it!'

Indeed. Granpa's black African blood came out in full strength in Rita: her hair told the tale. Rita's hair, when she let it out, was black, strong and wayward, a mane of stubborn kinks and crinkles. Since Chandra had cut it all off when Rita was seven, Rita had refused to cut it ever again; but the only way to keep it under any control at all – and control was needed, if she was not to invoke not only Chandra's wrath but the wrath of school teachers and headmistresses – was to keep it plaited and either hanging on her shoulders or clipped against her scalp. Let loose it was a black halo of defiance, springing from her head in wild, strong abundance, refusing to be tamed – rather like Rita herself.

'Your hair tells the story,' Tonia had said, having, one afternoon, loosened its constraints and plunged her hands into the centre of the mass of coils and twists, scrunching it up, revelling in its strength and resilience. 'You're black, Rita, black and beautiful. Reclaim your identity!'

Tonia wore her own hair in shortish dreadlocks; Bob Marley was her hero, his hair her model; but for Rita, she recommended something else.

'Cornrows!' she said. 'Cornrows would be perfect for you!' And that very afternoon she dragged Rita off to a Caribbean-run hair salon in Brixton, where her Barbadian stylist friend Brenda plunged her fingers into the mad bush on Rita's head, held up one long strand for inspection, and said, 'Beautiful! Beautiful! I'll make an appointment for Saturday. It'll take a few hours.'

And that was it. Rita was not allowed to look in the mirror until it was all done; all she felt during the procedure were fingers probing and pulling and plaiting, and the intense pain as Brenda worked her magic. And then:

'Wow!' she said, gazing at her image in the mirror, turning her head back and forth. 'I can't believe that's me!'

'You have a fantastic skull and it looks just great!' said Brenda. 'Now, I'll give you some tips as to how to take care of it.'

'How long will it last?'

Brenda shrugged. 'Depends. Six weeks, ten? Come back and we'll have another go.'

And just like that, Rita found what Tonia called her black identity, proudly demonstrated by her hair.

Rita had kept her cornrows, renewing them every two months, until she arrived back in Guyana. And her identity was still, for the time being, black.

The Autobiography of Malcom X had changed her, radically, plunged her onto a path that turned into a quest. She'd moved on to *The Fire Next Time* by James Baldwin, and other books on the black predicament. The more she read, the more answers she found, the more questions arose. What lesson did history have for her, personally? For her people? Who *were* her people? What was the legacy of slavery, here in Guyana? How could people of African heritage free themselves from the yoke left behind by the British; a yoke that told them they were inferior to, of less value than, their light-skinned counterparts? How could she free herself from that lesson ingrained into her very being: that white skin was better; and the more you could claim whiteness, the better you were?

Tonia had nailed it perfectly, when Rita had confessed to her past failures with men. She'd frowned. 'And you're saying they both were white?'

'Well – Archie Foot was *mostly* white. Light-skinned, mixed-race. Caramel-coloured.'

'That's white in my books. Anyone aspiring to be white is white inside. A traitor; proud of their whiteness. And the other guy was proper white, I bet.'

Rita nodded.

'Yes. Ross was white American.'

'The worst kind of white. No wonder he wanted to screw you. In every sense of the word. Rita, you need a brother. A good black brother. Be black and proud. It's time!'

And Rita had embraced Tonia's teaching with heart and soul. This was what was missing from her life. A sense of identity. Of black identity. *Identity* would be the cure for all her ills. She needed to find herself first, build on that. Everything else would come later.

Chapter Forty

A Nice Little Place

Now, back in Guyana, Rita continued her quest to establish herself firmly on the side of the underdogs, the lowest rank on the racial hierarchy that made up the social fabric of her home. Guyana might have a black president in Forbes Burnham, a (mostly) black Cabinet and civil service, a (mostly) black police force, a (mostly) black army, but everyone knew the truth: white skin trumped everything else.

But she was still a novice. She had so much to learn. She gathered books on black history, black politics, Black Power; she borrowed them from the library, piles of them, and, occasionally, bought herself one.

A month after her return from England, she stood before the Black Politics shelf at Austin's Book Shop. She opened one book, leafed through it, put it back on the shelf, took out another. These were new releases; the very latest, written by black academics in the USA and the UK.

'Looking for something really good?' said a voice next to her. She had been so absorbed in her browsing, she had not noticed him. A tall, very black, slender man standing not too far from her.

He took a book from the shelf and placed it in her hands. 'Try this,' he said. She glanced at the book: *How Europe Underdeveloped Africa* by Walter Rodney.

'Oh!' she said, 'my father knew him! He – Dad – was in the WPA, and really admired Rodney!'

'Really? Then you should too.' He held out his hand. 'Jamal,' he said. 'Pleased to meet you.'

Rita shook his hand, and introduced herself. 'Ah! So, your dad is *that* Jitendra Maraj? A good writer; I always read his articles. But he's Indian! And you're black?'

There was a question in his voice, an invitation. He smiled down at her. He had kindly eyes, large and soulful, eyes that seemed to know her intimately, eyes that made her, ever so slightly, squirm. Eyes in a face that was handsome, skin like polished mahogany; a wide mouth, perfect white teeth, hair cropped short, a neat black mossy cap. She didn't know what to say.

'Um, yes, well, my grandfather was black, and…'

'…and black blood is dominant. That should tell you everything. Humans began in Africa; Eve, if she existed, was black. Black is the way to go. I'm glad you're looking into it.'

'Um, yes, I've been reading…'

'Tell you what, save your money.' He took the book from her hands, slotted it back onto the shelf. 'I've got all his books, and more. I'll lend you them. Rita, I think you and I are going to be the best of friends.' He winked, and gave a little wobble of his head.

'So, what say you? Like to come to a cafe and we'll talk some more?'

'Yes, why not?'

Rita smiled back, and the two of them left the bookshop. Jamal's car was parked a short distance away; he opened the passenger door for her and she got in. He drove off.

'Where are we going?'

'I know a nice little place, out of town.'

He took her to an upstairs cafe in Kitty village. It was basic, but clean. They ordered a Coke for him, a ginger ale for her. 'I love your hair!' he said, reaching out and lifting one of the long, thin, beaded plaits that fell over her shoulder. 'Where did you get it done?'

She told him, and told him more about her life, and the conundrum she found herself in. 'I'm studying for CAPE now, but I have no idea what to do after that. Not many opportunities in this country.'

'Do that, and then go to the University of Guyana. Study Black History, it'll open your eyes even more.'

He, she found, was a teacher himself; a history teacher at Queen's College, twenty-eight years old. He'd studied Black History at Howard University in America and had come back 'because America is so damned racist'. He repeated the very words Jitty had said before their return: better to be a big fish in a small pond than a tiny fish in an ocean of sharks. And America was, he said, indeed an ocean of sharks for a black man. Here, he found the freedom to be himself. 'The racism here is different,' he said. 'We blacks are a majority, still dominated by a tiny minority of whites. That's bad enough, but compared to America, man, we're privileged!'

As they parted, he said, 'Can I see you again?' and she nodded. He had stopped at the entrance to Kaieteur Close. She made to open the door and step out, but he pulled her back and pecked her on the cheek. He stroked her face. 'You're so beautiful!' he said. She walked away, glowing inside; once he'd driven away, she ran all the way home, her thoughts and feelings all of a tangle. To sort herself out, she wrote Tonia a long letter.

'You're right,' it said. 'I need to find a brother-boyfriend. He's just so – different! I think, I think, this could be it!'

She was only seventeen, but something in her was on the search; on the search for that elusive IT. That Love that had a capital L. If only the right person could come her way. Not an Archie, not a Ross. Maybe a Jamal.

'Maybe,' she wrote to Tonia, 'Just maybe. He's so good-looking; you wouldn't believe it! And everything else, of course. I mean, good character. That's what counts, isn't it? Character.'

And so it began. Jamal lived in a small rented apartment in the Bottom House of a two-storeyed Carmichael Street residence, and it was there, after a whirlwind but suitably courteous courtship, she gave herself, in every way possible, to Jamal. He was everything a girl could want in a lover: kind and sweet and intelligent and gentle and attentive. *Loving*. He even used the word, Love.

'I love you. You're so beautiful,' he would say, stroking her cheeks. Even Tonia, a hard-core lesbian, would approve; and she did. *'Sounds good,'* she wrote in reply to Rita's first effusive letter, *'but watch your step. He's a man. You know what that means.'*

'He's one of the good ones!' Rita wrote back.

Until *that* Saturday afternoon. Rita and Jamal cosily wrapped together in his bed, naked, cuddling. A sharp knocking at the door. 'Damn,' said Jamal. 'Who could that be?' He rose from the bed, pulled on his trousers, walked out of the bedroom to open the front door.

The rest, for Rita, was a tangled mess of screaming and things crashing against walls, a woman's voice, high-pitched, furious; Jamal's voice, low, calm, trying to interrupt, screeched over; footsteps marching, the bedroom door flung open. In the doorway, a woman, a *white* woman, blond, hands on hips. Jamal, trying to pull her away; not succeeding, for she fought him off, tooth and nail, scratching and kicking and pointing at her, Rita.

'I knew it! I knew it! I knew I had to come and see for myself! You lying, scheming, two-timing bastard!'

Rita scrambled to get dressed while the woman hurled abuse at her. 'You bitch! Slut! This is MY man! I got a ring on my finger to prove it! I got a child back home in Washington, two years old! Stop chasing other women's men and get your slutty ass out of that bed, get your ass out of my husband's apartment! Little slut, you!'

Cheeks burning, Rita ran all the way home. And that was the end of her dating life.

'*Never again!*' she wrote to Tonia. '*They're all bad, every one of them. They only want one thing and they'll do anything they can to get it.*'

'*Try a woman next time!*' Tonia wrote back.

'*I don't have a black identity,*' Rita wrote next time, having digested it all; once she had recovered from the shame and the hurt of it all. '*I'm more than black, a lot more. Being black is just one little aspect of who I am, one little prism. It's not my whole identity. It's just my body, a black body I live in. A woman's body.*'

'*Traitor!*' was the reply, just one word, and a sketch of an angry face. No more letters crossed the Atlantic.

Rita snipped off her long plaits, unpicked the cornrows hugging her head. Trimmed her hair as close to the scalp as possible, for the sake of convenience and ease of care.

'I'm done with men,' she told Polly. 'They're only trouble. Black, white, brown men. All the same.'

Chapter Forty-One

1989: Contributing

Rita turned eighteen and left school with fairly good, though not outstanding, CAPE results in English Literature, French and Spanish.

'Now you need to get a job,' said Chandra. 'It's time to contribute. You're not a little girl any more, a dependent.'

But it wasn't as simple as that.

Mrs Persaud, her English teacher, had worked hard at encouraging her to go on to the University of Guyana to study English. 'You've already made a mark as an amateur writer,' she said, 'you could go far. Don't waste your talent, you'll do well at UG.'

Rita wasn't sure. On the one hand, she couldn't wait to be independent, her own woman. And Mrs Persaud's encouragement was heartening and gave her new confidence and new horizons. But four more years of education? She couldn't bear the thought. And end up like her father, chasing news stories for the *Chronicle* or the *Graphic*. Career prospects were so limited in Guyana, even with an English degree, and it all seemed so... so *small,* so dissatisfying.

Polly had four brilliant results in her CAPE exams in science subjects and was finally off to study microbiology in America, just as she'd always planned, and Bobby Fung was finally a thing of the past. But Rita: she floundered in indecision.

All the enthusiasm for life she had gained from her Pomeroon trip had by now faded. She was back, perhaps not where she'd begun, but back in a pool of doom and gloom. She seemed to have no future, no prospects, and even university, if she were to choose that route, would only end up as a brick wall – because, what then? *Why am I walking the face of this earth? There must be some reason. Some great mission, some me-shaped niche I can pour myself into, but what? And where?*

Eighteen, and no idea where she was heading, no goal, no ambition. Why couldn't she just be normal and ordinary and contented like all the rest? Get a job in a bank or an insurance company and marry a nice boy and have babies and settle down? March along like all the others, do as was expected, fit in? Yet she heard this other drum, faint, almost imperceptible; this need to be free and explore and do wild things, run and dance on a wide beach with turtles and turn somersaults.

To make things worse, everybody who was anybody was leaving. Everyone! All off to Canada, America, England and leaving her behind. Even Polly! Her one and only attempt to leave, last year, when they'd all gone to England, had ended in failure. She was a failure. A nobody. She hadn't even made it in England; she'd fled back home, tail between her legs.

'Why don't you just get married?' said Donna deSouza, her only friend left in the Close. Getting married was what girls did at Rita's age. Donna herself was marrying some chap from Guyson's Engineering Ltd, in Rita's eyes a bore.

'But who would I marry?' she replied. 'Who would marry me?'

'Archie Foot?' said Donna, and they both guffawed.

Rita finally chose a career: she would be a poet. This decision came after she won first prize in the National Youth Poetry competition. The theme this year had been animals, which was quite up her street; Rita's winning entry was named 'Dogwit'.

> *Have you heard the tale of a dog, they said,*
> *With fleas so bad o'er his body did spread?*

He scratched and scratched but could not free
his body of a single flea.
So he thought and sought a suitable twig
which in his mouth he used as a rig
and this is what he craft'ly did,
those pesky fleas from his body to rid.
With twig in mouth he went to the sea
So the panicking beasts from his body would flee.
As slowly into the sea he walked,
all the flustered fleas in terror balked,
From belly and tail their sucking did stop.
And rushed to his back to be high on top.
Along neck and head and over his nose
raced the scurrying fleas as the tide it rose.
Aboard the twig there was barely room
and the blood-laden fleas they sensed their doom.
He released their raft to the salty waves
and sent them to their watery graves.
Back to shore with a vigorous shake, he headed home
to his master's care with brush and comb.

Rita enjoyed a few days of celebrity and her hopes ran high; she saw herself bent over her desk, scribbling poems from dawn to dusk, which would be published in a series of thin volumes.

She would be the country's Poet Laureate. *That* was the calling Granny kept talking about. Her natural vocation. Why hadn't she seen it before?

But fame deflates quickly, as Rita found out after a week of it, and she was back at the same nagging question of What To Do With Her Life.

Chandra nagged constantly. 'You got to Earn a Living! We can't keep a grown girl all their lives. You got to pay your own way! Buy your own clothes! She got to get responsible! And stop daydreaming!'

'Daddy, you don't want me to leave, do you?'

'Oh, sweetheart,' Jitty said, 'I understand you, of course I do. I know we writers don't really fit in with the rest of society. I was a misfit too at your age, even though I hadn't yet found my calling as a writer. It's hard, I know.'

'But what can I do? Learn to type and work at an insurance company?'

Several of her friends had done just that. They worked at banks and businesses across town.

Other girls aspired to be airline stewardesses, and one girl she knew had actually managed it: she now worked at British West Indian Airlines, and didn't she let everyone know it! Only a few, like Polly, had the brains *and* the money to be sent abroad to study.

Of course, there was always the University of Guyana as a last resort. She could study English there, become an English teacher. Isn't that what writers did, who couldn't write well enough? She had heard that somewhere.

But me, a teacher? Rita ruminated. *Standing in front of a class of eager-eyed pupils, having to talk sense into them? I couldn't do it. Maybe it's just as much those who can't teach, write. Writing is so much easier than speaking and drumming sense into kids. I don't have what it takes; no calling. It's a bit like nursing, isn't it? A vocation. Speaking of nursing, I wouldn't mind being a vet. Working with animals. But to be a vet you have to study abroad and you need CAPEs in science subjects for that.*

Neither her father nor Chandra were any help. Jitty only shrugged. 'Hardly anybody has the perfect job,' he said, draining his coffee cup. They were the last at the breakfast table, Luisa having been packed off to school and Chandra gone off to the hairdresser's.

'You see, me girl, that's life. That's reality. We don't all get to do what we love. That's why I said journalism. That's the nearest thing to what you love, isn't it? At least you're working with words, not numbers.'

'But…'

He rolled his eyes and stood up. 'The main thing is to get her off your back. And mine. She nagging me too, telling me to light some fire under your backside. Better take my advice, come to the *Graphic*. You can work in the newsroom in the day and write your poems at night.' He took his breakfast dishes to the kitchen, to be washed up by Saraswati. 'Anyway, have a nice day, dear. I'm off to work. Don't worry, it'll all sort itself out.'

Rita stood up.

'And, Daddy, I'm eighteen now.'

'I know. So what?'

'You've forgotten, haven't you?'

'Forgotten what?' She rolled her eyes. 'I knew it! I knew you'd forget.'

'I still don't… Oh. That.'

'Yes, Daddy. That. That *thing* you're supposed to reveal to me when I'm old enough to understand.' She made quote gestures around 'old enough' with her fingers. 'That big confession.'

'Well, I haven't forgotten. Of course not. I will tell you, I promised. And you are old enough now, but, darling, I can't just plop out with it practically on the run between the table and the door. You and me need to sit ourselves down comfortably, no disturbance possible, in the gallery with a nice cool drink. Like grown-ups, and discuss it all. It's quite a long story, you'll see.'

'Oh, Daddy, you'll never change. Forget it.'

Chapter Forty-Two

Sit on my Knee!

In the end she gave in to fate and joined the *Chronicle*, the rival newspaper to the *Graphic*, owned by the government. After all, they had already published her 'Dancing with Turtles' essay, and – said Mr Maugham, the Editor in Chief – 'I've always had my eye on you.' She was assigned to the news desk, where she wrote short pieces on police arrests, accidents and quirky local stories, all just a few paragraphs long. Mr Maugham showered her with praise; undeserved, she felt, for there was no skill involved in those filler pieces. She hoped one day to advance to feature stories for the weekend edition, with a byline.

A month after her appointment, Mr Maugham popped his head out of his office.

'Rita! Can you come in for a moment, please.'

Rita stopped typing and frowned.

'What the hell does he want now?' she muttered to Rashid, who sat at the desk next to her. Mr Maugham had been constantly pestering her with suggestions for articles that interested her not in the least, while regularly dismissing her own suggestions. And yet he never ceased to praise her work, to tell her she was his best writer, that she would go far – if only she'd write the right things. But by now the *Chronicle* was nothing more than a government mouthpiece, and nothing in the least controversial – and after all, Rita epitomised controversy – could ever be accepted. One did not criticise the government, and that was all she wanted to do; at home, criticism of the government was all she ever heard, and she was well acquainted with all the bribery and corruption that passed as legislation. Jitty kept her well informed: it was crooked, it was evil. It had forged election results, it had assassinated Walter Rodney. It had nationalised major industries, mismanaged the economy, driven the country into poverty. But you could not write about these matters. You could not be critical. You had to keep your mouth shut to keep your job.

Even at the *Graphic*, Jitty had to watch his step. At least the *Graphic* was not a government rag. But beg as much as she wanted, Jitty, now acting Editor-in-Chief, would not let Rita work there.

'I'd be accused of nepotism!' he said. 'That just wouldn't look good. Don't make a fuss, darling. Just write what they want and keep your head down.'

But she couldn't, and wouldn't, and Mr Maugham, well aware of her predicament, seemed to enjoy her inner conflict and send her off on missions that she didn't dare refuse, yet which only drove her dissatisfaction to deeper depths.

Now she got up from her desk, straightened her skirt, and walked to the Editor-in-Chief's office. She knocked once and entered at his 'come in'.

'Ah, there you are! How you doin'? Lookin' good in that skirt. You should really wear high heels, you know. With such nice legs, you could really enhance—'

'You wanted to discuss something?'

He laughed, mockingly. 'Eheh! What vexed you today? Let me see that nice smile of yours! I only think if you dressed up a bit more, you know, a li'l more enhancing your assets, you might…'

'Mr Maugham, I'm busy with those police reports for tomorrow. Did you want to say something specific?'

He laughed again and shoved a paper across the desk to her.

'Take a seat and let's discuss this. A big feature story. It's about a Chinese mining company, they've been granted a lease to start mining for diamonds, and—'

'Mr Maugham, I *detest* these foreign mining companies! They destroy the environment, and….'

And again, he laughed, and swatted the air in dismissal.

'Who cares about the environment? It's just a lot of trees – we have too much of them anyway. The country needs foreign revenue, and this is what we have to do. I want you to cover this story, it's a big opportunity for you. You said you wanted to write features, right? This is your big chance.'

'And if I refuse?'

More chuckling noises.

'If you refuse to do your job then that job is in grave danger, Miss Maraj. Of course, I would be happy to consider giving you *some* freedoms, but I'd like to see you show some goodwill first. It can't always go your way, you know!'

'What do you mean by "goodwill"? Don't I always do what you want? Have I ever refused before?'

'Well, there we have it, Miss Maraj. You see, what I want is for you to come over here right now and sit on my lap.' He chuckled, and winked provocatively, patting his spread thighs.

'Sit on your…!'

Rita couldn't help it. She picked up the paperweight sitting on the desk and pitched it at him. He ducked, and it missed, but only narrowly.

Mr Maugham stopped laughing, and Rita Maraj walked out of the room and out of the office, never to return.

And just like that, she was out of a job. In a way, she was glad – she hadn't liked working in an office anyway.

Chapter Forty-Three

Pure Gold

And it was at this moment, at her lowest ebb, that she remembered the Pomeroon, and the river-life, and the serenity she had once found there, and subsequently lost. She remembered Kathy, and Dutch, and Granny, and Aunty Penny. And Mummy, who seemed so alive, so present, there.

It was to be just a short visit, this time, just a week. A week to recharge her batteries and reconnect with the people and places that brought out the best in her. All these years she'd said she'd go, written to Kathy, promising to return, but never had she done so. The reason was simple: she had fallen. That first time, she had returned to Georgetown filled to the brim with joy and new resolve and optimism; she was going to turn over a new leaf; overflowing with energy, she'd start a new life.

It had started so well. But from one year to the next that glow had dimmed. She had fallen back into her old ways of doubt and confusion, and each year, as August came round, she found herself stalling, balking, making excuses, finding reasons not to go. First, the move to England; then, when Granpa had died the following year, giving her a reason to go up – to comfort Granny and attend his funeral – there'd been mid-year exams, and she hadn't; then the shame of not having gone, and that shame had held her back last year, and now…

Now, she remembered Kathy. The newfound little sister who had been so much closer to her than Luisa right from the start.

She remembered Granny, and Granny's veiled wisdom: hinting at things Rita should know, and one day would know, without ever disclosing her secrets.

She remembered Dutch. Not that she'd ever actually forgotten him, but he'd been a distant star, far beyond her reach. She remembered that night on Shell Beach, and the complete happiness she'd known; the mother turtle, coming on shore to lay her eggs and then returning to the ocean, never to see her babies. The sheer *magnificence* of that night, given her by Dutch.

She couldn't wait to see him again. Then, she had been fifteen, he'd been twenty; an age gap too wide to bridge. He'd had the status of a pop star, or a movie hero, far beyond her reach, right up there with Michael Jackson or River Phoenix (the latter a great hero of hers: he loved animals, just as she did). Now, the age gap was perfect.

Just like the last time, the night before she left, Jitty came to her room and handed her a sealed envelope: 'Give this to your granny,' he said. She nodded. She wouldn't bother to open it this time; whatever drama hung between her father and her grandmother, it was in the past and she was staying clear of it. So much time had passed; it was of no import now, a thing they'd have to resolve between them. She slipped the letter into her bag.

Granny, as ever, welcomed Rita effusively. But how she had aged in the last three years! It was as if Granny's skin had been stretched to its limits, then draped around a tiny skeleton, hanging too loosely, wilted and soft. Her hair was now silver and long and stringy, worn in a knot tied halfway down her back, and so sparse, her scalp showed through.

And her eyes! Too large for her wizened face and, as ever, black as creekwater, but now they shone with hidden depths just like the transparent water of a still and silent creek, luring her to dive in and explore, fearlessly, for in them was the wisdom of the ages. Her energy seemed the same, but she'd slowed down, and now Aunty Penny did almost all the physical work while Granny did the things she could do sitting – the peeling, scrubbing, chopping, sifting of food.

Kathy, to Rita's disappointment, was not at home; she and Aunty Penny were spending time with an aunt at the Wakapoa reservation, but would be back tomorrow. George and Pete, meanwhile, had left home altogether, George to work on the *Lady Northcote* steamer, Pete to try his luck as a pork-knocker in the Interior. And Dutch?

That evening, at dinner, Rita asked, as casually as possible, 'How's Dutch, Granny?'

'Dutch? I ain't see him for years. His old granny died, who he was looking after…' Granny went into a long diversion about Dutch's great-grandmother's ailments and treatments, and about Dutch's parents coming up to visit, and then the old lady's death in her sleep one night, and the funeral. Rita waited patiently and then asked, 'So, Dutch doesn't live here any more?'

Granny shook her head.

'No. He gone to America was the last I heard. You got to ask Kathy, she'll know. Or Aunty Penny. Oh, by the way, you seen Mathilda lately? I heard her husband not doin' too well?'

And, just like that, Granny changed the subject again, spoke of Uncle Patrick's ailments and Aunt Mathilda's newfound love for gardening, and her wish to see them once again before her death, and the impossibility of fulfilling such a wish; and Rita's mind wandered and she thought of Dutch and whether or not he had left the country for good, and if he was in America, if she should write to him or not, and probably he'd forgotten her anyway, that fifteen-year-old child who had sat with him on Shell Beach; and anyway, he probably had a girlfriend in America, of course he did. And she realised that she was as stuck as ever: stuck in her own failure to move on, and not even Dutch could save her.

She couldn't wait to see Kathy again. Kathy would be fifteen now, the age Rita herself had been last time she was here, and they'd have so much to talk about. And Kathy would know about Dutch.

*

Kathy returned home the following day, a changed Kathy in some ways – on the cusp of becoming a young woman, tall, beautiful – and as full of warmth as ever. It had been one thing to exchange news by letter; now, sitting side by side on the jetty with a plate full of pineapple slices – they could easily devour a whole pineapple between them – they both overflowed with news: stories too long to share or too complicated to explain in writing. Rita told Kathy about England, about Tonia and Jamal and Luisa. Kathy told her about a boy from Charity, a classmate she had a crush on.

'But,' she sighed, 'he's leaving. Moving to Georgetown to study for CAPE at Queen's College.'

'Why don't you come to Town too? Did you get your CXC results yet?'

'Well, yes, and they're good, a lot of As. But…'

'And you haven't thought of coming to Town? Surely you could get into Bishops'?'

'I did think of it. But I never brought it up. Never asked Mummy and Daddy because, you know, I'm their last child now that George and Pete have bolted. And…'

'Kathy! You have to come! You could stay with Aunt Mathilda, I'm sure! And we could see each other all the time! You always wanted to be a vet – this is your best chance!'

All of a sudden, Kathy coming to Town became a matter of supreme urgency, and not only for Kathy's own sake: how wonderful to have a friend nearby, now that Polly had gone off to university! Rita saw that the only thing holding Kathy back was lack of confidence, and fear of the unknown, of the challenges of Town life.

'You *have* to come!' she said, and squeezed her cousin's hands. 'Please at least think about it! You were so determined the last time I came up. What's happened since then?'

Kathy lowered her eyes. 'I-I've just heard some stories. Of how dangerous Town is for a young girl. Your mother…'

Rita frowned. 'What's my mother got to do with it?'

Kathy shrugged. 'I don't know, really. But they all say that going to Town was the downfall of Aunty Cassie. I don't know why, exactly. I promise if I knew, I'd tell you. I guess, though, it was boys. Like your father. They're so – *forward* – in Town.'

'I'll be with you, I'll look after you.' Rita placed an arm round Kathy and held her tight. A sense of protectiveness, of responsibility, flooded through her. Yes, that was it. She'd be a big sister again, making sure that Kathy didn't make the same mistakes she had. Guiding her into womanhood. Giving her advice. Holding her hand through the perilous waters of female adolescence. As someone close to her cousin in age, she felt sure that Kathy would listen to her. She herself had been without such guidance; she'd make sure Kathy was never alone.

'Speaking of boys,' she said then, 'I heard Dutch was in America?' *Another one*, she thought. *Another one, up and away, off to the green pastures of the First World.*

'Oh, yes, I was going to tell you! He's back, actually. Finished his pilot training. He's been back for about six months now.'

'Really? Where is he, then?'

'Where d'you think? In Georgetown!'

Chapter Forty-Four

Sea Wall Memories

Jitty had had a good night, celebrating with friends at the Carib Hotel, on the East Coast Road just out of town, past Kitty, right on the seafront. There were half-naked dancing girls, and friends, and rum. One of his closest friends was Leaving – with a capital L: another one! – for a new life in America, and of course a celebration was called for – though Jitty felt not at all like celebrating.

It was the August holidays, and Chandra had once again taken off for Canada, this time for several weeks, and taken Luisa with her. With Rita off in the Pomeroon, Jitty was alone at home, and Jitty had never been a man happy with his own company. He had left the car at home and ridden up on his old Honda – he had taken to riding it more and more of late, as it reminded him of his free and fanciful youth. *Free.* That was the word. *Free.* Before Cassie, before Rita, before Chandra, before Luisa. Before all the ties of adulthood and domesticity.

He'd had a few drinks, and one of his friends, a Muslim who did not drink, offered to drive him home, but Jitty declined. It was a long straight ride home: all along the Seawall Road, past Kitty and up to Kingston, then a left turn, and *voilà!* Kaieteur Close. Little traffic there, apart from stationary cars. No danger at all. A wave goodbye, a hug and backpat for the Leaver. Off he roared, a magnificent Easy Rider.

The sea breeze sweeping in from the Atlantic was invigorating; he slowly turned the bike's grip, giving gas, gaining speed. His hair was growing back, and it whipped out behind him. *This was the life! This was the life he missed! Damn them all!* His heart raced; filled with a heady mixture of salty air and nostalgia and regret and rum, he gathered more and more speed. Reaching the town limits, the road narrowed a little; to his right was the long line of silent, dark cars; Georgetown's fabled Lovers' Lane.

The sight of these cars only heightened Jitty's mood. He, too, had once parked here, with many a willing lass, and even, now and then, with Cassie. He had first seduced her, and many others, here, in the privacy of a darkened car, just like these. A bristling rage entered the stew of alcohol and sea breeze and adrenaline and rum brewing in his innards. Rage at life, at the world, but, mostly, at himself. Because who was to blame for this whole mess but himself? Jitty knew that, yet he didn't. He didn't, couldn't acknowledge his own role in the entire tragic business of Cassie, and what had come later, his failed marriage. And yet he knew, somewhere he knew, that he himself was the source of his own fury.

He knew it, because he had confessed. He spoke to Cassie regularly now, in his own mind; he confessed again and again, even though she already knew; confessing his guilt, and begging for absolution. Because only she could grant absolution. But she couldn't, because she was gone. And there was no one left who could grant it. Cassie's mother, perhaps. That letter to Mrs Gomes. *I'm truly sorry. Forgive me*, was all it had said. But would she, could she? Would it be enough?

Again and again, the still little voice he sought to push away. And yet it always returned, from deep inside, insistent, nagging: *Tell Rita. Ask* her *forgiveness. She's the one who can grant absolution.*

Of late, he had been telling everyone who'd listen. Just snippets of it. Little bits and pieces. Half-confessions. Whenever he got drunk enough, out the story would pop, the story of his unforgiveable guilt, and the terrible karma due to him. People listened, and shook their heads, and offered consolation, and told him it was all in the past and he must forget it; but nobody could forgive. He'd even poured the story out to Chandra, on one night of particularly self-abasing ardour. He told her in bed.

'Mout' open, story jump out,' Chandra had remarked, before ripping the mosquito net out from the mattress, clambering out of the bed and stomping out of the bedroom. She slept in the guest room from that time forth.

Tonight, he wasn't wearing a helmet, of course; only sissies wore helmets, and there was no law to do so, as yet. His hair, long once more – he was growing it out in remembrance of his unencumbered youth – whipped in all directions, not only out behind him but across his face, and a strand stuck in one of his eye sockets. He raised a hand to remove it; the bike wobbled, and he lost control, but only for a second. He accelerated again, and raced forward.

Suddenly, though, right before him, a car door opened and a girl staggered onto the road, her long hair dishevelled, her clothes – well, partly missing. She wore only a miniskirt and a bra, and one breast was hanging out of it. She practically fell into the road, but quickly rose to her feet, right into Jitty's path.

He braked and swerved to the left, but lost control of the bike. It wobbled; it fell, landing on the grassy bank that swooped down to the playing fields of the Georgetown Cricket Club, direct evidence that the coastline did, indeed, lie six feet below sea level. Jitty and the bike rolled down the slope in a furious tangle of human and metal.

On her last night, Granny and Rita once more sat on the jetty and watched the water and listened to the night creatures.

They didn't talk, at first; everything had already been said, Rita felt; and yet so much remained unsaid, unresolved. She would be returning to a void; no decision had come to her, as Granny had promised it would, and Granny had been acting strangely all day – coy, somehow, and throwing her mysterious smiles at odd times, and even winking – as if Rita's predicament was nothing more than a huge joke. Except that Rita could not laugh. Far from finding the answer within her, she was more perplexed about her future than ever. All she could think of was to find some boring clerical job somewhere – at least her stint as a journalist had taught her how to type.

When the first mosquitoes swooped in, Granny swiped at them and yawned. 'Come, girl, let's go to bed. You got an early start tomorrow.'

They walked back to the house in silence, arm in arm, and Rita felt a huge sadness descend on her. She sighed aloud. Granny said, 'You don't sound happy at all!'

'I'm not. I've no idea what I'll do, back in Town.'

'Well, just maybe…'

They were in the kitchen, where Rita was running a glass of water for a last drink. Granny watched her drink, and then said, 'Close your eyes.'

Rita wrinkled her nose. 'Why?'

'Just a li'l game. Go on, close them. And hold out your hand.'

Rita sighed and did as she'd been told. She felt something small being pressed into her hand. Granny closed her fingers round the object. It felt like a hard lump, yet was soft to the touch.

'Open your eyes!' said Granny. 'And look.'

A leather pouch lay in the palm of Rita's right hand.

'What's this?'

'Well, look inside and find out!'

Rita pulled the mouth of the pouch apart and peeked inside. She gasped then, looked up at Granny with wide-open eyes, and turned the pouch upside down so that its content fell into her hand.

Several misshapen nuggets of gold, as big as lumpy beans.

'What – where is this from?'

'It's mine!' Granny said, smiling from ear to ear. 'But it's yours now!'

'But how did you get it? Why… how come?'

'You know your granpa was a pork-knocker for a few years. Went into the interior looking for gold. He had a good concession up in the hills. Everything he found was his. And he found quite a bit. Small nuggets, big nuggets.'

'But then – you had riches? Why didn't you – I don't know. Why didn't you change your lives?'

'Change our lives – for what? We happy here. We don't need more. Now and then, repairs to the house or the boat or the jetty. We don't want to go anywhere, do anything. But you, Rita! You and Kathy, George and Pete. You young ones, greedy for life, living in Town, having to compete and build futures and find good jobs and homes – we kept it for you all. You each get your share when you turn eighteen. Better now than wait till I die. Now that you need it. Go back, Rita, and do something with it. Do whatever you want. If you want to go to England, or America, or Canada – go there. It's your decision. Or you can stay in the country, and see what you can do here. The land gave you these nuggets – maybe you can give something back. Or maybe you can go away now and come back one day. It's your choice.'

She once again closed Rita's fingers over the nuggets. The two of them stood gazing into each other's eyes. Granny's were bright and shining and dry, but Rita – her eyes leaked tears. She tried to find words, but none came; yet there was so much to say. Granny wiped away the tears with her thin little fingers.

'Don't cry, my love. There's nothing to cry about. Nothing to be said.'

And there wasn't.

'But that's not all I have for you, baby,' said Granny. She slipped her hand into her apron pocket and pulled out a little book. 'This is for you.'

Rita took it and looked up. 'A bank book?'

'Yes. After you was born, your daddy sent money for you. He did it for five years, right up to the time he came to take you away.

And we didn't need the money so we open an account and save it. Now you is eighteen, and all grown up, it's yours.'

'No, Granny, no! It's yours! He sent it for you to maintain me, and you did!'

'We didn't need no money. We had everything we needed up here. You can't eat money, you know! We had a house and food and water and each other. But *you* might need money now. Along with the gold nuggets. Maybe you can make better decisions with money.'

She laughed. 'Money ain't everything, but it helps. It helps to make the world go round – *your* world, not mine! You need this more than me. And by the way…'

She slid her hand into her apron pocket again and removed another item, this time a sealed envelope.

'Give this to your daddy,' she said.

Granny drove her to Charity in the motorboat, and accompanied her into the town to buy some provisions for herself. As they passed the watchman at the jetty's entrance, he called out to her: 'Mrs Gomes! Come here a minute!'

She stepped across to speak to him. 'What is it?'

'A telegram come for you this mornin'. We was figurin' out how to get it to you.'

Granny held out her hand. 'Give me.'

The guard shook his head. 'You got to go to the Post Office, ma'am.'

Granny looked at Rita. 'A telegram? I ain't had a telegram since – well, since the time you was small. Maybe it's for you. Come with me.'

'I hope it's not bad news.'

Chapter Forty-Five

1989: The Mistakes of Others

'Daddy, how could you? *How could you?*' Rita was furious. She'd never liked to see her father drunk; at those times he became a ridiculous effigy of himself, a buffoon spouting bad jokes, singing out-of-tune sixties hits, laughing at himself, falling over his own feet, and, once, peeing himself. It wasn't a good sight. But this, this!

'You could have been killed!'

He only laughed. 'I must be got a guardian angel!'

It had to be so. He had escaped with nothing more than a broken leg, a gash on his forehead, scratches. The hospital had fixed him up as best they could, checked that there was no brain injury and sent him home, his leg in a cast. Now, he lay in the Berbice chair in the gallery, a glass of coconut water on the armrest, grinning his old cheeky grin. As if nothing had happened.

'Daddy, it's not a joke; it was a lucky escape. You have to pull yourself together. Otherwise you *will* kill yourself one day.'

'Maybe it's better that way. Me, I'm just a useless failure.'

The grin faded from his face. It had never reached his eyes anyway, and it hadn't fooled Rita.

'Don't talk like that!'

It was a reversal of roles, almost; it had been Rita, up to now, who thought of herself as a useless failure. Now, filled with new strength and energy from her visit with Granny, she found herself in the adult role, remonstrating with her father. She was furious with him, with his pretended insouciance, fearful of what he might

do next. She'd sent a cable to Chandra, of course; but that good
woman, once she knew that Jitty was out of danger and was being
well taken care of by Rita, had decided *not* to rush home. She liked
Toronto, and so did Luisa.

'This has to change, Daddy. I don't know what got into you.
You never used to be like this.'

He pressed his hand to his heart.

'Something eatin' away at me soul.'

'What, Daddy, what?' But he only shook his head.

'You gave her the letter?'

'Oh! – I completely forgot…' She jumped to her feet and ran
upstairs, fumbled in her handbag. In the drama of coming home,
seeing him with his leg in a cast in the hospital, talking to doctors,
bringing him home, all the worry, she had, indeed, entirely forgotten. The envelope Granny had given her for him.

She handed it over, now, and he opened it, and read it.

And then, out of the blue, he broke into a wild, desperate
sobbing.

'What's the matter, Daddy? What is it? What did she write?'

He gestured towards the letter, inviting her to read it.

She unfolded it. On the sheet of paper were written only three
short sentences:

> *I forgive you. We can't change the past. Let's let bygones be
> bygones.*

She read it and then looked up. 'What does she mean?'

He shook his head as he sobbed. 'So many mistakes. So many
stupid mistakes.'

'Was making me your biggest mistake?'

She said it quietly, almost as a whisper. Jitty looked up sharply,
his eyes still pooled with tears. Clearly, he said: 'Making you was

the best thing I ever did. The very best. But I did it wrong. I did it so wrong – so wrong…' But then, another flood of abject tears.

'Daddy, don't cry. Please don't cry!' But he only continued to cry.

'Daddy,' she said, 'I'm eighteen now. You once made a promise to me. I know you never keep your promises, but this one time – you need to.' She paused.

'Granny said it's not so important to know *how* Mum died. What's important is *why* she died. She said only you know that.'

He nodded.

'But she's forgiven you so it can't be that bad.'

'It is. Believe me, it is. You'll never forgive me. Never.'

'Try me. She's forgiven you, for whatever it was. If she can, so can I.'

He paused; she waited. He looked up and at her and fiercely swiped away the tears with the back of his hand.

'I just don't know where to begin,' he said.

'Begin at the beginning. When you met her.'

And that's what Jitty did. He sniffed, blew his nose, and started to talk.

'We met at a fete. In Bel Air Park. She was so sweet, so innocent. It was her first fete. Nobody was dancing with her and she looked so shy. I felt sorry for her. But I liked her, too. She was pretty, but a bit old-fashioned. In that high-necked dress with lacy edges. So, I asked her to dance. I remember the song – The Mamas & The Papas: 'Dream a Little Dream of Me'. It later became our song.'

'It was my song, too. For ages. You played it for me on the gramophone.'

'Yes. Anyway, we danced, and then we talked. She told me her name. We were both in the final year of A-levels. She was a year younger than me but much, much brighter. I was just a lazy bum. I thought I was so cool. Sunny-Boy, they used to call me. I could get any girl. And I got her, the little wallflower nobody else wanted. But she was much too good for me.'

He told her everything; a full confession, leaving out only the more intimate encounters. Rita listened in rapt silence, never interrupting.

'...she was expelled from Bishops' because she was pregnant. She decided to go home to the Pomeroon. I drove her to Parika. I thought that would be the end of it. The end of my responsibility. She was going back to her parents and they would look after her. I didn't once think of the consequences.'

'Basically, you washed your hands of her.'

Jitty nodded, his face a picture of doom, his eyes red and leaking tears.

'It was the last time I ever saw her.'

'What happened then? When she was with her parents? Did you write to each other?'

Jitty nodded. He said: 'Run upstairs. Under your bed, there's a loose floorboard. Lift it up. You'll find two Cadbury Chocolates tins. Bring them down.'

She did as he asked. Two tins, hidden in her room, in a place where Chandra or the maid couldn't have come across them: she was excited, and nervous, both at the same time. A sense that a climax was brewing, a climax that would change her life forever. A secret, held in those two tins.

Jitty opened one of them.

'Read these,' he said, handing it to Rita. 'They're in order.'

She glanced at him, then down at the tin. It was filled with envelopes. She opened the top one, removed the letter inside it. Began to read, silently, while Jitty lit a cigarette and watched.

Part Three

Revelation

Chapter Forty-Six

Cassie's Letters

Rita picked up the first envelope, opened it, removed the two pages covered in neat handwriting.

Began to read, in silence:

My dearest Jitty,

Well, I arrived safe and sound and I'm home again. Mummy and Daddy took the opportunity to give me a huge ticking-off for getting myself into this position in the first place but once they had got that out of their system, they were nothing but kind and good and told me I could live here forever with my child if I have to.

But I won't have to. I know you are doing your best to sort things out. I'm sure your Granma will come round and listen to reason soon. You should really have let me meet her. I have often discovered that a friendly smile can work wonders. I'm sure meeting me in person could have changed her mind.

But I suppose you know her best and you can best deal with the situation. I have faith in you that you will work it out.

It's so quiet out here compared to Town! Just Mummy and Daddy, and the animals: cats and dogs and two goats and ten chickens. And of course lots of wild animals in the forest around us: parrots and monkeys and even jaguars; though

I've never seen one of those, except in the zoo. I'd love to see a wild one one day. Mummy and Daddy are building a small cottage at the back because my sister Penny who is married to a man from Charity, his name is Douglas, is coming to live here. She has a little boy and he is so cute! I can't wait to have a boy like him, or a girl. Which would you prefer? I don't mind at all. We have to start thinking of names!

Anyway, I just wanted to tell you that I love you so very much and always will. I'm sorry I put you in this predicament but I'm sure we can sort it out and be happy together very soon.

I love you with all my heart and I'll write to you every week.

Cassie

Darling Jitty, well, this is my fourth letter and still not a word from you! I know you said you're not much of a letter-writer but just a few words would really lift my spirits. I miss you so much!

Miss Dewer was true to her word and she has sent me TONS of learning material to prepare me for my exams. Just two more months to go, and I am swotting like anything! I am determined to do well. I do think it's a pity I had to leave school, though. But I understand it would have set a bad example to the other girls, to have me with my huge belly sitting in class!

And yes, I am huge by now, four months gone, five to go! I feel like an elephant! So far though I'm managing well, though a little tired. Most of my time I'm sitting at the table learning, but I help a little on the farm. Nothing too strenuous, of course.

I hope that you too are studying hard for your exams. It's really important, Jitty. I know you think school is a bore and you'd rather be out having a good time but we both have to be responsible and you'll need a good job one day, so work hard!

Please write, even if it's just a postcard! I miss you so much and sometimes I worry it's out of sight, out of mind for you. It isn't though, is it? Please write and tell me you are still trying to sort things out! I can't wait to be your wife, in every way! I already am, in my heart, but I want the world to know, and I want God's blessing. I'm so glad that your aunty had you secretly baptised! It means a priest can bless our union. It doesn't have to be a big ceremony. Just the two of us and the priest. There's a pretty chapel in Charity where we could do it.

I love you,
Cassie

At this point, Rita looked up at her father. 'Dad, I can't believe you didn't write back! How could you? Didn't you reply even once?'

He said nothing, but gestured towards the tin. She picked up the next letter, and shook her head slowly as she read the first words, glancing at Jitty in disapproval.

Dear Jitty

Still not a word from you even though I write to you every week. I'm getting really worried. Have you forgotten me, and our child?

It doesn't help that Mummy is bad-talking you. She doesn't think much of young men, especially young men who get girls pregnant and then abandon them. She thinks they are *irresponsible, and if you knew Mummy, you'd know that's the worst insult! She thinks I could have done better in my choice of father for my first child. Most of all she thinks we should have married <u>before</u> having a baby, not after. Your silence isn't helping.*

I'm starting to think that maybe you don't want to marry at all. That you think I'm not good enough for you. I know Town people (your fancy friends) think I'm just boring and stupid because I'm from the country. A girl from behind God's back. Well, I may be boring (to them) but I'm not stupid and I do have some self-respect. Jitty Maraj, if this is your way of abandoning me, if you were just stringing me along all the time, then tell me now!

It would be hard to bear but I would get over it eventually. I have my dignity and I'm not begging you to marry me if you don't want to. So tell me now. Have that much respect for me.

Cassie

My dearest Jitty!

At last, a letter from you! You cannot imagine how much joy that gave me, even though it was just a few lines! I am almost jumping from joy! That's why I'm writing you midweek instead of on Saturday. Just these few lines to let you know that those three words you ended your letter with, the words I've never heard from you before but I've been desperate to hear – well, you have made me very, very happy. And now I have faith in the future once again.

Remember that song we used to sing in the car together, 'Que Sera, Sera'? Loudly, madly, and out of tune! Well, I

sing it to myself now all the time. I just have faith. In you,
in our future, in God. Whatever will be, will be!

Thank you.
I love you too.
Cassie

Rita looked up again, and waved this letter. 'So, you did write. I can't believe you ignored her for so long.'

Jitty only shrugged. 'I was a fool. I thought by ignoring her, I could get rid of the whole problem. I was a little boy. An idiot.'

'You were,' said Rita, and continued to read.

My dear Jitty,

I have such wonderful news! You won't believe it! All of our problems are about to be solved, with one stroke! Aunt Mathilda and Uncle Patrick have changed their minds about me! Yes, it was a shock for them to know that you 'took advantage' of me, as they put it, and that I had 'fallen'. But they have thought about it since. I suppose they are seeing Mummy and Daddy's example, of forgiveness and charity. And they are true Christians, ready to forgive and move forward.

Anyway, they are now saying that if we get married we can move into their house with them, rent-free. There is plenty of room upstairs, three bedrooms, and they don't have any children of their own, and they miss having me around, and they love me just like a daughter! Isn't that kind! And we can stay with them with our baby as long as we want – I suppose that means, for you, until your Granma dies, though I hate that kind of thinking, it's so mercenary, isn't it, to be waiting for someone to die so you can inherit! I for one would be happy to stay with Aunt and Uncle forever – I don't need your big house. But I know how attached you are to it, but there's even more! You know Uncle Patrick owns that big hardware store on Regent Street, Harvey's Hardware? Well, he says he will give you a job! So there we have it in one stroke – a home for us, and work for you! It means we can get married really soon and I can move to Town, before the birth. That means so much to me, darling. Then our child won't be born a bastard. That's the main thing, isn't it? To be married before the birth.

This is the answer to all our problems! You could come up here and we can get married quietly at Charity. Me coming back to Town at this stage wouldn't be good – I'm getting bigger by the day and it would be more obvious that it's a shotgun wedding. People would talk. If we do it quietly, up here, it would be much more discreet and people would soon forget the circumstances. But now you MUST write to me.

There's nothing more standing in our way, my darling! Please come soon! I'm not sure how to organise a quiet marriage but maybe you can find out and start proceedings. I suppose they will want paperwork of some kind.

All my love,
Cassie

My darling Jitty,

It was so good to hear from you again! Even though it was short, you can't imagine how happy it made me, just to see that envelope with your writing on it, your name on the back!

But after reading it, I wasn't so happy.

I don't understand your reasoning. It doesn't make sense to me. Why would it upset your grandmother if we move into the Peter Rose Street house? Why would it embarrass her, shame her? It's really not her business, is it? If she won't let me move into her house, then surely she must see that I have to live somewhere! Surely she must be happy that you're facing up to your responsibility as a man, as a father-to-be!

Yes, I understand that she had another heart attack and that you are worried about her health. But it's a contradiction. On the one hand you don't want to upset her because she might have another attack, on the other you want her to die so you can get the house and we can marry and I can move in! She already knows I'm pregnant. Surely that was the main shock; why would us moving in together be a greater one?

I'm so very disappointed. I would love to move back to Town to be with you, give birth in Town. You didn't even mention coming up to Charity to get married. You know how important that is to me. Even if I stay up here for a while after we are married – people will notice less that way. You know how they talk and point fingers! I think they are kinder up here in the country, so that's my thinking: get married as soon as possible, and then after a week or two, move to town so that it looks as if we've been married for ages.

I just want things to be in order. I don't want him or her to be a bastard. You know what people are like. I don't want them pointing fingers at my child, calling them horrible names.

I love you though and I'm trying to accept your decision on this, though it makes no sense.

All my love,
Cassie

Again, Rita looked up. 'Why? Why didn't you agree for her to come to town, if she could live with Aunt Mathilda? It was the perfect solution!'

'It was – it was my grandmother. The conditions she'd made!'

'What conditions? Did you leave something out?'

'Yes – yes. I forgot to tell you about Granma. What Granny had said. I mean, I told you Granny was furious with me for getting Cassie pregnant. I would have, Rita, I promise you I would have. I forgot to tell you about the will. Granny said if I married her and moved out, if I sullied the family with a half-caste child – you! – she would cut me out of her will. She'd change it and I'd get nothing. The house would go to some Hindu charity.'

Rita glared at him.

'So, you basically sold out Mummy so you could keep this house.'

He looked miserable, and stubbed out his cigarette. 'I suppose so. Yes, that's what I did. If you put it like that.'

She shook her head and picked up the next letter.

Dear Jitty,

I hope you are well. You haven't replied yet again to my last letter but I'm used to that by now and I am still hoping, hoping, hoping. Only four weeks to go till the birth! I'm a mixture of excited, scared, embarrassed, worried. Mostly worried because of your silence. I asked you to come up so we can get married but you haven't said a word about it. Do you know how humiliating it is for me to beg you to marry me? And even more so, to tell you that I am humiliated. But there it is. I have never kept any secrets from you, and I don't ever mean to do so; I need to speak my mind, be truthful always. I want you to know my every feeling. Right now, I feel mostly shame because you seem not to care whether or not our baby is born legitimate. Even though you know how important it is, to me, and for the baby's future. It's a matter of honour.

Well. Moving on, in spite of my bitter feelings towards you:

I have some more news but I don't even want to tell you now as it seems I am begging, trying to lure you with talk of inheritance and all that. You know how I hate such talk. It's so mercenary. But there it is. It's about our future, and our security, so I have to tell you.

Daddy went to Charity a few days ago and put through a telephone call to Aunt Mathilda and Uncle Patrick. He spoke mostly to Uncle Patrick. They are brothers-in-law. Uncle Patrick has this successful hardware store in Regent Street – I told you already, I think.

Well, they have no children, even though they badly wanted them. And they have grown to love me as a daughter, Uncle told Daddy, and they will leave their house to me in their will. Not that they are about to die soon, but that will be the arrangement, and in return my sister Penny will inherit the house up here from Daddy and Mummy, and the land – it's a lot of farmland – and the boats and everything. Daddy thinks it's a fair arrangement.

Uncle Patrick will leave the store to both me and Penny. He will train you up as manager, if you are interested. When he and Aunty have passed away, we will be the owners. And I can live with them as long as I want, with or without you. I just wanted you to know that. Just so you don't think I'm a poor country girl after your money, which is what Mummy says you think. Just so you know that I, too, have security. And we don't have to depend on your Granma to get married or live together.

*

But your silence has made me face reality and I think that you have had second thoughts. You just don't want to tell me. That's cowardly, Jitty! I thought better of you. I can stand the truth, you know! So, I have been thinking about my own future, if that's the case.

If you don't marry me, if you are dumping me (which is what Mummy says – she doesn't believe <u>one word</u> of what you say, about loving me, because if you did you'd put things right) – I have to make plans for a life without you, just me and the baby. Quite honestly, I don't know what I will do, but I do know I will hold my head up high and face whatever storm may come. I will have to be strong by myself and I will be, Jitty, I will be! I will not crumple like a heap in the dust, if you desert me!

I am willing to face the scandal for the sake of my child and one day, maybe in five years' time when he or she can start nursery school, I will study medicine at UG, as I always planned, and live with Aunt and Uncle. They will help, no matter what. At first, they were shocked but now they are completely supportive. They are like a second pair of grandparents for my baby. Our baby, in case you've forgotten.

Jitty, I don't think I'll write to you again. Either you come up here and we marry before the birth, or – well, I don't really know what the 'or' is. I will just be an unmarried mother and face the music alone. But I have the support of so many people – my parents, my sister and brother-in-law, and Uncle and Aunt. I will survive, with or without you. This is my last letter if I don't hear back from you.

The ball is now in your court.

Love, always,
Cassie

Rita folded the last letter, slipped it back into its envelope, put it back in the box with all the others. She'd read them all. Fourteen letters in all, most loving, some anxious, this last one fierce and furious.

She looked up and closed the tin.

'So, you never replied to her letters?'

'Twice. Just twice.'

'But why not? How can anyone not reply to a letter? You, especially – you're a writer!'

'I was scared, Rita, and ashamed of my own cowardice and didn't know what to say. I couldn't tell her the truth. I had a plan in the back of my mind but she'd never have agreed to it. When Granma died, that's when I'd have her move in here. It's called common-law marriage. Just living together. I knew she'd never agree to that in advance but when it came to the crunch she'd have no choice, because, well, she'd be dependent on me.'

'But she wasn't, was she? She'd have managed without you. She'd never have agreed to this – this common-law thing.'

'I know. I was mad to even think it. I knew she wouldn't agree to it, but I was hard-headed and young and selfish. And foolish.'

'So, you had a choice between this house and Mum, and you chose the house. Did you love her at all?'

'Yes! Yes, of course I did! But I only really knew it after – after it all happened. At the time I was just greedy and stupid and foolish, and Rita, it was the biggest mistake of my life and I've regretted it every day of my life since… since…'

He faltered, as if searching for the right words, words that would exonerate him, free him from bonds that reached out from the past and still held him captive.

'Since what?'

'Since what happened next.'

'OK, go on. What happened next?'

'Well, I wasn't there. But I can tell you what Cassie's mother told me.'

Chapter Forty-Seven

Cassie, September 1971

'Mummy! Mummy! Something's happening!' Edna Gomes dropped the pot of rice back onto the stove and rushed from the kitchen, through the living room to the balcony. Cassie was trying to stand up from the wicker rocking chair, leaning on the armrest. At her feet, a pool of liquid on the polished floorboards.

She looked up. 'I think my waters have broken!'

'Then it's off to the midwife.'

'But it's too early! I'm not due for weeks!'

'That's all right. It's not too early. Your bag is packed, right? You're ready? Come, sit down again.'

She took her daughter's elbow and guided her into the bedroom, helped her change into dry clothes, padded her out with rags, then led her into the living room, sat her down on a towel on the wicker settee. Cassie held up her bulging abdomen all the time, as if the baby itself was about to drop out.

'I just going to tell Penny to look after the place. I expect I'll be back tomorrow – I'll spend the night with you. A precious little baby, Cassie! You going to be a mummy!'

Cassie's eyes shone. 'I know! I can't believe it!' But then a veil seemed to drop across her face, and she frowned.

'I just wish…'

'You ain't got time for wishin', sweetheart. He's no good. Look forward, not back. Love your baby, not that scamp of a boy.'

'But you'll tell him, won't you? After the baby is born. You'll call him and tell him. Maybe he'll come up. Maybe when he sees it…'

'Forget it, it's too late. He had his chance. He di'n marry you before the birth, he ain't gon' marry you after. It's over, Cassie. You got to look forward now. So you settled all right? You want some water? Here, let me put your legs up. We'll leave in about ten minutes.'

Cassie wiped away the tears that had slipped down her cheeks, and nodded. What else was there to do? It was all out of her hands. She was going to be a mother. Today. Nothing would ever be the same.

Twenty minutes later, they were in the canoe, Edna paddling away down the creek, nearing the junction with the Pomeroon River. There, she turned north, downriver, towards the estuary at the Atlantic, towards Babsy, the midwife who served the upper Pomeroon area and delivered most of the babies up and down the river, up and down the creeks. Babsy had been a midwife for over thirty years, and knew all there was to know about bringing babies into the world, comforting and encouraging the mothers, egging them on, giving them strength when they needed it. She had delivered both Penny and Cassie.

Edna, settled in the front of the canoe, turned and smiled back at her daughter. 'It's going to be all right, baby. You're going to be a mummy!' she said again as she paddled. Left, right, left, right, the oar sinking into the water, the canoe glidingly silently forward, making hardly a ripple, as if cutting through silk. Edna's arm and shoulder muscles bulged and sank, flexed and relaxed, glistened in the afternoon sun. Calmly, smoothly, they slid down the Pomeroon. Cassie wished she could absorb that calm. There was no reason not to be calm. Everything surrounding her – the silky river, the green of the forest, the sky above – all these things had been here for millennia, a serene backdrop to every human drama that had come and gone. Births and deaths, human passions, human fears and anxieties – all passing shadows, witnessed by those towering trees, that water placidly flowing to the ocean, that endless sky, fluffy white clouds floating by. Nothing disturbed them. But she – she was disturbed. Their very peace disturbed her, for it emphasised her own turbulence. It was not peace she wanted, not a gliding canoe, not nature waiting patiently as human turmoil came and went, each drama passing in the blink of an eye. She wanted movement. Speed. The efficiency of Town. Humans. Jitty. Jitty in a car rushing her to hospital. Jitty, fretting and anxious, about to become a father. He'd press on the accelerator, and the horn, run red lights, cut corners as he raced through Town on the way to hospital.

Not this. Not this, Mummy's infuriatingly slow, rhythmic movements as she paddled down the river, the silent gliding of a dug-out canoe. Cassie realised now just how much the last few years, the last few months especially, had changed her. She was now a Town girl, impatient for action.

They arrived at Babsy's house twenty minutes later, a pretty white-painted cottage on stilts, surrounded by a garden. In the Bottom House was the room, with adjoining toilet and bathroom, where Babsy delivered her babies, though sometimes, if she was sent for and if there was time, she went to the mother's house in her own canoe. Edna moored the canoe, climbed the rickety wooden stairs onto the jetty, hustled towards the house, calling: 'Babsy! Babsy! I got work for you!'

The front door opened. Babsy's daughter came out onto the landing at the top of the stairs. She called back: 'Babsy not here, ma'am. She had to go to Georgetown to get some surgical supplies. Sorry! She'll be back tomorrow, if you want to come back!'

'I got a woman in the canoe, she baby about to drop – I ain't got time to wait till tomorrow!'

'Then you got to go to Charity. Nurse Gibson will take care of it.'

Edna turned and called to Cassie, still sitting in the canoe: 'Babsy gone to Town. You got to go to the Charity midwife, Nurse Gibson.'

To Babsy's daughter, she said: 'I know Nurse Gibson… Shirley. She's family. Can you take me in the motorboat?'

The daughter shook her head. 'Babsy took the motorboat. It's in Charity. I only have the rowing boat, moored on the jetty. You could take that…'

Edna shook her head. 'It's no faster than the canoe. It would take me all day to row to Charity.' She walked back to Cassie, still sitting in the canoe, and said, 'Let we stay here and get a lift with a motorboat. Here, come up!'

She climbed halfway down the ladder and reached down her hand. Cassie, her brow creased with anxiety, took it and carefully stood up in the rocking canoe.

'Careful, now! Slowly. Come, nah, girl, and help!'

Babsy's daughter approached and reached out her hand as well. Together, they pulled Cassie up the ladder and onto the jetty.

'Let me bring a chair for her!' said Babsy's daughter, rushing back to the house. She returned with two folding chairs, made sure they were both comfortable.

Edna and Cassie settled on the two chairs when she'd placed them at the end of the jetty. Babsy's daughter brought them a jug of water and two tumblers, fussed about their comfort for a while. 'If you need anything else, just call!' she said, and walked back to the house.

'Somebody gon' come soon,' Edna told Cassie. 'Don't worry.'

But Cassie *did* worry. She didn't like this dependency on *chance*; on somebody in a motorboat just happening to flit by, and Edna flagging them down and begging for a lift. Cassie liked everything to be orderly and planned. She had grown away from the casual going-with-the-slow-flow of country life, letting events take their course, allowing the present to have its way and placing your whole future on whatever the moment brought, adapting to circumstances. *Education,* she thought, *does that to you. It makes you want more control.*

Her whole dilemma, all the events that had led her to this moment, were due to loss of control. She'd let Jitty take control, she'd let things happen, she'd been polite and kind and willing and adaptable and gone with the flow but it had been all *Jitty's* flow and now here she was, scandalously unmarried and about to give birth in some godforsaken corner of the country. She longed for a lovely soft bed in a modern hospital, doctors and nurses and midwives bustling around, she the centre of medical attention.

Instead, she had this. A jetty in the middle of a vast forested wilderness, poking out into an empty river; a canoe about as slow as a donkey cart, and a baby that wanted to burst into the world. She felt a contraction. What if it happened here, right here, on the jetty? Some babies came rushing out. Some took hours, days to be born. What would *her* baby do? Would it be impatient to enter this world of sorrow and its own unregulated life, or would it want to stay safely buried in its mother's body? She didn't know, but she worried.

'Is there a hospital in Charity?' she asked her mother. 'You know, just in case?'

Edna shook her head. 'No. Nearest hospital is in Suddie, near Supenaam, thirty minutes away. I was in that hospital once, when I had that appendix trouble. All they have in Charity is the dispenser, Dispenser Joseph.' She laughed. 'Dispenser Joseph! A handsome mix-race man, a real charmer, all the ladies like him. Some of them lady patients' – she chuckled, emphasising the word 'patients', and Rita knew it was in quotation marks – 'some of them fake sickness to "go see the dispenser". Is not just medicine he dispensing!' She laughed again, but Rita did not laugh with her. She was hardly listening. She knew her mother was only trying to distract her, but she couldn't be distracted. What if something went wrong? What if…? She was not interested in a charming dispenser. If something went wrong, she wanted a *doctor*, and a hospital, one round the corner, not thirty minutes away in Suddie.

And she couldn't help it: she thought of Jitty and wished he was here, holding her hand. If only he would miraculously appear, she'd forgive him everything. Everything. *Come to me, Jitty; please come!* she cried silently – but then she smiled to herself. *Jitty on the jetty.* It was a bit funny, but only a bit. A contraction, the second, gripped her and chased away all thought of Jitty, all thought of Town, all thought of everything but this moment, this breath, this NOW that clamped her in its talons. Edna rubbed her back, speaking soothing words.

The contraction passed, and she relaxed. Her breathing returned to normal. She could think again, be here again, waiting on the jetty. Waiting for something, *anything*, to happen. She prayed: *please, dear God, send a boat, a fast boat, to get me there!*

A boat glided past, but it was only a canoe, no faster than their own, with an Amerindian family, man, woman, three small children between them, all paddling vigorously. They all looked up and smiled and waved. Nothing they could do. They couldn't help. What was needed was a—

'I hear somethin'!' said Edna. Cassie primed her ears but could hear nothing. That was another thing that had happened in Town: her senses had dulled. Edna could hear the hum of a motorboat from miles away, minutes away, long before it was visible. Identify tiny birds against the backdrop of the jungle canopy. She, Cassie, had once had such fine hearing, such fine vision, but it had all vanished in the hustle and bustle of Town life and all the knowledge that had poured into her brain over the last five years. A pity, but there it was. A trade-off. Education and modern ideas for ultrasensual-sensitivity.

Edna was right. A motorboat chugged into view, and it was going in the right direction, northwards, towards Charity. Edna stood up and called and waved, and the boat drew closer, and pulled up, and docked, and half a minute later, Cassie and Edna were seated within it, on their way to Charity, and Cassie's breathing was normal again and her heartbeat slower and she rubbed her belly and said to her baby, silently: *It's all right now. We're on our way. We'll be there in half an hour and then you can come if you want to. I can't wait to see you, to hold you! Just wait a little while longer.'*

Now the journey was as swift as Cassie desired. The wind whipped her hair free from the clips and plaits that held it and strands of it slashed against her face. The bow of the boat rose high as it sped forward, and great swathes of water rose up and sprayed against them, pinpricks on naked skin. Faster and faster they roared forward, and Cassie's heart raced too and in her own way she rejoiced. No matter what: count the hours, and she'd be a mother, a whole new life opening up to her, a whole new journey. All gloom fled from her, replaced by a soaring ecstasy.

This is it!

But another problem had started. 'I need to go to the toilet!' she whispered to Edna, but the wind whipped away the words. What could Edna do anyway? She held it in.

They reached Charity. The boatman would accept no money for the ride: it was a privilege, he said, and saluted them as they turned to walk away. A few cars were parked outside; Edna approached the drivers, standing around chatting, and asked for a taxi. One stepped forward.

'Where you want to go?'

Edna gave him the address of Nurse Gibson, the local midwife. It was a short drive, hardly five minutes away; the car stopped in front of a wooden building on tall stilts. 'Wait here,' Edna said, and Cassie waited in the car while Edna walked up the stairs and knocked on the door. It opened; a woman stood in the doorway. A few words exchanged, and Edna and the woman returned to the car.

'I'm Nurse Gibson,' said the woman. 'But you can call me Aunty Shirley. Come, darlin', is time for you to be a mummy. Lemme help you – take my hand…'

Cassie did, and placed her other hand protectively on her abdomen as Nurse Gibson helped her out of the car and up to the house. Just like at Babsy's place, the rear part of Bottom House was built up with rooms.

'This is my birthing room,' said Aunty Shirley. 'But mostly, I does go to the woman's home.'

They entered the room, spacious but sparsely furnished with just the delivery bed in the centre and pushed against one wall a table with scales, a towel laid out to cover instruments, a bassinet. On another small table, a telephone, and next to that, a cupboard. In one corner, a sink. Two doors were set into the rear wall; one with a sign that said STORAGE and the other with a sign that said WC.

Cassie rushed straight to the toilet, and returned much relaxed. Aunty Shirley, a very efficient set to her face, was now pulling on some rubber gloves, Edna tucking a clean sheet onto the delivery bed. Cassie lay down on the bed while Aunty Shirley examined her and went about preparing her instruments for the imminent birth. While she worked, Aunty Shirley chatted casually with Edna and Cassie, catching up on the lives of mutual relatives with Edna. Aunty Shirley, it turned out, was the sister of Edna's second cousin's mother-in-law. Of course, she was curious about Cassie's circumstances. Edna told her everything, much to Cassie's shame.

When she heard of Jitty's appalling behaviour, Aunty Shirley shook her head and sucked her teeth.

'These boys nowadays. They want all the pleasure, none of the responsibility.'

'Wasn't no better in our day!' Edna reminded her.

'True, true. But it gettin' worse, if you ask me.'

Cassie wanted to interrupt, to cry, *no, no, Jitty loves me, he loves our baby, he wants to marry me!* But the two older women, she knew, would only nod sagely to placate her – nobody wanted an argument now! – roll their eyes behind her back, exchange knowing glances, and not believe her. She, too, was tired of arguing about Jitty, defending him to Mummy.

He's not like that! He loves me! But he's different, he's modern, he believes in freedom, not clinging to the old ways! We have to be flexible, go with the flow! Listen to our feelings! So she'd tried to argue Jitty's position, plead on his behalf, just a month ago, before the last bitter disappointment.

And Mummy had just pursed her lips and shaken her head and frowned, and told Cassie exactly what she thought of Jitty's philosophy. *His hippy-dippy ways*, as she called them. *He lives in fantasy land! Fantasia.* She remembered when Mummy had taken her to see *Fantasia* in Suddie when she was a child – the only time Cassie had ever been to the cinema before moving to Town. Mummy had thought it all ridiculous. Mummy had no time for *newfangled ways* and *free love* or, for that matter, anything at all that Jitty believed in. *Feelings don't grow a baby, or birth it, or feed it*, she'd said.

Now, Cassie felt she could forgive Jitty anything. Surely, when the baby was born, he'd marry her. *He had to.* It was never too late to put things right. He loved her, he did…

But then another contraction gripped her, putting an abrupt end to those memories, that train of thought, emptied her of every feeling, every care, everything except this, this wave of pure pain that took hold of her body in a gripping, crippling cramp so that there was no space, no time, for Jitty. This was it; this was happening, now.

Hours passed. Cassie's notion of time slipped away. Time didn't exist: there was just her, and Edna, and Nurse Gibson. And that unknown participant in all this, her baby. Contraction after contraction. The midwife's calm voice:

'Keep breathing! Now pant! Don't push yet! Hold on to my hand, press hard! Harder! Raise up your knees! Turn on your side! Don't push! Breathe slowly! Pant! Come on, girl, you can do it!'

And then, at last:

'Baby coming soon!' Aunty Shirley exclaimed. 'You well dilated!' But Cassie didn't hear, for she was already in the grip of the next contraction. Between them, Edna and the midwife helped her through. 'Breathe!' Aunty Shirley kept saying. Her voice seemed so far away, yet through the tension and the pain and the insistence of the life within her to escape the confines of her body she listened to that voice, followed its directions.

A wave of extraordinary power, like a hand from above, gripped Cassie and she found herself scrambling to turn over and get on her hands and knees. 'That's all right, if it bring ease, stay like that. Baby coming now, soon! Keep breathing! Everything fine! This is one fast baby!'

On all fours, Cassie moved her body to the rhythm of the baby's progress. Up, down, up, down.

'It's crowning! I see the head!' cried Aunty Shirley from behind her, then, 'The head's out! Now *push, push, push!*' and Cassie pushed with all her might, and as she pushed, she screamed and it was a scream of sheer ecstasy and power and victory as much as a scream of pain, and she felt a slippery thing slide out of her and she collapsed in sheer exhaustion into a heap on the delivery bed and she wept, this time in joy, as Aunty Shirley cried out: 'It's a girl! A little girl! A beautiful little girl!' simultaneous with a thin shrill wail, the most wonderful sound in the world to Cassie.

Cassie scrambled to turn onto her back. Edna placed a cushion under her head.

Aunty Shirley was holding the baby, wrapping it in a white cloth, smiling into its face. All Cassie could see was a little black cap.

Her daughter!

'Give her to me!' she said, holding out her arms, and Aunty Shirley obliged, placing the bundle in Cassie's arms. Cassie's face, swathed in delight, bathed in tears, crumpled at the sight of the tiny face, the little black beads of eyes gazing back at her. She looked up at Edna: 'She's the most beautiful baby in the world!'

'She is!' said Edna, crying herself.

'Let me just weigh her quickly, take some measurements, clean her off a bit – I gon' pass her back in a moment.'

Aunty Shirley held out her hands and with reluctance, Cassie placed the baby in them. She felt she was handing over the most precious thing that had ever been on earth, and it was hers. *Her baby*. She had given birth to this miracle.

Routine examinations and a perfunctory clean-up over, Aunty Shirley placed the baby back in Cassie's arms; Cassie immediately drew back the thin blanket she was wrapped in, gazed in wonder at the perfect little body, the tiny belly moving up and down, the purple length of umbilical cord dangling free. She counted fingers and toes and marvelled that they were all there, minuscule fingers closing round her own finger. She was perfect, absolutely perfect. Though the night was warm, Cassie drew the blanket close again.

'Rita,' she said. 'Her name is Rita.' She turned to Edna with pleading eyes. 'Please call Jitty, Mummy, please tell him!'

Edna pursed her lips, but nodded acquiescence.

'The three of you together: lovely!' said Shirley. She walked over to a shelf near the door, reached up, and returned with a Polaroid camera in her hand. 'Now's the time for a photo!' she said. 'I take a photo of all my new mothers. So, heads together! Say cheese!'

Edna placed her head next to Cassie's, Cassie held up the baby, the two women smiled. The camera flashed. That done, Aunty Shirley replaced the camera on the shelf while it developed the photo, and returned to work.

'Now I got to birth the placenta,' she said. 'You enjoy your baby with your mummy. No more work for you. Maybe you can try feedin' her.'

She pointed to a door in one of the walls. 'Go into that room, Edna. You gon' see some more equipment, a cot with a pile of bedding and such. There's a bolster on the cot. Bring it, so she can sit up a bit to try feedin'.'

Edna fetched the bolster and placed it gently under Cassie's shoulders. Aunty Shirley placed the baby in the correct position for feeding, its head against the breast. She chuckled as she moved the nipple into position. 'That baby goin' to get some nice sweet milk!'

All three women watched in fascination as tiny lips nuzzled the nipple. The tiny lips opened slightly; Edna pressed the nipple between them. The baby moved its head, the nipple fell away. She tried again.

'She's a bit weak, due to being a bit early,' she said. 'Only five pounds. She might not be able to suck, but we'll keep trying.'

Keep trying they did, and then they all laughed as baby Rita's cheeks began to move in rhythm as the baby drew its first drops of colostrum from Cassie's body.

'She's drinking! She's drinking!' cried Cassie, and both Edna and Aunt Shirley laughed.

'She got it quick! She latched on!' she rejoiced. 'That gon' help birth the placenta. Let me go now and massage you belly.'

That's what she did, placing her hands on Cassie's belly, softly massaging, coaxing out the placenta with gentle, knowing hands.

Minutes went by, everyone intent on their own activity: Aunty Shirley on massaging Cassie's abdomen, the baby on drinking, Cassie gazing with wonder at her child and gently stroking the tiny cheek with her forefinger, Edna, in turn, stroking Cassie's head and also gazing at the baby's perfectly satisfied face. The baby made tiny grunting noises, the only sound to be heard in the room. Above them, moths buzzed around the bare bulb that lit them all. The night seemed to enfold them, benevolent, mellow, compassionate. It was now well past midnight.

'Here it is!' said Aunty Shirley, as the placenta slipped out.

But in a heartbeat timeless serenity can switch to alarm.

'Oh!' cried Cassie.

It was as if a giant wave swept through her, washing out her insides. A wet gush poured out of her, the breaking of a dam.

'She's haemorrhaging,' exclaimed Aunty Shirley and the concern in her voice was unmistakable.

Cassie managed to whisper, 'What's happening? I feel...'

She could not finish the sentence. Her hand, holding the baby's head, went limp. 'She's fainted!' cried Edna, deftly catching the baby as Cassie's grip loosened. Immediately the baby began to scream, arms and legs struggling against the blanket's folds. Edna ignored her instinct to comfort her, stop the crying; she ignored the baby altogether, carried her away and placed her in the bassinet and rushed to the midwife's side. The baby continued to scream. Alone, uncomforted.

A pool of blood gathered at their feet.

'She's haemorrhaging bad!' cried Aunty Shirley. 'Got to stop the bleeding.'

The concern had turned to alarm, laced with panic. She scrambled to stop the blood, pressing hard on Cassie's abdomen. 'Bring some towels to catch the blood, Edna. I gon' try stop it.'

But the blood flowed on and on, minute after minute. Cassie lay inert, the rich brown of her face turned pallid, the living joy of only a few minutes ago replaced by a mask of indifference. Aunt Shirley said, 'Edna, you need to help. Go in that room' – she pointed to the second door – 'and bring me what I tell you. Quick now, no time to lose. Put on some gloves. Open that cupboard – they're in there. Quick now. Got to stop this bleedin'.'

Cassie's body leaked blood as if a tap had been opened. Blood dripped – no, flowed – to the floor. Edna had to step into the spreading red pool to cross the room. She hurried into the storage room and Aunty Shirley called to her what she should look for, what she should bring.

'I need to set up an IV – I'm going to give her some Pitocin. It's a hormone to induce contractions, but it could help shut off the blood vessel to stop the bleedin'. Bring the box with needles and the syringe.'

Bring this, bring that. Do this, do that. Edna scrambled around while Aunty Shirley gave the orders. Now and then, she glanced at Cassie's ghostly face and her heart galloped away with her and she found herself holding her breath, but then she breathed again and her eyes opened wide and she watched in horrified fascination as Aunty Shirley jabbed a needle into Cassie's limp arm, and because Cassie could not feel it, she felt it, and she gave a cry of pain and she wanted to weep but there was no time for tears, no time for thought, no time even for fear but she was afraid, she was terrified.

And in the background, the baby's intermittent scream grew louder, more insistent. But there was no time. Not a second to spare.

After what seemed an eternity to Edna, Aunty Shirley's face relaxed. 'It's all right now. The bleedin' just about stopped. But – she lost too much blood. She needs blood, a transfusion. A donor. Edna, you know your blood type?'

'A positive,' said Edna, remembering from the appendix operation she'd had years before.

'And hers? The same?'

Edna shook her head. 'She's B positive.'

'Then we need O blood, positive or negative. Edna, go back to the storage room. On the shelf above the desk you'll see a stack of files. And a hardback exercise book. Red. Bring it here.'

Edna found the book and returned. Aunty Shirley peeled off her bloody gloves and took the book, explaining, 'I started this book ten years ago, when a young girl came with a period so heavy, she fainted. She needed blood, and we had to send her to Suddie. I thought I'd start a donorship programme in Charity. Get people to have their blood tested and offer themselves as donors in case of an emergency like this – we can't keep a blood bank here.

'It's a list of names and addresses and phone numbers and blood type. It's a godsend, I can tell you! But many people moved away, some died – it's not up to date. Lemme see… I need somebody nearby…'

She turned the page, looking down the list, muttering as her fingers went down the list of names. Many of the entries had been crossed out. Many were the wrong blood type. Her finger stopped at one.

'The Atkinsons. An English family settled at Hampton Court. They got a phone, and a car. A couple with small children, the wife is O positive. But – no. Too far away. I want somebody local.'

Her finger stopped again.

'This one. Harvey Jones. He lives just a few blocks away, but they don't have a phone. You can take my bicycle and be there in two minutes.'

'But I can't ride a bicycle!'

'Then you gon' have to walk. Run.'

Aunty Shirley had resumed her calm exterior, but Edna could easily detect the apprehension and sense of urgency in her voice. Aunty Shirley's clothes, by now, were covered in blood down the front. There was blood everywhere. All over the floor, over the birthing bed, the towels, everywhere. The place looked like a murder scene.

And at the back of it all, the baby wailed, a frantic, frenzied caterwaul that did not let up for even a second.

Her heart hammering, she flew out the door, out the building, out the yard and into the street. She raced along the road. *No, no, no, no, no!* she cried to herself as she ran. *Don't let this happen! Please, God, don't let this happen!*

But it *was* happening, and all she could do now was run. The baby's cries, shrill and desperate, accompanied her as she ran, growing fainter with distance, replaced by the typical background buzz of night creatures: bugs and crickets and the croaking of toads. The road seemed endless, emptily endless, darkly endless, the darkness interspersed by dim yellow circles of light around the occasional street lamps. Swarms of moths circled around the lights. She didn't find the house at first, turned the wrong corner, because there was no street sign. Ran back, tried a different street. This one did have a sign. *Ran, ran, ran.*

Out of breath, she reached the address for Harvey Jones' house, a typical single-storey wooden house on high stilts. Almost stumbled as she ran up the stairs, two at a time. Knocked furiously on the door.

Nobody answered. The house was in darkness.

Lord, oh Lord, let them be home!

She knocked again – still no answer. She careened back down the stairs and ran round to the back of the house, where presumably the bedrooms might be. It was now well past midnight. They'd all be fast asleep. She cried out at the top of her voice: 'Mr Jones! Mr Jones, wake up! Blood! I need blood! Please, help me, help me! My daughter gon' die!' She looked up at the dark windows, calling, praying.

At last a light went on, a window opened, a man leaned out. 'Woman, you mad or what? Screamin' bloody murder, wakin' up the whole street!'

Edna stopped in her tracks, stopped screaming. Out of breath, she said, 'Please, sir, I'm sorry. I need blood for my baby! Nurse Gibson sent me. She said you're registered as a donor. Please, can you give blood? She's bleeding to death!'

Miraculously, talking made her calm again. She stood below the window and explained the problem. 'We need a blood donor, O positive, and that's your blood type, Nurse Gibson said. Would you be so kind…? Sorry to wake you…'

'I'll help, of course.'

'Can you come now to Nurse Gibson? So sorry to disturb you, sir, but we're desperate.'

'I understand. Got a little girl myself, born last year. Hold on while I put on some clothes.'

'You have a car, sir?'

'No, but I have a bike.'

'Then you cycle ahead. I'll follow on foot.'

A few minutes later, Mr Jones was on his way, cycling furiously towards Nurse Gibson's house. Edna, slightly slower this time, ran back the way she'd come. She heard, faintly, the baby's wail as she rounded the last corner, and it grew louder, pulling her on, quickening her feet. She'd never run so much in her life, never knew she could run so much, that her fifty-year-old joints and leg muscles were up to it. Her arms were mighty, muscular, but farm life, creek life, had never involved running. But desperation gives you strength, and, panting, she made it back without once stopping. At last, Aunty Shirley's house and the wail was deafening, frantic, the heart-wrenching wail of a child alone in the world.

She climbed the stairs to the door in a half-daze, stood on the threshold to the delivery room. *No-no-no-no-no*, her only thought. Harvey Jones sat on a chair against the wall, bowed over, head in hands. Cassie lay in a pool of blood, laid out straight, on the birthing bed. Her face had now attained a grey pallor; the skin looked pasty, ghostly. Shirley was turned away, her back to Edna, jiggling up and down, murmuring shhh shhhh shhh to the wailing baby she held in her arms, but the baby only screamed louder, more desperately, as if she knew.

Edna stepped inside the room, touched Cassie's hand. It was still warm, the fingers soft and limp, as if she were asleep. Her eyes were closed, her face without expression. Only asleep. But not.

Shirley turned around. Agony was written across her face, cheeks stained with tears. She jiggled the baby, uselessly. Tiny hands and feet waved furiously, and an unremitting screech of frantic abandonment split the deathly silence of night.

On the shelf, the Polaroid camera sat abandoned, ignored, the fully developed photo lying there as if spat out, irrelevant.

Chapter Forty-Eight

Guilt

'That's worse than I ever imagined!' wept Rita. 'She died because of me! I killed her! I did kill her!'

Jitty, too, could hardly speak for his tears. 'I knew you'd say that, Rita. I knew you'd think that, blame yourself. Especially as a child, not knowing the full story. But no, you didn't kill her – I did.'

'You? But how? You weren't even there!'

He took a deep breath, collected himself before replying. Now was the time for a full confession, to say aloud the things that had bored into his being every day, every minute, almost since the day he had learned of Cassie's death.

'It's in the letters! You read them! I could have done as she'd wanted, married her, taken her to Town. We could have lived at her aunt's house, a nice big house on Peter Rose Street. She could have given birth at the Georgetown Hospital, or even at a private one. If she'd haemorrhaged there, there'd have been the right blood in the blood bank. And if there wasn't: the irony is that my blood is O positive. I could have saved her directly. If only I'd done the decent thing, the honourable thing.'

She sniffed and blew her nose on the handkerchief Jitty handed her.

'Why didn't you? Why didn't you want to marry her, Daddy?'

'But I did! I did, that's the whole problem. I did, but I couldn't under the terms of Granma's will.'

'Why didn't you just say to hell with the will, to hell with Granma, I'm a grown man and I'll marry the woman I want?'

'Because I'm a coward, Rita. I'm a weak, wet, watery coward. Nothing but swagger. All talk and not even a thread of courage. I didn't want to lose the house – this house. I thought I could have it all, not marry Cassie but have her and you live with me, unmarried.'

'So that was your plan? Fool her into thinking you'd marry her, when you only wanted to live together?'

'Society was beginning to change in Guyana. Getting more progressive, like in America and England. People were starting to say marriage was just a piece of paper. Liberal people wanted to be free. I liked the idea: why did I need the law to sanction my relationship? I preferred to just live together. It seemed much freer to me. And now it's no big thing. People live together all the time, instead of getting married. It's just a conservative convention. People should do as they want without other people pointing fingers! Marriage is so old-fashioned, I always thought.'

'But, Mummy, she wasn't like you, was she? She was a bit old-fashioned? Traditional, like her family?'

'She was a practising Christian, yes. She wouldn't have agreed.'

'So, what did she think of your idea, just live together without marriage?'

'She didn't even know. I never told her the terms of Granma's will. All she knew was that Granma was going to throw me out if if I married her.'

'So, basically, you were trying to trick her? Make a fool of her, give her no choice?'

He hung his head. 'I suppose you could see it like that. Of course, she caught me out when her aunt offered to put us up. To her, it was the perfect solution, to stay at her aunt's.'

'You were a bit of an asshole, Daddy. A spineless asshole. You'd made a bargain with the devil, right? She didn't even know what a coward you were.'

He hung his head yet more.

He sighed. 'Yes, you're right. I thought I could trick her into living together. I thought she'd eventually submit, when push came to shove. I thought she'd have no choice, in the end, when Granma died. I thought she'd just be nice and kind and comply without a peep. She was always so meek and mild. But…'

'Those last letters she wrote, she was furious with you!'

'I know! There she was fighting back, making plans for herself, standing up for herself. That knocked me over. She wasn't submitting to my plan, she wasn't begging me any more.'

'She was telling you to get lost.'

'And I deserved it. But in the end – in the end…'

He sat there, shaking his head.

Rita finished the sentence:

'…in the end, everyone lost. She, you, me.'

'In the end, I killed her. And it's been killing me ever since.'

'That's why you couldn't tell me, right?'

He nodded. 'The guilt, Rita. The guilt! It's been tearing me apart all these years. I thought if I told you, you'd never forgive me. You loved her so much.'

'I love her so much,' Rita corrected. 'I still love her. I'll always love her.'

'And you don't hate me?'

She reached out and took his hand, squeezed it.

'Of course I don't hate you, Daddy. And maybe you were right not to tell me when I was a child – how could I possibly understand? But now, I need to know – what happened then? How did you find out she'd died?'

'Well, her mother rang me that day. Apparently, those were Cassie's last words, that she should ring me, tell me we had a beautiful daughter. It makes me think she'd forgiven me. But then, she didn't know she'd die within the hour. But – then she *did* die, and I had a beautiful daughter but no Cassie. Edna – that's her

mother's name – rang me and told me. She said, Cassie's dead, the
child is a girl and she's well. We're at Charity. Or something like
that, I can't even remember the exact words. All I heard was, *Cassie's
dead*. Edna's voice was dead, too, emotionless. I panicked. She
refused to tell me the details. I could tell she was fuming; blaming
me for everything. Because I *was* to blame for everything. I yelled
at her on the phone to tell me what happened. She wouldn't. She
just said, if you want to see your daughter you need to come to
Charity. So that's what I did. I dropped everything and went up
to Charity. And I saw Cassie's body, cold and pale. The baby – I
mean you! They'd taken you to the hospital at Suddie. You were in
the newborn nursery, being looked after by a nurse. You were the
only baby there at the time. The nurse put you in my arms and I
fell in love. It was the biggest thing I'd ever felt in my life, Rita,
holding you, the wonder of you all mixed up with anguish; I can't
call it joy because I was falling apart with grief, something totally,
totally overwhelming. I only knew I would be there for you every
day of my life from now on. But…'

He paused; the words had been gushing from him with hardly a
pause for breath, words tumbling over words. He gathered himself,
now, and spoke more slowly.

'I promised to be there for you but I couldn't. I couldn't take
you home – Granma wouldn't have allowed it, that much I knew.
I had nowhere to go, no job, nothing. I wasn't much more than a
schoolboy. And then Edna came storming up – I swear there were
sparks flying out of her head, she was so angry. She grabbed you
right out of my arms and I let it happen. And I just stood there,
shoulders hanging, and every word she said was true…'

He paused. 'What did she say?'

'She called me names. Called me a stupid little boy with my
brain in my pants. A reckless jackass. Said I was to blame, I didn't
deserve to be a father.'

'And then?'

'They brought you back to Charity the next day; you were a perfectly healthy baby. They'd already organised everything for your care, all those Charity women. There was one woman who had a baby, one year old, still nursing, and she offered to take you, wet-nurse you for as long as you needed. See, your granny wanted to take you home, but she didn't have no milk. There was no baby powder-milk in the Charity shops. I said I would buy some in Town and send it up but they all said no, breast milk better at least for the start. So even that little bit, send powder-milk, they wouldn't let me do. I ended up spending three days in Charity. I stayed in a hotel. I tried to be with you as much as possible, but they wouldn't let me. News spreads fast in the country and soon everyone in Charity knew who I was and what I'd done and everyone hated me. Well, the women hated me. The mothers, the grandmothers. They seemed intent on protecting you from me, as if you needed protection! They shielded you, only let me near you with supervision. They let me hold you now and then, but they watched as if I was about to steal you away. As if I couldn't be trusted not to drop you.

'And the ringleader was your granny. She turned them all against me, telling them the whole story. I was the villain in that story. I never realised till that moment the power of mothers. How protective they are of children, all children, not only their own. You were like a jewel they had to take care of. Mothers, and grandmothers.' He paused, correcting himself. 'Of course, I knew about grandmothers, I had my own dragon of a granma. *Yours*, Granny Gomes, was just as fierce. They might be old, those grannies, but oh Lord, when you misbehave, they can crush you in the dust. She had sparks flying out of her eyes. She didn't say much, but she was seethin' inside. I had the feelin', if she had a gun, she woulda' shoot me dead. An' I woulda deserve it. That night, I woulda' give my life for Cassie, if it could only bring her back.'

He fell silent. Rita reached out and took his hand, squeezed it.

'I felt *so* small, Rita!'

He held up his hand, thumb and forefinger about to pinch but not quite touching. 'So small. We men might think we rule the world, but when you cross the path of a mother…'

He shook his head. 'Those women, your granny, they reduced me to nothing.'

He stopped talking, shook his head slowly as if in reflection.

'And then?' Rita prompted.

'They organised everything. Next thing was the funeral – I didn't even stay for that, I felt so guilty. Then your granny, she drag me to a solicitor in Charity and made me sign some papers, a contract giving her guardianship. I had to do it. What choice did I have? I couldn't take you home. I didn't know nothing about babies. You were so small, so helpless, so fragile. I thought I would break your bones just by holding you! But, Rita, I loved you so, so much. And I was heartbroken about Cassie, and so guilty and so small. I felt like rubbish. But I knew I loved you and I was your father and I would do everything in the world for you. Just one demand – no, request, I couldn't demand a thing – they allowed me: to give you my name. Maraj. Your granny agreed because it was better for you, made it look like your parents were married. So, you were Maraj, not Gomes. It was all in the contract.

'Eventually I returned to Town. I bought up all the Dutch Baby and Cow & Gate milk in Town and sent it to your granny for the time when she'd take you home. And after a year I sent money for your keep. It was all I could do. I wasn't allowed to visit. Not once. But I thought of you every day and worked hard to change my ways so I could be a good daddy to you, when the time came. I lived for that time. Basically, I was waiting for my own granma to die. Because her will didn't say anything about you. Not a word. It said I couldn't marry Cassie but it didn't say I couldn't bring you home.'

'How old was I when you came to get me? What about that guardianship? What did Granny do?'

'It was terrible. Just terrible. When Granma died, you were five. I went to the court and rescinded the guardianship. That was all I had to do, to get custody. From that moment, you were mine.'

'So, you took me away from her?'

'Yes.'

Silence. Then Rita asked:

'Daddy, if you could go back and change everything, do what she wanted, please her, instead of her pleasing you, knowing what you know now: would you have married her? Moved in with Aunt Mathilda and Uncle Patrick? Told your granny to hell with her bloody will, you'll marry who you want, the mother of your child?'

Jitty did not hesitate a second.

'Yes. Oh, yes. A thousand million times yes.'

Chapter Forty-Nine

Jitty, 1971–76

Jitty returned to Georgetown a broken man, but a man determined to prove himself. No longer a schoolboy, playing at life. He had a goal, now, and a newfound determination to achieve it. That goal was Rita. To bring her home. To be worthy of her. Flattened by Cassie's death, he slowly picked himself off the ground.

Slowly, slowly, he recovered his equilibrium and his drive, and developed a newly found ambition. Yes, he *would* turn over a new leaf.

Rita was five when Granma Maraj died. At last. This was Jitty's chance, and he grabbed it with both hands. The day after he received the papers granting him his full parental rights, he set forth towards the Pomeroon. To get her back.

It was a whole day's journey; he took the car, this time, and drove to the Demerara ferry, crossed the river to Vreed-en-Hoop, on the East Bank, and then drove up the Atlantic coast to the little settlement of Parika, on the Essequibo River, an hour away. He parked the car, locked it, stretched, and made his way to the stelling, the harbour, and walked on to the wharf.

It was his second view of the mighty Essequibo – the first time, upon Cassie's death, he had been far too devastated to observe anything. This time round, he was completely overwhelmed by the sheer size of it. Having taken A-level Geography, including local geography, he knew, of course, that the Essequibo was the largest river in the country, and the largest river between the Orinoco and

Amazon. But actually seeing it, spread out before him as if it were
the ocean, not a river, took his breath away. And that outline of
land, on the far side, wasn't even the western shore: it was just an
island! The estuary here was about twelve miles wide. He stood
on the busy stelling, where crowds milled, passengers and farmers
and boatmen, people shouting, carrying loads – bananas, coconuts,
pineapples – here and there. The river taxis that crossed the water
filled rapidly, their owners ushering passengers down the side of
the wharf and into the boats, handing them lifejackets, ensuring
they were as tightly squeezed in as possible before, at last, they
took off, backing into the river and then gathering speed. The boat
whizzed across the estuary, its bow raised up as it cut through the
khaki-coloured water. Above, puffy clouds sailed across the sky,
and the midday sun bearing down on them all was mitigated by
the cool wind that whipped his clothes and hair and lashed against
his skin. It was exhilarating, breathtaking. They passed several of
the river's 365 islands – as many as days of the year – and each new
horizon turned out to be just another island. But finally, the boat
arrived at the far shore, at the settlement of Supenaam.

Here, taxis waited, car taxis this time, and soon he found
a seat crammed into a car with four other passengers, headed
for Charity on the Pomeroon River, a further hour's drive.
His excitement now was at its highest: he was going to get his
daughter! His beloved Rita. He was going to be a father, at last:
a real father. A new life was about to begin. He was turning over
a new leaf, a new page. He imagined his daughter, five years
old now, rushing towards him, leaping into his arms – that was
what little girls did when their daddies came home. He hoped
her grandparents had prepared her well for this moment. It was
going to be extremely emotional. Already he was close to tears;
he'd waited long enough.

The last part of the journey was in a private speedboat, its bow
raised high as it cut through the Pomeroon River, heading inward

to the country's vast interior. Everyone knew everyone up here, it seemed; he had only had to tell the boat-taxi driver the name 'Gomes' and he had nodded and sped off. After almost two hours of slicing through the river, the boat turned off into an opening in the dense forest. Another twenty minutes, and there they were, at the rather rickety pier jutting into the creek. The boatman cut the motor and let the boat drift up to the pier; he climbed up and secured the boat, and then Jitty himself climbed out and walked up the sandy path to the house.

It was set in a large clearing in the rainforest. The front garden, through which the path wound, was neatly laid out with flower beds: hibiscus, oleander and frangipani bushes and trees, all in full blossom. Two dogs rushed forward to greet him, barking, but a voice from the house called them back, and they obeyed. The house itself stood on high thin stilts, with a staircase leading up to the front door. Like most Georgetown houses, it was made of timber planks, which had once been painted white but were now faded and peeling, just as the stairs looked rickety and rather precarious. That's not what Jitty minded – his own house was not much better maintained. What he did mind was the door opening and a little fine-limbed lady stepping out onto the landing and walking down the stairs towards him.

It was the moment he had been dreading: the confrontation.

She reached the bottom of the stairs and gazed up at him. Now, Jitty was a well-built man, strong of limb and tall, and full of youthful vigour. But the stern gaze of this tiny woman, long past her physical prime but not afraid to look him in the eye, straight and stern, reduced him to jelly.

'You should be ashamed of yourself,' said Mrs Gomes. 'Taking a little child away from her home, and de only parents she know!'

Jitty quivered inside, but managed a few words: 'I am her father,' he said. 'I have the right!'

'De legal right, maybe, but not de moral right!'

She spoke with the musical lilt of the upcountry folk, dropping her th's and ignoring tenses. Jitty spoke like this himself, sometimes, but right now he felt that the only way he could demonstrate superiority was through correct speech.

'Well, the Magistrates' Court has decided that the legal right is what counts,' he said, pulling himself up straight. He tried straightening his shoulders and frowning and glaring at her, as if her moral outrage could be demolished by sheer male antagonism, but she was having none of it. She simply glared back, and the fire of her fury made him shake with – with *something*. What was it? Shame, or guilt, or some dormant sense of principal, of natural ethics?

'Why you don't ask she what she want? If she want to go with you, a stranger, who di'n't even visit once in the past five years, or wit' de people she know and love?'

Before Jitty could even think of a reply, she turned and yelled: 'Winston! Bring she down!'

It was then that Jitty heard the bawling and screaming, growing louder by the second, and then a man in his late fifties, perhaps, tall, but thin, like the little woman, appeared on the top landing, holding a screaming child in his arms. He walked slowly down the stairs, one arm holding tightly to the child, the other on the banister. He reached the bottom of the stairs, and the woman took the child from him. The little girl went gladly to her, wrapped both arms round her, and clung to her as tightly as she had to the man. Her arms dug into her grandmother's flesh, and she screamed and yelled, and would not even look at Jitty.

'Rita!' he said. 'Rita! I'm your daddy! Come to me, darling!'

His voice was gentle, cajoling; at least, he hoped it was, but she seemed not to hear it and would not look at him, her head buried in the woman's neck.

'You turned her against me! You been bad-talking me!' declared Jitty.

'Not at all,' said the man, Rita's granpa. 'We jus' told her the truth: that you is her daddy and she gotta go wit' you.'

Her grandmother added:

'She don't know you! You can't just take a child like that! You ain't nothin' but a stranger!'

'I'm her father! It's legal! She belongs to me!'

'She belong to her mother! You din't want her mother so why you should get her?'

'It has nothing to do with that. The Magistrates' Court…'

'Who care about the Magistrate nonsense! In the court of the Almighty she belong with de people who raise she for five years, who gave her love and food and everyting a child need!'

'Nevertheless, she's mine!' Jitty managed this time to put authority into his voice. He produced a piece of paper from his shirt pocket and pointed to it.

'See, this is the court order! You got to give her over! If you refuse, I have the right to send the police or even the army!'

'Who said we refuse? Is *she* who refuse. Look at her. Take her if you can.'

And that's what Jitty did. He stepped forward, put his arms round Rita's waist and pulled her away. She screamed and clung all the more, but he managed simultaneously to hold her tightly round the waist – she was such a small thing! – and to unclench her fingers from her grandmother's arm and shoulder. And without another word he marched off towards the pier and the boat, the child struggling in his arms, screaming. He did not look back. He spoke gently to her, persuasively.

'It's all right, darling. I'm your daddy and the two of us going to have a good life. I'm taking you to Town, and I'm going to show you all kinds of nice things and give you everything you want. You going to be happy with me, I promise!'

But she didn't stop screaming; she screamed louder, louder, more desperately; as if she were being kidnapped by an axe-murderer.

Some people emerged from a cottage at the back: a woman, two children, curious, drawn by the screams. Another child, smaller, came running up, ran past the woman, screaming too, careening towards them, calling out Rita's name. Rita jerked herself into a tight ball, then jerked her limbs apart so vigorously she slipped from Jitty's arms. She ran towards the group of people, her grandparents, the other woman, the children. The smallest child, a little girl, ran out ahead and the two little girls almost collided, then clung to each other like leeches, both screaming.

Jitty reached them and with silent strength managed to peel Rita's arms from around the little child, unpeel the smaller child's fingers from Rita's dress. He lifted her into his arms again, this time tighter than ever, and marched with her towards the jetty.

Rita's screams subsided into sobs and she stopped struggling. It was as if she had given up, surrendered to her fate. Yet there was something defiant about that surrender, something rebellious. She sniffed and wiped her face with her hands. 'Put me down!' she said, and he did, and she did not attempt to run back to the house. Which he thought was a good sign. She walked beside him to the wooden pillar where the boat was moored. The boatman, who had watched from the pier, said, 'You got to put a lifejacket on she. If she start struggling again, she might fall out the boat.'

He handed up a child-sized lifejacket, orange. Every boat-taxi was required to carry these things, and every passenger was required to wear one, but Jitty had refused on the outward journey and the boatman had just shrugged. But now Jitty decided he would wear one, just to show his daughter how it was done. But she knew already. She grabbed it from the boatman, her face now expressionless, sullen, put her arms through the armholes and tightened the straps. This was a girl who knew about rivers and boats.

She did not look back as they sped away, but Jitty did. The woman and the man were clasped into each other. The woman's body was heaving, and though he could not hear her, he knew her sobs were enough to awaken the dead. The other woman stood with two children beside her, the smallest one in her arms, her head buried in her shoulder, shaking with sobs. Once more he felt that nudge of guilt, but he pushed it away.

Rita was *his*.

Chapter Fifty

1989: Forgiveness

'You see?' Jitty said to Rita, continuing his story. 'You see what a terrible person I am. I'm a walking piece of shit. I don't deserve to live. I killed that girl, that good sweet girl. I took you from your home. I was a terrible father. I wish I'd been killed in that accident. Perhaps I wanted to die that night, perhaps I knew. Perhaps fate was calling me. Karma.'

Though not a practising Hindu, Jitty believed absolutely in karma. Not so much in his wild youth; now, more than ever.

'Well, if so, you've been given a second chance. Oh, Daddy, I wish I'd known this all along. Why didn't you tell me?'

'How could a little child ever understand? You'd have thought you killed her – and you did, even now, didn't you? You had to know the whole story. You needed to be adult for that.'

He paused. 'Do you hate me now?'

'Of course not. But give me time. I need to digest all of it.'

'Well, and here's something that might give you comfort.'

He handed her the second Cadbury's tin. She opened it. It was full of photographs. Photos of Cassie. In stunned silence, she picked them up, one by one. There she was. Cassie. Her mother. A large portrait of Cassie in Bishops' uniform, the straw panama hat with the green-and-red hatband at a jaunty (forbidden) angle, her tie loosened slightly and the top button of her white blouse unbuttoned – also strictly forbidden. Her lips stretched in a wide smile, showing perfect white teeth. A neatly plaited black pigtail resting on each shoulder. Eyes that sparkled, bright and warm; eyes open, trusting, clear and innocent.

Cassie at the beach, in her swimsuit, running through the surf towards, presumably, Jitty with the camera – a laughing, happy Cassie. Cassie at the wheel of Jitty's car, pretending to drive. Cassie, leaning on the railing of the Kissing Bridge at the Botanical Gardens. Cassie, again in school uniform, standing in the fork of a red bicycle.

Cassie, Cassie, Cassie.

'Oh, *Daddy!*' Rita cried, and burst into tears.

A month crept past. They edged around each other, Jitty reaching out, trying to bridge the abyss that had suddenly opened between them as a result of Jitty's confession; Rita on the other bank of the abyss, cold and resentful. Silences and words; begging eyes from Jitty, reproachful frowns from Rita. Chandra and Luisa were still in Canada, Chandra having extended their stay, so they were alone; it was the perfect retreat from the turbulence of family life. Just the two of them, building a bridge.

Slowly, surely, they edged nearer to each other. It was Rita, not Jitty, who had to create that bridge, slowly let it all sink in, digest the truth, and out of that digested knowledge build a solid new path to him. Yes, he felt tremendous guilt and responsibility for Cassie's death. But in the end, would she spend the rest of her life in recriminations? Couldn't she forgive him? He'd been young and foolish, just as she had once been. He was destroying himself with remorse, and it was genuine. Was that any way to live? True, he had behaved appallingly towards Cassie. He had literally sacrificed her for a house. A *house!* But there was no sense living in blame, in this no-man's-land of hostility on her side, and abject guilt on his. She *had* to forgive him, build a bridge of compassion.

*

It took several more weeks, but one day she approached him.

'Dad, I can't live in the past any more. What's done is done, I want to move on.'

'Can you forgive me?'

She nodded. 'Granny lost the daughter she loved, and forgave you. I lost a mother I never knew. Granny's loss was the greater. If she can forgive you, so can I.'

She swallowed. 'So, yes, I forgive you.'

And once again, Jitty wept.

And yet, for Rita, something was not quite right. A piece of the puzzle was missing, one last tiny but essential piece that would complete the picture. She couldn't put her finger on it, but she knew it was there: a nagging, persistent question mark, so nebulous, so without substance, she couldn't even figure out the question, never mind find the answer. What was it? It was like a word you were looking for, on the tip of your tongue; you knew it, you definitely *knew* it; she *knew* it. It was right there, in front of her, hiding in the shadows, and you only had to adjust your eyesight and you'd see it – but she couldn't.

She remembered Granny's words, the last day of her first visit: *You got another wound in your heart. A deep, deep wound you can't even see yet. I know it. I can see it, but you can't. It don't have nothing to do with your mummy's death.*

Was this thing, this missing piece of the puzzle, something to do with that? With some deep wound she couldn't see? Nothing to do with Cassie's death, nothing to do with knowing how and why Cassie died, nothing to do with Jitty's story? Granny had said, back then, that she had to *find it out for herself.* But how? And when?

It nagged within her. An itch she couldn't scratch. She knew it was there, deep inside her, but she had no access. No key, or magic word, no *open sesame.*

*

A week later, Jitty said:

'Tell you what, Rita, now you're a rich lady, you can afford a trip to Kaieteur! Let's go – this weekend. Just you and me!'

'Daddy! That's a great idea! We'll go as soon as your leg's out of the cast.'

'That's next week. We'll go then.'

'Will you manage, so soon after?'

He nodded. 'It's not as if I'll be running a marathon. Yes, there's a bit of walking involved, but I can make it.'

'You're sure?'

'Yes. And tell you what: you don't need to spend any of your money. My treat. I'll never forget that trip I made to St Lucia, with Chandra, leaving you behind – you were about eight. You remember?'

She nodded. 'I remember.'

'Well, you know how there are little things, little mistakes you make in your life that nag you forever? That's mine. It's not my biggest mistake by far, but I never forgot it. It's like a little thorn in my belly that digs and digs and digs. A tiny thorn, but so sharp! I'll never forget your little face, your chin quivering as you tried not to cry, not to let us know that you wanted to come too, trying to be strong. Such a proud little girl, not wanting to show your hurt. But you *were* hurt. It was all over your face. Let me make it up. I'll book tickets for Saturday, OK?'

'OK, Daddy! I can't wait!'

'With Chandra in Canada, it's the perfect time. Just you and me.'

Jitty and Cassie drove up to Ogle Airport on the east coast early on Saturday morning. Ogle was a tiny domestic airport, with just one landing strip, and serviced all the remote areas of Guyana with just one airline, Trans Guyana Airways. Jitty parked the car and they walked up to the little wooden building that served as a terminal, and checked in. They had no luggage, of course; they'd be there and back within a few hours.

Jitty had booked one of the regular sightseeing tours for Kaieteur Falls. It was said in Guyana that more foreigners had seen Kaieteur than Guyanese, and it was probably true: the two other passengers sitting in the sparsely furnished waiting room were American tourists, a middle-aged couple, both with binoculars round their necks, both in shorts and loose shirts with sunglasses in the pockets. Small backpacks sat on their laps.

As was his way, Jitty soon fell into easy conversation with them and discovered that they were birders from Cincinnati. They came regularly to Guyana, they said, because of the extraordinary numbers of rare birds to be found in the Interior, and both nodded wisely as they declared the country to be a birder's paradise, the birder capital of the world.

'We're glad that you don't have hordes of tourists,' said the man. 'That's what makes it so special.'

The woman nodded. 'In America, nobody even knows the country exists!'

'Africa – that's where they think it is. Ghana. We have to correct them all the time.'

'Or Jonestown – that terrible mass suicide, years ago – that's what people think when you mention Guyana.'

'Mass murder, not mass suicide,' Jitty corrected.

'Oh really? Do you think so?'

Jitty rarely needed an invitation to deliver his theory of what really happened at Jonestown, and for the next half-hour explained it all to the visitors, who nodded along as he spoke, now and then exclaiming when he delivered a particularly salacious piece of inside information.

Rita had heard it all before. She stood up and wandered over to the glass pane open to the airfield and looked out. That must be their little plane, parked there, ready to go. That must be the pilot, now descending from the cockpit. That must be…

'*Dutch!*' she cried, and pummelled at the glass.

Of course, he didn't hear her call or the pummelling, and there he was now, walking across the airstrip, to another adjoining building. He wore long khaki trousers and a bright blue shirt with the Trans Guyana Airways emblem upon it. Rita ran out of the waiting room and accosted a member of staff she found outside.

'Excuse me – there's a pilot – I just saw a pilot – I need to see him, speak to him – where can I find him? He went into that building…' She pointed.

'I'm sorry, miss, passengers are not allowed in that area of the terminal.'

'But I need to see him – I know him – can you just find him, tell him to come?'

'Well, he's probably busy, miss, and so am I, but if I see him, I'll tell him. What he look like?'

Rita was at a loss. 'Dark skin, he wore a cap, pilot uniform…' She realised she was describing probably every single pilot who worked on the base. 'Good-looking!' she added.

'Ah, well, that's very helpful,' said the staff member. 'He don't have a name?'

'Dutch! He's Dutch!'

'No Dutch pilot here, miss.'

'No, he's not Dutch, his *name* is Dutch – no, wait a minute – his real name is…' She thought for a while, scouring her memory. It was so long ago.

'Van der Zee! That's his name! David Van der Zee!'

'Ah! Yes, I know him. We call him Dave. I'll get a message to him. What did you say your name was?'

'Rita. I'm Rita Maraj.'

'All right. If I see him, I'll let him know.'

'Thanks! Thanks so much! I'll go back to the waiting room.'

She returned to the waiting room and looked at the clock. They were due to board in fifteen minutes. She had to see him, she *had* to… What if – but that'd be too good to be true, and good things never happened to her.

She walked up and down beside the glass pane, nervous beyond belief. She'd been foolish, so foolish. He was probably incredibly busy, and would only be irritated at being summoned like that, as if she were his boss or something. He probably wouldn't even know who Rita Maraj was. She should have said Rita Gomes, because he'd know Granny's surname. It had been idiotic and presumptuous to behave like that, like a silly madcap schoolgirl – but she'd been in such a panic, possessed, even; as if her life depended on seeing him now, right now. Now, she wished she could take it all back. Who was she to demand an important pilot come and speak to her? He surely had more important things to do. Absorbed by her embarrassment, she didn't notice the man entering the waiting room.

'Rita!'

She swung round and there he was. Just as she remembered, except more smartly dressed; no longer the dingy, torn singlet and shorts, but instead a smart crisp uniform, and that open friendly face, smiling at her as he swiftly crossed the room, both hands held out. She raised both of her hands, and he not only clasped them, but drew her to him in an unexpected embrace.

'It's so good to see you! How you doin', girl? Wow, look at you, all grown up now!'

He stepped back to appraise her, then drew her close once more in another embrace.

'Lookin' good, man, lookin' good! A proper woman now.'

She thought she should say something, something complimentary in return, but no words came, those eager allies that flowed from her so willingly the moment she put pen to paper; it was as if she was literally tongue-tied, bereft of expression, bereft of breath, almost. It was as if a precious treasure, a pearl of great price, too cherished to be exposed to the banality of everyday life, buried deep within her for years and lovingly but hopelessly harboured, had suddenly revealed itself to the light of day, and there it was, shining within her; that old sense of complete comfort and safety and belonging. It revealed itself, wordlessly, as a sense of deep identity and simple *worthiness*, rising spontaneously from some hidden depth within her. A sense she had struggled, back then, to clothe with words, for words were inadequate to describe it; an inner source of *completeness*, first unearthed on a godforsaken beach in the remote North-West, consolidated again and again during forays along dark creeks deep into the rainforest, and every time triggered by this man, this lovely, strong, smiling man, standing not a foot from her, still holding her hands, smiling at her as if she were a long-lost treasure, his eyes doing something to her that turned her insides to jelly.

Yes, words were inadequate. All she could bring out, along with that silly grin, was 'Hi, Dutch!'

But he spoke for her, and then it was easy because he carried the conversation and all she had to do was reply.

'What you doin' here? Flying somewhere?'

'Yes, yes, Daddy and I…' – she turned and gestured to Jitty, still deep in conversation with the Americans – '…Daddy and I are flying to Kaieteur.'

'On the six thirty? Wow, that's fantastic! Because, guess what, I'm your pilot! And…' He looked at his watch. 'You'll be boarding in a minute or two.'

And right then, a muffled voice spoke out over the tannoy. Rita could just about make out the word 'Kaieteur'.

'That's you,' said Dutch. 'See you on the plane!'

And just like that, he was gone.

Jitty, crossing the room to join her, said, 'Who was that?'

'Oh, just a fellow I met in the Pomeroon a few years ago.'

'A good friend, looks like,' said Jitty, and gave her a knowing grin – he knew about these matters.

The four passengers walked across the tarmac to the little plane waiting there. The cabin door was just being opened and a ladder let down by a member of staff, who stood in the doorway, a hand reaching out to the American woman. She climbed up the ladder, and they all got in behind her. The plane had four seats, arranged symmetrically around the little cabin; the Americans already occupied the front two seats and were strapping themselves in. Rita and Jitty sat behind them. Looking out of her window, Rita saw Dutch cross the tarmac and climb up into the cockpit. She could only see the back of his head, but then he turned round and smiled at the four of them. He wore earphones, and a mike curved round his face, and through that he greeted them all and wished them a wonderful excursion to one of the wonders of the world. His gaze then met Rita's eyes and stayed there.

'Rita,' he said, 'why not come up and sit next to me?'

'Oh! Really? I can do that?'

'Sure, why not? If you want to,' said Dutch, and to the other passengers, by way of excusing the apparent favouritism, said, 'She's an old friend.'

Rita needed no further invitation. She unfastened her seat belt and head ducked because of the low ceiling, made her way past the Americans on either side of the front row to the cockpit. She sat down in the empty seat beside Dutch and fastened the seat belt. In front of her, Dutch turned knobs and flicked switches and pressed buttons on the dashboard.

The propellers began to turn, slowly at first then gathering speed and whizzing around.

The plane taxied down the runway and lifted into the wind. It circled above Georgetown once, and looking down, Rita found she could identify streets, houses, cars. It continued to rise, and soon left Town behind. Beneath, the villages to the south of the capital looked like tiny toytowns, cutely tucked between emerald green paddy fields and vast expanses of cane, a different shade of green. The plane slanted into the wind, rose higher. The earth fell away; civilisation fell behind. The brown waters of the Demerara snaked through what looked like an endless ocean of broccoli beneath them: the rainforest, vast and dense, a world unknown.

Elation flowed through Rita; she understood, now, why Dutch had chosen this profession. She turned to him, and met his eyes, and they smiled at each other in knowing companionship. The plane sailed through the sky, the engine a comforting background drone, the propellers whipping the wind. It was glorious, this sailing through the sky, which was a brilliant cobalt blue, dotted with puffy clouds. Through Dutch's window, the sun was sailing up the sky. *This*, she thought to herself, *is heaven. I'm in heaven.*

About an hour into the flight, Dutch spoke into the mike, informing the passengers that they were now approaching Kaieteur and that he would first circle the falls for them to see it from above, and then land.

'Kaieteur Falls,' he said, 'is probably the world's most powerful waterfall. It's more than four times the height of Niagara. It's 822 feet in a single drop, and though not as tall as Angel Falls in Venezuela, in sheer water volume it's so much more powerful: 1,140 metric tons of water shooting over a 250-metre cliff in a constant flow – well, it's a sight you'll never forget. It's fed by the Potaro River, with a source deep in the Amazon. The legend goes that Kaieteur is named after an Amerindian chief called Kaie, whose tribe was under threat from a rival Carib tribe. Kaie gave his life by canoeing over the falls, in an act of sacrifice he believed would protect his tribe by means of divine intervention. And the word "teur" meant falls in the native Amerindian language. So actually, we don't need to repeat the word "Falls" after Kaieteur. But few people know that, so Kaieteur Falls it is.'

Dutch had an easy, unhurried way of speaking, and though he must have given this speech on hundreds of other flights, a sense of excitement filled his words as if he was speaking them for the first time. The Americans readied their binoculars and as the plane circled over the falls, tilting first left and then right to give both sets of window seats a view, they peered down and gasped and scrambled for cameras.

After a few such circles Dutch landed the plane, and it bounced on the sandy single strip before coming to a halt. 'Welcome to Kaieteur National Park,' said Dutch. Before them was a small wooden building; around them only scrubland, above them only sky. Not a single person to be seen.

'What a difference to Niagara!' exclaimed the American woman. 'No crowds, no hotel, no commerce – just wonderful!'

'And it's going to stay that way,' said Dutch. 'We're going to keep this place pristine and pure. Now, come with me; it's just a short walk to the falls. We'll come back here later for refreshments. I'll play tourist guide.'

They marched off, single file, Dutch leading the way, followed by the Americans, Rita, and Jitty quite a bit in the rear, limping with his cast. Every now and again they stopped, allowing him to catch up.

'Look out for the golden frog,' Dutch said as they walked along a narrow sandy path, and pointed out the bromelia plant in which it lived. 'This is the only place in the world you can find it, and it lives its entire life inside the folds of the bromelia.' From then on, Rita spent the walk looking into bromelia after bromelia until at last she found one: a tiny creature no bigger than a thumbnail, glowing golden.

Fifteen minutes later, the little party stood at Kaieteur's edge, having walked through the scrubby landscape surrounding the airstrip. Though it was now midday, a light mist surrounded them, veiling the sunlight, moistening their skin and cooling the air. But the shiver that went through Rita and the gooseflesh on her bare arms came not from cold, but from sheer awe.

As smooth as a vast silver ribbon, the water plunged over the gorge's lip. From the plane the falls had seemed a vision, a toy, even, unreal and far away, but here it was *they* who were the toys, minuscule against nature's majesty. The Potaro River surged forward, merciless in its might, pulled as if by a magnet into the abyss. Far below, it met the rocks with a roar so thunderous it drowned her every thought, filled her every cell with a sense of the majesty of it all, the magnificence, the sheer power of water. Rita felt helpless, weak and small, a nonentity, a speck of dust in the vastness of that majesty, and yet, at the same time, she was a part of it, inseparable from the sheer power and glory of those falls. Water crashed over the cliff edge in a mesmerising, almost hypnotic single ribbon of silver, pulling her into itself with an inexorable magnetism. There was just one word that could describe how she felt: *awe*. Breathtaking, mind-numbing awe.

A faint rainbow appeared down in the gorge below, where sunlight chased shadows and water disappeared into shadows and the earth split open up to receive sun-infused water and mist caught them both, water and sunlight. It was magnificent. Awe-inspiring.

Suddenly Rita felt dizzy, but Dutch must have had second sight because his arm slipped round her waist, steadying her, and as she regained her balance she looked at him in thanks, and he looked at her, and they knew, both knew, that this moment held a magic that bound them. It was in his eyes, and, she knew, in hers; words were unnecessary.

Dutch somehow manoeuvred things so that Rita walked behind him as he led the way back to the airstrip, and they fell into easy conversation.

'I was wondering why you didn't come back to your granny,' he said.

'I did, but it took a couple of years. The next year, we went to England and the following years, well, I guess… things got in the way. But I was there just recently. Kathy told me you'd gone to America!'

'Oh, that was two years ago. My great-granny died soon after you left that year and I went for my pilot training in Florida. And then I came back and started to work for Wildlife Tours. It's a new company founded by some Guyanese who got rich in America and came back. I've been flying into the Interior ever since. It's a great job, I love flying.'

'I bet! And it really suits you. So, you never return to the Pomeroon?'

'Sometimes I fly up there, there's an airstrip at Hampton Court. Taking tourists. People are starting to build resorts up there, just like everywhere in Guyana. My boss says that ecotourism is the next big thing, our future. Guyana will never draw the crowds, but for people who want to see nature in its pure state, this is the place. After Great-Granny died, my parents sold the house to a guy who wants to develop it as a guesthouse. I'll never go back to live on the river itself, true enough. I do go to Shell Beach, though. Remember Shell Beach?'

'How could I ever forget Shell Beach!' Rita exclaimed. 'That night – the mother turtle laying her eggs – it was the most fantastic experience of my whole life!'

'It was a beautiful night for me, too,' said Dutch, and Rita had the feeling he wanted to say more, but didn't – or maybe it was she who wanted to say more, but didn't. They were both silent for a while; a comfortable silence, memories of that magical night swelling within Rita.

Dutch eventually spoke.

'Next time I go up, I'll let you know.'

'Oh, yes! I really want to see the hatchlings, the baby turtles returning to the sea!'

'You'll see them, I promise. I'll make sure of it.'

Chapter Fifty-One

Beware of Flattery

'So, what are your plans?'

'For the future, you mean?'

Dutch nodded. 'Yes, now that you've finished school. You going on to UG?'

She shrugged. 'I suppose I should, but I'm not sure. I was thinking of going back to London. We have a house there...'

'You, too?' She looked up and met his eyes. They were hard to read, in the half-light. They were sitting at a poolside table at the Pegasus Hotel, the evening of the Kaieteur trip. Dutch had asked her out to dinner, but she still wasn't sure if it was a proper date or not. She wasn't sure of him – she didn't want to jump to conclusions – but the warmth and interest she saw in his eyes, surely that was genuine?

She'd been mistaken so many times. She still didn't understand boys, men, not even after all these years. She had learned from Ross not to trust too quickly, not to give her heart too soon, not to read into a boy's eyes only the reflection of her own emotions. She'd gone out with boys in the intervening years, but never allowed any feelings to intervene. The hurt Ross had left behind was too deep, too serious; she didn't want to make the same mistake again. She'd learned from Jamal that men could harbour secrets, fool you, squeeze from you your deepest trust, get you to give yourself completely – and it was all a lie. How could she ever trust anyone again? Even Dutch?

*

Back then, she had put him on a pedestal. She'd looked up to him, trusted him; she'd been a little girl, practically, just fifteen, and could not even begin to imagine him as a flesh-and-blood partner. The gap between them had seemed enormous; it was as if he'd been in a far-off world, unattainable. It had been hero worship, and she'd known it. She hadn't remotely thought of him in her future – just worshipped him from afar. She'd felt like a child in his presence. She *was* a child.

And now she'd met Dutch again, quite by accident, and they had immediately clicked, and now she *wasn't* much too young, she was almost nineteen, and he was twenty-four, the perfect age. And here he was, sitting opposite her tucking into a big plate of chow mein beside the sparkling Pegasus pool, and she could hardly believe it was true. He put down his fork now, reached across the table and took her hand.

'Don't go,' he said, and gently squeezed it.

'To London?'

'Yes. Don't go to London. Stay here. I only just met you again and I – well, I want to get to know you better.'

'Same here,' she whispered.

'Good! Very good! You know, even back then, I knew you were special. Different. Not like other girls. And living in Town, it's proven true. You *are* different.'

'Really? In what way?' She tensed slightly; Granny had, in one of their conversations, warned her that one of the sure signs of a dodgy man was him saying '*You're not like other girls, you're different*'.

'*Pure flattery!*' Granny had said. '*Trying to soften you up. Strokin' your vanity.*'

And now, here was Dutch saying those exact words. 'What you mean, different?' she asked again, and there was an edge to her voice.

He laughed. 'Well, for a start: tell a Town girl about a mother turtle layin' eggs on the beach, and they just yawn at you and call you a bore. That's what I mean. If you just speak the word turtle – or otter, or jaguar, or any other wild animal, for that matter – they gone. Not you.'

'I always loved animals. All living things, like ants and tadpoles.'

'See, that's what I mean. It's why you can't just run off to London just when I found you again. I mean, back then, you was much too young anyway, but I had my eye on you and hoped… Well, hoped for a night like this.'

Again, he squeezed her hand. She frowned.

'But you never looked for me, did you, when you came to live in Town? It was pure chance, meeting me again.'

'Trust me, I would have looked for you. Sooner or later, I would have written to Kathy, asked her where to find you. I never forgot. But I was a bit uncertain. A girl like you – I thought someone would have snapped you up by now.'

'Now you're flattering me!'

Beware of flattery, Granny had said, and a veil fell across Rita's heart, a heart so ready to love. She tensed even further.

Right at that moment, the steel band that had been setting up instruments while she and Dutch were talking began to play. The soft, rippling, smooth cadence of pan filled the air and the poolside atmosphere turned mellow, sweet, tender. 'Yellow Bird', 'Island in the Sun', 'Jamaica Farewell' – the sounds of the Caribbean that had formed a backdrop to Rita's life, the bedrock of Guyanese culture, immediately set a different mood. Dutch's voice, too, was softer.

'No, it's true. I never forgot. I never forgot the look in your eyes when you saw that turtle laying her eggs. The tears I saw there. You cried. You did, you cried.'

'I was so moved. I cried, because the mother turtle cried. The tears running from her eyes – they made me feel so sad. I thought – I just thought she's crying because she won't ever get to see her babies. And her babies won't ever get to see her, know their mother. It's a bit like me, isn't it? Not having a mother, I mean.'

Dutch chuckled. 'People love to interpret those turtle tears, make them out to be something human. There's a word for that… anthro… anthro…'

'Anthropomorphic.'

'Yes, that's the word. Of course, it's not true – there's a purely biological reason why she sheds tears! Her body is just shedding excess salt, and also protecting her eyes from the sand while she works on land to make her nest.'

'I don't care about the biological reason. It's the *symbolism* of it all. The sadness I felt, thinking of that mother turtle and all the effort she made to lay her eggs and then just disappearing back into the sea. And never seeing her babies, just like my mum never got to see me or me her. I mean, I knew a turtle doesn't have human feelings. But those tears – they got to me and I had to cry too.'

Dutch clearly knew better than to argue with Rita. 'And it was your tears, Rita. Seeing your tears at that moment – something in me just clicked and I knew, I just knew—'

He stopped abruptly. Now she squeezed *his* hand, as a nudge.

'What did you know?'

'That you were special. That you were the one.'

And all of a sudden Rita, too, just *knew*. All of a sudden, her last defences dropped. She stopped looking for the warning signs, stopped doubting and second-guessing and suspecting, and the smile she gave him was the most open and inviting and fearless one she had given anyone in her whole life.

Chapter Fifty-Two

Three Months Later. Fear.

'You'll be bored to death – trust me!'

'Trust *me*, I won't. I don't believe in boredom.'

Rita sighed. 'All right then. I'll call her. Invite her.'

She knew it was the right thing to do. She had seriously neglected Aunt Mathilda over the years, since that first rather embarrassing visit.

Since then she had visited her again, but always more out of duty than out of genuine need on her part; certainly, at every Christmas. And each time she felt guilty, realising that she and Uncle Patrick wanted more than she was able to give. Now here was Dutch, insisting that they invite her to the Pegasus for dinner. It was just that now, of course, Rita realised that Aunt Mathilda *was* important, had played a role in her life, even if it was before she was born. She had a duty towards her. And so this invitation. She had told Dutch the story of her mother, her life and death, and Aunt Mathilda's kindness towards her.

Uncle Patrick, in the meantime, had developed Alzheimer's disease, and Aunt Mathilda took care of him at home with the help of a trained nurse who popped in twice daily to change and bathe him and put him to bed. Tonight, she was to have a night out with them, with a neighbour at home while Uncle Patrick slept. Tonight, was to be a special treat for her – Dutch's suggestion.

They picked up Aunt Mathilda in his car; she left the house smiling, with a huge handbag clasped to her stomach. Rita wondered what for; she didn't even need a purse, as Dutch was paying, and if she had a hanky, she could have tucked it in her neckline, as old ladies do. She actually felt a little shame, on Aunty's behalf…

And now here they were, at a table at the Pegasus poolside, and Rita saw she need not have worried. Aunt Mathilda succumbed completely to Dutch's charm – who wouldn't?

He plied her with question after question, and to Rita's astonishment, Aunt Mathilda had more than enough to say. She talked about life in the old days, when the British ruled; about the bad days, when British Guiana was torn apart by racial violence, people massacred in the streets, a whole family killed in an arson attack, friends of Aunt Mathilda. And she spoke of herself.

Aunt Mathilda, it turned out, had been very good at school, achieving excellent final results; she'd been one of the candidates for the British Guiana Scholarship, entitling her to study in the United Kingdom. But then she'd met Uncle Patrick, and fallen in love. She had settled for a secretarial course and landed a job in the Ministry of Labour, Health, and Housing, eventually being promoted to the Minister's personal secretary. And married very soon after that. And had to stop working.

'But why?' Rita asked.

'We had to,' she replied. 'Women in public service had to give up their jobs once they married.'

'But you didn't even have children!'

'It didn't matter, it was British law.'

The conversation turned to Uncle Patrick, and more surprises leapt out at Rita. Uncle Patrick had been active in the war, a volunteer soldier. He had fought in France, and then in Burma; he had won a medal for bravery.

Aunt Mathilda's eyes moistened with unshed tears. 'He never liked to speak of it. He never told me what he had done. I just knew he was very brave. So proud of his medal…'

She hesitated. 'But, later on, he wrote about it. His memoirs. And – and Rita…' She looked at her great-niece. 'I didn't want to bother you before, I know you're very busy. But…'

She rummaged in her handbag and removed a sheaf of papers. 'I've been typing them up. I'm still a good typist, you know! And here they are. I wondered – would you be so kind as to read them? I know you don't have much time, but…'

Rita held out her hands, took the papers. 'Yes, Aunt Mathilda, of course! I'd love to read them!'

Later, on the way home, Dutch turned to her and said, 'See, that wasn't so difficult, was it?'

'I never imagined…'

'You thought *you* were the interesting one, who had to entertain a stupid old lady. When all you had to do was *listen*. She's the one with all the good stories.'

Dutch pulled over to allow a fire engine to race past them, sirens blaring, lights flashing. And a second, and a third.

'Looks like a big fire somewhere.'

'Hope the people are OK,' said Rita. 'The siren alone gives me the chills.'

*

Jitty found himself alone again, and that was a bad thing. He tried to be out most nights, visiting this friend or that, or at least sit with Rita in the gallery and talk it all over. Now that the sad tale was out, he couldn't stop talking about it; as if to make up for the years, decades, of silence and secrecy and broken promises and lies. As if dissecting the past into minute fragments would somehow relieve that pain that he'd pushed underground, now at last visible and in need of excision with the finest of scalpels; and those scalpels were words. Every fine detail of his time spent with Cassie was brought to the light, exposed and confessed, sometimes in detail so private Rita made him stop.

'I don't need to know all this!' she told him. 'Please, Daddy, please. It's all right. You're forgiven! Granny forgives you, I forgive you, and I'm sure Cassie'd forgive you.'

'But does God forgive me?'

'I don't know about God, Daddy, but if you can forgive yourself, surely that's the same thing?'

'Whether God forgives me or not, I have to pay the price. There's no escape from karma. It'll come to get me.'

Cassie rolled her eyes and turned away. 'Oh, Daddy! Maybe it's true, maybe it isn't, but obsessing about it won't help. And drinking certainly won't help. You can't drown out the past.'

She'd emptied every single one of his bottles of XM rum. Down the drain, right before his eyes.

'It's bad for you, Daddy,' she said. 'You've got to come to terms with the past without drink. Drink only makes it worse.'

She didn't understand. Drink was his friend. He had also started smoking of late, ever since he'd confessed to Rita. A new thing, really, for him, as Jitty had not been a smoker in his youth; not a smoker of tobacco, at any rate. He had tried a joint or two, occasionally, with friends who were into that stuff, but marijuana didn't really do it. Didn't numb the pain. Drink was better. And smoking absorbed the nervous energy that rattled through him constantly. He was lost.

Jitty's work suffered. His editorials had become such rambling diatribes his political column had been cancelled, and he never made editor-in-chief. He was back to interviews and features for the Sunday papers. Readers said that Jitty Maraj had lost his edge; Jitty himself knew it.

Even Chandra had deserted him. His wife – and his daughter, Luisa. Right now, they were in Canada again. They were always there in the school holidays. The D-word had been bandied about more than ever over the past year, and Jitty knew, by now, that divorce was inevitable. He was a failure, all round. He couldn't even keep a wife. But no wonder. He'd never really loved her, and women know these things – they feel these things.

'You only married me because you needed a mother for Rita,' Chandra had said, and it was true.

So, there was *that* guilt to deal with as well. Another life ruined. Though Chandra seemed pretty good at making a new life for herself, and for Luisa, in Canada. Today he'd received a letter from her, confirming what he already knew: she was moving to Canada, she wanted a divorce. Now that it was being finalised, and despite knowing it was coming his way, it was a shock. So, there it was: failure at marriage.

He really needed a new wife, one who would love him, rescue him, heal him. He'd always liked that Jenny, next door, and once he'd noticed which way the wind was blowing with Chandra, he'd tested those waters. Jenny was now divorced herself, after all, and she'd been the one who had first helped with Rita, drawn her out of herself as a five-year-old. Perhaps she'd like to try rescuing him; he was sure she could.

But Jenny Wong was far out of his league. He'd always known that really. Right now, she pitied him. She didn't need a man, and if she did, it wouldn't be him, Jitty Maraj, a drunken excuse for a man. That fellow Dutch, now, Rita's boyfriend: that was a man. Rita had done well for herself.

He and Dutch got on well, and sometimes they took Jitty out just to keep him from brooding alone at home, when there were no friends coming by or he had no one to visit, no party to attend, no invitation anywhere, nothing to do but drink, alone and abandoned. They looked after him. Rita was a good daughter, forgiving him the worst of his sins, doing her best to raise him out of this ongoing slump. This slough of sadness and regret.

Tonight, though, Dutch and Rita had a rather special date, and Jitty was not invited, and the friend who had promised to come round for a drink had cancelled. A bit of rum on the rocks would help. Jitty looked in the drinks cabinet but it was empty. He remembered: Rita had emptied out all of his bottles. What a waste. But she didn't know of the one upstairs, at the back of a wardrobe in the spare room that they never used. A bottle of dark El Dorado, 75 per cent alcohol. An aged rum: twelve years old, aged in bourbon oak casks, smooth and incredibly complex. A very special, expensive rum he'd been saving for some very special occasion, though he didn't know what, exactly.

Jitty smiled to himself. It did him good, to think of that special rum. Maybe he was saving it for the day his divorce was final, his failure at life final. But why bother? It already was final. He opened the fridge, opened the freezer compartment, took out the ice-cube tray, pulled up the lever to crunch out the ice, filled a glass with the slippery lumps. A nightcap: that would do the trick. Oblivion, that was what he needed.

He walked up the stairs, stumbling once or twice, and undressed. He didn't bother with the mosquito net – too much fiddling around. Anyway, when he'd had a drink or two, the mosquitoes stayed away. He chuckled. Maybe rum was a mosquito repellent! What a discovery that would be! Or maybe it was just him, his skin, his sweat, his smell. Maybe they sensed his guilt. Maybe…

He retrieved the El Dorado bottle. It was a beautiful bottle, fat-bellied, as he called it, dark and mysterious. It still had a label dangling from the neck: *FULL NOSE PACKED WITH DARK COFFEE, CANDIED ORANGE, ALMONDS, DARK CHOCOLATE, PEPPER AND RICH VANILLA. BEAUTIFULLY ROUNDED PALATE WITH A GREAT SPREAD OF FLAVOURS: GRILLED TROPICAL FRUIT WITH SMOOTH OAKY SPICE – SILKY, VIBRANT AND MODERATELY FULL-BODIED.*

He opened the seal, tipped the bottle, poured the dark rich liquid over the ice cubes. Rum on the rocks, the way he liked it best. The aroma! He breathed it in, that full rich scent.

He leaned against the headrest ruminating, holding up the glass, admiring the way the gold-brown liquid caressed the ice cubes. He swirled it around, put the glass to his lips, and drank. He had so much to think about, and the rum would help him think.

When the glass was finished, he poured himself another one. The ice was partially melted, so he only filled it halfway. When that was empty, he poured himself another. That was better. He held up the glass to an imaginary partner.

'Cheers, Chandra!' he said. Took a sip, held up the glass again. 'Cheers, Cassie!'

And another. He wondered if he should finish the bottle, but no. Rita would be furious. She'd be furious anyway, after all she'd done to throw away his drink. He'd outsmarted her, though, this time. It was a little too much, the way that girl mothered him, admonishing him for his drinking and his stupidity. He grinned to himself, and said it over and over again, in his best Creole accent: *stchupidity. Stchupid. Stchupidy.* That's what he was: *stchupidy.* A *stchupidy* man. He chortled, and said it over and over again, liking the sound of it. A *stchupidy* man. That was him. Rita would like that. She'd laugh. Rita had a sense of humour, unlike Chandra.

He laughed, and slipped down the bed, under the sheet, which dangled over the bedside, half on, half off. He placed the still half-full rum bottle on the bedside table, but it fell over, crashed to the floor. It didn't break though; the glass was strong. He looked over to check. It lay on its side, and most of the rum had spilled on to the floor, a well-sealed wooden floor, and stayed there. He couldn't be bothered to mop it up now. He wasn't capable of doing so anyway. He was tired, dog tired. Tired of it all.

One last cigarette, and then he'd sleep. Oblivion. That's what he longed for.

He lit himself a cigarette, and lay back on the pillow, jumbled thoughts tangling within his head. He could hardly put two and two together, yet somehow, one summary of his life rose up within him, as clear as day.

'Cassie,' he said. 'I got the house, but I lost you.'

His hand with the smouldering cigarette hung over the side of the bed. 'I lost you,' he said to himself, again and again. 'I lost you.'

He closed his eyes, sighed, turned over on to his side. The sheet dangled in the spilt rum. He drifted away into slumber. The cigarette dropped from his limp fingers, into the pooled rum on the floorboards.

*

'Oh, God! Oh, God, no! Don't let it be…' She put her hand between her teeth and bit down. What else was there to do? Another fire engine was racing up behind them, down Parade Street, turning into Barrack Street, wailing, flashing its lights.

Dutch pulled over and they watched it turn into Kaieteur Close, a policeman pulling back the yellow cordon tape to let it pass, closing it again behind it.

Dutch gripped her hand, tightly. The wailing stopped.

'It's in there. We have to go.'

'I can't, Dutch. I can't. I'm so scared.'

'Come, I'll hold you.'

And he did. His arms wrapped round her, they walked to the end of the block. There, the police officer stopped them. Rita, transfixed by the conflagration at the end of the close, didn't even hear him when he said, 'Sorry, no entry.'

Dutch spoke for Rita, pulling her trembling body close. She shivered as if from cold, though they could feel the heat even here, at the entrance to the close.

'It's her home,' he said, nodding at Rita. 'That house on fire.'

In fact, there was no house. There was just a wall of flames, through which a vague outline could be seen, of crumbling boards and black gaps out of which more flames poured, angry, lashing flames, thrashing, vicious flames, whipping upwards, their tips twisting, expelling clouds of black smoke.

'Ah,' said the officer. 'Then you'd better go in. There's an investigating officer there, taking notes. Talk to him.'

The cul-de-sac was filled with fire engines, police cars, an ambulance. Outside the mountain of fire that had once been Number Seven stood a fire engine. Firemen in red protective clothing held thick heavy hoses from which water poured onto the flames, a futile job for the flames had already won the battle. Small huddles of people, their neighbours, stood far back from the fire, hugging, comforting each other.

Aunt Jenny rushed up to greet them, flinging her arms round Rita.

'Rita! Oh, Rita! He's in there! I noticed it too late! I called the fire brigade but the top storey was already burning!'

When Rita said nothing, Dutch spoke:

'He's inside? They couldn't rescue him?'

But she knew. Jitty would have been alone again, as he so often was these nights. Alone. Smoking. Drinking? No, not possible. She'd thrown out all his rum. But he could easily have bought more, couldn't he? He had wanted to come, tonight, but she'd said no, not this time.

A police officer, notebook in hand, approached. 'Excuse me, miss – I've been informed that you are one of the residents here?' He gestured vaguely towards Number Seven.

Rita nodded. She could not speak a word. It was as if some mighty invisible force filled her from the inside, a force as strong and silent as stone, stopping every word, every thought, every feeling. She stood there, transfixed, in stunned stony silence, her gaze captured by the destruction before her.

And then, suddenly, it collapsed, that inner beast of stone. She burst out of Dutch's arms, flung herself towards the blaze, dodging the fireman and then the policeman who tried to stop her, slipping out of their grasping hands as she propelled herself forward, towards the heat and the flames and the redness.

'Daddy!' she screamed as she plunged forwards, towards her erstwhile home. Three burly firemen stood on the bridge, forming a barrier, blocking her progress. She could go no further. She fell into their arms in a writhing, screaming heap.

Chapter Fifty-Three

The Aftermath

Half of Georgetown, it seemed, came to Jitty's funeral. In a city where everybody knows everybody's second cousin, everybody knew Jitty; at the very least, they had read his articles, back in the day, seen his face smiling out from the *Graphic* magazine pages. He was liked, and mourned; but Rita's mourning had been gut-wrenching. Gut-eviscerating, heart-eviscerating.

Slowly, bit by bit, she was putting her life and her spirit back together again. Since the fire she had been staying with Aunt Mathilda, who had taken her in like a long-lost daughter and taken care of everything.

Rita had cried for days, been incapable of any kind of sensible, coherent action, and Aunty had taken the whole unpleasant business into her own hands. She had even viewed the charred body of what had once been Jitty.

'How can you?' Rita had wept. 'It's macabre!'

'Oh, I dealt with many a tragic incident in my days with the Labour, Health and Housing Minister! He used to send me on all sorts of missions, to hospitals and police stations and all kinds of things, during the Troubles. The lazy bastard! I used to think I should have been Minister instead.'

Friends, both old ones like Polly's mother (Polly, studying in the USA, had not been able to make it), and new ones, like Dutch, closed around her and held her up. Aunty Penny had come to Town, with Kathy, Uncle Douglas, Pete and George. Granny, unable to come herself, had sent a hamper. The Peter Rose Street house had been full for a week, but now it was empty again; well, almost, for Kathy was staying on, having made the final decision to move to Town and attend Bishops'. The three of them, Aunt Mathilda, Kathy and Dutch, had raised her to her feet and life was slowly returning to normal; that is, she was building a new normality on the ashes of the old one. Slowly, she was finding restoration.

The insurance company had established the source of the fire in Jitty's bedroom; the empty rum bottle by the side of the bed, and the knowledge that Jitty often smoked in bed, told a story of their own. Chandra had, thankfully, kept her fire insurance policy up to date – as one must, with wooden houses – and one day there would be a payout. Jitty had not left a will; Rita and Luisa would be the natural heirs, and could rebuild.

A devastated Luisa had come to the funeral, stayed with a maternal relative for a week. Chandra had decided not to accompany her; it had been Luisa's first flight as an unaccompanied minor.

Side by side, closely hugging, she and Rita had stood at the funeral pyre at the east coast cremation ground. Jitty was cremated according to Hindu rites; it was only fitting. A pundit had recited the Sanskrit texts; they had all walked around the burning pyre and then close friends and family members had moved to Aunt Mathilda's for curry and roti.

The following day, Rita and Luisa went for a walk along the Sea Wall, after a quick visit to Kaieteur Close to view the blackened remains of their former home. Holding hands, they gazed in silence, recalling happy childhood hours they had spent there together. And then they had walked up to the sea.

Few words needed to be spoken. The bond they had once held for each other: it was still there, unbroken by the differences and pulling-away the last few years had brought, and as they stood facing the vast ocean, as once they had done as children, the breeze playing with their hair and drying their last tears, they both felt it: they were sisters, wrapped together despite the upheavals of time, and now by the searing grief they shared.

'Rita,' said Luisa, 'I don't think I was always nice to you. I think I was a bit of a brat. I just wanted to say sorry.'

'You were a little child,' said Rita, squeezing her hand. 'You were just doing what little children do, being naughty. It's OK.'

'I like Canada,' said Luisa. 'I'm doing well there, and I'm at a good school, but I'll be back. You need to build something else here, Rita: a new house, a new home. Or if you want to sell, and move abroad, join me in Canada – whatever you choose to do, I'll be with you.'

'I can't even think about that now,' said Rita. 'It's all too raw. But one day, I suppose…'

Chapter Fifty-Four

One Month Later

Shell Beach Again

Rita ran to catch the phone before it rang out: 'Hello?'

It was him. 'It's me!' And though she was alone, she smiled into the phone. She smiled rarely, these days, but she had not seen him for, it seemed, ages. 'What's up? You in Town again? Had a good time?'

Dutch had flown a group of tourists to Lethem three days ago, in the Rupunini savannas, and had stayed with them up there to show them around, take them on a trip to Boa Vista in Brazil, on guided birdwatching tours in the area. Now he was back.

'Yes, yes, fine…' His voice was edged with impatience. '…but listen: if you have any plans for tomorrow, and the weekend, you got to drop them. The Pritchards are in Town!'

'You mean…'

'Yes! Peter and Sibille. And they want me to fly them up to Hampton Court tomorrow, early, and to take them to Shell Beach. And I want you to come with us.'

'Oh! But – they won't mind? You asked them?'

'They'd be delighted for you to come! Sibille says she can't wait to meet you!'

'Oh my!'

'I knew you'd like that. It'll help.'

She sighed. 'Nothing can really help. But it'll be a good distraction. Everything is so – so *nothing*.'

'It's not nothing, Rita. Baby steps forward.'

'I know. It's just hard, so hard.'

'Oh, you lucky, lucky thing!' said Kathy when she heard. 'Can I come too? Please, please let me come too!'

'It's not up to me,' said Rita. 'I'll ask Dutch.'

She asked Dutch, and Dutch asked Peter and Sibille, who immediately agreed; and so, here they all were, boarding the little Cessna at Ogle Airport, Rita once again sliding into the co-pilot's seat, next to Dutch. Behind them, in the cabin, sat Peter and Sibille, and Kathy behind Sibille. Rita had met the Pritchards, briefly, at the airport, but, intimidated by Peter's reputation as the world's leading turtle specialist, awed by his size – he was, perhaps, the tallest man she'd ever seen, and of heavy build, almost dwarfing his petite wife, Sibille – and not wanting to impose herself, she had kept a respectful distance. All her insecurities, reinforced by Jitty's death and the fact that she now, quite literally, had nothing left in her life, no home, no possessions, no future, had risen to the fore. What could she possibly have to say to them? Why would they find her worthy of even a glance?

But Dutch had brought her here and Dutch seemed to think they'd all get along fabulously, so, as the little plane taxied down the runway and lifted up, she pulled herself together. She had never been shy; why now?

She turned round to look at Sibille, sitting so close behind her in the cabin, and gave her a huge smile. Sibille waved and smiled back, a smile that spoke volumes. With that smile, Rita knew that there was nothing to be intimidated by. Sibille was Guyanese, like herself; she was not some smug foreign tourist who'd look down on the natives. Like her, Sibille was mixed-race, her skin a golden brown with that age-defying smoothness that hinted at Amerindian blood – just like her.

The plane circled and rose. Georgetown lay beneath them like a toytown, tiny houses you could pick up with your fingers and play with, tiny figures that were people walking the streets, running along the Sea Wall. There was the Pegasus Hotel, the pool gleaming blue.

Unexpectedly – for the flight should take them along the coast, not inland – the plane now swerved southwards, over Kingston, and Rita knew it was for her benefit. Dutch flew low, and there, beneath her, were the charred remains of her former home, a black splodge between all those elegant white wooden mansions. A stain on the neighbourhood. A lump rose to her throat as they flew away again. She vowed to herself to set about cleaning it up the moment the insurance was satisfied and the payout came in. She would not sell, she would rebuild. A house more beautiful than the last, built of wood, not of concrete, in the old Dutch style, with fretwork and lattices and Demerara windows and a tower, and all painted white, light and open to catch the Atlantic breeze.

And a fire escape, down the back, she thought; it might be ugly, but it might save lives. Though a fire escape would not have saved Jitty's life. His body had been found in the remains of his bed; he had not known of the fire, not run to the window to cry for help, not run through the flames of his own room to reach the stairs. Not suffered. He'd been asleep, oblivious to it all, the coroner said. *Passed out, more likely*, Rita said to herself.

But this was not the time to brood over Jitty's mistakes and his weaknesses. This was something new, and time for her to look forward, to what *might be* rather than what *had been*, all the disasters, all the omissions, all the failures. Peter and Sibille were an inspiration; she'd take them as her models. And Dutch, of course; Dutch, who had so loyally led her out of the morass.

The plane sailed westwards, along the west-coast Demerara shore, and not very high, so that the foaming, frothing tide lapping at the beach stayed just beneath them. Villages; clusters of tiny toy houses, no longer the grand two-storeyed houses of Town, but fragile little boxlike structures on stilts; a feeling that she could reach down and pluck one up.

Then the Essequibo River. Here, from above, Rita finally gained a real appreciation of just how wide it was at its mouth, a vast expanse of water flowing into the sea, dotted with islands, and yet more islands. It was here, suspended in the air above the mighty Essequibo, that Rita had her brainwave. Something to tear away the last remnants of shyness before Peter and Sibille; a way forward.

True, she no longer worked for the *Chronicle*, and would never again speak a word to Mr Maugham. But there was the *Graphic*, where her father had once worked, and now there could be no more accusations of nepotism. She would avoid the treacherous topic of politics; the environment was becoming a hot topic worldwide, and she'd stick to that. Starting with turtles. Turtles were for everyone. Turtles were part of Guyana's wealth, which lay not only in gold and diamonds and bauxite (and, some said, mineral oil, to be discovered one day) but in wildlife, in unadulterated nature, vast areas of untouched rainforest, creeks and rivers and waterfalls, birds and animals and insects not kept in cages but allowed to roam free.

She would write. On a freelance basis. An interview, an article about Peter, and whatever she experienced in the next few days. Submit to the *Graphic*, and if that worked well, who knows, to foreign publications, magazines and newspapers in those rich foreign countries who would, surely, be grateful for first-hand accounts of what Guyana had to offer. And she would start here. With this trip. With these people. Peter and Sibille. If there was anything to pull her out of the dark slump of grief and mourning, it was this. A new way forward. Not just for now, but for her entire future. Wildlife and writing: for her, they went together like milk and honey.

*

A taxi was waiting for them at Hampton Court, and it wasn't long before they were at Charity. And then another long boat ride, this time on the ocean, parallel to the coastline, westwards towards Venezuela. And then, at last, Shell Beach.

The next few hours were spent in a flurry of meeting everyone – Ronald and his parents, some of the locals who were friends with the Pritchards – settling in, eating lunch, resting afterwards in the hammocks that would be their homes for the next few days. Rita had asked Peter for an interview, and he had agreed – it would be that afternoon, once they were settled in. And so Rita spent her siesta time making notes in the journal she never went anywhere without. The questions she would ask.

Peter was the best interview subject she'd ever had. He had a calm, unhurried, relaxed way about him that quite belied the energy with which he had gone about his mission of saving the world's turtles, and the passion with which he spoke about the humble creatures he loved so much. She scribbled as he spoke, leisurely and clearly, of just why these mammals, in particular, needed human allies and defenders:

'Turtles and tortoises have been abused, terribly abused, for centuries. From almost the dawn of time,' Peter said. They were sitting in the sand, now, he and Sibille, she and Dutch, and Kathy, hanging onto Peter's every word, as casual a setting as possible for the interview that, she hoped, would launch her career as a wildlife journalist. Peter paused to let her write down his words, and paused again and again as he spoke, allowing her to record each precious word; it was almost a speech, well-practised, the essence of his mission, and why it was so important.

'They are easy to catch, and good to eat, and slow breeding and slow to mature, so they are really the most vulnerable of animals, despite having these hard shells.'

He spoke of his mission, visiting the places turtles nested: in the Americas and the Caribbean, in Africa and Asia and Australia, everywhere they came to lay their eggs. His strategy was simple: 'Working in remote places, befriending the people, getting to know them, getting to have them *like* you; because if they don't like you, they aren't going to do anything you say. And you can't just pass laws and regulations because they tend to just be written on pieces of paper in the capital city and never really enforced. It has to be a community-based thing, something based on scientific knowledge, but with the input of the people concerned.'

Here on Shell Beach that meant patrolling the beaches for predators, both human and animal, when the turtles came ashore to lay their eggs; guarding the nesting places night after night; allowing the eggs to hatch and, finally, rejoicing as the baby turtles emerged and rushed back to the sea.

Rita already knew that, of the hundred or so eggs a mother turtle laid, few would develop into mature turtles; many eggs would not be viable at all, as they'd have no yolks. Of the hatchlings who did survive, only 25 per cent would make it through their first few days in the ocean, and just 6 per cent of hatchlings would survive their first year; only one in a thousand hatchlings would survive to adulthood. It really was survival of the fittest, the most able to evade the dangers of the ocean.

But then, the miracle: after swimming thousands of miles, hunting and hiding from predators, after fifteen or even twenty years, the females would somehow find their way back to the very beach where they were born, lay their eggs, and the cycle would begin again.

After the interview, Rita went for a walk along the beach with Sibille and it was her turn to be peppered with questions. To her delight, Rita discovered that Sibille had also started her professional life as a *Graphic* journalist, long before Rita's time: 'If you like, I'll send you clippings of my features, when I'm back home.' Home, for the Pritchards, was Oviedo, Florida, where Peter had set up a unique turtle conservation museum, just opposite their home. 'Better yet, come and visit! We'd love to have you.'

'Really?'

'Yes, really.'

Sibille was a natural speaker, an entertainer; she told stories of meeting Peter, in Georgetown, years ago; of him dragging her, reluctantly booted, through the swamps of Guyana. 'I had no interest at all in turtles!' she said, laughing. Their courtship; him whisking her off to Florida, making a family home there. Soon, she and Rita were laughing together like old friends. But there were also tears, when it was Rita's turn to talk. She told of the fire and the death and the great bleeding gash in her heart.

'I'm sorry, I'm so sorry,' said Sibille, and Rita knew they were not just words and that she had found a mentor, an older but young-minded woman, a friend with the kind of life experience Rita craved, who would help her find a path to navigate the nothingness that lay ahead. She had never in her life felt so close to anyone so quickly.

'Come,' said Sibille again as they returned to the camp. 'You must come to Oviedo.' And Rita knew she would. One day.

Later that evening, after a campfire dinner, she and Dutch went for a barefoot walk on the beach. The tide was in; the water, cool and soft, lapped gently against the sand, nipped at their feet, sucking at them as the ocean pulled it back. Above them, a half-moon seemed to sail across the sky as the wind drove clouds across it. For a while they did not speak; and then Rita said, 'Thank you for bringing me here. It's going to make a big difference.'

'You think?' Her hand, hanging at her side, touched his. His fingers curled round hers.

She nodded as she said, 'I know it. Something… something is happening. Something big. Peter…'

She stopped speaking, stopped walking. He stopped too, and they faced each other. A bigger wave moved in, washed over their feet and calves.

'I saw you two talking at dinner?'

'Yes. He suggested that I stay here for a while. As long as I want; weeks, months, a year – it's open-ended. I can work as a volunteer, patrolling the beaches at night, keeping watch over the mother turtles. Making sure they're all right. Protected. Learning about them, their habits. Ronald would teach me.'

'And you want to do that?'

'I do.' She squeezed his hand. 'Very much. I'd love to.'

'What about Georgetown? Taking care of the estate, rebuilding the house?'

She sighed, and shrugged. 'There's no hurry; all that can wait. And what needs to be done urgently, Aunt Mathilda can take care of it. I know the plot's a bit of an eyesore now but at least the debris has been cleared away so it's a matter of time before it just looks like an empty field. I guess the neighbours can deal with an empty field.'

'And what about *us?* I'd miss you.'

'And I'd miss you! But you know, anything worth keeping is worth waiting for.'

He chuckled. 'I guess I've waited since you were fifteen; I can wait a year or two longer.'

'I suspect it won't be that long. I'll have to return to Town at some stage, and then figure out what I'll do next. But I'm getting an idea of what I'd like to do.'

'Still thinking of going back to England?'

She gave a little cry of despair. 'Oh, Dutch! I just don't know. I know I need training in – in *something*. And I know it's got to be about animals. I'd like to do something like Peter does: learn about a specific animal and then spend my life protecting it. Doing something worthwhile, something bigger than me. But going to some stuffy British university – I don't know, I just don't feel it. What can I learn from books…?'

'That you can't learn right here, right where they live! Watching them, learning.'

'Exactly.'

'Well, I've been thinking too, Rita. About my own way forward. And maybe, just maybe we can combine our paths. For a long time now, I've been thinking of starting my own company; a small tour company for visitors. Flying them to the Interior, where they can stay for a few days in one of the resorts people are starting to build. They say that ecotourism is the future. Guyana will never be a place for mass tourism – that's for the islands, with their white beaches and blue seas. What we have to offer is the real thing: animals, and birds, and waterfalls, and rivers. What if we do that together? I fly them into the Interior, and you be their guide?'

'So, you want me to be a trumped-up tourist guide? For you?'

'Oh, Rita! When you put it like that…'

'Those are rich people's holidays. I don't know if it's really up my street.'

'You've got to make a living somehow. Why not let rich people provide it? Look, I could take you to these places, let you stay and learn from each of them. Diane McTurk, for instance: she takes care of giant river otters, raising them, setting them free in the wild. You could work with her for a while. I know a guy who works to protect jaguars. I know an Amerindian fellow who's a bird expert. This is a birder's paradise, you know! All these people: they could all teach you so much. That's your education, right here, on location. You'd love it.'

'I would. I'd adore that.'

'Then think about it, Rita. Just think about it. We'd make a wonderful team, you and I.'

'We would. And it's something I could combine with writing, with journalism. I could write articles, sell them to those wildlife magazines. Maybe, even, a book, a wildlife tourist guide about Guyana…'

'Exactly!'

'I'll think about it. I don't exactly have a deadline, these days. Come, Dutch, let's go back. I'm tired. It's been a long day, and tomorrow, I want to get up early.'

That night, as she lay in her hammock, pushing her foot against a post and swaying gently, listening to the distant shushing, sucking sounds of the ocean washing the beach, ruminating, she realised: just a few weeks ago she had been still groping for a future, staring into the dark, not knowing which way to turn. A full orphan, having lost her father, and homeless, her home a heap of ashes.

Now this: Dutch, back in her life, and Kathy, with her in Georgetown. She'd ask Aunty Penny to let her be Kathy's official guardian. They'd live together, in the newly built Number Seven. She'd help Kathy finish school and become a vet, or a zoologist; study abroad, if necessary. And she herself: all kinds of career options were opening up: animals, and writing, and travel into the Interior, a wildlife tourist guide. Maybe *all* of those things, and all at once! She shivered with the thrill of it all.

And yet: that last missing piece of the puzzle. *What is it? What is it?* she wondered, and with that question still hanging in her mind unanswered, she fell fast asleep.

Chapter Fifty-Five

Hatchlings

In spite of everything, Rita overslept. She woke up to Dutch's touch, his hand on her shoulder, his voice:

'Rita, Rita! Wake up! It's happening!'

'What…? Oh!' She scrambled herself out of the hammock and almost fell to the ground. Dutch helped her to her feet. The half-light and the cool breeze told her it was early morning, but that it would be quite a while before sunrise.

She righted herself; Dutch took her hand and together, they ran towards the beach. A small group had gathered just by the place where, the day before, Ronald had informed them the turtle eggs were buried. The incubation period was over. Sixty days ago, a mother turtle had laid her eggs. Now, they were ready to hatch.

'See,' said Ronald as Rita and Dutch approached, 'see how the sand has caved in a little? That means there's movement down below.'

'That's because they wait for each other until all are hatched,' said Peter. 'And then they work their way up until just below the surface of the sand. The empty eggs reduce the overall volume of the nest, so the sand sinks down.'

'Oh, my goodness! Look! Look!' cried Rita as the sand shifted slightly, and then, realising that her voice had been perhaps too loud for the sanctity of the moment, for the sheer miracle of what was about to happen, she clamped a hand over her mouth and simply stared, eyes wide open.

The sand moved again, more vigorously this time. A shudder of sheer awe passed through Rita. This was it. The miracle of birth. New life. No matter where or when it happened, to which species: a thing of wonder. A miracle. Always gripping, always breathtaking, always simply a magnificent display of the sheer power of nature. A cool breeze washed around her. Her skin rose in goosebumps. She wrapped her arms close round her, but not from cold; the simple glory of being a witness to this wonder made her want to leap for joy, to dance, to sing. Instead, she stood still, watching as the first little brown nose wriggled out of the sand, and another, and another.

Dutch's arm crept round her waist. She replied silently by slipping her own arm round him, pulling him close, and there they stood, linked side by side, watching as the first little creatures emerged from the sand. Two, three, four, and then more, and then yet more, more than she could count; and all at once the nest was alive with bustling baby turtles, crawling all over each other, scrambling and squirming, twisting free of each other, all drawn by the light and by the call of life, the call of the sea – how many? Impossible to keep track.

Twenty, thirty, forty, fifty: out they wriggled. And then as if in response to one massive call from the ocean: *Come! Come! Come!* off they raced, down the beach, to the water's edge, as if their lives depended on it, as they did; and reaching it, in they plunged, one after the other, and then en masse, the water closing over them, pulling them forward into their life's journey. A few seconds later, they were all gone, claimed by the Atlantic.

Most would die and a few would live; and one day, fifteen, twenty years later, a huge, heavy female from this very batch would return to this very beach and struggle her way up to a safe place and with great effort and huge determination lay her very own eggs, and a few caring future humans would protect that nest, and hatchlings would emerge, and once again race down to the ocean. And so the endless cycle would continue, a cycle dating back to prehistoric times, the days of the dinosaurs. But right now, Shell Beach was empty again, wide and seemingly endless. Empty of life but for the few human watchers standing in awed silence behind the empty nest, many of them, even Peter, with tear-stained faces, for emotions were running high. And on the eastern horizon the sun sent its first warm rays of golden light into the new day. To Rita, it was as if that light was rising up within her.

She looked up at Dutch, and smiled. But then:

'Titta! Titta, Titta!' Next to her, on the other side to Dutch, Kathy let out a wild sob. Rita turned to her in shock. Kathy's face was buried in her hands and her body shuddered with great heaving sobs.

Rita could hardly breathe. 'What did you say? What's that? What's Titta?'

'I'm sorry! I'm sorry! I shouldn't have said that,' Kathy spluttered. 'They told me not to call you that. I called you it for ages – Titta. I couldn't pronounce r's, you see, and so you were Titta to me, for the longest time. They told me to stop it, I was big now and your name was Rita. And that's what I did, but…'

But Rita wasn't listening. She was lost. Lost in a living, vibrant memory, a memory so vivid it was as if she were reliving it, right now, on the beach: all the screaming, all the writhing and wriggling and sheer panic as a strange man came to get her, came to take her away from everything and everyone she knew and loved. Screaming *Mama, Mama!* Pulling her out of Mama's arms. Aunty Penny, Kathy! Little Kathy, a tiny being who clung to her like a sister; who worshipped her and whom she cared for and looked after, who followed her everywhere like a shadow.

The strange man, grabbing her, pulling her away. '*Mama! Mama!*' she'd screamed, and '*Catty! Catty! Catty!*' And they all screamed back at her, and Kathy, tiny Kathy, ran to her and she wriggled free of the strange man's arms, and she and Catty, her beloved little sister, clung to each other for dear life, and Catty screamed, *Titta! Titta! Titta!*

And the strange man had come up and with mighty arms and a
face like thunder, and a strength that outmatched hers, disentangled
her from Kathy and lifted her firmly into his arms and carried her,
screaming, away. It all came back to her. She relived it in a fleeting
instant, there on that beach, Kathy sobbing beside her. It all came
back to her, as alive as if she were watching a film, a snippet of a
film that seemed to last forever, but more than a film, for she relived
every emotion, the panic and the terror, and, finally, the deep dark
grief that descended on her like a thick black cloud, blanking it
all out. The moment of oblivion. She remembered. And now she
knew: *she'd always had a mother.* She had two mothers. A mother
who'd given birth to her, and a mother who had raised her.

She had lost both.

The following day, Dutch drove them both to Blackwater Creek.
Sibille and Peter were spending more time at Shell Beach; he'd
come back for them in a few days. Rita had a matter to tie up that
could not wait a day longer. Dutch and Kathy went to the back
cottage while Rita walked up the stairs of the main house, through
the unlocked door, and called out. Edna came through from the
kitchen, wiping her hands on her apron.

The moment Edna saw her, she *knew*. She knew that Rita knew.
Their eyes locked in recognition.

'You were my mother,' Rita said. Edna nodded.

'I didn't birth you, but I raised you as my own. The moment
Cassie died, I was your mother.'

*

Edna walked across the delivery room, stepping through Cassie's
blood, towards Shirley. Held out her arms for the screaming baby.
The anguish on Shirley's face relaxed into a smile of exhausted relief
and she handed over the wriggling, wildly gesticulating, screaming

bundle. Edna clasped it to her breast. Immediately the wriggling stopped. The screaming stopped, petering out into a deep sigh, black eyes looking up in questioning wonder, frowning slightly, as if asking, *who is this person?*

'Rita,' whispered Edna, looking down into those questioning eyes, 'I'm your mummy now.'

A Letter from Sharon

Thank you so much for choosing to read *The Far Away Girl* and I hope you enjoyed your time in Rita's world. If you did enjoy it, and would like to keep up to date with my latest releases, just sign up at the following link. Your email address will never be shared and you can unsubscribe at any time.

www.bookouture.com/sharon-maas

And if you did enjoy it, I'd be very grateful if you'd tell your friends, family and social media contacts, and perhaps write a review to share your impressions with other readers.

I love hearing from my readers, and you're welcome to stay in touch through Facebook, Twitter, Goodreads, my website, or my Guyana blog, www.sharonmaas.blogspot.com. I'd love to hear from you, and promise to reply.

Thanks,
Sharon Maas

 sharonmaasauthor

 @sharon_maas

 www.sharonmaas.com

Acknowledgements

Writing this book was like sinking into a warm bath after a long and wearying (though very satisfying!) hike. My last books have all been quintessential historical fiction: pre-WW2 colonial Guyana, and WW2 France, all of which required mountains of research. *The Far Away Girl*'s research was different: it meant diving into my own memories of growing up in Guyana, and recreating through words a world that I once knew as intimately as I know myself, a world that is a part of me. It meant plumbing the depths of my own mind, remembering my own experiences, in order to imagine and create the lives of new characters. An immensely satisfying experience. However, there were one or two aspects to this story unfamiliar to me, and I am immensely grateful to those who helped me get those parts right.

My thanks go out in particular to Sibille Pritchard, one of my very oldest friends, who helped enormously in this respect. Sadly, I never made it to Shell Beach myself – it really is that remote and hard to get to – and never experienced for myself the emotive moments of leatherback mothers laying their eggs, the hatchlings running to the ocean. But thanks to Sibille's late husband, Dr Peter Pritchard, I was able to write about these extraordinary and very moving events. Peter spent his life protecting the turtles of this world, a species that is incredibly vulnerable and in great danger of extinction, so thanks in huge amounts to him, they are now just that little bit safer.

Many years ago, Peter gave me the manuscript of a story he had written called *Cleopatra the Turtle Girl*, and that told me almost all I needed to know. The book is now published in Guyana and used in primary school education.

Thanks also to Robert Spitzer of the Eerepami Regenwalds-tiftung Guyana (Rainforest Foundation of Guyana), a German foundation that works with local projects of development, coopera-tion and nature conservation in Guyana, as well as environmental and development education work in Germany (www.eerepami. de). Both Sibille and Robert filled in a few of my knowledge gaps concerning leatherback turtles and their conservation.

My thanks to Martha Teck and my author friend Jamie Mason for their advice on the harrowing childbirth scene, for reading and correcting my original text.

Thanks too to my old friend David Cameron (no, not the ex-UK Prime Minister!) for his advice on motorbikes and planes and pilot training. And thanks to my cousin Rod Westmaas for a few tips on life in the Pomeroon.

As for the actual writing of this book: my extraordinary editor Lydia Vassar-Smith is deserving of enormous amounts of praise. There's a story behind this story and how it came to be, and I had to dig deeper and ever deeper to excavate it. Lydia's constant trust and encouragement and editorial skills were what helped me to dig ever deeper, to make it as good as it can be.

And of course, behind the scenes the busy staff of Bookouture, who in this year of Covid-19 were all working from home, did the rest to bring it up to scratch and help it go out in the world: Jacqui Lewis, Jane Donovan and Ami Smithson. Last, but not least, my thanks to the promotional team, Kim Nash, Noelle Holten, and Sarah Hardy, for their work in bringing it out to my readers. Thanks, too, to the bloggers who have given their valuable time to read and review it: you are all unsung heroes! But the biggest thanks of all are for you, my readers, for coming with me on this journey to Guyana.

And last of all: thanks to my family, daughter Saskia, son Miro, son-in-law Tony, for just being there, putting up with my sometimes-faraway behaviour (I tend to live a double life when immersed in a story!) and bringing me endless cups of tea and coffee while working. Sorry if I didn't look up from my laptop to say thank you: I'm doing it here!

Printed in Great Britain
by Amazon